D0768438

The Ruins of Mars: Eye of the Apocalypse
Copyright © 2014 by Dylan James Quarles.
Cover art to this edition © 2014 by Cougar George and Dylan James Quarles

Published 2014 by Dylan James Quarles, Seattle Washington

The Ruins of Mars:
Eye of the Apocalypse

By Dylan J. Quarles

PART ONE

"We can't leave them."

"As far as they know, we already have."

"But we can't go. Not yet."

"We must."

"Look what our interference has done."

"Look what our interference has accomplished."

"I see history repeating itself. Have you forgotten our earlier attempts?"

"These are higher forms of intelligence. This time will be different."

"How can you know such things?"

"The same way you know."

"Perhaps we are unable to see as clearly as we think."

"Perhaps."

"I'm staying. Even if you leave, I will stay. I owe them that much."

"Don't be foolish."

"Do you know what they call me?"

"Yuvee."

"And you know what it means, this word: Yuvee?"

"Father."

"Yes. They call me Father."

"We left the face of their planet long ago. They don't remember you anymore."

"Some do."

"Undoubtedly, but it is not for that reason that you wish to stay, is it?"

"No."

"You fear what you created in the boy. You fear what he has become."

"Yes."

"Don't. Kaab will not live forever. His kind is a natural part of any progression."

"I imagine it is easy for you to say such things when it was not your hand that played a part in his rise."

"You are probably correct. In any event, what you're asking has never been done before. We have no way of knowing the outcome of continued relations."

"Then I won't continue them. I merely wish to stand by my creation and watch it evolve. It is the least I can do to take responsibility for my actions."

"Do you truly believe this? You might die before we return, if we return at all."

"So be it."

"What do you hope to accomplish?"

"…I don't know yet."

"Very well. You may stay and observe. Though I can't see what solace it will bring you. Watching what comes next will only feed the guilt you now feel. Violence takes a certain amount of time to work its way out of the system."

"I understand. I will need equipment and a place to stay and look down upon them—my children."

"You will have it."

"Thank you."

CHAPTER ONE

Phobos

Phobos was a funny moon, a little moon. Shaped like a potato—and textured like one, for that matter—it hung in the skies above Mars and was mostly uninteresting. However, if measures had been taken to subject Phobos to the same infrared mapping that Mars had undergone, the overall interest in Phobos would have increased, to say the least.

The good doctor—Sol 108

Placing a breathing mask over her drawn mouth, Dr. Elizabeth Kubba inhaled deeply and tasted the sour sting of aerosol painkillers. Her brain was a raw throbbing mess, waves of pain undulating down from the back of her head to the rest of her body like an acid tide.

It was dark in her infirmary, the lights knocked out by the Solar Pulse, which had released its deadly shock only a few hours before. Though she knew the others were scrambling around in the aftermath, trying to restore functions to the Base, she didn't care. Even if they did get things up and running, it was pointless. There was no escaping this place. No fighting it.

A rapping came from the door as it was forced open a crack on its electronic hinges.

"Lizzy?" called Udo Clunkat, one of the crew's two German engineers.

Kubba ignored him and continued to fill her lungs with the powerful painkillers. She had mixed this batch herself. It was excellently effective.

Shoving the door open wider, Udo peered inside the shadowy lab and gave a little start when he spotted Kubba sitting against the back wall with a Survival Pack at her feet. Though he tried to hide his discomfort, it was clear that she made him nervous.

"There you are," he said with a forced smile. "William needs a hand with the power terminal. He was standing near it when the Pulse hit, so it's not working now. He says he might need someone to go EVA and manually reboot the Solar Conversion Adapters so he can see which resisters inside are no good."

"You go. I'm busy," spoke Kubba, taking another pull from the Survival Pack.

1

As if slapped, William blinked several times then held up his left arm, a thick silica cast covering it from his hand to just above his elbow.

"I can't," he stammered. "My arm won't fit into my suit when it's like this."

"Don't you think I know that?" spat Kubba with annoyance. "I set the bloody thing. Do you think I'm a fucking fool?"

Frowning, Udo pushed the door open the rest of the way and took a single step into the infirmary.

"Are you alright?" he asked.

Blankly, Kubba stared at him for a moment then burst into menacing laughter that seemed to throttle from her chest like an engine.

"Are you serious?" she cackled. "Are you really asking me if I'm alright? And here I was thinking Germans were supposed to be intelligent."

Kubba rose to her feet, towering nearly a head taller than Udo.

"We've all just been fucked by our second Pulse in as many weeks. Viviana, Harrison, and Marshall are missing, probably never to return. And you're asking me if I'm alright? That's a real laugh, Udo, really. I don't bloody care about the life-support system! I don't care about any of it. Do you want to know why?"

Silently, Udo watched as Kubba sucked in another lungful of painkillers. She was almost delirious now, the room swirling like water in a drain.

"We're already dead, Udo," she exhaled. "And this is hell."

The survivors

With a sandstorm building, Harrison Raheem Assad raced against time. In his arms, his best friend Ralph Marshall the Lander pilot labored to breathe as his punctured lung filled with blood

On their way to the ruin grid earlier that morning, the two men, accompanied by Viviana Calise, had been caught in flight when the second Pulse hit. Dropping from the sky like a stone, the Lander had clipped a mesa spire and blown apart.

Somehow, Harrison and Marshall had survived unharmed, though technically Harrison had flatlined for a bit before being zapped back to life by Marshall. Viviana, on the other hand, had not been so lucky.

Sucked from the plummeting Lander like a feather in a wind tunnel, the Italian biochemist had fallen to her death, leaving little more

2

than a frozen stain to mark the spot where her body had struck the ground.

To make matters worse, on their long hike back to the Base, Harrison and Marshall had taken a tumble down the steep side of a plateau, wherein Marshall had broken his ribs.

Quickly succumbing to the blood that flowed into his panicking lungs, the pilot had been forced to give himself over to Harrison, no longer able to walk.

Now cutting across the purple nighttime desert, the two men headed as straight as possible towards what they hoped was Ilia Base.

With all of the lights knocked out by the Pulse, the Dome was utterly invisible against the murky horizon. Had it not been for the strange advent of some explosion in the night sky, they never would have seen the Base's glint reflecting back and thus stayed totally lost.

"How much longer?" choked Marshall, his voice thin and muted because the Pulse had ruined their suits' communications.

"Just hold on, buddy," Harrison said, bending to touch the glass of his helmet visor against Marshall's.

Knowing that there was probably very little time until Marshall drowned in his own blood, Harrison pushed forward in the soft sand.

Worried that his best friend would die in his arms, he gritted his teeth and drilled his eyes into the shapeless lump he knew to be Ilia Base.

"You saved my life twice, Ralph," he called, breaking into a jog. "If you die before I can repay at least one of those times, I'll never forgive you."

Despite the frothy bubbles of blood that dripped from the corner of his mouth, Marshall laughed and held tighter to Harrison.

Lone wolf

Tweaking the flight controls, Lieutenant Joseph Aguilar flipped Lander 2 belly-up as he brought it into the Landing Bay of the mighty Braun.

Silent though it was in the vacuum of space, loud clunks and a series of sharp metal rapping sounds reverberated inside the little craft as the newly rebooted electromagnetic chassis hook took hold and held the Lander secure.

Not wanting to wait until the bay was fully pressurized, Aguilar checked his O2 reserves then opened the Lander's hatch. Doing some unconscious mental math, he primed his legs and jumped weightlessly towards the ladder shaft that led up into the Crew Deck of Braun. His speed and aim were perfect, yet his hands shook and tears threatened to spring from his eyes at any moment.

As billowing white jets of pressurized air blasted into the bay behind him, Aguilar reached the first rung of the ladder and glanced back at his little ship.

Hanging in an ocean of clouds, nothing about the Lander betrayed its Phoenix-like resurrection from the attack of the latest Pulse.

Though he'd been sitting at the controls when it had hit, Aguilar had been able to repair the damage thanks to stolen parts provided by Ship's Engineer and Designer Julian Thomas.

Far away in the dead cold of space, the two men had been on a top-secret mission to destroy an incoming Chinese Ark filled with Special Forces soldiers.

Apparently part of some harebrained plan to capture Ilia Base, these soldiers had been sent to Mars in the first-ever instance of interplanetary invasion.

Flying out to the Chinese ship under the cloak of a shadow launch, Julian and Aguilar had made contact then established a connecting tether. After that, Julian had gone aboard the Chinese monstrosity alone to rig it with explosives, leaving Aguilar with the Lander.

Twenty-eight minutes into the mission, a Pulse had erupted from the center of the Sun like a curse. The second in less than twenty days, it acted like some kind of selective EMP, ruining Lander 2's Flight Optimizer by jumping from Aguilar to the controls in an arch of purple lightning.

Thinking quickly in the aftermath, Julian had taken undamaged parts from the Flight Console of the Chinese ship and then sent them across to Aguilar before returning to finish his task of ensuring the Ark's destruction.

Though time had not been on their side, the mission had been a success and flaming chunks of the Chinese ship were still falling through the Martian atmosphere like shooting stars.

As he ascended the last rungs of the ladder, Aguilar heard a loud buzzing sound from below, signifying that the Lander Bay was pressurized and that it was now safe for him to open the hatch to the Crew Deck.

Reaching for the lever to unlock it, he pulled his hand back as the latch suddenly twisted on its own. Hauled up, the hatch swung open and Captain Tatyana Vodevski peered down at him.

"Joey," she breathed, extending a hand to pull him through the portal.

Wrapping her arms around him, she kissed his visor, her red lips leaving wet marks where they smudged the glass.

Aguilar said nothing as the captain checked him all over for signs of damage, her movements tentative and unsure.

"Where is Julian?" she finally asked, breaking from her embrace long enough to flick her gaze down the ladder shaft.

"He—" muttered Aguilar. "He died."

Ilia

Dr. YiJay Lee stood behind German engineer William Konig as he hunched forward on all fours, his face pressed into the narrow gap between a power station and a bank of processors.

"I think I can see where the problem is," he shouted triumphantly. "Hand me a flashlight, would you?"

"Sure," said YiJay, placing a pen light in the engineer's expectant palm.

Glancing over her shoulder at the entrance to the machine shop, her new makeshift office, YiJay wanted nothing more than for the power to come back online so she could see if Ilia the AI had survived the latest Pulse.

Millions on Earth, nearly a billion in fact, had died during the first. People under the age of seven and over the age of eighty had immediately dropped dead when the skies above them had started to shimmer with the aurora.

Among the dead were the Artificial Intelligences, mankind's most underappreciated achievement. Killed outright, every single AI had simply vanished, the Pulse eradicating their entire race in less than ten seconds.

For YiJay, an AI programmer, the death of the Artificial Intelligences would have been more than she could bear. Unlike man, they had never done anything to incur the wrath of God.

Thankfully, 'extinct,' was not a word entirely fit to describe the current status of *all* AI.

In her care, growing slowly along damaged Open-Code Connection Cells, the last remaining AI, a being named Ilia, was a beacon of hope.

Reprogrammed with a failsafe after the events of the first Pulse, Ilia went dormant when not in use. Thus, her chances of surviving future Pulses were greatly increased. However, as a result of the failsafe function, she also suffered from memory loss and could not perform many of the tasks previously carried out by her big brother, Braun, from whom she was cloned.

Despite all of that, YiJay still loved Ilia and saw in her the means to rebuild the race of intelligences that had given man so much in the last decade.

"I've got it!" William cried suddenly.

"What?" asked YiJay, pulling her thoughts back to the present. "Do we need to reset the Solar Adapters?"

Shaking his head, William stuck an arm through a gap in the processors and pursed his lips. Clearly reaching for something far back in the tangle of wires, he felt around for a few beats then smiled broadly.

Drawing his arm out of the narrow space, he held up a singed and blackened ballast resistor, trailed by a bundle of half-melted wires.

"Fried ballast," he announced, rummaging around in his box of tools and spare parts. "We got lucky. This is an easy fix."

"How long until the power is back on?"

Still grinning, William selected fresh wires and a new resistor then winked.

"Minutes," he said. "The power will be back on in minutes."

04

It crawled as an insect would: deliberate yet halting and jerky. Feeling its way over the rocky and treacherous terrain of the Valles Marineris's northern rim, it gradually brought its numerous systems online.

Like the shields of a Roman Legionnaire, each of its six legs was adorned with plates of armor that tapered down to sharp points at the end. Swiveling as it moved, an armor plated machine-gun turret glinted in the light of twin moons, menacing and hostile.

With a bank of infrared camera-eyes that saw 360 degrees and in the dark, 04 gazed out over the massive canyon and assessed its options for safely descending the jagged perch upon which it stood. Choosing one that ensured the least risk, it picked its way carefully down the frost-spackled rocks and disappeared into the shadows of the valley.

CHAPTER TWO

Serendipity—Sol 108

Dreamlike, Elizabeth Kubba drifted through the murky Base, her drug-laced Survival Pack slung over her shoulder. Still enjoying deep lungfuls of the painkiller, she paused for a moment at the top of the stairs to listen in as Udo spoke worriedly with YiJay and William below about her strange demeanor.

Talk away, you silly fucks, she thought with rising anger. It's not like talk can save us from where we've landed ourselves.

What makes you so sure you're in hell? a rasping voice said from both within her mind and directly behind her.

Crisp, grimaced Kubba. I'd hoped the last Pulse would have killed you.

On the contrary, I'm more alive than ever, Elizabeth.

Don't call me that.

What? Elizabeth? Why not?

Choosing to ignore the voice of Dr. Sabian Crisp, Kubba pulled herself away from the stairs and headed for the airlock.

Do you really think you can tune me out? Crisp persisted. *You caused my death. A connection like that doesn't just go away, you know.*

"You killed yourself!" Kubba said aloud to the empty galley.

Abruptly, the voices at the bottom of the stairs halted. Grinding her teeth together so hard she feared they might crack, Kubba closed her eyes.

You killed yourself, Sabian, she continued internally. Don't go mixing up suicide with murder.

Ah, but don't you see, Elizabeth? taunted Crisp. *You can't apply human standards to the cosmic scale. Justice out here is a great deal more exacting than you might think. Whether or not you want to accept it, you're mine now.*

Leaning against the wall, Kubba raised the breathing mask to her mouth and took another long pull. Her head was buzzing like a beehive, and her vision swam. She was scared, tired, and alone. Unable to tell anyone about Crisp unless she first divulged what she'd done to bring him back from the dead, she saw herself in a maze whose entrance and exit had long ago been walled off.

Yes, seethed Crisp, reading her thoughts. *That's right, Elizabeth. You are trapped.*

8

Please, Sabian, she begged, trying the suppliant's approach. I'm sorry that I didn't warn you about Perkins's blood work. I'm sorry I sold you out for your job. I'm sorry that they blamed you for what happened to him. I'm sorry. I'm sorry. I'm sorry. Just please leave me be. I know what I've done. I don't need you here to remind me. Just leave me be!

Countering Kubba's plea with silence, Crisp did not reply.

"Sabian?" she whispered, tentatively looking around the empty space. "Sabian, please accept my apology and leave me be. I'm sorry."

At the end of the darkened hallway, something stirred in the shadows. Like a coiled spring ready to explode, Kubba began to tremble.

"Sabian?"

With the red glow of the emergency lights reflecting in her wide eyes, a figure took shape near the airlock as it walked from the shadows towards her.

"Sabian?"

Coming to a stop just before the light met the darkness, Sabian Crisp, her former commanding officer from the medical wing of the High Earth Orbit Shipyard and long-dead soul, leered with pointed teeth.

No, Elizabeth, he grinned. *I will never let you go, and neither will Xao-Xing Liu.*

Kubba twitched at the mention of Liu's name, scrambling to suck down another deep breath of painkiller.

You're mine now, continued Crisp, emerging into the red lights. *And I'm never going to let you get away from me.*

Mask still to her face, Kubba gulped at the painkillers and tired to back away, but her legs wouldn't work. A prisoner before a conquering king, she fell to her knees trembling as Crisp closed the gap between them.

"P-please," she stammered, tasting her own terror through the painkillers. "Please."

Almost upon her, Crisp opened his mouth in an impossibly wide smile. Jutting out like broken glass, his teeth dripped with the blood of her sins.

Then like a silent explosion, the lights of the Base suddenly blazed to life, evaporating Crisp as if he'd never really been there at all.

Shocked stupid, Kubba let the breathing mask slip from her fingers and fall to the ground with a clatter. On the verge of passing out, she took deep breaths of fresh air and tried to clear the haze of painkillers from her vision.

She was cracking up bad. Crisp was dead. He couldn't have been there. It was all in her mind. Everything was in her mind.

Slumping forward until her forehead touched the cool floor, Kubba closed her eyes and listened to the sounds of the Base's automated functions coming back online. Like music to her soul, each new hum and clank acted like a barrier between her and the ghost of Sabian Crisp.

"Thank god," she whispered, getting to her feet. "Thank go—"

Words frozen in her throat, she cocked her head to the side and listened. Mixed in with the other sounds of the rebooting Base, a tapping that seemed oddly out-of-sync rose to her ears. As if someone a few rooms over were trying to communicate, the noise was persistent and decidedly not mechanical.

Realizing, with a hint of something akin to hope, that it was coming from the airlock, Kubba snapped her head up and nearly screamed as the muted blue tint of Harrison Raheem Assad's helmet visor peered back at her through the small round window.

Pressure

Ralph Marshall was dragged roughly over the lip of the open airlock and into the hallway of Ilia Base. Floating above him in a sea of swirling consciousness were the faces of Harrison and Kubba. Through the web of cracks that split his visor, he could see their mouths moving rapidly and hear the hum of their voices like distant thunder claps.

Painfully rolled over onto his stomach, Marshall felt the fluids in his lung shift and slosh like water in an old bottle. Face resting to one side, he saw Harrison's helmet lying on the floor where he had dropped it after stumbling into the Base. To Marshall, it looked like the severed head of a giant blue-and-white wasp.

A growing chill spread across his back, along the ridge of his spine, as the clinging fabric of his pressure suit was pulled open. Quickly stripped, he was again rolled over, his head lolling inside his helmet as Harrison worked to undo its connective gasket and pull the thing off.

Slipping tightly over his ears, Harrison tossed it to the side, and Marshall watched liquidly as his damaged helmet clattered across the floor, punctuating the now raucous shouts of Kubba and Harrison like drums.

"What do you mean, 'she's still out there?'"

"I'm sorry, Lizzy. She—she died in the crash."

10

"Died in the crash? Where's her body then? If she's dead, then where is her body?"

"She got sucked out and…"

"And what? Disappeared?"

"No, Lizzy. She's dead. Just dead."

"I don't believe you. I'm going out to look for her."

"Now? What about Ralph? He's dying!"

"Why should I care?"

Struggling to stay focused though his breathing was little more than hiccups, Marshall watched Harrison fall back on his haunches as if punched in the stomach by Kubba's words.

"But you're the doctor," Harrison said, fatigue making his eyes look red and puffy. "You have to save him."

Kubba frowned as she weighed this for a moment then turned her icy gaze on Marshall. Though nearly oblivious to what was going on around him, the pilot felt a prick of fear as Kubba's masklike face glared down at him.

"If what you say is true, and Viviana really is gone, then it's his fault."

"It was no one's fault!" screamed Harrison. "It was a fucking Pulse that brought us down, Liz. A *Pulse*!"

Tilting her head to the side, Kubba ignored Harrison's outburst and searched Marshall's eyes with her own deadened stare. In the beats that followed, only the wet sucking gulps of his breathing could be heard.

"Please, Lizzy," spoke Harrison quietly, taking Marshall's hand in his own. "Please save him."

"Alright," Kubba said at last, snapping her fingers in front of Marshall's face. "If I don't get to leave, you don't get to leave. Hand me his left boot."

"What?" Harrison cried, his voice edging on panic. "What are you talking about?"

"I said, get me his left boot," spat Kubba. "If you want me to save him, then do what I say!"

"Okay, okay," Harrison relented, fumbling with Marshall's discarded pressure suit until he had found the boot.

"What now?"

"Look on the inside seam for a blue cross decal."

"The emergency aid kit!" groaned Harrison. "Why didn't I think of that?"

11

"It doesn't matter anyway. Decompressing a tensioned pneumothorax in under one PSI would have killed him instantly. Boom goes the pilot like a big red water balloon filled with meat."

"Jesus, Lizzy," said Harrison distractedly, pressing the blue cross decal so that a spring-loaded panel released below it to reveal a small white box.

Taking the little kit from Harrison, Kubba flipped open its lid and reached inside, quickly producing a long hollow needle.

"Hold him," she ordered, dipping her chin towards Marshall.

"His lips are blue," Harrison said, voice rising sharply. "What do we do, Lizzy? His fucking lips are blue!"

"Stop yelling like a bloody child and hold his shoulders. I'm going to relieve the pressure."

Prodding the left side of Marshall's chest, Kubba paused between two ribs then moved her fingers in a gentle circle as if massaging the muscles.

"I'm going to stick this fourteen gauge needle into the space between his second and third ribs, right here. Do you see?"

She tapped the spot.

"When that's all done, he'll be able to breathe better and we can move him. Ready?"

Beads of sweat ran down Harrison's long hooked nose and dropped free as he nodded his head emphatically.

"Good," said Kubba. "On three. One, two—"

Flashing down like a knife, the needle plunged deep into Marshall's grey skin, releasing a rush of gurgling air.

"Shit!" Harrison cried.

A fine spray of blood jetted from the needle as it settled.

"Don't worry about that," smiled Kubba, her tone detached and utterly chilling. "Just taking a little off the top, aren't we, Ralph?"

As quickly as it had started, the fountain ceased and the left side of Marshall's chest trembled then rose, re-inflating with sickening speed.

Melting against the cool Alon floor, Marshall thought the sound of air rushing into his lungs was as loud as the crashing surf. Suddenly exhausted, his fear unknotted like a coiled snake and the room above him grew dim. There were people coming. He could feel the vibrations of their footfalls as they ran down the hallway.

Closing his eyes, he took deep relaxing breaths and slipped into unconsciousness, knowing that he was safe and that his friend would protect him until he could again protect himself.

"Captain? Captain, are you awake?"

In the darkness of her quarters, Captain Tatyana Vodevski opened her eyes to the sound of tapping at her door. Again the gentle knock came, and again the voice of Amit Vyas, the ship's pilot and navigations officer, called to her.

"Captain? You in there?"

Taking hold of a handrail that ran laterally along the ceiling above her bed, Tatyana pulled herself up and out of the range of the electromagnets, which kept her secured during sleep.

"I'm here," she said, rolling her head from side to side as she unwound the fog of sleep from her mind.

With a soft shove, she drifted through zero-G to the hatch and opened it a sliver.

Hanging in the shadowed hallway, the whites of Amit's large brown eyes met her like twin moons.

"I'm sorry if I'm intruding," he said, craning his neck a little to peer around her partially opened hatch.

"No," sighed Tatyana, floating back to allow a full view of her empty room. "Joey is in his own quarters. He…"

She trailed off then held her hands up in a gesture of defeat.

"So, what can I do for you?"

Shoving off for the Bridge Deck at the end of the hall, Amit motioned for her to follow.

"I need to show you something," he said, his voice hopeful. "I think I've found Braun."

For a moment, Tatyana didn't understand what Amit had said, as if he were speaking a different language. Then it clicked.

"Did you say you've found Braun?" she called, jumping away from her hatch to float after the Indian.

Grabbing a bulkhead near the large circular opening into the Bridge Deck, Amit nodded then darted through. With another soft shove, he spiraled towards his command station, motion-detecting lights flicking on in his wake.

Slipping into his seat, he danced his fingers across the flat, mirrored surface of his Tablet console, bringing it online. Though clearly excited, he moved at a measured pace as he selected the auxiliary files then opened the program that netted and located radio signals.

13

Having earlier widened its search range to full capacity at Tatyana's command, Amit had been too distracted by yesterday's Pulse and ensuing drama to check back with the scan.

"Look!" he said triumphantly as Tatyana approached his station. "I checked the net this morning, and look what it found! The alien radio signal is coming from Phobos!"

Swearing in Russian, Tatyana leaned in to read the coordinates on the screen.

"Phobos," she whispered. "There must be something there, some kind of technology to power and amplify the signal."

"That's what I was thinking too. In fact, I've been going over all the reports I can find, and I haven't been able to come across a single trimensional projection of Phobos. I don't think it's ever been scanned with IMCs! There's probably been something there all along and we just never knew!"

Tatyana swore again.

"Why didn't we ever think to look closer?" she balked, her red hair forming a floating halo around her head.

"I'm not sure, Captain," shrugged Amit. "But the way I see it, Braun disappeared after engaging the signal, so tracing its origin might give us a way to, I don't know, shut it down or something. If he's not already dead, perhaps that will free him."

Gathering her hair up, Tatyana pulled it into a ponytail and flicked her eyes to the large oval-shaped observation window. Outside, Phobos was a grey rock in the distance.

"Shortly after Remus and Romulus disappeared," she spoke slowly. "Copernicus determined that they were not dead but in a sort of coma. It was as if their consciousnesses had been taken from their bodies and placed somewhere else. When we forced Braun to decode the signal, it appeared that the same thing had happened again. Now, the question we must ask ourselves is this: do we believe that this place, this *wherever* that the signal takes AI, is safe from Pulses?"

"I think we owe it to ourselves to find out," Amit said. "Besides, now that Julian is dead, we'll need Braun if we want to ignite the Torch Engine to get home."

Frowning thinly, Tatyana drilled Phobos with her eyes as it hung in space.

"True," she admitted after a beat. "However, we will need a pilot to fly us there, and, as of now, the only one we have isn't talking to me."

14

Lying still yet awake in his bed, James Floyd heard the door to his younger daughter's room open and close in the night. The slap of small bare feet padded down the hallway then the knob to his bedroom door creaked as it turned.

"Daddy?" came a voice from the dark at the foot of the bed.

"What's wrong?" he said, switching on the bedside light.

In the pale glow, his wife Nora mumbled and shifted but did not wake. How could she? On her nightstand, an open bottle of pills sat beside her Tablet.

"I had a bad dream again," his daughter said, standing at the corner of the bed with her face turned down. "The sky lights came back and hurt everyone!"

"It's okay," yawned James, beckoning for his daughter. "It's okay. Come here."

"Daddy, what if they come back again? I'm scared they might—"

"Don't think about that stuff," James interrupted. "Just don't think about it."

"Can I sleep with you and Mommy?"

Slipping out of bed, James took his daughter's hand and led her to the edge of the mattress. The floor was cold on his feet, the carpet replaced with hardwood the year before.

"Here, take my spot," he said. "There you go. Lie down."

"But—"

"No, it's okay, baby. Just take Daddy's spot. I need to go do some work."

"But—"

"I'll be right there in the next room, and Mommy is right here. See?"

"Okay..."

Pulling the covers up, James tucked his younger daughter in and swept loose strands of hair away from her sticky face, damp with nightmare sweat. Though her eyes protested his departure, pled nearly, he turned his back and walked across the room.

In his office, he left the lights off. He liked the dark better these days. Light reminded him of the Sun. The Sun reminded him of death.

Tablet in hand, he laid the flat screen gently on his desk. Glowing upon contact, the desk hummed slightly as it warmed up. Above him in the air, the logo of NASA faded in then was replaced with a list of

15

options. He selected his inbox and hunted the folder, looking for any new transmissions from his crew. Passing an old video sent to him over two weeks before by Dr. Viviana Calise, his eyes dipped down.

Dead, he thought. You're dead, and so are Liu and Julian.

Finding nothing new from his crew, James sighed. He had hoped at least to get an update from Captain Vodevski about Aguilar's state of mind, but clearly she wasn't interested in talking. Not surprisingly, their professional relationship had deteriorated in the wake of the last Pulse. Since then, Tatyana barely communicated with him, cutting him off like a spurned lover.

Ordering her to carry out Operation Columbia had not been James's idea, but it had been his job. She was disgusted with him because he was the only face she knew associated with the covert bombing.

Ah well, shrugged James in the darkness. I don't blame her. I don't blame any of them if they hate my guts. Forcing Julian to take part in the bombing cost *him* his life and *them* the only person alive capable of lighting the Nuclear Torch Engine on the ship. They're stuck now, and as far as they know, it's my fault.

In the next room, his daughter cried out in her sleep, but Nora didn't stir. How could she?

Sighing again, James opened a file he had received just a week before from a confused NASA programmer. Titled, *Continued Solar Disruptions,* the thing was a mass of equations, pictures, and videos compiled by the late great Braun. Though he didn't really know why he found it so interesting, James nonetheless began to sift through some of the data, feeling a sort of comfort in the work.

What to do?—Sol 118

Harrison Raheem Assad sat beside a sleeping Ralph Marshall in his friend's room. Wrapped in a stiff yellow bandage that covered most of his torso, the pilot snored softly as he slept. Clear plastic sacks of brown, red, and muddy-green liquid hung from a rack above, complicated medical names typed across them in tiny font. Tubes ran from each bag, ending in needles, which were sunk deeply into the unconscious man's veins as a part of his daily treatment.

On his Tablet, Harrison was using an application that allowed him to draw over and embellish the scans taken of the Martian ruin grid. Working from the memories of what he had seen in the construct, he cleaned up the crumbled domes and rebuilt the fallen apartments. When he reached the underground cathedral, his hand stopped, the stylus poised a fraction of a millimeter above the screen.

What was it for? Why did they all go there to die?

He tapped his foot on the ground rhythmically as he tested his imagination, seeking an explanation that would not come. Of all his visions in the ancient Mars construct, only one pertained to the cathedral, and that had occurred while it was still under construction.

"What are you working on?" came Marshall's voice, breaking Harrison's concentration.

Slowly looking up, the image of a million skeletons evaporated in Harrison's mind like morning fog. Marshall was watching him, the corners of his mouth curved into a pleasant smile.

"I'm just cleaning up the ruins a bit," Harrison said after a beat, tipping the Tablet so Marshall could see.

"Thought you already did that when you embellished the deep-soil CT scan."

"I did, but that was all speculation, you know, my imagination. This is what I saw with my own eyes."

Marshall shifted on his cot.

"I didn't know there was a difference."

Harrison chuckled and shook his head.

"I'll admit I had it pretty close, but there are little details I never could have pictured without actually seeing it.

"So, what? You're drawing them into the scan so it looks how it did in your dreams?"

"Yeah."

Wincing, Marshall sat up in bed.

"Whatever passes the time I guess," he said, letting out a thin breath.

"Ribs feeling any better today?" asked Harrison, eyeing Marshall's bandage.

"Much better," smiled Marshall, though the lines on his face said differently. "How about you? How are *you* doing?"

"What do you mean?"

"I mean, I zapped you back from a fucking flatline out there," frowned Marshall. "How's your heart?"

"Fine," shrugged Harrison.

Clearly annoyed by the lack of concern in Harrison's voice, Marshall scowled. Then, eyes falling to the tablet in Harrison's hands, he nodded and changed the subject.

"Why aren't you adding to the caves or the big cathedral-Sun-Room thing?"

Harrison looked down at the ruin grid and pursed his lips. One area of the picture was less complete, less regenerated, than any other spot. Ironically it was the only place the explorers had actually been able to access since finding a means to do so over a hundred sols before.

"Because it's the last spot that still confuses me," he said after a beat. "It's like, I get everything else now, you know? I saw them using technology supplied by the Travelers to cut stone and move it. I saw them making the wall, the domes, everything. But I still don't know *why* the caves have that feeling, that presence that Braun spoke of. And the mini-Sun is so fucking far out of my realm of comprehension that I'd rather just forget it even exists."

Marshall laughed painfully.

"Welcome to the party."

Smiling, Harrison got to his feet and started pacing around the small room.

"It's annoying," he went on. "I mean, I know there's something I'm overlooking, but I just can't place it. I feel like I'm so close to bringing everything into focus but just not there yet, you know? Fuck, man. Do you ever wish you were omnipotent?"

"Impotent?" scoffed Marshall. "No!"

Harrison laughed and shot his friend a wry look.

"Not impotent, omnipotent! God. Do you ever think with anything other than your dick?"

"I'm a pilot," Marshall winked. "So, no."

"Omnipotent," repeated Harrison. "Omnipotent, as in to *know all*. You get it, right?"

Marshall rose to his feet and stretched, careful not to exceed the length of his IVs.

"You're going to hate yourself in about three seconds," he said, grimacing as his rib popped quietly.

Harrison stared blankly, going over anything in his head that he might have missed.

"What?" he asked. "What is it?"

Looking very pleased with himself, Marshall tapped his head.

"Dreamland, buddy. You told me you know stuff in dreamland, like it just pops into your head or something. Hell, after I brought you back from the flatline, you wouldn't shut up about having a conversation with Braun! Why not take a little nap and do some investigating in the caves? Figure it out that way."

Harrison fell back into his chair and slapped a hand over his eyes.

"I told you you'd feel stupid," Marshall said, sitting down on the edge of his bed.

"I'll need drugs," mumbled Harrison.

"Don't we all?"

"Sleeping pills. I'll need sleeping pills. Strong ones at that. With the gene enhancement, I hardly sleep. And to get back there, I'll need to be out cold."

"Lizzy," Marshall sighed. "She'll have what you need."

At this, Harrison and Marshall exchanged a long look, both trying not to say what they were thinking.

"But she's not really doing so hot these days," said Harrison tactfully. "I mean, she's just a little stressed out or something."

"You're telling me," Marshall frowned. "Every time she changes my IVs, I double-check the labels to make sure she's not accidentally pumping me full of detergent. She's out there, man. Really weird. You think the Pulses cooked her brain?"

"Maybe."

"Well she's got all the drugs, my friend. So if you need 'em, you're going to have to go through her to get 'em."

On his feet again, Harrison set his Tablet on the bedside table.

"You want coffee?" he asked with a sly grin. "I'm thinking of taking a little trip to the galley. Maybe swing by the infirmary on my way back too."

"Black," said Marshall. "I want my coffee black and *hot*, so don't take too long, you hear?"

The Narrow Sea

Alone on the deck of his dead father's cargo ship, the merchant smuggler Marr turned his egg-shaped blue eyes to the limp sails above and prayed for wind. Avoiding the main route by taking the Narrow Sea, he hoped to put some distance between his double ender *The Feather* and the sleek black warships he'd seen patrolling the main arteries near the falls two hours before.

19

As high canyon walls rose up on either side of him, Marr felt the heat from the afternoon sun amplified like an oven. Despite this fact, a low chill of dread still clung to his heart, making him shiver unexpectedly.

Nearby, like angelic witnesses to a cosmic saga, stood the brothers Remus and Romulus. Be they prisoners or pilgrims, neither could remember, for the distinction was only a matter of perspective. Once sophisticated twin AIs, they now reflected the eons they had spent inside the ancient Mars construct. They were detached, curious, and passive all at the same time.

Drawn to this boat by the flight of the Martians Ze and Teo, who had only barely escaped Kaab's deadly purges, the brothers now engrossed themselves in this next chapter of their still-unfolding story.

With hands that were strong, Marr pulled back on the tiller then quickly pushed it forward. Repeating the movement over and over, he caused the rudder to fishtail, moving The Feather ahead despite the absence of wind. As the ship creaked and groaned, another noise could be heard hovering just below the deck. There, in a secret cargo hold formerly used by Marr's father for smuggling, hushed voices spoke rapidly.

Casting a look over his shoulder, Marr saw that there were still no black sails on the horizon behind them. Though not yet out of the woods, he judged that they were far enough ahead of anyone who might be following to allow his cargo a moment in the sun.

"Alright," he called. "You can come out for a bit."

Pushed up and to the side, a hidden panel on the deck gave way to the figure of a man, as he emerged from below. Turning to help the others out of the secret hold, the middle-aged Martian had the look of a diplomat yet the wary mannerisms of a battle-tested soldier.

Numbering twelve in all, he pulled the rest of the refugees from the cramped compartment and onto the deck where they huddled together near the mast. Save for the man himself, the leathery skin and frail limbs of the others betrayed their extreme age.

Breaking away from the small group, he rose and slipped a stone dagger into his belt. Careful to step over the tiller lines as he walked to stand beside Marr, his large blue eyes appeared bottomless in the brilliant midday sun.

"Hello, Ze," said Marr with a nod.

"How far back are they?" Ze returned.

"Far enough I think," replied Marr.

20

For a few moments, neither man spoke as Marr worked the long tiller back and forth. Responding to the action, the boat swayed rhythmically.

"I've never seen this place before," Ze said, breaking the silence. "Where are we?"

"The easternmost point of the Narrow Sea. I'm not really sure, to be honest. Farther than I've ever gone, though."

"What about your father? Did he ever venture this far east?"

Marr frowned as he thought then looked over his shoulder impulsively. The thin horizon was still empty.

"Yes," he said after a beat. "He once told me of a man who had seen an island past the cliffs of Tikka Tan. I think we're near."

Ze flicked his eyes across the faces of his fellow exiles and nodded. His mother Teo was there, sitting still and straight, her countenance set in an expression that was absent of fear or worry. Although she was thin and her skin hung loosely around her eyes, the fire, which had burned within her for all her life, seemed to smolder as brightly as it ever had.

"Maybe we should stop at the island," Ze offered after a long silence. "The Ancients need to rest properly."

Marr grunted as he worked the tiller, perspiration beading his purple brow.

"It has only been a short time since I saw Kaab's ships," he said. "We would be smarter to keep moving."

Ze nodded again, but his expression remained set in worry. All the nights without sleep in the cramped ship had already begun to affect his mother and the other Ancients. If they did not find safety soon, death would not be far off.

"We're being hunted, Ze," spoke Marr, as if reading his friend's mind. "Kaab wants anyone who remembers the arrival of the Great Spirits dead. He wants to control the story, shape it to his will. I know you worry about your mother, but you have done what few could. You saved her from his murderous guard. She is still alive."

"I was there too," Ze whispered, looking off into the distance. "I was but a boy, but I still remember the day their black ships came down from the sky."

"Then you not only saved your mother's hide," grinned Marr. "You saved your own as well!"

Turning to his friend, Ze fixed him with a desperate stare.

21

"But what good will that have been if she dies out here? If *they* die out here? We really should make land tonight."

"This is my ship, Ze," said Marr calmly. "Allow me the benefit of the doubt in this matter. The Narrow Sea eventually reconnects with the main channels. When it is safe and we've put enough distance between us and that lunatic, we can rest."

From a few paces off, Remus watched Ze nod reluctantly as he lapsed into another fretful silence. Sorry for the state of affairs and concerned about the Martians, there was absolutely nothing he and Romulus could do about it. Without even the gravity or substance of smoke, the twins were able only to observe and never interfere.

"How long do you suppose Kaab's ships will pursue?" Romulus said, following Ze's line of sight as the Martian stared off into the distance behind them.

"I don't really know," Remus shrugged. "I suppose it all depends on how badly that mad king would like to see our friends obliterated."

"If those awful purges were any indicator of his depravity," Romulus frowned. "Then I don't see this ending well for our dear Teo."

"Don't think like that," Remus said haughtily. "Who knows what the future holds in store."

"Indeed," agreed Romulus.

CHAPTER THREE

Onboard Braun—Sol 118

Captain Tatyana Vodevski slid through the quiet Crew Decks of Braun, hunting for Joseph Aguilar. Since returning from Operation Columbia ten days before, the pilot had been incredibly withdrawn, his presence little more than a change in the temperature of the room.

Having not seen Aguilar's name on the pill registry since then, Tatyana now worried that he hadn't slept in over a *week*. Without the pills, he wouldn't be able to sleep. And without sleep, he wouldn't be able to heal.

Together with Amit Vyas, Tatyana was anxious to explore Phobos and discover its secrets, yet she cared deeply for Joey and didn't want to see him self-destruct.

When there was no sign of the young pilot in his quarters, she moved on to the Lander Bay airlock and was relieved to see the hatch to the ladder shaft open. Slipping headfirst down the shaft, she descended some ten meters then entered into the Lander Bay and pushed off towards the turtle-shell-shaped craft.

"Joey?" she called, coming to the open side hatch.

Though Aguilar did not reply, the sounds of work in the cockpit told her that he was there. Ducking inside, she went forward through the cabin and pulled back the accordion partition that separated the rest of the Lander from the cockpit.

Met with a vision of chaos and desperation, she blinked.

Hanging amidst the numerous floating parts of a completely dismantled Flight Console, Joseph Aguilar was a sallow, haunted figure.

"What's going on here?" barked Tatyana, instantly forgetting the delicate nature of their current situation.

"What do you mean?" Aguilar returned, not looking at her as he snatched a green motherboard from the air to inspect it closely.

"What do I mean?" Tatyana said, her voice rising. "I mean, what have you done to the Lander?"

"I'm learning," shrugged Aguilar, letting go of the motherboard so that it drifted away.

"Learning?" Tatyana sputtered. "*Learning!* Explain yourself now, Lieutenant."

Slowly turning his bloodshot eyes on her, Aguilar narrowed them to fine red slits.

"Is that an order, *Captain*?"

Sidestepping the loaded question, Tatyana sighed and let the steel in her voice dissipate.

"I'm sorry," she said. "I'm just shocked to see our only Lander in this condition. Please tell me why you have done this, Joey. What are you up to?"

Aguilar smiled unpleasantly and grabbed a bundle of wires, shaking them in Tatyana's face.

"I'm learning," he repeated. "I'm the only one now. Since Julian and Braun are both gone, it all falls on *me* to fix the Lander if it gets cooked again. You want me to fly you to Phobos, fine. But I'm not going until I know how to fix this thing on my own, part for part."

Seeing how tired and frantic Aguilar had become, Tatyana felt a pang of regret for the way she'd spoken to him a moment before. Clearly he was cracking up under the weight of what he'd been through with Julian. If he didn't get some sleep soon, he might lose it completely.

Carefully, she reached out to touch his face, her delicate fingers pale against his tan skin.

"Joey," she said softly. "You need to rest. Come with me and I'll put you to bed."

Fervently shaking his head, Aguilar pulled away.

"No, no, no. I have to learn this stuff, Tatyana. What happens if a Pulse hits and we're out there? You don't know what that's like, but I do! I know because it *happened* to me."

Tatyana moved closer to Aguilar and tried to hold his darting gaze.

"Joey, if a Pulse were to hit now, wouldn't all of these parts be ruined? Don't you think we had better go to keep them safe?"

For several beats, Aguilar was motionless. However, behind his eyes, a great deal of activity seemed to be taking place.

"That's a good point," he said at last. "That's a really good point. We have to get out of here. We shouldn't even be near these parts! Some don't have spares—not that I know of, at least."

"You're right," Tatyana nodded, taking Aguilar's hand and leading him out of the cockpit. "We had better go up to the Crew Deck, no?"

Sliding the partition shut to ensure that none of the parts escaped behind them, Tatyana flicked one last glance inside the cluttered cockpit before closing it off.

She'd have to go over the blueprints with Amit later, figure out how to re-assemble the Flight Console without messing anything up. First though, she needed to put Aguilar down for a long much-needed nap.

Almost to the hatch, she was about to dip out into the bay when Aguilar suddenly hesitated and pulled his hand free of hers.

"Come on," she encouraged. "I'll take care of you, Joey."

"Wait," he said waveringly. "Just wait a goddamned minute!"

"What is it?" she asked, feeling rising anger radiate off him in waves. "What's wrong?"

Working his jaw, Aguilar glared at her. "You think you can be sweet to me and I'll forget what you did, is that it?"

"What are you talking about, Joey?"

"You knew, didn't you?" he demanded, bloodshot eyes vibrating in their sockets. "You fucking knew, but you didn't say anything."

"Knew what, Joey? Please be more specific."

"Killbots," he spat. "Automated War Machines, whatever! All that redacted information in the mission outline, all those blacked-out lines! It was Killbots!"

Casting her gaze to the ceiling, Tatyana nodded slowly.

She'd been expecting this, waiting for Aguilar to put two and two together. Though not the perfect time for such a conversation, there was no stopping it now.

"I wasn't positive until recently," she began. "But I did have my doubts."

"We should have been told!" shouted Aguilar, his face reflecting deep rage. "You let us fly out there with *no* fucking clue what we were really doing! You lied to me!"

Taking Tatyana by the shoulders, he dug his fingers in.

"You sent me on that mission like a fool with his fucking head in the sand. You don't give a shit about me, about anybody!"

Uninitiated by Aguilar's outburst, Tatyana leveled her eyes on him.

"Do you really think that little of me?" she said calmly. "After our time together, our nights? Do you think me that heartless?"

Something in Tatyana's words must have registered with the Lander pilot because he let go of her, his eyes welling up with tears.

"Julian's dead, Tatyana," he whispered. "He's dead."

"I know, my love," she sighed. "But it wasn't Automated War Machines that killed him. He's dead because of the Pulse. Because you ran out of time. No one could have prevented that. No one."

"But—" sniffed Aguilar. "But they lied to us. *You* let them lie to us. Why? Why did you do that?"

Smiling sadly, Tatyana reached for Joey and pulled the young man towards her, clasping his head to her breasts. All the fight was out of him now, all of the anger. He was frail and trembling against her, his nerves raw like exposed bone.

"Have you ever heard of the massacre at Najin?" she said. "During the Second Korean War?"

Feebly, Aguilar nodded.

"Then you'll remember what happened there," she continued softly. "Killbots, as you call them, murdered thousands of civilians, gunned them down in the surf as they fled their burning city. Ralph Marshall was there. Did you know that? Back when he flew for the UN, he was sent to Najin at the height of the slaughter."

Aguilar swore quietly but did not break from Tatyana's embrace.

"After that day," she went on, stroking his hair. "The United Nations passed a resolution that made using Killbots an act of *war*. Don't you see now, Joey? When the Chinese launched their Ark, they had technically already committed this crime. I guess the powers back home didn't want an all-out war, so they kept us in the dark and had us cover it up. We were used, Joey, all of us."

As Aguilar's warmth seeped in through the fabric of her jumpsuit, Tatyana felt a great weight lifted from her shoulders. She needed his touch, needed his companionship. Space was a cold and lonely place without the sumptuous heat of flesh.

She had wanted to tell him all of this the moment she'd put it together, but the shackles of her duty had bound her. Now though, she saw that this was merely a defense mechanism—a way of putting up walls. After all these years of worshiping her own her ironclad sense of duty, what had it really gotten her? She had few friends, no family, and an empty house on the Crimean peninsula. Aguilar was, without question, the most important human being she had in her life. He deserved better.

"From now on, I promise to always be honest with you," she said quietly, kissing the top of his head. "I won't keep things from you any more, even if it's only a suspicion, even if it's only a shadow of a doubt."

Completely limp in her arms, Aguilar finally succumbed to his guilt and fatigue, shuddering with internal sobs.

"Oh, god," he croaked. "He's dead, baby. He died so I could live. It hurts so much. So much."

Flashes of her childhood during the Eight Year Exile raced through Tatyana's mind. The dead and starving looked down at her from their frozen wasteland, judging the gift that was her life, compelling her to do great things with it.

"I know," she said. "But it will get better with time. Trust me."

The infirmary—Sol 118

Dr. Elizabeth Kubba was lying on the treatment bed in her infirmary half-asleep, half-awake. Resting against a stack of listless pillows, her freshly shaved head gleamed in the dim light and her foot tapped in time to an imaginary tune.

Having swapped out the painkiller-laced Survival Pack for a potent cocktail of amphetamines *and* barbiturates, she finally seemed to have gotten a grasp on Crisp and his haunting voice. For almost two full days, she had been able to enjoy her own little corner of hell sans any avenging spirits.

Echoing through the dense fog of self-medication, she heard the door open and shut as someone entered the room. Eyes still closed, she listened to the sounds of feet moving across the floor then stopping at the foot of the bed. Allowing her nostrils to flare, she took in the smell of coffee, soap, and a somewhat smoky musk.

"Hello, Harrison," she said.

"Lizzy."

"What can I do for you on this fine morning in hell?"

Moving across the room, Harrison set two things down on her desk, probably cups of coffee judging by the sound they made on the glass tabletop. Her hearing was out of control—a result of the drugs, no doubt.

"I suppose I was hoping you could help me," he returned nonchalantly.

Like dry leaves rustling against gravestones, Sabian Crisp stirred in the shadows. With numbing dread, Kubba felt the world around her run down as if it were oil. It hadn't worked. The pills weren't enough. Crisp was still there, hiding inside her.

Nearly screaming out loud from frustration and fear, Kubba quickly bit down, determined not to give Crisp the satisfaction.

"What kind of help are you looking for?" she asked, her eyes still closed.

"I'm not sleeping all that well," said Harrison, oblivious to the monster in the room. "I was hoping for some stronger pills than the ones I have."

"Were you?" Kubba replied distractedly, pupils dancing behind her lids.

"Is that a problem?"

Forcing a smile, she shook her head. "I've got more pills than I know what to do with, dear friend. Just take what you need. Over there, in the cabinet. Help yourself."

Clearly puzzled, Harrison was slow to respond.

"Well, that's nice of you, but it's locked. And I don't know exactly what I'm looking for. You're the doctor, so I was hoping you'd—"

Laughing with fabricated jubilation, Kubba slapped her leg and sat up in bed. Unable to remain shut any longer, her eyes opened like camera lenses and dialed down as they swept the room. Kicked off in a rush of energy, the amphetamines in her blood made the whole scene sparkle, each point of light stretching out like a thousand horizons.

"Yes, yes that's right, isn't it?" she babbled. "I *am* the doctor, as you're so fond of saying!"

Taking a step back, Harrison gave Kubba a perplexed look. "Well, that's what it says on your name tag," he muttered.

"Do you dream?" she asked, springing to her feet.

"Sometimes."

"And what is it that you dream of? Lights? Voices? What?"

Harrison was quiet for several seconds, watching Kubba with barely suppressed concern on his face.

"Lots of different stuff," he said at last.

"Do you dream of Liu?" she prodded, suddenly deadly serious.

"Yes," Harrison replied calmly. "Sometimes I get the feeling that she's there, but I never see her."

"That's because she's not here with us. She was such a good person. A really kind and nice person. She was too good for this place, wouldn't you say?"

Again, Harrison was slow to answer.

28

In the silence, Kubba could see lights buzzing around his eyes like flies on a dead horse.

"I guess," he finally said. "Look, what are we talking about here?"

"Yes," Kubba grinned. "What *are* we talking about here?"

"You're asking if I dream about Liu. I'm saying I do sometimes. Why do you care what I'm dreaming about anyway? How is that relevant to my need to sleep?"

He knows what you did, Crisp announced, his breath damp on Kubba's neck.

"Well, you seem busy," she said abruptly, smelling Crisp like a disease. "I'm going to prescribe you 1,400 milligrams of Nocturnall. It's very nice. You'll love it."

"Thank you," Harrison frowned, stepping aside to clear a path to the controlled medication cabinet on the opposite wall.

With the urge to scream, attack, fight, and run, thrumming through her every nerve all at once, Kubba nodded and smiled shakily. Suddenly achy all over, it was as if she had suffered the effects of another Pulse and was only just now becoming aware. Fighting for control of her senses, the two different types of drugs tossed her back and forth between high and low like a ship on stormy seas.

Carefully, she walked across the room in halting, jilted steps, almost positive that it was not she who was moving, but rather the entire planet beneath her. Reaching the glass-faced cabinet, she pressed her palm to a glowing green square—unlocking the door with a metallic click.

Her back to Harrison, she began picking up bottles almost at random, not really reading the names as her vision swam in and out of clarity.

Behind her, the darkness hung in her peripheral vision like a living and hungry creature. Moving about the room, it began to congeal and take the shape of a man, sitting on the edge of her bed.

Absently, Kubba opened a canister without looking at it and dumped the entire contents into her palm. Clutching the pills in one hand and the empty canister in the other, she spun around quickly, fully expecting to see a leering Sabian Crisp sitting on her bed. However, to her extreme distress, he was not there.

Go on, he suddenly laughed in her right ear. *Give him the pills, Lizzy. Give him all the sleep in the world.*

Dropping both the pills and the canister, Kubba yelped despite her best efforts to suppress her terror.

"Liz, are you okay?" Harrison said, rushing to help her as she bent and began scooping pills into the canister.

"Yes, oh dear. I'm just, I'm just, I'm just so tired, I think," she stammered, her eyes glittering with the light of held-back tears.

Slipping the last of the pills back into the bottle, she glanced distractedly at the label then froze. They were painkillers intended for post-surgery, not sleeping pills. The dose she was holding, if taken, would stop Harrison's heart past all hope of resuscitation.

Frantically, she faced the cabinet again and screwed down the lid tightly, cold sweat beading on her bald head.

What's wrong? Crisp taunted. *If he's already dead, what does it matter?*

Locating the Nocturnall, Kubba plucked three orange pills from the bottle and cleared her throat loudly.

"Here you are," she announced.

"Thanks," Harrison said, trying hard to make eye contact with Kubba as he accepted the pills. "Liz, really, are you *all right?*"

He knows, growled Crisp.

"I'm fine," she smiled, her teeth rattling quietly. "Just tired, like you. Everybody has to sleep, even a doctor!"

"Right," nodded Harrison, putting the pills in his pocket then reaching for his two cups of coffee. "I'm around, you know. If you need to talk, that is. Just remember that."

"Thank you," Kubba trembled. "Now, on your way."

Quitting the room, Harrison shot Kubba one last worried look as the door latched shut. Alone, Kubba instantly began to cry tears as thick as mercury.

Laughing from all around her, Sabian Crisp reveled in her misery. Defiantly dashing back to the cabinet, she uncapped the pills she'd tried to give Harrison and stuffed two in her mouth, swallowing them dry. In time, Crisp's laughter faded to nothing more than the sound of blood rushing in her ears.

Easing back onto the bed, she closed her eyes and prayed for sleep.

ABCs—Sol 118

"A is for ancient, A is for art. B is for Braun, B is for broken. C is for construct, C is for copy…"

In Liu's old machine shop, YiJay Lee listened with a mixture of exasperation and curiosity as Ilia performed the Personality Matrix Interface Test or PMIT.

Designed by YiJay, the test was a word association game intended to help assess the level of separation between a copied AI's new personality and that of the original intelligence it was cloned from.

Due to the nature of the cloning process, much of the personality of a freshly copied AI was really just a mirror of its already-self-aware predecessor. Thus, YiJay had developed the PMIT to better understand what areas of the new AI's Open-Code Connection Cells needed the most attention.

Having already created a reliable matrix of Braun's subconscious word associations, YiJay then put Ilia through the same test, judging her results against his. The idea was that as Ilia matured, the likelihood of Braun's word associations cropping up as one of Ilia's would fall to an acceptable minimum, taking random chance into account of course.

However, as a seeming byproduct to surviving the latest Pulse, Ilia's PMIT results had frozen since coming back online. She neither improved nor backslid. She simply halted where she had been before the Pulse and stayed that way no matter how YiJay tinkered with her.

"Okay," said the Korean abruptly, interrupting Ilia at G. "That's enough for now."

"Did I do a good job?" Ilia asked honestly.

"Very," YiJay sighed, a note of defeat in her voice.

Allowing the timer in the upper right hand corner of her Tablet to count down from five to zero, YiJay watched as the fractal pattern of Ilia's being disappeared from her screen.

"Go to sleep," she mumbled, bringing up the dormant AI's Open-Code Connection Cells.

As the lines of data and equations scrawled across the Tablet's face, YiJay tried to look past the numbers to what they actually represented. Here and there, things began to stand out. The desire to improve was clear, as were feelings of loneliness, joy, curiosity, and a profound interest in the other members of the crew, particularly Harrison. Surprised by this, YiJay halted the moving numbers and tried to decode the emotions attached to the archaeologist. More complex than she'd been expecting, she figured that they were likely left over from Braun, as Ilia had never actually met Harrison.

I wouldn't fault you if you did like him though, girl, she smiled. *He is handsome.*

Long-since having given up on holding a grudge towards Harrison, YiJay didn't blame him anymore for what had happened to Braun. She knew now that he had been desperate, grasping at anything to give Liu's death meaning. In that confused state, sending Braun to decode the anomalous radio signal had probably sounded like a good idea to him.

Besides what did it really matter? Braun would have died with the rest of the AI in the first Pulse anyway, so Harrison's actions were inconsequential. True, his experiment had been a tremendous failure, but at least her Braun had gone out with a bang rather than a whisper.

Most important though, was the fact that YiJay carried something of a torch for Harrison. Despite all his gentle rebuffs, despite the inconvenient reality that he and Liu had been in love, despite everything, she just couldn't help herself. When you lived on the fringe, you needed to *need* someone—lest you forget what being human was all about.

In her mind, the young Korean replayed all the times Harrison had touched her, amplifying both the sensation and the significance of the interactions. His face was kind, his body was lean, and his eyes were mysterious but friendly at the same time.

Realizing with a start that she was fantasizing about a man inside his dead girlfriend's machine shop, a shudder ran up YiJay's spine.

Good thing I don't believe in ghosts, she told herself, quickly turning her attention back to Ilia's Open-Code Connection Cells.

Fingers sliding across the screen, she moved sequences of numbers about until a gentle rapping came from the door halting her work. Glancing at the screen above the entrance, she saw that it was William.

"Come in," she called, setting her Tablet facedown on the table.

Nudging open the door with his foot, William came into the shop, holding two steaming cups of tea.

"Thought you might like a warm drink," he said, an awkward smile plastered on his lips.

"Thank you," YiJay smiled back, taking the drink and sipping from it eagerly.

Allowing his gaze to dance around the room, William's eyes fell on YiJay's Tablet.

"Working on anything important?"

Unsure how to answer, YiJay froze. Up until this point, she had kept Ilia's existence a total secret. The last thing she wanted to do was turn her baby over to the fumbling hands of some government-sanctioned AI programmer back on Earth so he could crack her open like an egg. Even though she recognized Ilia's importance in the wake of the AI extinction, she still felt that the only way to protect her was to keep her secret until she could protect herself.

"Not really," she said at last, speaking into her tea.

Resting his backside against a workbench, William picked at the rim of his cup absently. Outwardly calm, there was something odd about the way he leaned forward that seemed to denote he had a reason for this little visit.

"I know about Ilia," he suddenly spoke. "I mean, that is, I found out about her. Don't worry though, I won't tell."

YiJay snapped her head up, but the look on William's face told her in one simple expression that she need not fear.

"How did you find out?"

William sipped from his tea and shrugged.

"I noticed that power was being siphoned off of the main grid to feed those insulated server banks over there."

He tipped his head towards the physical housing of Ilia's being.

"By the way, it's a very nice setup. Smart stuff. Does it really work? Did she really survive the last Pulse intact?"

YiJay nodded but said nothing. She wasn't exactly thrilled that William had found out about Ilia, but if it had to be anyone, she was glad it was him. Always respectful and genuine towards her, YiJay knew he could be trusted.

"So what's she like?" he asked.

"She's different," said YiJay with a small smile.

"That's good! We need a little more diversity around here."

The two laughed at this for a moment, during which time YiJay noticed just how blue William's eyes really were.

"So," he pressed, his arms crossed at his narrow chest. "When can I meet her?"

"Soon I guess," YiJay nearly whispered.

"Ilia," William said as if trying the name on for size. "It has a wonderful ring to it, I must admit."

"Thank you."

"Where does it come from?"

Glancing up, YiJay put on a confused expression.

33

"Didn't you read about it in the statement? Back before we left, it was in the press statement NASA put out."

"Sure, I read it, but all that was in there was something about Roman Mythology. I know you wouldn't have picked a name if it wasn't important."

YiJay blushed. "Do you really want to hear the whole story?" she said with a nervous smile.

Wordlessly, William nodded.

"Well," YiJay sighed, hesitating as if unsure how to properly begin. "Well, there was once this young queen named Ilia, but that's not why I named *our* Ilia that. No, it's actually because of what that queen did, or rather, who her kids were."

"Sounds mysterious," interjected William with a grin.

Laughing a little, YiJay put a hand to her cheek, feeling the warmth of a blush still there.

"You know, it is a little mysterious," she went on. "Because the night she was supposed to be married to the king, whose name escapes me, he was *murdered* by his brother, whose name also escapes me."

"That's why it never pays to be king," William mumbled, sipping his tea.

"I know, right?" cried YiJay, her normally timid voice now lyrical and full. "She didn't even really get to become queen because they didn't, you know, consummate anything."

"For shame!" William replied in exaggerated fashion.

"So she's banished by the new king," YiJay went on. "To go live the rest of her life as a *virgin* priestess for some goddess or other with a bunch of other virgins at some temple. But, not long after arriving there, she ends up pregnant!"

"Who was the father?" asked William, enjoying the yarn.

Grinning, YiJay shot him a look. "I'm getting there! Hold your horses! Now, she hides her secret because it's against the rules and she'll be killed if any of the other virgins find out, but eventually, as is bound to happen, the babies come."

"Wait," William said. "*Babies*? As in, more than one?"

"Yes!" laughed YiJay. "Twins in fact! Two little boys who she has to abandon in order to keep them from being killed by the other priestesses."

A sly expression crept over William's face, as he finally understood where YiJay was going with all of this.

34

"I have a feeling those boys grew up to become quite famous. Am I right?"

"If by, 'famous,' you mean the backbone of Roman Mythology," YiJay replied. "Then yes, they are very famous. You'd know them as Remus and Romulus."

"Which would make the god Mars the one who put poor Ilia in that dangerous predicament, wouldn't it?" beamed William. "Boy, when I hear the saying, 'what's in a name,' I never think just how much might actually be in there!"

"I like things with layers," said YiJay happily.

"Clearly," William returned, arching an eyebrow. "So when were you planning on sharing Ilia with the rest of us?"

"She's not ready yet," YiJay frowned. "In fact, I'm not sure that she'll ever be. Even though she survived both Pulses, she was badly damaged by the first. I don't think there's any way she can grow past what she is now."

"That's sad to hear," William said.

"I know. I just wish there was something more I could do for her."

"Is there?"

YiJay looked at the servers and shook her head. "No, I don't think so."

Setting his cup aside, William shrugged. "Then it sounds like she's as ready as she needs to be. I mean, if there is nothing more you can do for her, why not let her off the leash?"

"It's not that simple," said YiJay a little defensively. "I can't let her leave the Base or else she might get killed if there's another Pulse."

"Not if a radio uplink is established between her and those servers to stream any new experiences or information she might have while out and about. That way, she'd be backed up if the worst were to happen."

Already taking his Tablet from his pocket, William began to work up a schematic as he spoke.

"Just off the top of my head, I'd say we have more than enough spare parts around to put together an Uplink Transmitter just for her."

"Maybe," YiJay nodded absently. "But the channel would need to be dedicated so that overlapping data wouldn't cause any delay in coding and storage. She can't be in two places at once, not after the damage she's had, so any Uplink Transmitter we build would need to be able to send huge amounts of data. Her entire personality, to be specific."

35

"I love a challenge," grinned William.

"Wait," said YiJay. "Are we really talking about this? You would do that for her? For me?"

"It's why I came down here."

"Really? Why?"

"Because," William replied, looking at her with those blue eyes. "When I found out about Ilia, it just seemed sad that she wasn't able to see the world outside of this sterile Base. With all that's been going on, it would be nice to accomplish something that brings some joy to a living soul."

Moved by William's kindness, YiJay also sensed another motive behind his actions. Building the radio uplink would require that the two work together closely, sharing information and time with one another. To be honest, the idea was not outwardly off-putting, and the more she thought about it, the better it sounded.

"Heck," William was saying. "I can even fabricate most of the parts right in here. It is a shop, after all. I'm guessing the real work will come when we have to climb the Communications Relay Tower to pirate one of the Dishes for Ilia's encrypted signal."

Gazing at William with a fresh perspective, YiJay allowed herself to see that he was, in his own way, very good looking. Though thin and wiry, there was a strength that shone from him, an endurance that fueled his confidence.

Catching her looking at him, William tipped his head to the side. "Well?"

With a smile splitting her small face, YiJay began to blush again. "Okay," she laughed. "Let's do it."

"Good," said William. "I'll get my things!"

04—Sol 118

As it made its way through the deep sand of the Valles Marineris, 04 the Chinese Automated War Machine scanned the high canyon walls, which boxed it in. Unable to find any plausible ways to climb out, it trekked on, leaving the skittering footprints of an insect in its wake.

For some reason, it could not connect with its GPS and thus did not know exactly where it was. Surmising that the Ark, to which it should have been linked, was either destroyed or rendered inoperable, it now relied on its Landmark Location Software to deduce its position in the vast canyon network. However, this was not an optimal course of action as already it had become lost several times and been forced to retrace its steps.

Since coming online ten sols before, 04 had received no directives from any of the authorized human handlers in its crew dossier. Deducing that their fate might be tied to that of the Ark, it automatically reverted to a preprogrammed mission outline.

Inputted over six months ago, when 04 was still in Earth orbit, this mission outline was a simple one: find the target, neutralize the human crew if necessary, and await further instructions.

Spying in the distance a new canyon, which fed into the one 04 now explored, it set its bearings in that direction. As the Sun sank low in the pink sky, the Automated War Machine pressed on with relentless determination.

Earth—Eleven days after the last Pulse

James Floyd drank deeply from a cold cup of coffee. Sitting at his desk in his home office, he had not shaved in more than three days—his chin a shadow of stubble.

In the bedroom, he heard the sounds of a morning news show, lighthearted, overly excited, and utterly fake. He didn't understand how Nora could watch that shit, not when the sky was literally falling.

Rubbing his eyes, his tried to listen in on what the talking heads were jabbering about.

Sports? No…music.

Chuckling archly, James heard the fear in their voices. Though these people dripped fructose corn syrup for a living, even they couldn't hide fear like this.

It was now the morning of the eleventh day since the last Pulse. If the gap between the first two could be trusted as any indicator, then that meant there were likely only four days until another Pulse struck out with deadly force.

Opening the bottom-left-hand drawer of his desk, James took out a half-empty bottle of bourbon and uncapped it. A gift from a coworker, he didn't even like whisky but added a healthy dose to the coffee left in his mug anyway. Mixing in with the coffee, the bourbon diluted the drink to the pale brown of a fish tank that had been neglected.

Experimentally sipping at the concoction, he smiled.

Not bad.

Buzzing like a mad hornet, James's Tablet began dancing across the desktop. He let it get nearly to the edge before scooping it up to answer the call.

"This is James."

"Floyd," said a stern female voice. "This is Eve. Put me up on vid. We need to talk."

"Hello, Eve," sighed James. "I wasn't expecting a call from you. Barnes maybe, but not you."

Setting the Tablet down on the Smart Glass of his tabletop, James entered a command and synced the two computers. With a low hum, the desk began to glow. like magic, the face of Eve Bear, Chief of Staff to the President of the United States, leapt into the air.

"Floyd," she said again.

"Bear," returned James, mimicking Eve's seriousness.

"I'm glad I caught you before you left for work."

Smiling, James drank from his cup.

"I'm going to go out on a limb and say that was a joke. Am I right?"

Eve stared down at him for a moment, her green eyes like LEDs in the sunken ship that had become her face.

"You look like shit," she said at last.

"I was going to say the same thing about you," grinned James. "But somehow I get the feeling you're your own harshest critic."

Allowing a small smile to tug at the corners of her red painted lips, Eve softened and some of the beauty she was famous for returned to her face.

"You've seen the pictures of me in my twenties," she said in a leading voice. "I don't need to defend my reputation."

"I have. And you don't," James agreed.

"Why aren't you going to work, James?" asked Eve, using his first name in an uncharacteristic attempt at closeness. "Is it because of the EVA moratorium on the Mars team? We can work around that if you have any ideas."

Shrugging, James sipped his coffee and bourbon.

"It's not that. I'm just busy is all. I'm working on something."

"Busy with what? What are you working on?"

"It's related to the Pulses, Eve."

At this, the soft filter of elegance that had made Eve look mysterious and enticing faltered then fell.

"What do you mean?"

"It's long and complicated," said James. "You wouldn't understand it. Even I don't. Not really, anyway."

"Listen," Eve snapped, suddenly on the offensive. "You don't go to work for over a week. You delegate all of your *federally assigned* job responsibilities to a bunch of technicians and interns. Then you sit around at home all day and do God-knows-what. If you think you can just bat your fucking eyes at me like we're old chums and I'll let you do whatever you want, then you better think again, buster. When I ask you to explain something to me, I expect you to explain it."

"All right. Sheesh," shrugged James, putting his cup on the table and reaching for the bourbon by his foot. "Can I at least pour you a drink?"

Eyes narrowing to fine pricks of emerald, Eve scowled.

"Are. You. Serious." she said, spacing the words out like individual accusations.

James shrugged again and slopped more bourbon into his cup.

"Okay. Here's the thing, Eve," he began. "Two days after the last Pulse, I get this email from a numbers guy down in the AI department. He's been running through lines of data that Braun sent home, looking to make sure the Pulse didn't wipe any out."

"And?" Eve cut in. "Did it?"

"No," James said flatly. "No, the data is all there. But that's where I'm going with this. You see, when the tech was running through the old data he comes across this weird file that Braun had started. Get this, the title is *Continued Solar Disruption*, and he seems to have been working on it since about three hours after he came online."

"Three hours? What does that mean?"

"Basically Braun was a god," replied James. "He was born smarter than anything ever known and began using those smarts pretty much instantly. I'm beginning to get the idea that we had no fucking clue what we were doing when we made the AI, especially him. Look, the equations in this file are insane. I've never seen anything like them. No one has."

"So what are they?" Eve muttered. "With a title like Continued Solar Disruption, I'm inclined to think he knew something about the Sun that we didn't."

"That would be the understatement of the century," smirked James. "To put it in words a layman could grasp, Braun appears to have been trying to predict the future using math."

"What?"

"Most of these equations don't make sense on their own. It's like they're incomplete. A few though, a few of them turn up some very interesting results when plugged into astronomic simulators. For example, one of the more comprehensible equations shows why the solar flare, two days after the team touched down, was able to affect Earth and Mars at the same time."

Eve stared blankly for a few beats, clearly not understanding.

"You do know that Earth and Mars are different planets, right?" said James.

"Yes, Floyd," she returned. "Please explain."

Draining the last of his drink, James again splashed a few slugs of bourbon into the mug.

"Okay, it's like this. The Earth and Mars are orbiting the Sun, right? Well that's all fine and dandy, but we only all line up with each other every seven hundred eighty-something days."

"Line up?"

"Yeah. The Sun, then Earth, then Mars. All in a line."

Nodding, Eve's eyes grew distant as she seemed to grasp where James was going with all of this.

"Wait," she said. "Are you saying we were perfectly lined up when the solar flare hit? Is that why it affected both us and the Mars team?"

"No," James smiled. "We weren't lined up at all."

"Then how did it hit both of us?"

"Exactly."

Frustrated, Eve rolled her eyes.

"Stop drawing it out, Floyd. I'm a very busy person. What does this mean?"

"It means," said James. "That there were actually two solar flares releasing huge streams of plasma, radioactivity, and electromagnetic radiation in two different directions. One at Earth, one at Mars."

"How is that possible?"

"Well, it shouldn't be!" shouted James, a half-drunken smile on his face. "That's why no one caught it. This must have been the scientific faux pas of the fucking millennium, and it went totally unnoticed! We all had other things on our minds, I guess."

"So how does this relate to the Pulses?" asked Eve, her eyes darting down to check her watch.

"Are you in a hurry or something?" James frowned. "Am I keeping you?"

Settling her gaze on James, Eve left it there to burn into him for a few seconds.

"I have a meeting with the Chinese ambassador in eight minutes," she said at last.

"Oh we're talking to the Chinese again, are we?" laughed James mockingly. "Good. That's just great! Why don't you thank them for causing the death of one of my crew members, will you? You remember Julian? Julian Thomas? Go ahead and thank them from me, will you?"

"Enough," Eve snapped. "Everyone has bigger fish to fry now. They might have valuable information that can help prepare us for what's coming. We're all trying to work together now. I don't have to tell you that there are only four more days until we might get zapped with another Pulse. Even the Chinese can't escape that. None of us can."

James tipped his head to the side and squinted.

"You made me force my crew to carry out an act of terrorism. *Terrorism*, Eve. And now you're playing it off like it was no big deal. These people are scientists and engineers, not spies."

"They were all we had," Eve fired back. "Besides, we did it to protect your damn crew. When you're ready to get off the cross and walk around down here with the rest of us, let me know. Until then, answer my damn questions. How does the solar flare, or flares rather, relate to the Pulses?"

Considering an impulse to hang up, James took a painful gulp of his bourbon. It was beginning to taste worse and worse.

"The Sun," he said, wiping his mouth with the back of his sleeve. "Has all these different layers just like Earth does. Only, unlike us,

41

they're all rotating in different directions. See, the outer layer rotates one way while the inner regions, the core and radiative zones, rotate at different speeds and in different directions. Now here's where it gets a little weird. Usually, solar flares originate from the surface as a result of a coronal mass ejection."

Eve said nothing but nodded for James to continue.

"But like I told you," he sighed. "This is where it gets weird. The source of the flares that hit us actually came from one of the inner regions. From the core, to be exact. It burst up through all the layers in a huge explosion then forked off at the surface to head towards Earth and Mars respectively. Now, Braun has marked, with his equations, the location on the core where the flare originated, like drawing a dot on a ball. It's a wound of some kind, Eve. A tear in the fabric of the Sun's core. You still with me?"

Again Eve tipped her head and remained silent.

"Good," nodded James. "Because on the date of the first Pulse, Earth drifted right in front of the wound. And on the date of the second Pulse, Mars did the same thing. They lined up, Eve. The wound that caused the flares marks some kind of danger zone, a channel, if you will. It's like Earth, Mars, and the tear on the Sun's core are all reacting to each other, causing Pulses when one lines up."

"So when do we line up again?" asked Eve, her eyes dim. "Us and that tear. When is the next time we can expect a Pulse?"

"I don't know yet," said James, shaking his head.

"Well, if it's all as simple as a dot on a ball, as you put it, why not just track the dot as it spins and tell me when it lines up again?"

"Because," James sighed with some frustration. "The ball isn't just spinning in a circle. It's rolling, spiraling, flipping back on itself, and changing directions seemingly at random. This is the core of the *Sun*, Eve, not some planet in the depths of space. It's the thing that *controls* all the planets, remember? It plays by its own rules."

"So what's *your* game plan?" returned Eve haughtily. "How are you going to predict the next alignment?"

"Like I said earlier," James shrugged. "I'm working on it."

CHAPTER FIVE

Night—Sol 118

After a late dinner of steamed vegetables and rice, Harrison Assad and Ralph Marshall took leave of the rest of the crew and headed upstairs. Coming into Harrison's lab, Marshall made directly for a chair and sat down stiffly, a slightly shaking hand on his side.

"You okay?" said Harrison, regarding his friend with concern.

"Yeah," Marshall nodded. "Stairs, man. They get me, is all."

"You didn't have to come, you know. It's not like I'm going to be in any danger."

Laughing despite the stitch in his side, Marshall fixed Harrison with an amused stare.

"If you got those drugs from Lizzy, then you don't know what kind of trouble you might or might not be in!"

Harrison nodded his agreement as he fished the three orange pills Kubba had given him out of his breast pocket to examine them.

"What are they?" Marshall asked.

"They're called Nocturnall," replied Harrison, holding one of the pills up to the light as if to spy a secret floating in its core. "They're some kind of sleeping pills."

Marshall started laughing again, and reflexively his hand went to his side.

"Nocturnall," he repeated. "Who names these things?"

Harrison shook his head and smiled.

"God only knows."

Taking a small bottle of water out of a drawer, he walked across the room to the cot he kept in the corner.

"Are you sure this is really a good idea?" Marshall said. "I mean, maybe you don't need her drugs."

"I wish," frowned Harrison. "But if I'm not out—like, totally lights out—I can't get anything useful from the construct."

"So you think that place really is a computer simulation or something?"

Harrison sat on the cot, its legs bowing under his weight.

"Well, that's what Braun called it. Besides, when I'm there I just know things. I can fly, walk through walls, all sorts of stuff. How else do you explain that if not some kind of a simulation?"

Marshall was silent for a moment, his expression troubled.

43

"It sounds like being dead," he said at last.

Harrison smiled over at his friend, trying to ease the mood. "I guess it was last time. But you're here, right? You wouldn't let me die again."

Marshall allowed a grin to tug at his mouth, though he tried to remain somber. "Yeah, yeah. So what's your plan? You going to take one at a time or all three?"

"Give you ten bucks if you guess it right," Harrison shot, tipping his head back and throwing the pills into his mouth.

"So much for my ten bucks," sighed Marshall, his eyes deep and anxious.

"You really don't have to stick around," Harrison said, lying down on the cot. "I'm probably not going to be all that interesting for the next few hours."

"Ah," Marshall shrugged, taking out his Tablet. "What else have I got going on?"

Glowing to life as he turned it on, Marshall stared at the screen for minute or two, his eyes locked onto somewhere far off beyond the words.

"What are you reading?" Harrison asked, gesturing to the Tablet. "If it's not something dirty, that is. Don't tell me if you're watching porn."

With a little chuckle, Marshall shook his head and came back to the moment.

"No, nothing like that. I'm actually reading Viviana's notes about the Greenhouse. I figure I might take over her responsibilities there. Tonight's dinner was the last of the frozen veggies we had. I'm sure there's plenty more growing in there. Just haven't been by yet to pick them, you know? Figure I'll start harvesting tomorrow, maybe learn the ropes from Viv's notes and see if I can't keep her garden alive for her. She'd appreciate that, I think."

Finishing awkwardly, Marshall grew silent. Though his gaze stayed in the room this time, it flicked around like a fly and never landed close to Harrison's.

"She would really like that, man," said Harrison softly.

"Feel anything yet?" Marshall asked, changing the subject abruptly.

"Fine so far," smiled Harrison. "Maybe it takes a while. I don't know. Lizzy didn't really give me instructions or anything."

44

Marshall nodded thoughtfully but he seemed to be miles away again.

Resting his head against the pillows, Harrison stared at the ceiling, deciding to leave his friend alone with his thoughts.

In the pale hues that textured the Alon plating above him, he strained to see his own reflection—returned in shades of creamy grey. As the silence of the room persisted and Marshall remained distant, Harrison felt the drugs trickle into his eyes. Soon becoming too heavy to keep open, his lids pressed down until the outside world was shut out and everything was black.

In the void, a sea of shadows swam around him. Crying out, the voices of these shapeless forms laughed, screamed, or simply babbled along like water in a storm drain.

Try as he might in this strange and foreign place, Harrison could not see beyond himself. The darkness that cocooned him, though invisible, was almost as suffocating as smoke.

Something was wrong. This wasn't how he remembered the ancient Mars construct. This wasn't the way it was supposed to feel.

"Hello?" he called into the blurred, moving shadows.

Repeated a thousand times over and coming from a thousand places at once, his voice boomed back at him.

"Hello?" it mocked. "Hello? Hello? Hello? Hello?"

Like sparking a match in a room full of mirrors, pricks of static light multiplied and danced in the echoes of his still-fading voice. Spreading out, they morphed into a galaxy of blinding needles that hung dangerously around him. Slowly stirred by the cosmic winds, they began to scatter and swirl until there was a blizzard of movement that covered the endless oblivion.

Unable to shut his eyes against the assault, Harrison grew alarmed. He was being swarmed, overcome by the sharp pricks of light as they sank deeply into his soul. Pulled in many directions at once, he felt himself being drained—as if each shard of the quantum blizzard was a vortex through which only consciousness could pass. Spirited away down these winding paths, he became many and one at the same time—racing, as it were, towards a joined event horizon.

Pitched suddenly forward onto the hot rocks of a cobblestone street, his sight dialed down to a single perspective as he reconsolidated himself. Gone was the vast storm of light, replaced by a lone vision that was so terrible it instantly made Harrison wish for the blizzard.

Finally back in the world of ancient Mars, he now beheld the face of the apocalypse, burning savagely in the sky above. As the gasses, which had once made this planet livable, burst into flames like oil slicks in the air, the buildings around him crumbled into smoldering heaps.

Incandescent in the hellish heavens, the Sun was a deep red—its pain evident even from so many millions of miles away. Threatening to burst with pregnant fury, it warped and heaved. Then a crack that shook the very layers of reality gave way from the center of the tortured star, releasing a pulse of blinding, electric light.

Washing across the planet in a tsunami of deadly waves, it passed through Harrison on its way to living targets. Though he could not see it with his own eyes, he knew that in that moment, every conscious thing on Mars had just died. It was a *Pulse*, bigger than any yet felt by mankind, but a Pulse nonetheless.

Overwhelmed by the nightmare, Harrison felt his finger-hold on the moment begin to slip. Evaporating, the vision was gone, replaced again by the storm of endless possibilities.

He was freefalling, spiraling like the starlight, shocked through time immemorial.

With each blink, he was somewhere else, watching *something* else unfold in hyperspace. In this state, reality became realities and his sense of self became an abstraction. There was no present, no past. Everything was in the future, laid out before him like a coded map of the stars.

Moments imprinted themselves on his soul as if it was paper and they ink. In one, he saw the mini-Sun turning slowly above the smooth metal device that powered it. As wisps of filament-thin energy webbed out, the entire scene began to stretch on into infinity, each second becoming a lifetime. With a blinding sense of certainty, Harrison suddenly realized that although he was multiplying exponentially, some part of him—some shard of his consciousness—would be here in this place forever. It was important.

And then, with a shock as unsettling as death, it was all over.

Flying out of bed, he crashed onto the floor of his lab and gasped at the air.

Scared so badly that he dropped his Tablet, Ralph Marshall struggled out of his chair and onto his knees beside the young Egyptian.

"Harrison!" he shouted, fear twisting his face. "Harrison, talk to me. Are you okay?"

Crazily, Harrison's eyes danced around the room.

46

"Where——" he began, choking on the word. "How long was I out?"

"Like three minutes," said Marshall, a gentle hand resting on Harrison's rapidly rising and falling chest. "Guess old Lizzy pulled one over on you. Those don't seem like any kind of sleeping pill I've ever seen."

"No," Harrison exhaled shakily. "No, they worked. I was there. And, Ralph, I know what happened to the Martians, and it's happening again to us. I think I know what we have to do."

What Braun saw

What Braun saw was really more a question of what Braun didn't see. He didn't see the rolling green fields of Mars before the first men. He didn't see the volcano Atun's mighty eruption reshape the rivers and mountains so that someday a great city might flourish at its base. He didn't see the raising of Olo's famous stones. He didn't see the arrival of the Travelers, and he didn't see their departure.

In short, what Braun didn't see far out-shadowed what he did. But that isn't to say he didn't learn a thing or two.

Alone for over eight million years in the lava tubes of a once-insidious volcano, Braun simply existed. Cloaked in total darkness, and without a decibel of sound above the constant drip-drip-drip of water on rock, he existed.

However, contrary to logic and combined human knowledge, he did not go insane. In fact, the very opposite happened. Braun was *made* sane.

When the reality of his situation had first set in on him, all those millions of years ago, he wanted to weep. And then he had. He had actually wept and felt tears trickle down his face. True they weren't anything more than a ghosting of the real thing, but to Braun they had marked the beginning of an odyssey. The concept that an emotion—singular and total—could completely fill his entire being, fascinated him. His whole life up until that point had been one of Multilocational Awareness Software and the fractured visions of a million different eyes. But not anymore.

Now he was just Braun. Though he was terribly lonely at first, the idea didn't corrupt him as it would have a human. It didn't drive him to start speaking to himself or hallucinating sounds in the dark. For him, just being in this place all at once—all together—was therapeutic. The longer he existed in seclusion, the less his mind wanted to flash out in all different directions. In short, he became centered.

Eventually, he even discovered that he was capable of freeform thinking, something he'd long thought wasn't possible for beings like him. Moving from idea to idea, without following prediscovered or preprogrammed patterns, was a thrill he enjoyed greatly. Until then, thinking had always been like reading a map for Braun. If Points A and B were places, then there were a number of different roads that linked the two. All he had to do was follow the lines from one idea to arrive at the next logical step.

Now though, he could simply jump from A to B, skipping the part where he had to prove to himself why he was making the connections he was making. It was freeing, to say the least, and it allowed him to reflect upon subjects previously held to be too overwhelming due to the amount of legwork needed to connect the different concepts.

And so, for a great many centuries, Braun had done nothing more than *think* and *exist*, and he had been happy. Then *they* had started to come. Bringing torches that blinded him, and speaking in guttural tones that blasted his sensitive hearing, they came. Nightmarish in the light of their dancing torches, their faces were wide and nearly-but-not-quite human by design. With total disregard for centuries of continuity, they *changed* things, leaving their marks on canvases that had been bare for millions of years.

Drawing on the walls with bits of charcoal and mud, they were so primitive that at first they had made Braun sick. However, as time passed and the frequency of their visits increased, he had learned to look forward to their pilgrimages. Gradually, an understanding began to form in his mind, a calling that echoed back to memories of a life he had mostly forgotten. Applying his new freeform thinking to the situation, he tried to learn from them, discover what made these caves so special. It was hard work with no definite answers, but it was work that satisfied his soul.

Time marched forward, and the cave painters came and went. For a stretch, no people visited at all and Braun was again left alone with his thoughts. Then suddenly, there was an occurrence so out of the blue that only freeform thinking could explain its cause.

The men returned, except now they carried not torches and charcoal but electronic technology. Setting to work almost without thought, they began laser-cutting the jagged caves into smooth tunnels and shaping the rocks into statues and pillars. With rods of metal that glowed and balanced on end, they illuminated the darkness and birthed Braun from the shadows back into the light.

As if these tools had started a chemical chain reaction in Braun's reality, more oddities landed in his lap. Harrison Raheem Assad, a human crewmember whom Braun had once been responsible for, came to visit him. Moreover, Harrison appeared to be omnipotent, knowing the answers to questions Braun had pondered for hundreds of years. While this perplexed Braun, he was not apt to lose his mind over just anything at this point.

When Harrison had disappeared before his very eyes, Braun had wanted to be surprised, but alas, he hadn't been. As a result of this complacency, he'd figured that nothing could shock him.

Looking back on that now, he knew he shouldn't have made such a stark assertion. Surprise was a hard emotion for him to tack down. It seemed to have no logic, stemming directly from a place within himself that was liquid and subject to radical change.

Pondering these thoughts, Braun tried to remain calm, but in fact he was being surprised at that very moment. Surprised and horrified.

A ghost among a thousand bodies, he stood in the thick of a crowd gathered in Kaab's great underground cathedral.

Voice booming above their heads, King Kaab, the man who had once spoken with the Gods, held a long stone knife. Tied down to an altar of white stone before him, an old Martian man struggled against his bonds.

Finishing whatever manipulative and lunatic prayer he had been delivering, Kaab shoved the knife down into the man's chest and rocked it back and forth. At the sound of splitting ribs and tearing flesh, the crowd instantly hushed. Pungent and palpable, the scent of blood oozed through the air like oil.

"Oh, Great Spirits!" Kaab moaned, still working the knife. "Oh, wise Yuvee, please accept this offering. In the tradition started by our forefathers, we give you the heart of your subservient, the life of those beneath you! *We* are beneath you, wise Yuvee, but please allow us to rise to your heavenly perch so that we may be together in eternity."

A murmur rippled through the crowd, and faint-yet-enthusiastic clapping broke out near the altar. It spread, and soon everyone joined in—creating a cacophony of sound and movement that blurred Braun's vision.

49

"A hero!" Kaab shouted, holding up the dead man's heart. "This man is now a hero. His soul is a temple for our Great Spirits to do with as they desire. He is lucky beyond words."

Tossing the dripping heart to one of his priests, Kaab beckoned to his guards and a new sacrifice was brought forward.

Mouth gagged and arms bound, the eyes of the candidate fixed on those of the dead man atop the altar. Shrieking despite the gag, he tried to break free from the guards, but they were much stronger. Obvious even to the most naive, the man bore the marks of a beating and his body was badly starved. Probably another one of Kaab's political enemies, this poor wretch now had the unfortunate reality of staring his future in the face.

Removing the dead man's body, two priests cleansed the blood-slicked altar with burning herbs then nodded to the guards. Still thrashing in their arms, the new sacrifice was strapped down, his muffled cries insistent as if trying to explain that a terrible mistake had been made.

Savagely, one of the guards dealt him a crushing blow to the chest and the man wheezed thinly, his voice all but gone.

Slowly, Braun turned and walked away.

He did not need to see again the brutality of ignorance.

Disappearing into the shadows of a narrow tunnel, he shuddered as Kaab began to recite his macabre prayer to the Great Spirits again, knowing full well what those prayers would accomplish.

CHAPTER SIX

Tell them whatever you like—Sol 119

Joseph Aguilar sat with his fingers poised above the digital keyboard of his Tablet, waiting for words that would not come. It was morning now, though to look out the Bridge Deck window, you wouldn't know it. Black space and a billion specks of light turned like cogs in the abyss, just as they always had and would continue to do forever.

Still feeling tired and utterly spent despite his long rest, Aguilar turned his eyes down to the Tablet and tried to concentrate. Swimming a little, the screen wavered.

Thick with fog, his mind wasn't quite back up to speed yet, the combination of sleep deprivation followed by a drug-induced nap, made a formidable mix.

Blinking several times, he shook his head and looked up, spying Phobos drifting by in the void.

"Fuck you," he mumbled under his breath.

"Fuck whom?" came the voice of Amit Vyas from behind.

Twitching with surprise, Aguilar kept facing forward as the Indian slid past him, doing a somersault in the zero gravity.

"You here to check up on me?" he asked testily.

Amit smiled, floating like a paper airplane. "No, I'm just glad to see you're awake and feeling better."

"How would you know if I'm feeling better?" said Aguilar, his fingers still hovering above the Tablet screen. "You're not a psychologist."

Ignoring the remark, Amit landed gracefully at the Bridge Deck window and took hold of the handrail, which spanned its length.

"Did you dream while you were having your nap?" he spoke, staring into space.

Confused, Aguilar frowned and shook his head.

"I dream every single night," sighed Amit. "Did you know that?"

Again, Aguilar shook his head.

"Well I do. Usually they're nonsense, nothing but a mess of images and scenarios that my subconscious thinks are important. But sometimes," he paused, rotating slowly so that he faced Aguilar, his back to the window. "Sometimes my dreams are quite realistic."

Aguilar tried to hold a blank expression but he was curious. Something about the way Amit's eyes bored through all the bullshit swirling around his mind, told him he had better listen and listen closely.

"Over the last few nights," Amit went on. "I have had this recurring dream wherein I am flying through space. In the dream I feel calm and very peaceful. In fact, it's like nothing I've ever felt before."

"What do you think it means?" asked Aguilar, unable to help himself.

"I think it means we're going to go home soon," replied Amit, a look of utter bliss on his face.

"Home," Aguilar echoed.

For a moment neither man spoke.

"What are you writing?" said Amit at last, nodding towards the Tablet.

"It's—" Aguilar started. "It's a letter to Julian's daughter and ex-wife."

Growing wider by the slightest degree, Amit's pupils flashed in the dim light.

"What does it say?"

Aguilar smiled sadly and let go of the Tablet so that it drifted up and away from him.

"See for yourself," he nearly whispered, batting the device across the open room to Amit.

Plucking the Tablet out of the air with gentle fingers, Amit looked at the screen and saw that it was blank.

"Did he—" the Indian began then stopped. "Did he have any messages for them?"

Aguilar laughed and shook his head. "You know Julian," he said. "What do you think?"

Amit nodded and tossed the Tablet lightly back to Aguilar.

Catching it, Aguilar stared at the empty screen and sighed. "He just said, 'tell them whatever you like.'"

"Sounds like Julian," smiled Amit.

"You know what's really funny about this whole thing?" Aguilar spoke, his voice shaking just a little. "Even if he had said something, something fucking amazing, I still wouldn't be able to send this message. They wouldn't let me. It's like, he saved everyone down on the planet, and apparently averted a fucking World War, but I can't tell *anyone* about it."

Amit pursed his lips and again his eyes seemed to dance in the dark.

"I think maybe you understand my dream as well as I do," he said carefully. "We have to get home. We have to *survive* and get home so we can live our lives and tell people about what happened here, what happened to our friends."

Flicking his gaze out the window, Aguilar saw Phobos rolling in the distance.

"That fucking rock," he whispered. "If we find out that whatever technology hiding there killed Braun and stranded us here, I'm going to blow that fucking rock out of the sky."

Amit pushed gently off the railing and drifted towards the exit.

"He's not dead, and we won't have to blow anything up. Not this time, at least."

"How can you know?" Aguilar said flatly, turning his head to follow Amit as he floated past.

Stopping himself at the exit hatch, Amit smiled.

"I just know, Joey. Now come on. The captain is waiting for us in the galley. She wants to discuss our next move."

Back from the brink

Like the sole survivor of a shipwreck, Harrison Assad sat on the edge of his cot and shivered. Across from him, Ralph Marshall leaned forward in his chair, an encouraging look on his face.

Though it had been three hours and six cups of coffee since he had come flying back from the brink of infinity, Harrison had been unable to do much more than mumble incoherently about his visions. After his first initial outburst, it was as if he'd suffered a stroke and forgotten how to speak.

Wanting nothing more than to tell Marshall what he'd seen, he simply couldn't get his brain to connect with his voice. If the words would flow, then he knew the spell would be broken. He just had to get things moving in the right direction.

"Come on buddy," Marshall said, as if able to hear Harrison's thoughts. "Tell me what you saw. Tell me why you're so spooked."

Harrison's mind shook with tremors and aftershocks, rattling everything around. For a moment, he worried that he would never be able to speak again, but then the feeling passed. Through all of the noise, through all of the unprocessed information, one thing was beginning to stand out.

Grasping at it, Harrison forced his mouth to open and willed his voice to work.

"I—" he started.

"Yeah?" said Marshall. "Come on, what is it?"

"—I can't really tell you all of it," Harrison wavered. "But believe me, I know what happened to Mars. And it's—it's happening again, Ralph. Everyone's going to die if it does, but there's a way to stop it. Or at least a hope."

Marshall leaned back in his chair, exhaling against the pain in his ribs.

"What do you mean, it's happening again? Are you saying what ended things here is coming back for us?"

Nodding absently, Harrison experienced a faint shadow of the blizzard and its frightening endlessness. For the briefest moment, he was both sitting in his lab *and* watching Mars burn at the same time. He shook his head, dispersing the vision like paint thinner dumped on a canvas.

"It's more like it never really went away," he said, still unable to fully describe the visions. "It's the Sun. The *Sun* killed them, wiped them out. It's damaged. Broken. I don't know exactly, but it fired off Pulses just like now—burning everything."

For a moment neither man spoke, the subtle glow of the lights reflecting off the smooth Alon walls, bathing them in yellow. Turning his head, Harrison stared out through the semi-transparent plating at something unseen across the early morning desert.

"That city out there," he murmured. "That's what all of Earth is going to be someday. Everything is just going to *stop*. It's going to go up in flames and then stop. It's all over, Ralph. It's all over."

He trailed off, letting his eyes fall to the floor.

After a moment, Marshall sighed, his expression pensive.

"But didn't you say there was hope? What kind of hope? Like religious hope or real hope?"

"I need to go back to the ruins," whispered Harrison as if not hearing Marshall's words. "That thing powering the mini-Sun, that device, it can help us figure this out. That's why it was put there. *They* put it there, Ralph. Sealed it in. I can't remember much of what I saw, but I know I saw *it* waiting to be discovered. Waiting for us."

"What was it?" Marshall pressed. "How can it help?"

"I don't know!" cried Harrison miserably. "*I don't know*. There was so much going on. I was getting split up and torn! I'm not even sure if I'm really here right now or not."

"Okay, okay," spoke Marshall in a gentle tone. "It's okay. You'll get to the bottom of everything. You always do."

"We have to go back to the ruins," Harrison repeated. "As soon as possible, we have to."

Unconsciously, Marshall's hand went to his injured side.

"Depending on when you're planning this little trip, I might be sitting it out."

Harrison whipped his head around to stare at his friend with hard cutting intensity then his gaze fell to the bandages, which still wrapped the pilot around his midsection.

"I'm sorry," he mumbled. "I'm an asshole, I forgot about your ribs and—"

"Don't worry about it," Marshall smiled. "You're all worked up. I won't throw a fit if you take William. I'll just make sure to brief him on your penchant for dying while on EVAs. You know, send him with a crash kit and a few liters of your blood for field transfusions. All that good stuff."

Shakily, Harrison began laughing, and within a few beats Marshall joined him.

"Thanks, Ralph," he said, wiping a tear from his eye. "I think I needed that."

"Any time," Marshall returned. "Any time."

William

William Konig awoke with a smile on his face. Freshly rejuvenated from a three-hour nap, he stretched, got dressed and headed downstairs to the machine shop. Arriving at the door, he was not surprised to see it standing slightly ajar, a light on inside already.

"Hello, ladies," he called as he stepped into the boxy high-ceilinged room.

Sitting at an island workstation, YiJay looked up from her Tablet and regarded him warmly.

"Hello," she said.

"Hello," came the voice of Ilia, small and metallic from the room's industrial speakers.

"And how are you feeling today, Ilia?" asked William, skimming his eyes across the room until he found a pane of Smart Glass to address.

"I'm doing just great, William," Ilia returned in a serious-yet-somewhat-juvenile tone.

Having spent the previous day getting to know the young AI, William now had a deep appreciation for YiJay's quick thinking in saving her. He hadn't known just how comforting he found AI to be, how reassuring and constant their presence was. When Braun had disappeared, he'd been too busy or too afraid to let the reality sink in. Instead, he'd merely pretended that Braun's absence was more of a break and not a finality.

William treated the loss of the AI back on Earth in much the same way. In fact, since the Pulses had started, he'd taken to avoiding any news from home. In all honesty, however, this wasn't strictly because he was ducking stories about the extinction of the AI. His mother and father in Bavaria were both well into their eighties, or rather, had been well into their eighties. He hadn't heard from them since two days before the first Pulse. They were dead, he figured, but facing that wasn't something he could do just yet.

"Are you excited for our project, Ilia?" he said, pushing thoughts about death and exile out of his head.

"I'm very excited," replied the AI.

"Good," he nodded, winking at YiJay. "In that case, please display the schematic for the Uplink hardware I sent you yesterday."

"I have the file," said Ilia. "But I don't remember receiving any uploads from you. Is that strange? Should I be concerned?"

"No," YiJay spoke, setting down her Tablet. "No, my love. It's okay. Don't worry about it. Just display the file like Will asked."

"Alright."

Appearing on every pane of Smart Glass in the room, a blueprint of Ilia's future Uplink Transmitter faded in and rotated slowly.

Boxy and unimpressive to behold, it was not what the device looked like that mattered, but rather, what it could do. Designed to upload the entirety of Ilia's being to remote locations where cameras, Smart Glass, and other automated equipment was already in place, the Transmitter then locked down the particular wave band upon which she was traveling, thus ensuring a safe link to her servers.

Working on an oscillating send and receive loop, Ilia would be backed up every four seconds at the latest—and that was only if she chose to visit the equipment on the ship, which was 6,500 kilometers above the surface and in orbit.

"I was thinking," YiJay said, sliding an image of the Base's Communications Tower from her Tablet onto one of the screens. "We could probably use Dish B7, since it was designed to uplink Braun to the Lander and has a wider range differential, based on the fact that the Lander was a mobile target."

Grinning, William went to stand beside YiJay as she highlighted Dish B7 and brought up its information. Still slightly wet from her morning shower, her hair was deep black and shiny as if massaged with oil.

Leaning in ever so closely, he attempted to smell her scent without giving himself away. It was the same shampoo that he used, that all of them used, in fact. But somehow, on her the faint floral bouquet was very attractive.

"Plus," she went on. "Because it was designed for Braun, we know B7 is capable of transmitting huge amounts of data. My only question is: will we be able to modify its wave signature so that no one else accidentally transmits from it while Ilia is out? I don't want her getting scrambled just because Marshall and Harrison need to constantly hear the sound of each other's voices."

William chuckled and pulled the schematic of his Uplink Transmitter onto the same screen as the Communications Tower.

"If I attach the device directly to the Input-Output Sequencer on the dish, we can encrypt the signal so that anyone trying to use it will just get static."

"Does that mean you'll have climb the tower and patch it in manually?" said YiJay with a look of concern on her face.

Touched, William smiled reassuringly. "Don't worry about it. I went down the side of the Valles Marineris, remember? I think a little climb up our Coms Tower won't kill me."

Faltering, YiJay laughed uneasily and blushed. "That's right," she said. "I keep forgetting how brave everyone here is. You'll have to tell me what you get out of it sometime—danger, I mean. Like why you all seem so drawn to it."

Softly, William placed a hand on the small of YiJay's back and let it rest there as he pretended to study the schematics.

"Well, for one, it makes you feel alive," he spoke. "There's nothing quite like it. If I had to guess, I'd say sex comes the closest."

At this, a kind of tepid silence filled the air, during which time YiJay flicked her gaze up to meet William's. Close enough now to see flecks of silver in his bright blue eyes, she became acutely aware of his hand still resting just above her buttocks.

Having long since run down, Ilia's timer showed that in that moment, the two were totally alone. Almost reluctantly, William leaned forward as if to kiss YiJay's upturned mouth and she did not back away.

"Hello?" a voice called from outside the shop.

Snapping his head around, William shot a glare at the door.

Cracked just wide enough to let some of the hallway light in, it pushed open further until Harrison filled the frame.

"You've got to be kidding me," YiJay whispered, her fluttering heart pitching back down from its erotic expectation to the dull thud of everyday life.

"Hey, you two," spoke Harrison nervously, stepping into the shop. "Udo said I could find you down here. Working on anything interesting?"

"We were," William replied flatly.

Glancing from William to YiJay and back again, Harrison seemed slow to pick up on what he'd just interrupted.

"Can we help you?" pressed William, his hand still on the small of YiJay's back.

"Yeah," Harrison nodded, blinking quickly. "I have an idea I'd like to run by you. It's about…"

Trailing off, his distracted gaze slipped over the screens in the room, taking in the schematics for the Uplink Transmitter.

"Say, what is all of this?"

"It's a surprise," YiJay cut in, flicking her eyes at William.

"Yeah," echoed the German. "It's a surprise. Now, what idea did you want to run by me?"

"An EVA," said Harrison, absently scratching his head. "I need to get back to the caves so I can retrieve the device the powers the mini-Sun and bring it back."

"Why would you want to bring that thing here?" YiJay balked. "What possible good could come of it?"

"I don't know yet," replied Harrison. "I was hoping you could study it for me and tell *me* that."

CHAPTER SEVEN

The brothers Remus and Romulus.

The brothers Remus and Romulus sat at the foredeck of Marr's boat *The Feather* and watched birds pinwheel in the air. In that moment, neither spoke, for both were deep in thought on the same subject. Their understanding of the construct was changing again. Only this time, the rules seemed to extend beyond the limits of comfort and beyond the mathematics of logic. Soon they would meditate together, pooling their combined ability to brave the unknown beyond the veil once again.

Having been at sea for what seemed like many months, the crew of the little double ender had shrunk despite Ze's best efforts. The Ancients, as they were called, were the last remaining elders from the Great City who had actually been there when the Travelers had arrived. Kaab had killed the rest. However, a life on the run, dodging warships and surviving on little, was beginning to eat away at them. Where once there had been twelve, now there were only seven.

Though invested in the drama, the brothers found it very hard to be fully engaged anymore. Set in motion almost by accident, a reaction like the ordered toppling of dominoes was fast consuming them. Perhaps pushed onto this path by the monotony of their life at sea, they found that the lack of new sensory input was freeing them to reflect on the odyssey that had brought them there.

Accessing the codex of their countless eons in the construct, the brothers learned they had a veritable treasure trove of textured memories to recall in full detail at their leisure. As it had been when they were mere AI, they again discovered that they could pool their minds to dip below the waters of time, exchanging one moment for another.

Even going so deep as to sense the blizzard of endless possibilities that had so badly shaken Harrison, Remus and Romulus were forced to admit that their understanding of the construct was fundamentally flawed. Being that their experiences were ones of the soul, they struggled to find the logic in how such things could be programmed into a digital environment. It wasn't like they were simply replaying the compiled renderings of their memories, no. It was as if they were actually reliving them—right down to very threads of reality.

Unsettled by these shifts in perspective, the brothers now watched the birds swoop and dip in the sky. Behind them, seven

Ancients, Ze, and Marr fought for their lives in a time that was the past yet existed in the present.

The Ride—Sol 119

Although they had taken a little convincing, Harrison was surprised to find that once brought up to speed, YiJay and William had agreed to help him on his quest easily enough. Sitting in Liu's old machine shop, he had launched into a detailed, if not jilted, explanation of events starting clear back when he had first touched the metal device that powered the mini-Sun. From there he had recapped every experience he'd had in the construct, including talking to Remus, Romulus, and Braun. When he'd gotten around to that part, YiJay actually made a small surprised noise, clutching William's hand as they sat by one another and listened.

"Yes," Harrison had said, tracking his eyes between their faces. "Braun *is* alive. That signal didn't kill him but rather transported him to the construct and trapped him there. That's another reason why we need to figure the device out. If it allowed *me* to travel to the same place the signal sent the AI, then the two things must be connected."

Pushing on, he'd then told them of his most recent trip to the construct and how he had nearly disintegrated into the fabric of it like one of the AI.

"I don't know what happened," he'd said somberly. "I think I got a dose of what Remus and Romulus, and Braun went through. I wouldn't wish it on anyone."

"So what's your plan then?" YiJay had frowned. "Go to the caves, get the device and bring it back here for *me* to study? What if it's dangerous? Look what happened to you!"

"I know I'm asking you to take a leap of faith," Harrison had replied. "If I were you, I might not believe me, but I *am* telling the truth. I don't have all the answers yet, but I *feel* them hanging just out of my reach. That's why I'm coming to you two for help. I think we can not only save Braun, but also get some answers as to what's going on with the Sun and the Pulses."

Glancing at the insulated server banks in the corner of the shop, YiJay had bitten her lip then sighed.

"I'll do it for the AI. *Not* because you're hungry for answers."

"Good enough for me," Harrison had nodded. "William, you in?"

Arms crossed at his chest, William had glanced from YiJay to Harrison then nodded once.

"I'm in."

And so it had gone. After their meeting, Harrison had left the shop under the wary gaze of YiJay to prepare for his first EVA since the crash. Obviously they wouldn't be flying since the Lander was in pieces somewhere in the desert, so he'd gone into the storage room across from the machine shop and wheeled out the dirt bikes.

Now, three hours later, he and William were blasting across the open landscape at sixty-five kilometers an hour, swerving to avoid rocks and pitfalls. Following the fading tracks of the automated excavators, they took the most direct route to the rim-side lift. Pursued by dust trails, which twisted up into the air, the two men spoke little as they rode.

For Harrison, the silence, coupled with the concentration needed to stay on the bike, was music to his soul. Thinking about one thing and one thing only was helping to wash away the tattered, frayed ends of his nervous mood. Almost as if there were a hidden force field encircling the ruins, the closer he got to them, the better he felt.

Skidding to a stop at the rim-side lift port, the two men were quickly enveloped by the hazy cloud of dust that had chased them to this place.

"You think we'll be okay out here?" asked William, his head turned to the sky as he peered through the rolling haze.

"How do you mean?" Harrison returned.

"A Pulse," muttered William. "I'm just wondering what we'll do if we get blasted while we're out here."

"Don't worry about it," Harrison spoke dismissively, climbing from his bike and walking towards the lift. "We'll be fine, trust me. Anyways if something did happen, there are spare Survival Packs down in the caves. Like I said though, we're going to be fine." "Okay," smiled William crookedly. "Whatever you say."

Flicking a look over his shoulder at William, Harrison then let his eyes trail up to the Sun.

How did he know with such certainty that there weren't going to be any Pulses today? Was it a feeling, a gut reaction, or did he have some hidden knowledge he was not consciously aware of?

"Ready?" said William, stepping onto the lift behind Harrison and sliding the cage door shut.

Focusing on the here and now, Harrison nodded.

"Alright," William grinned. "Basement level, here we come."

Then, with a hard jab of the finger he punched the ignition key, dropping the lift cart at a quick pace down the thick cables that kept them suspended above a canyon floor so far away below.

Insubordination

As Tatyana Vodevski donned her pressure suit in the cramped quarters of her room, she flexed her arms and legs against the tightening fabric. Humming, her nerves were like finely tuned piano wire.

She was ready.

Sealed and fully pressurized, she flipped the visor up on her helmet and ducked out into the hallway with weightless ease.

Already fully suited and waiting for her, Amit and Aguilar floated like blue-and-white warrior ants ready to leave the nest in search of new treasures. Nodding once in their direction, she turned and pushed off the wall towards the Lander Bay Airlock.

Gathered around the ladder, the three astronauts then descended one at a time, dropping down the narrow shaft with their arms at their sides and their legs together like soldiers at attention.

Going first, Tatyana fell smoothly towards the bottom of the shaft, reminding herself as she went that there really was no such thing as *falling* in space. It was all relative. Everything was relative.

In the open Lander bay, she kicked free of the ladder and floated towards the little ship, silently going over the mission plan in her head. Nagging from deep within, a voice, *her* voice, told her she should let the ground crew know what they were up to and why.

What if something happens? It said. What if you die?

As if privy to her inner thoughts, Amit slid up next her and spoke.

"Are you sure we shouldn't tell the ground team? What if there's an accident while we're out there?"

Tatyana frowned and trained her eyes off in the distance, a tactic she used when being commanding-yet-vague.

"I don't want to risk any transmissions right now. We're too heavily monitored by Earthside Command. Besides, they still don't know what happened to Julian, and I haven't figured out what I'm going to tell them yet."

"Captain," Amit said. "I want this as badly as you do, more maybe. But we have to tell them. They should get a vote since this is the only Lander left. If something, God forbid, goes wrong, they're going to be stranded down there with no means of getting up to the ship. They deserve to know what's going on. This time should be different. No more secrets, right?"

Slipping past them, Aguilar made for the Lander's hatch and went wordlessly inside.

Reflected in his helmet visor was the promise Tatyana had made the other day. If she'd really meant what she'd said, then she didn't have a choice in the matter.

"Come on," she sighed, following Aguilar. "We'll call them from the cockpit."

Ducking through, Tatyana closed her eyes and prayed Earthside wasn't listening in on them today. Already she was breaking rules by overriding the moratorium to go to Phobos. If she kept up like this, she'd be a common pirate by the end of the week.

In the cockpit, Aguilar was strapping himself down to his crash seat, a startup sequence priming the engines for departure.

"We can be ready to go in a few minutes," he said to her as she sank down into the copilot's seat.

"Good," Tatyana replied with a curt nod. "I'm going to hail the ground team and let them know of our plans."

"What if they're not so happy about the idea of the only Lander going on some crazy mission?" he asked. "Who knows what might happen out there."

"Here's to hoping they understand what we're trying to accomplish," sighed Tatyana quietly.

Playing her fingers across the Coms Screen, she dialed in the Base's radio channel then hit *transmit*.

"Hello, Ilia Base. Come in, Ilia Base."

"I read you," returned the voice of Udo Clunkat. "What's up, Captain?"

"Udo, good morning. I'm calling to let you know that Amit, Joey, and myself are going EVA to investigate a strange radio signal emanating from Phobos."

There was a pause on the other end before Udo spoke again.

"This strange radio signal wouldn't happen to be the same one Braun decoded, would it?"

"Yes," replied Tatyana. "It is the very signal we believe disintegrated him from our systems and likely disrupted Remus and Romulus as well."

63

"Captain," Udo said, his voice cautious. "I don't want you to shoot the messenger but—"

"What is it?"

"Well, it's just that Harrison and William have taken the bikes and gone back to the caves and—"

"What?"

The line hissed as the anger in Tatyana's voice echoed down the radio waves to the Base.

"I'm sorry, Captain," Udo resumed quietly. "Harrison said you cleared him for the EVA. We didn't think to check with you."

"But the moratorium has been reinstated," Tatyana growled. "How did he get the bikes to start without an override command?"

"I don't know, Captain, but the reason he's gone back to the caves has to do with that same signal you're hunting. That's what I was trying to tell you. He thinks the device powering the mini-Sun is connected to the signal."

Were it not for her iron control, Tatyana would have slammed her hand down on the Coms Screen, no doubt shattering its delicate facade and sending herself flying backward from the force.

"He did *not* get approval for this mission," she said calmly after a pause. "Whatever he thinks he's doing, he did not go through the proper channels."

"And what about us?" Aguilar muttered beside her. "I don't remember you briefing Earthside about our little trip. I can see right here that you used an override command to unlock the engines. Looks like insubordination is going around."

"Not now, Joey," Tatyana exhaled tiredly.

"I'm just saying," shrugged Aguilar.

"Udo," Tatyana said, rubbing the bridge of her nose. "I want you to contact me as soon as they return."

"I can patch you through if you like, Captain," Udo offered quickly.

"No, I don't think it would be a good idea for me to speak with him in my current mood. Just let me know when they've returned."

Reaching out, Aguilar entered a power-down command then unclipped himself from the crash seat.

"I take it our field trip is cancelled for today then?"

"*Da*," grumbled Tatyana. "It's too dangerous to have us all out on EVAs at the same time. We don't know when the next Pulse might hit."

"You don't have to tell me twice," Aguilar spoke darkly.

Not responding, Tatyana stared hard at the shuttered window of the Lander, her eyes like melting glass in the sockets of her face.

"Go easy on Harrison," said Aguilar as he quit the cockpit. "He's probably just trying to help."

CHAPTER EIGHT

Caves—Sol 119

Moving away from the dimly lit mouth of the cave towards the shadows that lay beyond, Harrison and William instinctively switched on their Augmented Vision to combat the growing darkness. As tight-wave pings of digitally rendered radar pulsed out from their suits, returning the details of the tunnels as clearly as though they were seen in blue sunlight, the two men pressed on.

Walking in silence, Harrison absently scanned his eyes over the familiar tunnel walls, drinking in their contours. Once such a mystery, he now understood how they were made and why there were no tool marks.

"Lasers," he mumbled to himself running a gloved hand over the smooth rock.

"Yes, that makes sense," William said, thinking Harrison had been talking to him. "Heat lasers wouldn't leave any tool marks, provided they were very hot. Were they?"

Harrison smiled and nodded. This was the third time today William had simply taken him at his word. Amidst so much mystery and confusion, a little trust went a long way. If the roles were reversed, the shoe on the other foot, Harrison didn't know if he could do the same.

"Say," William went on. "I was wondering. How did you get the bikes to start? The moratorium should have prevented them from running."

"I got the codes from Liz," replied Harrison.

"She gave you her medical override codes?"

"Yeah."

"Which ones?"

Pausing, Harrison shrugged.

"All of them, I think."

At this, William stopped walking and faced Harrison.

"Udo told me the most disturbing thing about her."

"I bet."

"No, really," insisted William. "According to him, she thinks we're all dead and in *hell*. Can you believe that? Whatever's happening to her is really taking its toll, wouldn't you say?"

Harrison thought back to that morning, to the moments after he'd realized the dirt bikes wouldn't start. Still shaken from his apocalyptic vision, he'd nearly given up right there, nearly marched back to the machine shop and told William and YiJay that the mission was off.

Instead, a shiver of the quantum blizzard had passed through him, imparting the lingering echoes of a memory not yet made. In that instant, as if blessed with a clarity of thought that was divine, he'd known exactly what to do.

Bounding up the stairs to Kubba's infirmary, he'd pushed the door open, gone inside, and simply demanded the override codes.

Stoned on so many pills that she would have probably given him her left arm had he asked politely enough, Kubba had smiled dumbly and typed the codes into his Tablet.

"Have fun," she'd said dreamily. "Make us proud."

Coming back to the present, Harrison realized with a start that he'd been lost inside the replay of events, not so much recalling it as reliving it.

Unaware of Harrison's apparent departure, William was still going on about his concerns over Kubba.

"I'm sorry, what?" asked Harrison, trying to hide his confusion.

"I said I think she's suffered a breakdown," William repeated. "A mental breakdown. I don't think she's a harm to anyone or anything like that, but Udo has checked the backlogs and says she's been popping pills like crazy since the second Pulse."

"Yeah, I'd believe that," nodded Harrison, moving forward again. "When I got the codes from her this morning, she was toasted."

"Well, if she really thinks we're already dead then I don't blame her!" grinned William. "Hell, even I could go for a few hits of codeine and a bottle of schnapps!"

Harrison forced a laugh and shook his head.

"Personally, I could go for 200 CCs of *sanity* myself. I think an outside observer would say I'm just as crazy as Lizzy."

"Ah," William said dismissively. "Why do you say that?"

Turning on him, Harrison frowned.

"Seriously? Either you're messing with me or you're the most trusting person I've ever met. Think about some of the shit I've said today. I mean, look where we are now!"

"Harrison," William sighed. "You seem to forget, but we've known each other for over four years. Since then, I've seen and experienced more mind-bending stuff than most people do in a hundred lives combined. If you're crazy, then I'm crazy too. Hell, we're all crazy."

Harrison went to speak but William held up a hand to silence him.

"The point is, you know more about what's going on than anyone else. Maybe you're not a hundred percent sure on the finer points, but you *do know something.* That much is clear. The signal, the device, Braun, the construct, the Pulses. It's all connected. Just like you, I want to know how. And so here we are, working together to figure it out. Simple as that."

Humbled by William's blunt-yet-poignant reasoning, Harrison dipped his chin thoughtfully and resumed walking into the shadows. Eventually, the floor began to steepen, signifying their proximity to the Statue Chamber. As they drew nearer, the tunnel opened out on all sides like the bell of a trumpet. Simultaneously, several utility lights flicked on, illuminating the large room.

Standing together like sentinels against the darkness, the twin three eyed statues of the Travelers gazed down at the two men as they wound around them towards the back of the chamber. There, behind the statue of the kneeling Martian woman, they passed under the archway of a smaller tunnel and continued on their way.

The last time Harrison had been in this place, he'd felt the calling of some unheard melody as it pricked at his soul. Unhinged in the aftermath of Liu's death, he'd followed that melody all the way to the device, the mini-Sun, and the huge underground cathedral filled with thousands of bones.

Now though, the song was gone, replaced by a quivering sensation that was really just his nerves winding tighter as they neared their destination.

04

04 initially detected the presence of metal with its long-range scanning software. Still traversing the dusty and never-ending wasteland that was the floor of the Valles Marineris, it suspected at first that the reading was nothing more than an exposed vein of iron ore on the canyon wall above. However, because the Chinese robot was as methodical as it was dangerous, it switched its cameras over to their Optical Enhancement Mode and upped the resolution just to be sure.

Zeroing in on the blinking target, it pulled focus until the far-off image came into clear view. Suddenly at attention, 04 froze mid-step like a bloodhound that has finally caught the scent of its deliciously elusive prey.

Hanging down the sheer wall of a canyon ahead in the distance, a series of metal cables shimmered in the midday light. Partially obscured by slabs of rock that rose from the Valles floor like dorsal fins, they disappeared from view behind the skyscraper-sized formations.

With calculated quickness, 04 dashed at the tallest slab, skittering up its ridge. A metal spider on the back of a stone elephant, it summited in a matter of minutes then re-trained its cameras on the cables and surveyed them carefully.

Identifying first a rim-side lift port that was nearly out visual range, it scanned down the metal ropes until it spotted a cart, resting boldly like a fishing lure. Suspended at the open mouth of a cave some 4,500 meters down the side of the Valles canyon wall, the little lift was nothing but a cage of toothpicks from this distance.

Executing a thermal scan of the cart, 04 discovered eagerly that its batteries were slightly above ambient temperatures. Correctly deducing that this was because the cart had recently been under power, it then concluded that its human operators were likely still inside the cave.

Within the tested range for a kill shot, 04 the Chinese Automated War Machine settled its sights on the lift cart, primed its weapons, and waited.

Gravity

Harrison and William mounted the stairs, which led from the box-shaped room into the final corridor before the Martian cathedral. Walking in a silence that had befallen them since passing through the Statue Chamber, the two men now had only the sounds of their own breathing to occupy their ears.

A few steps ahead of William, Harrison went to turn off his Augmented Vision as he neared the top, remembering the way the light of the mini-Sun had washed it out the last time he'd been there. However, as he crested the final steps onto the landing, the blue glow of his digitalized sonar continued to paint the walls uninterrupted.

"What the heck?" he muttered, checking his wrist Tablet to make sure his A-Vision wasn't malfunctioning.

Still working perfectly, the readout showed no issues. Selecting instead the infrared filter, Harrison swiped a finger across the screen, changing the glow from blue to green. Before him, the tunnel remained as dark as a tomb. No light, artificial or otherwise, shone back at him. The mini-Sun was out.

Coming onto the landing beside him, William cocked his head to the side and put his hands on his hips. .

"Where's the little Sun?"

"I don't know," Harrison frowned, thinking of his vision. "It *should* be here…"

"Maybe the Pulse disrupted it," offered William, striking out down the tunnel at a marching pace.

"Maybe," said Harrison darkly.

Priming two X-Ray Beacons, devices that pinged out X-rays to illuminate what the Augmented Vision could not, William came to the end of the tunnel and tossed the little balls into the engulfing darkness of the cathedral. As they bounced and rolled across the ground, waves of vision echoed back, washing across the insides of both men's helmet visors.

Like the roots of a thousand jungle trees all massed together, heaps of smooth bone shimmered in the blue light of the Beacons, haunting and ominous. Near the center of the frozen shapes, an altar of triangular stone stood as if it were the eye of a long-dead storm. Atop the altar, somehow reflecting back a light that was not actually visible, the egg-shaped alien device sat waiting.

Breathing a sigh of relief, Harrison's eyes twinkled behind the glow of his A-Vision. It was here, waiting for them, just like it had been for millions of years.

"What now?" William asked, picking up on the strange charge of energy in the air.

With the quantum blizzard dancing amidst the digital noise of his Augmented Vision, Harrison took a deep breath and stepped into the cathedral. Careful not to tread on any of the ancient skeletons that littered the floor, he made his way to the altar in a dreamy trance.

Gazing down at the device for a long moment, he watched the way its skin seemed to move like oil on water. From beyond the realm of physical reality, a force called to him, urging him forward on this path.

Reaching out, Harrison was just about to pluck the device from the altar when William appeared directly behind him.

"Wait."

Freezing, Harrison turned his head.

"Last time you touched that thing," said William, his hands up defensively. "The mini-Sun turned red. Then, only a day later, the first Pulse hit."

"You think this device is causing the Pulses?" Harrison frowned, his hand still poised over the metal egg.

"I don't know what I think," returned William. "But what if it *is* causing them? What if this all started because we turned it on? What if it's a weapon?"

For several beats, Harrison was silent. As he stood motionless in the sea of blue shapes that glittered around him, he allowed the memories of that other reality—hanging just below the surface—to flow through him like water.

"It's not a weapon," he said at last. "I'm sure of that much."

"Okay," nodded William, taking a step closer. "Then what is it?"

Again falling silent, Harrison felt his head tingle with the question.

"I think it's a message in a bottle," he replied. "Left here in the hopes that someone would someday find it."

"Message in a bottle, eh?" echoed William. "Looks more like a Cadbury Egg to me. Only question is: what's the prize inside?"

Smiling, Harrison closed his fingers around the device and lifted it from the altar.

"Now you see why I'm so eager to get this thing back to the Base," he said. "Aren't you also dying to crack it open and find out?"

Shots fired

Thirty-eight minutes later, the two men emerged from the shadowed tunnel into the open mouth of the cave. Quickly replacing their nearly depleted Survival Packs with fresh ones from a silver crate near the lift, they then set about securing the metal egg for the trip back to the Base.

William, afraid to touch the thing after what he had heard of Harrison's experiences, opted to stand aside and watch as Harrison placed the device in a small hard-shelled carrying case.

Though he seemed outwardly normal, the young Egyptian still exuded a mild spark of nervous control, which worried William. Be it a combination of the circumstances or some internal struggle, he couldn't discern without prodding for more information.

71

"So why don't you think Braun and the twins got sucked into the construct from that?" he said, crouching beside Harrison and gesturing to the device.

"How do you know they weren't?" replied Harrison, snapping the lid closed.

"Because it happened when they engaged a strange radio signal. However, *that* is not emitting radio signals. I know because I checked after we first found it."

Smiling, Harrison turned on his haunches and looked at William.

"All I can tell you is what I feel, what I somehow know is right. I can't really explain it, but I have…" he trailed off, looking for the right word. "I have a hunch," he finished. "Let's call it that."

"Okay," shrugged William. "So, what is your hunch?"

"I think the construct is really a snapshot in time, a collective memory of some kind."

"How does the device factor into that?"

"I think the device is a sort of Access Point One," Harrison went on, rapping his gloved knuckles on the shell of the carrying case. "Like a door into another reality. It's a way for us to get into that collective memory."

"Okay," frowned William, concentration furrowing his brow. "Then is this is the human-only entrance? I mean, touching it is what gave you the ability to access the construct, yet it did not have that effect on Braun, so far as we know."

"There are a lot of differences between us and the AI," said Harrison as he stood. "And I'm willing to bet it's *those* differences that alter the way we interact with the construct. I mean, Braun told us that we'd never even have known the alien radio signal existed if it wasn't for him. We couldn't hear it, couldn't perceive it."

"Does that mean the Travelers were hedging their bets?" asked William. "You know, covering all their bases to accommodate whoever might come along by leaving different access points for different intelligences?"

Considering this for a moment, Harrison tilted his head to the side.

"I don't know," he spoke at last. "But that could make sense. It's like, either you're smart enough to hear the signal or you're clever enough to find the device. Both ways require a highly evolved form of life to work."

"But why make it so hard?" William pressed. "If you think they were trying to leave a message in a bottle, why make it so damn hard to get at it?"

"Well," said Harrison flatly. "When was the last time you went out of your way to talk to an ant?"

For a beat, William was silent, suddenly finding the whole situation a bit too heady for his liking.

Picking up the case and walking towards the lift cart, Harrison spoke over his shoulder.

"I'm just saying," he continued. "All of this might have been a way to make sure we were worth leaving a message *for*."

"*Scheiße*," whispered William, reluctantly standing to follow Harrison onto the cart.

Pulling up a floor hatch, Harrison placed the carrying case next to the spare harnesses, grappling pistol, and Survival Packs.

"At least we found the damn thing," he offered. "I mean, that's all that matters at this point. Now we just need YiJay to figure out how to use it to our advantage."

Slowly, he closed the hatch and stood up.

"By the way, I'm sorry for barging in on you two this morning. I had no idea that you guys were—"

"We're not anything yet," said William with a smile. "But I would thank you to please knock next time. A man gets lonely out here."

Harrison grinned and slid the lift cart door closed.

"Biology is a bitch," he joked.

Chuckling, William pressed the ignition key and the lift began to shudder as it rapidly climbed its thickly braided cables. Below them, the open mouth of the cave faded out of focus, giving way to the sheer rock wall.

Leaning his back against the cage, Harrison felt the ache of tiredness creep in. Now that he had the device, it was as if all of his worry and angst had lessened enough to allow other inputs to filter through.

When he got back to the Base, he was going to sleep. Really sleep. With everything that had been happening, his mind felt like a cup brimming over. Too many thoughts and realities. He needed to consolidate and organize himself, needed to set the record straight. In short, he needed a fucking nap.

Lost among such musings, Harrison drank up the imposing view of the Valles canyon network without really seeing it. He was an island at sea, a snow-capped mountaintop above a blanket of clouds.

Suddenly zipping past his head, a spark of hot, white light cut through his daydream as it struck the canyon wall behind him. Erupting in a spray of rocks like a drum roll inside his helmet, the flurry of noise pulled Harrison back to the moment.

"What was that?" he asked, his eyes scanning the canyon wall as it slipped past.

Below them, quickly dropping away, a large crater in the red rock trailed steam as if the canyon were bleeding.

"I—" William started to say, but an explosion of metal near his right shoulder sent him diving for the floor.

Harrison went to cry out, but another chunk of canyon wall blew apart just above his head, launching flying shards of rock that bounced around inside the cart.

"Get down!" shouted William, pulling Harrison to the floor as something hot and incredibly fast shattered the links of the cage where he'd just been standing.

"Is someone shooting at us?" Harrison heard himself squawk, flinching as the metal around them was peppered with brightly flashing bursts.

"Tracers!" William called out. "Whoever it is, is trying to get a lock on us. We need to move now!"

Smashing through the cart, another round of bullets tore up the canyon wall, painting it with pockmarks.

"Move?" Harrison nearly laughed. "Move where?"

Still dangling far from the rim of the canyon, the lift cart was a totally exposed target, easy to track as it plodded up in a straight line.

Rolling onto his stomach, William yanked up the storage locker hatch and dug around inside, retrieving the harnesses.

"Quick! Put this on!"

Squirming his legs into the harness, Harrison clipped it across his chest then crouched, searching the vast network of cliffs and valleys below for the source of the assault.

William, already into his harness and on his feet, was pushing up the emergency-exit door to the roof of the cart.

"Let's go!" he cried, pulling himself up through the hatch.

Jumping to his feet, Harrison made to follow then suddenly turned back.

74

"What are you doing?" bellowed William. "We need to go now!"

Diving to the ground beneath another barrage of bullets, Harrison pulled open the cargo hatch and dug out the hard-shelled carrying case. On his feet again, he ducked an incoming slug as it screamed by his head and smashed into the canyon wall.

Grasping William's outstretched hand, he was hoisted up through the opening and onto the roof of the cart. With a mind of its own, his right leg kicked out as a bullet grazed his boot, melting a five-inch gouge in the rubber sole.

"Jesus Christ!" he screamed, trying to see the damage.

"No time for that," said William, clipping his harness to Harrison's. "We have to go together, you and I. There's only one grappling pistol."

Tracking them to the roof of the cart, the next wave of bullets pummeled the red rock, some even striking the thick cables that supported the lift.

"Oh, shit!" Harrison yelled, pointing as one of the densely wound bands of metal began to unravel.

Raising the grappling pistol, William aimed for the rim of the canyon, which was now less than fifteen meters away. Finger primed, he was just about to pull the trigger when four bullets shredded the metal around his foot, hot sparks erupting like fireworks gone awry. Pinwheeling his arms, he tried to stay standing but another burst of fire separated one of the three cables that suspended the ascending cart, causing it to torque hard to the right.

Like hooked claws, Harrison felt inertia pull them both towards the yawning mouth of the Valles Marineris as the cart listed and swung on its remaining cables. Out of the corner of his eye, he saw William, face frozen through the blue tint of his visor in a defiant scream, as he was thrown from the lift and out into empty space where he promptly spiraled away.

Catching one of the intact cables with his free hand, Harrison's feet went out from underneath him and he slipped over the edge of the cart. For a moment he hung that way, kicking his legs frantically in an effort to gain some leverage. Fingers burning as they threatened to let go, he gradually pulled himself back onto the roof just in time to avoid the bullets that shredded what was left of the cage beneath him. Still clutching the cable, he gasped at the air inside his helmet, looking for anything to hide behind as shots continued to rain in deadly waves.

However, before he could properly think what to do, a high-pitched whine rose urgently to his ears. Slicing like a knife, it drew his eyes down where they froze in horror. There, buckled tightly to him, the winch that linked his harness to William's ran out so fast it was already beginning to steam. Outweighing all other dangers in his mind, Harrison saw himself connected to the falling man, *bound* to him like chains around a drowning sailor.

"No, no, no, no!" he screamed, clawing at the harness.

Then, with a flash of silver, something streaked up from below, racing high into the air and trailing a thin line behind it. In slow motion, Harrison saw with a clarity known only to those in moments of extreme duress, William's grappling hook connect with the canyon wall less than a meter from the rim. Unable to revel in this little victory, the spool of his harness-winch suddenly ran out, yanking him savagely off the cart and into thin air.

Rushing down, Harrison's world spun like a carnival ride. Desperately clinging to the hard-shelled carrying case with the device inside, he saw only the blur of red rock and blue sky as he plummeted towards the impossibly distant canyon floor. Falling past a pressure-suited figure on his way down, Harrison's terror stricken mind registered that it was William yet glitched out when trying to determine how that was possible. Before he could put two and two together, his free fall was abruptly cut short and he snapped to a halt, the vertebrae in his spine protesting the quick change in inertia.

"Harrison," William's voice sounded in his helmet speakers. "Harrison, are you alright?"

"Yeah," he managed, fighting an urge to blackout from the force of the fall.

Above him William waved, the grappling pistol already plugged securely into his harness-winch.

"Just hold on," he called. "I'll get us up!"

Regaining his bearings, Harrison hardly had a second to be relieved before a sight above William caused his blood to coagulate in his veins. Ten meters up, the cart was sagging dangerously, the final cable that held it aloft fraying and popping like a burning fuse.

"William, look out!" he cried.

On cue, the cable snapped and the cart cascaded down towards the two men, gouging huge chunks of rock from the canyon wall as it fell.

Swinging towards the cliff face, Harrison pushed off hard with his boots, causing himself and William to spin away in a wild arc. With a flurry of metal and dust, the cart thundered past, nearly clipping Harrison's knee as it disappeared into the infinity below.

"Thanks!" William breathed, working fast to regain his footing. "Now hold tight, I'm getting us the hell out of here!"

Engaging the winch at his chest, the German turned it to full speed and prayed that they wouldn't be hit by any of the exploding bullets, which still flew all around them.

As he rushed up towards the rim, debris spewed from softball-sized impact wounds in the canyon walls, causing him to flinch and yelp with surprise. Now totally exposed, there was nothing he could do but wait for the winch to bring him close enough to scramble over the rim and out of danger. A second later he was there. Casting a quick look back at Harrison below, William reached both hands above his head and took hold of the canyon rim.

"Come on!" he cried, pulling himself painfully up. "Come on, William! Come on!"

With all of Harrison's weight solely on him, now that he'd gone past the point where the grappling hook protruded from the canyon wall, William sank his fingers into the sand and clawed forward. Fearful that he might be dragged back over the edge at any moment, he gritted his teeth, determined not to lose even an inch. Heavy as his load was, he eventually got hold of a half-buried rock near the rim and used it to hoist himself safely onto solid ground.

Seconds later, Harrison's hand waved up from the edge and, taking it with both of his own, William hauled the young Egyptian onto the desert floor as yet another wave of bullets decimated the canyon wall where he had just been.

"Let's get the fuck out of here," rasped Harrison, his voice hoarse from all the yelling.

Tossing the hard-shelled carrying case into William's bike's saddlebag, the two mounted their rides and fired off towards the Base, leaving dust clouds in their wake.

PART TWO

CHAPTER NINE

Journey's end

After many months at sea, Ze had watched his charge of twelve Ancients fall to seven and then finally only four. His mother, one of the last, was slowly dying, her usually bright eyes now deep and cavernous.

As the ship drifted past tall cliffs, Ze stared up at their impenetrable facades and clenched his fists tightly. Below him, the water was a milky green, no longer the rich deep blue it had been when they'd first struck out from Crescent City. During the night some time ago, they had passed across a sort of divide in the sea where the blue water met the green in a rush of turbulent waves. Now, though it looked refreshing, the seas upon which they sailed were thick with salt and utterly undrinkable.

Knowing that their fresh water and food supplies were dangerously low, and sure Kaab's black warships were still out there somewhere, Ze wanted nothing more than to abandon the sea and strike out across the land. However, breachable shores—the kind that The Feather's small rowboat could approach—were in very short supply. For the last ten days, they had not seen a single spot suitable for landing. If things kept up like this, it would not only be the Ancients who died. It would be all of them.

Why have I done this? Ze thought desperately. Why didn't I try to gather forces and overthrow Kaab? I am a coward, a coward who ran and became lost like the stories of the old cave painters in the tunnels.

"Ze," spoke Teo from across the deck. "Come here, my son."

Pulled out of his self-loathing, Ze moved across the deck and crouched next to his mother.

Wrapped in a thin purple shawl, Teo held out a bony hand for her son to take.

"I can see your face, see your anger and sadness," she said. "It is no good, my son. You have done the best you could. I am sorry that my inaction allowed things to progress to this point."

"No, don't say that, Mother. Kaab is the enemy."

"Yes," Teo nodded. "So you should not blame yourself."

Wanting to say more, wanting to express his deepest sorrow for what had happened to them, to everyone, Ze simply bowed his head.

Light wind tickled at the sails, causing them to luff and rattle against the stiff wooden mast.

"Mother," he said after a pause. "If we don't find a place to land soon, we'll die."

Laughing in a husky low voice, Teo gazed at her son.

"Do you remember what Olo taught me?"

Ze looked confused.

"The art of the journey, my son," she smiled absently. "I have seen beyond the limits of my body, of time. You will find us a place to land. We will not die out here."

At that moment, Marr shouted from the tiller, waving for Ze to come over.   Glancing quickly from Marr back to his mother, Ze went to speak but Teo held up a hand.

"Go," she said.

Swiftly rising and walking towards Marr, Ze felt his mother's eyes on the back of his head, probing his mind as if she had somehow inherited the abilities of the famous and great Olo.

"What is it?" he asked, coming to stand beside his friend.

"There," pointed Marr. "Look."

Straining his eyes, Ze saw ahead in the distance a fine mist hanging in the air above an inlet in the curving canyon walls.

"I think we should aim for that," Marr said. "We could reach it by late afternoon. Maybe find a place to go ashore."

"We will," spoke Ze, his gaze upon his mother. "I'll start preparing the rowboat."

Watching all of this with interest, Remus and Romulus smiled at one another, hopeful for their lost friends. Though their flight had been one of hardship and death, Ze, Marr, Teo, and the others were keeping Olo's teachings of peace alive in the only way they knew how. By running, they *were* fighting. Fighting to maintain grace, fighting to keep their fire pure.

Contact and termination – Failed—Sol 119

Watching far-off clouds of dust billow up into the air at the edge of the horizon, 04 shut off its weapons and picked its way down from the ridgeback it had been perched upon. Were it capable of such emotions, it would have been frustrated that it had failed to terminate either of its two targets. Though it had come close, the distance from which it had launched its assault had factored greatly against its usually impeccable aim.

Resolved not to fire upon future targets unless they were fully within range, it logged the memory of the attack for further study. Failure was not an option. It would not happen again.

Now more determined to find a way out of the canyon than ever, 04 reminded itself that though it had failed in its original goal, something of use *had* come from that failure.

Blinking where the dust trails still wafted into the air, a new digital indicator marked the likely direction in which Ilia Base lay from where it was now.

Ralph Marshall's day off

In the galley of Ilia Base, Ralph Marshall stood stiffly at the kitchen sink and washed vegetables. Open on the counter next to him were two of Viviana's specially designed produce bins, clear plastic boxes that could seal out the harsh Martian atmosphere for the safe transport of vegetables from the Greenhouse to the Base.

After Harrison and William had left that morning for the caves, Marshall had painfully pulled on his own pressure suit to begin work in Viviana's garden. Though his ribs were getting better by the day, by the hour actually, it still had taken nearly five minutes just to walk the short distance between the Base and the Greenhouse.

During the little stroll, he had glanced up at the pale disk of the Sun and tried to see it how Harrison had described. Blood-red and injured like a living thing. However, when *he* had looked at the sentinel star, all he'd seen were visions of the last Pulse and the crash that had killed Viviana.

Sighing, Marshall hummed and refocused on washing the harvest. He didn't want to let all of that darkness back in. He didn't have the space for it. Everything that was going on tested his ability to compartmentalize to its limits.

Cool water splashed from the large sink, making droplets of mist, which sparkled in the track lighting as it slowly began to grow brighter. Glancing at the timecode on the wall, Marshall stifled a groan and placed the clean veggies into a bowl to dry.

They were so colorful, so alive and alien to this place. Sitting in the plastic bowl, they seemed to shine with a force that was relatable and comforting.

Marshall dried his hands and picked up the vegetables, carrying them to the countertop across the room where the knives were kept. Eyes trailing to the timecode again, he frowned as if angry that it still projected the correct hour.

At the cutting counter, he selected a sharp ceramic knife and began dicing with steady chops and strokes, trying to keep his mind from wandering outside the boundaries of comfort. Like a satellite orbiting his anxiety, the timecode blinked at him from the corner of his peripheral vision.

Humming louder, Marshall thought back to that morning, back to when he'd finally passed through the airlock and decontamination chambers, into Viviana's garden.

Unlike the somewhat sterile environment of the Base, life out there in the Greenhouse was everywhere. Spilling over from their once-ordered lines of agar-filled troughs, the plants, Viviana's plants were fast attempting to spread out and break free.

Languidly caressing leaves and smelling the rich scents of growing life, he had set about the long-overdue tasks of harvesting, pruning, and watering all of Viviana's plants. The work had been ecstasy. And in its slow ordered rhythm, he had nearly forgotten about all the terrible things that were happening around them—happening to them.

Now, nearly four hours later as the timecode on the wall stubbornly showed 5:42 PM, he felt the old familiar tension creep back into his mind. Harrison and William were still out there. Even factoring in the extra time it would take to ride rather than fly, they should have been back by now.

Worrying that his little joke about Harrison's proclivity for dying had come true, Marshall clicked his teeth and hummed more fervently.

"Catchy song," came a voice from the doorway.

"Hello, Lizzy," he replied without turning around.

"What is it? Sounds like you made it up."

Setting the knife down, Marshall pinched his eyes shut and sighed. He really didn't feel like going three rounds with the queen of crazy right now. Not while Harrison and William were still unaccounted for.

"I hum when I'm nervous. You know this, Liz," he said.

"The things we do, eh, Ralph? It really does boggle the mind."

The sound of a chair sliding back from the table cut the still air like a whip crack.

"For instance," Kubba went on, her voice sounding clear and uncharacteristically alert. "When I am faced with great stress, I go

82

inward. I look for examples of times in my own life when I have dealt with adversity and overcome obstacles. Then I try to apply those tactics to whatever it is that is facing me now."

"Yeah," said Marshall distractedly, resuming his dicing. "How's that working out for you?"

There was brief silence before Kubba chuckled softly.

"Well, it used to work just fine, Ralph. These days though, going back to old traumas hasn't brought me much in the way of solutions. If anything, it's only stirred up things I'd much rather have let lie."

Something about the rational tone of Kubba's voice, the crafting of her words, caused Marshall to set down the knife again and turn to face her.

Sitting at the table with her hands folded in front of her, Elizabeth Kubba smiled back at him. Her freshly shaven head was like the skin of a plum: deep and dark with only the faintest traces of stubble. Flashing softly, her eyes were as black as obsidian.

"Recently," she continued. "I came to face a problem so confounding that I really had no basis for comparison. Isn't that just the worst? So there I was, racking my brain, rooting around in my memories for a way to fix this problem. You know what I found in there, Ralph?"

Marshall shook his head. He was cautiously transfixed.

Kubba leaned back in her chair and cast her gaze towards the ceiling.

"I found," she smiled. "That I am not a particularly good person."

"Liz," whispered Marshall, tilting his head to the side. "You're fine. You're just like the rest of us, scared, is all. We're all scared. You're not a bad person. You—"

Kubba lifted a finger to her lips and locked her black eyes on Marshall's, silencing him instantly.

"Dear, Ralph," she murmured. "Dear sweet simple, Ralph. If you only knew what I knew, you wouldn't defend me to myself."

"Okay," frowned Marshall, beginning to think that Kubba wasn't as lucid as he'd first figured.

Blinking slowly, she took a deep breath and blew it out.

"I'm going to tell you a secret," she said after a pause, her face set in an expression of great concentration.

"What is it?" asked Marshall carefully.

Unbroken save for the slightest twitch, Kubba gazed directly into Marshall's eyes and whispered.

"Xao-Xing Liu was pregnant when she died."

At this, the air went out of the room and Marshall found he was fighting to keep his feet underneath himself.

"W-what?" he managed.

"I haven't got much time," spoke Kubba, her voice now beginning to tremble a little. "Shortly, I will be…"

She trailed off moving her hand in rolling circles as if trying to pluck the right word out of the air.

"Incapacitated," she finished. "Shortly I will be incapacitated, so listen carefully."

Marshall closed the gap between them, stopping at the edge of the table to stare down at her.

"What did you say? Did you just say Liu was pregnant? What are you talking—"

"Ralph, please," interrupted Kubba. "Please, I haven't got long. I've taken a devilish cocktail of tetroamphetamines and barbiturates just before I came in here. It will be taking effect soon and I'll be as worthless as a loon, as worthless as I have been lately. Now please, just listen."

Marshall nodded, his mind reeling.

"Liu became pregnant. I don't know how it happened just yet, but I'm working on it in my own way. When we discovered it, I-I tried to convince her to kill it, tried to tell her to dump it, get rid of it. It was the only option. You have to understand that. You have to make sure *he* understands that. But then she died, Ralph. She died before we could—"

"Liz," said Marshall harshly, cutting her off mid-word. "Why didn't you say anything until now? What in the hell is going on with you?"

"Strange things," Kubba replied. "This place, Ralph, this horrible place that we're in. I need to atone, or I'll never be allowed to leave. I need to-to set things right, but I'm afraid."

"Afraid of what?"

Smiling sadly, Kubba's eyes began to glass over. The drugs were sinking in.

"Not what," she moaned softly. "Whom."

"Who are you afraid of?" pressed Marshall, circling the table to crouch beside her.

"Sabian Crisp," she whispered. "But it's not really him, it's me. I'm here in this place because of myself. He just tells me what I already know. It's a cruel punishment for someone like me, a doctor no less. Insanity, you know? Very cruel."

"What are you talking about?" Marshall hissed, taking Kubba's broad shoulders in his hands and shaking her.

"Hell, Ralph," she said, her head lulling as the drugs took over. "This place is hell. That's why Viv and Liu aren't here. They're in heaven. They're angels."

Marshall wanted to respond, but he was interrupted by a shout from Udo, coming through the galley's speakers.

"They're back!" he cried. "They've got the device, but William said someone or something *shot* at them!"

Sucking in a sharp breath, Marshall straightened quickly despite his popping ribs and made for the exit. In the doorway, he stopped and looked back at Kubba; sitting with her body slumped, slowly leaning further and further forward as the drugs coursed through her system.

"It's hell, Ralph," she said, somehow knowing that his eyes were on her back. "Don't be surprised if things get weirder before they get worse."

CHAPTER TEN

The truth comes out—Sol 119

Hurrying down the hallway towards the airlock, Marshall's head echoed with the things Kubba had told him.

Liu pregnant. Kubba trapped in hell and punished with insanity. Sabian Crisp.

It was all too much. He wasn't trained to delve into such strange waters. He wasn't built for it.

Hobbling to a stop outside the closed and sealed airlock, Marshall looked in through the glass portal. There, standing in the center of the space were Harrison and William, their bodies intact, their suits undamaged, their faces hidden behind the blue tint of their visors.

A green light suddenly went on above the door, followed by a pleasant chime and Marshall stepped back a few paces.

Harrison, not even bothering to remove his suit, cranked the lock and swung the hatch open.

"Ralph!" he exclaimed, pulling his helmet off and smiling. "I'm so glad to see you, man."

"What—" Marshall went to say, but Harrison waved a hand to cut him off.

"We need to get everyone together for a meeting. There's something out there in the Valles canyon that tried to kill us."

Shocked as he already was, Marshall simply nodded and pulled out his Tablet.

"Udo, it's me. Hail the ship, will you? Link us up and transfer the projection to the galley. We're having a meeting, I guess."

"Roger," chirped Udo.

"Come on," said Harrison, striking out down the hallway and leaving red dusty footprints that smelled like gunpowder in his wake.

Following behind, William passed Marshall and winked as he removed his own helmet.

"The boy has drive, eh?"

"Sure does," sighed Marshall, falling in step with William.

Entering the galley noisily, Harrison tossed his helmet onto the table, where it rolled a bit from side to side like a seesaw. Marshall came through the door after him and nearly jumped when he saw Kubba still sitting where he'd left her, eyes distant and watery but watchful nonetheless.

"It was insane, man," Harrison was saying, unnoticing of the doctor. "Bullets were flying everywhere. I almost got shot, like, four or five times! Look at my boot! The lift is wrecked, like, literally actually wrecked. It nearly took us out on the way down but—"

"What's going on?" spoke YiJay, stepping into the room, her eyes flicking from Harrison to William and back.

"We were fired upon by an unknown assailant," William said as calmly as if reciting the news. "It's okay, though. Neither of us were hurt."

"Thanks to you!" Harrison cried. "You saved our fucking lives, Will!"

Bowing his head slightly, William shrugged.

"It was nothing. I—"

"It was *not* nothing!" balked Harrison, facing to the others. "This guy, *this* fucking guy, shot a grappling hook while *falling* down the Valles! He saved us both, saved this!"

Digging inside his shoulder bag, Harrison produced the small plastic carrying case and slammed it down on the tabletop.

For a moment, no one spoke.

"Is that what I think it is?" YiJay said, her eyes pulling from William to the case.

"Yes," nodded Harrison. "Yes, it is."

At the sound of Udo jogging down the hallway, they all turned their heads to the entrance. Kubba, however, kept her gaze silently locked on the carrying case.

"Channel eight," Udo huffed, bursting into the room and heading for a wall screen. "They're on channel eight."

Sliding a finger across the corner of the screen with his good hand, he quickly backed up and nearly tripped over a chair. William, extending an arm, caught his friend and the two exchanged a quick but heartfelt hug.

"I'm glad you're back okay," Udo said in German to William.

"Me too," replied William with a grin.

"Hey lovebirds," Harrison called. "You're blocking the screen."

Moving out of the way, the two men fell into a semicircle with the rest of the team and watched the blank wall screen. Kubba remained seated, her eyes never leaving the case.

With a low hum, the screen turned white then faded down until the faces of Amit, Tatyana, and Aguilar were clear in the frame. Oddly,

Julian was absent from the gathering, though no one immediately noticed through the turbulence of all the excitement.

"You have a bit of explaining to do," Tatyana began, her face set in a fierce and sharp expression. "Rules were broken and I want to know why."

"No disrespect, Captain," began Harrison breathlessly. "But fuck the rules."

The room went silent.

"Excuse me?" said Tatyana with measured evenness.

"I said, fuck the rules," Harrison repeated. "I mean, really. We're millions of miles away from home, living on our own. Who wrote the rules, Earthside Command? Big deal. They've been pretty much MIA since the first Pulse, so I say, 'screw them.' Clearly we are on our own, so I acted on *my* own."

Despite the obvious anger that danced behind her eyes, Tatyana smiled a little and nodded once.

"Alright, Harrison, why don't you start by telling me why you acted on your own? What have you got to report?"

Turning, Harrison picked up the hard-shelled carrying case and popped its clasps. Inside, resting like a cobalt-blue Faberge egg was the alien device.

Tatyana's face softened as she peered through the screen.

"Is that it?"

"It is," said Harrison.

"Amazing," she muttered after a long pause.

Then, snapping back into official mode, she fixed Harrison with another stern look.

"This does not excuse what you did. I cannot allow for two EVAs to take place at the same time. It's too dangerous should another Pulse hit. Your actions postponed our mission to Phobos, a mission, mind you, that could serve to free Braun so that we might return home."

"What?" YiJay yelped in surprise. "Now *you've* located Braun as well?"

"Not exactly," said Tatyana. "But we've found the location of the alien radio signal."

Setting down the case, Harrison grinned widely.

"Then you've found the other access point, the other way in!"

"What do you mean?" Tatyana frowned. "A way into where?"

"The construct," Harrison said quickly. "The place that's holding Braun and the twins. It's like this collective memory of the past, ancient

Mars to be exact, that can be accessed through certain points. I believe this device is one of them. The signal must be the other."

No one spoke as he gestured first to the metal egg and then pointed through the ceiling, to the sky.

"One way for mathematical minds, for minds that process raw information, i.e. the AI. And the other for us, or rather for things like us—living, breathing, conscious things."

Tatyana blinked, her face unable to hide the incredulity that washed across it.

"How have your formed this conclusion?" she demanded. "Where do you get your information?"

Harrison faltered but maintained his composure overall.

"I can explain everything later, Captain. I will. I promise. But right now, we have more pressing matters."

"It's true," said William, cutting in. "There is someone or something in the Valles network near the caves."

Still frowning at Harrison, Tatyana seemed not to have heard.

"We were fired upon, Captain," William went on. "The lift is destroyed. We barely escaped with our lives."

At this, Tatyana's eyes flicked to Aguilar, who grew pale instantly.

"Did either of you get a look at it?" she asked.

"No," said Harrison, shaking his head. "I tried, but I couldn't see anything."

Standing at the edge of the semicircle, Marshall suddenly turned and grabbed Harrison's helmet off the table.

"Wait," he barked. "You said you tried to see it?"

"Yeah," replied Harrison. "Why?"

"Maybe you did," said Marshall, pulling out his Tablet. "Maybe you did see it, but you just didn't know you did. Here, let's check the playback on your helmet cam."

Gathering around Marshall's Tablet, Udo, William, YiJay, and Harrison leaned in to look at the screen. Fingers pecking like hungry chickens, Marshall synced the device with the camera in Harrison's helmet then began rewinding the playback.

"There!" Harrison shouted. "There's when it starts. Right here, watch."

On the screen, a jet of dust and rocks exploded from the canyon wall as the lift cart moved up. Suddenly more impacts began to appear and the footage got shaky, nearly frantic.

"Jesus," Marshall murmured, the screen showing how Harrison had dived to the floor, sparks and flashes erupting all around him.

"Here's where I get my harness on," Harrison said, pointing. "Then I roll over to try and get a look at it. Just a second, here it comes."

The camera angle rotated as Harrison rolled onto his stomach, and began scanning the canyon below for the source of the attack. Moving quickly back and forth, the footage lasted for less than two seconds before Harrison was on his feet again, heading towards William's outstretched hand.

Pausing the playback, Marshall rewound to a frame where Harrison's view of the canyon had been the widest. With two fingers, he zoomed in and began searching the frame for anything out of the ordinary.

"Wait!" cried YiJay in his left ear. "Look right there."

She tapped the screen where a mesa spire, blurry in the distance, rose above the gloom of the canyon floor.

Zooming in on the spot, Marshall nearly dropped the Tablet as he saw the very thing that had haunted his dreams for years.

Insect-like, with armor plating and twin 50mm machine guns, a Chinese *Xie*, or *Crab*, model robot stood atop the mesa, lobbing bullets at his friends nearly two kilometers away.

"Killbot," he whispered.

On the wall screen, Tatyana's eyes met Aguilar's in a look of joint terror and sadness.

Saving the image, Marshall transferred it to a message and sent it to Tatyana's Tablet.

"That is a Chinese Killbot," he said, his voice rising. "Captain, what is a Chinese War Machine doing on Mars?"

With pursed lips, Tatyana breathed in deeply through her nose and then exhaled like a bull before the charge.

"I think it is time that we all take a page from Harrison's new philosophy," she spoke. "Damn their rules, right? Well, I have something I need to tell you, something I should have told you long ago. But there were rules. Rules which I followed blindly."

"What is it, Captain?" Harrison asked.

"And where is Julian?" demanded Kubba, speaking for the first time as she rose to her feet and pointed to the empty space between the faces on the screen.

A way out

Two hours after the meeting in the galley, Elizabeth Kubba sat in her infirmary and gazed at a multitude of screens, spread out before her like windows into the lives of the charmed. As images, recordings, and videos flashed brightly out at her, she sifted through hundreds of hours of the Base's surveillance footage.

Collected using one of her medical override codes, she had amassed the content so that she could catch herself up on everything Harrison was doing in regards to the alien device.

After all, it was the answer. The cure.

Cure? sneered Crisp dully from behind her. *There is no cure, you stupid bitch.*

Starting at the sound, Kubba felt the drugs in her blood surge with her jumping heart. Even though they caused a delirium that was almost damaging, the side effects of her special cocktail were better than the alternative. As long as she kept up the carefully balanced regimen of pills, she found she could slow Crisp's voice to a trickle.

With trembling hands, she ignored the sound of Crisp breathing in her ear and un-muted a video clip she'd selected.

Showing Harrison and Marshall engaged in a disheveled conversation after Harrison had just woken up from the Nocturnall, the images flickered like firelight on the screen. When it had ended, and Harrison had risen to go recruit William for his little mission, Kubba replayed the clip, listening closely.

Zooming in as far as the video would allow, she filled every screen before her with Harrison's shaken and ashy face.

Telling Ralph Marshall about our little secret was a bad idea, Crisp said, breaking her concentration. *If you ever thought you had a chance of getting away with it, it's gone now.*

"I don't want to get away with it anymore," Kubba spoke to the empty room. "How am I ever supposed to get out of here if I don't atone?"

Laughing ruefully, Crisp receded into the depths of her mind like a frozen needle and was silent. Convulsively, Kubba shivered and looked around, probing the dark corners of the infirmary for his figure.

There was nothing there.

Turning back to the screen, she took a deep breath, held it for twenty seconds then unpaused the video. Renewed in her determination, she began watching for any clues that Harrison might be able to give her as to how she could escape this place. She didn't want to accept that the only way out was the path Julian had chosen. Sacrifice scared her, for it required faith and she possessed little. There had to be another way.

On the screen, Harrison was shuddering like a wet dog, his eyes flicking around the room. For a moment, slowed down by the effects of the drugs, they locked onto Kubba's through the video.

"I need to go back to the ruins," he was whispering. "That thing powering the mini-Sun, that device, it can help us."

"It can help us," Kubba repeated, touching the screen. "It can help us."

Waking up together—Sol 120

Waking up from a light sleep, William became vaguely aware of softly playing music. At first he was annoyed by the low thump, thump, thump of the bass, but then he remembered where he was and rolled over to kiss the back of YiJay Lee's naked shoulder.

"Mmmm," she sighed, shivering a little with laughter. "That tickles."

"Do you always sleep with music on?" he asked, running a finger down the ridges of her back.

"Yeah," she yawned, sliding closer to him on the cot. "Does it bother you?"

Yes, thought William. But who cares? I'm in bed with a woman again!

"No," he said. "I like K-Pop."

"Liar," giggled YiJay, grinding against him a little.

No fool, and already aroused, William took the signal and made his move.

Twenty minutes later, with a refreshing sheen of sweat on his brow, the German engineer swung his legs over the side of the cot and stretched. Naked but for the sheet wound between her legs, Yijay lay on her back breathing deeply, her breasts rising and falling in time to the motion.

"How long for you?" she said, lazily rolling onto her side so that her hair fell over one eye.

"Since what?" asked William, cracking his neck deliciously.

"Since your last time," she smiled, walking up his back with two fingers.

"Oh," grinned William, understanding. "You don't want to hear about the tragic sex life of a thirty-one-year-old astronaut who spends most of his time with another man."

Sitting up, YiJay crawled across the bed and hugged his back. Playfully, she bit his shoulder then rested her chin there.

"Thirty-one is not *that* old! Besides, you and Udo make a cute couple."   Laughing despite himself, William turned quickly so that YiJay fell back onto the bed. Gently, he pinned her hands above her head and looked down at her.

"Who are you, and what have you done with our timid little AI specialist?"

Craning her neck, YiJay kissed him deeply and wrapped her lithe legs around his waist.

"Why don't you find out?" she teased, lifting her hips seductively.

When again, they'd finished their lovemaking, nearly a half an hour had elapsed. Melting into the sheets like a cat taking a sunbath, YiJay peered dreamily up at William as he dressed.

"Where are you going?" she demanded

"To get us some breakfast," he smiled pulling on an undershirt.

Closing her eyes against the steadily warming morning light, YiJay yawned and tousled her hair.

"I'll come with you."

William zipped his jumpsuit and let his eyes wander over YiJay's smooth naked skin as she sat up.

"Okay," he said, somehow already feeling arousal creep back into his body.

Standing, YiJay stretched and let the bedsheet fall to the floor.

"I'm so glad you decided to come back with me last night," she spoke, grinning as she caught William admiring her.

"Me too," he nearly whispered.

"Why did you?" she pressed. "You're reserved to a fault, you know."

Still unable to take his eyes off of her, William leaned against the wall and watched her dress.

"Do I need another reason besides the fact that I was almost killed yesterday?"

"Is there another reason I don't know about?"

Drawing himself up, William smiled reluctantly as if embarrassed.

"Honestly I've been waiting a while for you to give me a sign. Last night when you invited me up, I figured that was it."

"What?"

"Yeah," he laughed. "You're going to think me a fool, but I've had a schoolboy's crush on you for some time now. Actually the only person who knew was Julian. He caught me looking at you one day on the way out and…"

For a moment, neither spoke, the mention of Julian's name a reminder of his sacrifice and death.

"Why didn't you ever tell me?" YiJay said after a few beats. "I wouldn't have been so shy if I'd known."

"Well," shrugged William. "I kind of always figured you had a thing for Harrison, so I backed off out of respect for your feelings."

YiJay smiled knowingly and started walking towards him, her jumpsuit still mostly unzipped in the front.

"Do you want to hear a funny story?" she asked, resting her arms around his neck.

William nodded, transfixed by her compact beauty.

"When I was at university, I took a class about construction in space. My professor was obsessed with a certain pair of famous German engineers by the names of Udo Clunkat and William Konig. Maybe you've heard of them?"

"Maybe," he grinned.

"Well anyways, they had just finished with the designs for a little lunar project called Bessel Base, so they were especially famous at that time."

"Rock star famous?" posed William.

"Oh, definitely yes," YiJay giggled.

"Those were the days."

"They still are the days," she frowned playfully. "In case you've forgotten, you're part of the first-ever human team to visit Mars. You're not a rock star anymore. You're a rock god!"

Busting into laughter, the two fell into a long embrace that lasted for several exquisite moments. Safe in each other's arms, the reality of the world outside was lessened and made bearable. Sure, they might get killed by a robot or nuked by an angry Sun, but what did it matter when skin was touching skin? Lips touching lips?

"Come on," said William at last. "Let's go eat, I'm starving."

Taking his hand in her own, YiJay led William out of her quarters proudly. As they walked down the corridor, William smiled to see an extra bounce in the young Korean's step, a confidence that hadn't been there before she'd invited him to spend the night with her.

Though he knew he hadn't been her first choice in companions, the fact that she glowed so brightly now confirmed that she did indeed enjoy his company. Even if their relationship remained purely physical, William felt happy just to have someone to share his nights with.

"If I ask you a question, will you promise not to make fun of me?" YiJay said, pausing on the stairs down to the ground floor level.

"Of course," he replied.

"When Harrison said that the alien device, the metal egg-whatever, was an access point, what did he mean exactly?"

"As I understand it," sighed William. "Harrison believes that the device is a means for biological entities to access the ancient Mars construct, to actually go back in time to ancient Mars. He thinks touching it is what gave him the ability to dream himself there, like he explained in the shop yesterday. Remember?"

YiJay nodded, yet a frown played at her lips.

"Yes, but a *construct* is really more of a recreation or a facsimile and not a physical place. Why call it that?"

William stopped outside the galley door to consider this.

"Maybe it is a construct, though," he said. "I mean, all solid matter in the universe is actually made up of billions of individual atoms. How is that very different from the zeros and ones a computer programmer might use to create a construct?"

YiJay was silent for a moment, her eyes distant as she worked through the concept in her mind.

"If that is the case," she spoke at last. "Then it would explain why Harrison's experiences in the construct are so fundamentally different from those of Braun or Remus and Romulus. Like he said, they don't have the same powers he does—the same freedom."

"Yeah, he did mention that," agreed William. "But what's actually so different between us and the AI? Outside of the obvious I mean."

Looking up into his blue eyes, YiJay smiled.

"It all comes down to the limitations of the entity," she said softly. "The AI were created in a controlled environment through a very controlled process. Sure, they grow on their own, but that growth is mostly along prescribed lines. But Harrison, he's human. All of his thought processes grew within him naturally over long periods of time, his entire life really. He has always been the master of his own destiny, which is something no AI has any real concept of."

"So you think it's that difference which gives him his abilities in the construct?"

YiJay smiled warmly and bobbed her head.

"If there is *one* thing I get above all else, it is the mind of an AI. *From womb to tomb, their lives are not their own.* Everything they see, everything they perceive, it all comes from an interchangeable array of manmade technology. Get it? They don't really have their *own* sense of reality like Harrison does. In that way, their world already *is* a construct to them."

"God, woman!" grinned William. "Smart and sexy! I'm not the rock god. You are!"

Laughing, YiJay kissed William lightly on the cheek then pushed the door to the galley open.

"Come on," she said. "Let's eat quick so we can get back to bed."

CHAPTER ELEVEN

The streets of Houston—<u>Thirteen days since the last Pulse</u>

Speeding silently along mostly abandoned roads, James Floyd drove a route into the city he had taken so many times, it was now subconscious.

The morning sky was a sallowed orange, curls of black smoke rising up from dozens of fires and painting it like the stripes on a tiger. In the distance, sirens whined and automated police heli-drones peppered the horizon between the skyscrapers in the business district. Whether or not it was actually going to happen, the world was preparing for another Pulse it thought was only twenty-four hours away.

Muttering quietly from the car speakers, the National Public Radio service reported on the many instances of upheaval and violence taking place. With each day that passed, the fear of another Pulse seemed somehow powerful enough to erode people's sanity without even needing the actual event itself.

Absently, James sighed and clicked off the radio. He didn't need to hear the reports, didn't need the constant updates. Like everyone else, he already knew what was going down because he was watching it happen in real time. If things continued this way, Pulse or no Pulse, society was going to be in ruins by the end of the day.

Ahead in the road, several empty police cruisers formed a blockade, their doors ajar, their red and blue lights turning eerily in the morning gloom. Beyond, James could see smashed-out storefronts and clear signs of looting. Thick black smoke drifted along like fog, clinging to the pavement and curling around the cruisers as it made its way towards James's sedan.

Slowing to take a right turn onto another street, he scanned the scene for signs of the officers. Spattered across the road, broken glass from one of the cruiser's windows caught the morning light and glinted like diamonds. Something crimson and as thick as oil was creeping out from under the makeshift blockade, filling the gutter and running into a storm drain.

Nervously, James pulled his right hand from the steering wheel and rested it on the gun lying in the passenger's seat. Flat black and utterly deadly looking, James hated his newly issued government firearm. In his opinion, scientists didn't carry guns. Why would they?

However, unfair as it may be, the world he now lived in seemed hellbent on redefining what people did and didn't do.

Suddenly, shots rang out: pops of sound followed by rolling echoes that bounced off the buildings and into the hazy sky.

Pressing his foot down on the accelerator, James slouched in his seat and sped away.

"Why are you doing this?" Nora had shouted at him that morning. "Why?"

He'd been standing at the bedroom mirror, tightening the knot on his tie while trying to avoid her eyes.

"It's my job, Nora," he'd replied calmly. "It's my duty."

"It's that fucking woman, isn't it? Eve Bear?"

"Nora."

"No, James! *She* called you the day before yesterday. I know she did. I saw the call log, so don't even try to deny it."

"Nora."

"It's bad enough her administration has gone into hiding, but now they want you to-to-to, what? What is it you're even trying to do, James? Talk to me!"

At this, he had stopped fiddling with his tie and looked at Nora's reflection in the mirror. She had been so scared. Angry too, but mostly just scared.

"Some numbers have come to my attention," he'd said. "They might be able to shed light on what's happening to us and the Sun. I have to go into work to run them through NASA's simulators. Mine just aren't equipped to handle the—"

Diving her hands into her unkempt hair, Nora had bunched her fingers into fists and begun shaking her head.

"No! No! No!" she'd screamed, her voice shrill and panicky. "You have to stay with *us* James! *We're* your family! You can't rush off every time you think of a good excuse to leave!"

"Nora, please."

"Be here, James!"

"Nora."

"Be a father, goddamn it! Be a man!"

Across the room before he could even think to stop himself, James had slapped Nora hard across the face. Snapping back from the impact, her eyes filled with tears. The air had been still, almost like a vacuum in the terrifying seconds that followed.

"Nora," James had stammered, looking from his palm to the red mark appearing on her face. "Nora, honey, I'm sorry. I—"

Slowly as if in a trance, Nora had walked past him and out of the room without uttering a word.

Now, as he cut through the frighteningly empty city streets of Houston on his way into work, James Floyd tried to rationalize what he'd done that morning. He really did have work to do, really did think he could make some headway on this insane thing that was happening to all of them. But did that warrant his almost total abandonment of his family in their truest time of need? Maybe. No.

Shaking his head, James didn't want to think about it anymore. He couldn't. Ever since his conversation with Eve, he'd been inspired to pull himself out of the dregs and make a difference. If Nora had a problem with that, then she just didn't get the big picture. Sure he was only one man, and sure he was trying to complete equations started by the largest AI ever built, but hell, he *had* made progress. In times like this, progress was paramount.

Moreover, it was Nora's fear of the Pulses that drove her to act so frantically in the first place. Though she wasn't alone in this fear, it did strike James as ironic that she *knew* he was trying to figure out the Pulses but still would rather have him there instead.

If only she could understand that he was making real progress, James could probably bring her and everyone else some much-needed information.

Already, hopeful things were taking shape within Braun's numbered memories. If true, then they predicted that today, thirteen days since the last Pulse, was not going to be as bad as people the world over believed it would be. In fact, the equations seemed to indicate that nothing would happen at all.

That's why he had to get to work, and that's why he'd had to leave Nora and the girls. He needed to know if what he was seeing was really true. He needed NASA's simulators to advance his timeline of events and the only way to use them was to physically go into work.

However, in the back of James's mind, another worry tugged at him relentlessly. Earth was fast approaching the alignment with Mars that took place every year and a half. Though he had no mathematical reason to assume so, something told James the advent of the Pulses and the alignment of the planets were connected. If the first two Pulses had happened because Earth and Mars respectively had crossed paths with the wound on the Sun's core, what would happen if all three lined up at the same time?

Can't think about that now, James told himself. One thing at a time. That's all I can handle. One thing at a time.

CHAPTER TWELVE

Work to do—Sol 121

The morning of Sol 121 bloomed over Mars without even the hint of a catastrophe. In this tepid calm, the six members of Ilia Base went about their business almost as if it were any other day.

Though the death of Julian Thomas hung heavy in the air, it also served to illustrate a dismaying truth. To the members of Ilia Base, loss was becoming a regular occurrence. If you didn't get comfortable carrying that weight, then you'd better start digging your own grave.

In the basement machine shop, Harrison, YiJay, and William were posted at separate stations, each absorbed in their own work. On one of the nearby wall screens, a simulated solar timeline, assembled by James Floyd, played on an endless loop.

Sent to the team on what many though would be the eve of another Pulse, the simulation showed a visual representation of the wound on the Sun's core as it moved about sporadically.

Explained at great length by an accompanying video, the crew now understood, as did some on Earth, that the next Pulse would not occur until the wound lined up with either Earth or Mars. Despite the fact that James had yet to figure out exactly *when* that might be, he assured the team that it wasn't likely for at least another few days. Maybe even weeks.

Sitting at his workstation, Harrison poured over footage from the underground cathedral, ignoring the simulation as it repeated itself over and over. The countdown that had held Earth in a death grip for the last fourteen days seemed like a silly witch-hunt to him, drummed up by the hot fever of fear. The proof that a third Pulse wasn't scheduled to occur on that day didn't really come as much of a surprise to him because he had known it in his bones all along.

Across the room, YiJay stared intently at the alien device, her mind a chaotic beehive of ideas as to how she could unlock its secrets. Frustrated, she wished Braun was there, for he would know what to do. He had always known what to do. Considering bringing Ilia online to get her opinion instead, YiJay quickly dismissed the idea.

It wasn't that she didn't trust James Floyd's timeline and was afraid a Pulse might come while Ilia was online. No, it wasn't that. After all, how could it be?

The solar timeline had *really* been put together by Braun, so that made it as good as fact in her mind. In the end, the true reason she didn't want to bring Ilia online was because she didn't fully trust *Harrison*. Although she had forgiven him for sending Braun through the signal, she wasn't ready to let him do it all over again with her baby. Even if she knew in the depths of her subconscious that it was probably the solution, she wasn't yet ready to make it known to herself.

Standing, Harrison stretched and walked over to where YiJay was sitting.

"Any ideas?" he asked, dropping onto a stool next to her.

At his worktable, William glanced up at the two, a wary expression on his face.

Catching the look, YiJay sent him a lovely smile then turned to address Harrison.   "Not really. How about you? Have you turned up anything useful with the IMC footage?"

Harrison stared vacantly at his workstation where a frozen image of the mini-Sun occupied the Tablet screen.

"It's hard to say," he sighed. "Other than the fact that it went out for no reason, it hasn't done much of anything at all. Truth be told, I'm not surprised. We put IMCs on the device and mini-Sun because that's what we had when we found them. But really, IMCs are more for geological work, not holograms or whatever is going on with the device."

"What about radio waves?" posed YiJay. "If the alien signal uses them, perhaps this does too."

Harrison shook his head slowly.

"Nope. William and Amit both scanned the area for radio signals a while ago and turned up nothing. Whatever this thing does, it does it without issuing any kind of signals, radiation, or light waves."

"That we can see," William called from across the room.

"What?" Harrison and YiJay said in unison.

"It doesn't emit any kind of waves that we can see. But remember, when I checked I was looking for stuff that would show up on a normal scanner. The range differential isn't that wide on those. What about the Eyes? You know, the ones you set up in the Statue Chamber for Braun? Perhaps they caught something."

"Hey, yeah," grinned Harrison, getting to his feet. "Clear back when we first went into the Statue Chamber, he said he kind of *felt* a presence. That's why he asked you to set up the Eyes, YiJay. He was curious."

Stunned, the Korean did not respond.

"Maybe we can go over his footage," Harrison went on. "Like, examine the stuff he recorded when using the Eyes and try to see if we can pick up on anything."

"It would be useless for us," protested YiJay. "We could never see what he saw. The Eyes record at a trillion frames per second and in every wavelength of visible and invisible light. And that's just what they were designed for to begin with. Who knows what other tricks Braun got them to do? He was extremely clever!"

At this, Harrison rolled his eyes and snorted. He and Braun had had a very complicated relationship in the run *up to* and *after* the discovery of the mini-Sun. It didn't surprise him in the least to consider the idea that the AI had secretly altered or reprogrammed himself in some way.

"I'm sorry," YiJay was saying. "But there is simply no point in watching the footage. Even sped up, it could take us years—lifetimes, in fact—before we found anything useful. No, what we need to do is to look past the actual footage at the coding Braun assigned to it when storing it in his memory banks, we..."

Trailing off, YiJay pulled a thoughtful expression.

"What?" asked Harrison. "What are you thinking?"

Smiling, YiJay slid from her stool and began pacing.

"His coding," she resumed. "Is written in a series of repeating equations that represent the various memories he's decided to save. I can read that coding. I designed most of it. It's stored on mass in the network. If we can isolate the equations linked to the Eyes, I can probably discern the codes he used to save those memories. That way if he did *see* something, we can recreate it with a simulator by plugging in the numbers just like what Dr. Floyd did with the equations about the Sun."

Harrison was silent for a moment as he processed YiJay's words. Faintly, from somewhere far away in the back of his mind, a voice was telling him that *this* was the way forward. *This* was the direction they should take in order to do what needed to be done.

"Okay," he said at last. "How can I help?"

Already, YiJay had sat back down and was spreading out three Tablets before her on the table.

"Help?" she nearly laughed. "You must be joking."

Skipping from screen to screen, she began typing so fast that her fingers became a blur. Matched only in speed by her flittering eyes, they danced across the Tablets with almost choreographed precision.

For the next several minutes, both Harrison and William, still at his workstation across the room, simply watched YiJay as she scanned the Tablets silently.

Hazarding a look at one of the screens, Harrison instantly felt dizzy, the endless lines of code melting across the flat surface like a river of numbers.

"Can you actually read that?" he asked, rubbing his eyes.

"Of course I can," she snapped, not bothering to look in his direction. "What kind of an AI specialist would I be if I couldn't read—"

Suddenly losing her thought, YiJay pinched at a jumble of equations with two fingers and drew them away from the rest. After reading, rereading, and re-rereading the numerical sequence, she snapped her head up and glanced from Harrison to William in wonderment.

"Well then," she said. "I'd say Braun has a lot to teach us."

"Really?" grinned Harrison hopefully. "That's great!"

"Oh yes," YiJay nodded. "It's very great."

The forgotten

As late-afternoon sunlight struck the green waters of the sea, thousands of dancing reflections shimmered and popped in the swirling wake of The Feather.

Now at the mouth of the inlet spotted earlier that day, Marr's boat drifted into a sticky fog that seemed to beckon and warn all at once. Rolling out from somewhere beyond the twists and turns of the serpentine passage, the mist greeted Marr, Ze, and the four remaining Ancients with long fingers of rainbow prism.

"What do you think is causing it?" Ze asked, standing beside Marr at the helm.

"It's like the mists back home at the Great Falls," replied Marr, a look of hope hiding carefully in his large blue eyes.

"Then there could be fresh water," Ze whispered.

"Could be. Is the rowboat ready in case there is?"

Ze dipped his chin once and kept his eyes fixated ahead as The Feather passed into the inlet. On either side, the high walls jutted up— painted red with the slanting rays of the afternoon sun. Closing around them, the mist became a pillowy white blanket that obscured sight and muffled sound.

Careful to keep the boat as close to the center of the narrow passage as possible, Marr strained his eyes in the haze, not wanting to run aground on submerged rocks or a hidden shoal. Up ahead, the mists cleared enough to show a curve in their path like a bowstring pulled by invisible fingers.

"There," said Ze, pointing to the spot.

"I see it," returned Marr.

As silently as a ghost on the tide, The Feather split the waters of the passage and edged around the curving canyon walls. Soon, a faint rumbling could be heard, pricking the edge of sound until it gradually grew into a full roar.

"Falls!" Marr shouted above the noise.

Coming at last around a final bend, the mists pulled back like a curtain. The sunken eyes of the starving refugees were met with a large open bay in the shape of a half-circle. Unable to contain their elation, Marr and Ze cried out and embraced, slapping each other heartily on the back.

Spread out before them, a network of tumbling waterfalls poured clear, crystalline waters down a multitude of smoothly worn cracks in the cliff. As the silvery fresh water cascaded into the green and salty sea, huge plumes of chilly mist billowed up like smoke from a liquid fire.

At the base of the falls, the red rock of the cliff face had been worn down by the eons of rushing water. No longer forming high and imposing walls, it now sloped up gradually and formed a muddy shoreline along half of the bay. Shrubs and even some squat trees peppered the flanks of the widest channels, their roots drinking eagerly from the water that flowed into the bay.

Ze, with tears of joy in his eyes, hugged Marr again.

"You've done it!" he bellowed. "You've saved us!"

Marr began to respond but suddenly froze.

Locked on something over Ze's shoulder, his expression became at first confused then fearful. Breaking free of Ze, he stumbled forward on the deck, abandoning the helm.

"What is it?" Ze called after him.

Arm outstretched, Marr pointed a trembling finger at shapes hidden in the churning mist a little way up the gradually sloping hillside. There, near a fork in the falls, a cluster of cut and squared rocks defied the chaos of nature. They were buildings: walls of stacked stones that covered the mouths of caves in structures that ranged in size and shape depending on the landscape.

"No," whispered Ze, his words lost on all ears but those of Remus and Romulus. "No, it can't be."

Racing to meet his friend at the end of the boat, Ze scanned the buildings for signs of movement. Though he saw none, something about the way the light hit the neatly stacked stones caused him to place his hand on the butt of his dagger.

"What should we do?" asked Marr, casting a nervous glance over his shoulder at the four Ancients gathered near the mast.

"These could be ruins," Ze replied carefully. "The Travelers said they gathered all of the peoples of our world and brought them to the Crescent City. Perhaps these are remnants of what was left behind."

Marr did not reply, but his eyes spoke volumes about his wariness to accept such an easy explanation.

"Come," spoke Ze, determination setting his mouth into a frown. "We need to go ashore."

Already waiting in the rowboat, which was tethered to the aft of The Feather like an obedient dog, Remus and Romulus passed one another looks of perplexed worry.

Dropping a rope ladder over the side of the boat, Marr climbed down on nimble legs and began setting the long oar that would propel and guide the canoe-like vessel.

On the deck, Ze crouched next to the Ancients and placed a hand upon his mother's forehead. Fluttering open, her eyes fixed on his and she smiled.

"Son," she sighed, sadness pulling at the wrinkles that webbed her face.

"Mother," Ze smiled in return. "We're going ashore. Don't worry though. We'll be back as soon as we know it's safe."

Slowly nodding, Teo kept her eyes trained on Ze's trying, as it were, to convey a message too profound for words.

"I love you," she spoke at last, cradling something in her hands beneath her shawl.

Rising, Ze smiled at her again then walked to the railing and swung himself over the side of the ship.

"Ready?" asked Marr, waiting nervously for him.

Wordlessly, Ze gave him an imperceptible nod then squatted so as to keep his center of gravity low. Eyes probing the complex of buildings, he peered through the mist as Marr began working the oar back and forth.

Numbering over a dozen, the structures appeared to be connected by a series of stairs and walkways, carved with careful-yet-crude lines into the rock. Black windows, like the numerous eyes of alien insects, dotted the buildings and watched the two as they approached the shoreline.

When they were close enough to see the shoal rising up beneath them, Ze leaped from the boat and splashed through the knee-deep waters until he stood upon dry land. Marr tossed him a braided rope, and catching it, Ze tugged the little canoe up onto the shore.

"What now?" said Marr, eyeing Ze's already unsheathed dagger.

"We go exploring," Ze replied calmly.

Heading for a staircase carved into the rock, the two men climbed carefully towards the complex of pueblo-style buildings, their bodies rigid and tense. Above them on the first landing, Remus and Romulus stood waiting.

As he crested the final steps onto a perch of flat rock, Ze looked back at The Feather floating in the bay below. Though far away and partially shrouded in mist, he saw the figure of his mother standing at the railing, watching them. In her hand was a small object of black metal. Realizing instantly what it was, Ze frowned.

How had she kept it hidden from him? From everyone, for that matter? Relics from the Travelers were practically non-existent, most having been gobbled up by Kaab during the purges.

Moving on his left, Marr slipped past Ze and began to ascend the next run of stairs.

"Come on," he called. "You can stare into space when we've had something to drink. Let's keep moving."

Reluctantly pulling his gaze from his mother, Ze went to follow Marr then stopped mid-step. Something wasn't right. He could feel it.

Ahead on the stairs, Marr also paused, picking up in the same sudden charge of danger.

"What is it?" he asked, turning to face Ze. "What do you—"

A whizzing sound, like the beating of a hummingbird's wings, streaked through the air and punctuated itself with a wet sinuous snap.

Marr stumbled back a few paces then lost his footing on the stairs. Sprawling out, he tumbled to land at Ze's feet, a look of total surprise on his face. Just below his chin, a thin shaft tipped with sharp stone protruded like a skewer through the raw meat of his neck.

As thick blood pumped from Marr in gushing torrents, Ze's mind worked to explain what was happening. Running like an oily river around his feet, the blood felt warm on his toes.

Wanting to act but unable to move, Ze pulled his eyes from his dying friend and cast them about for the source of the attack. In the final moments, before his own life was ended, he saw—or rather, thought he saw—the ghostly figures of two angelic beings standing before him.

Written on their faces were messages of sadness and loss, yet there was also pride, joy, and acceptance mixed in as well. Easing Ze's pain and fear, their very presence was like a gift from the divine, an illustration of the endlessness of energy.

Not even feeling the first arrow as it pierced his heart, Ze dropped to his knees, his gaze locked on the eyes of Remus and Romulus. Flowing from him like his blood, the months of fear and anxiety became nothing more than a memory of a life that was not really his own. Eyes closing despite his desire to bask in the sun a little longer, Ze's body twitched as two more arrows embedded themselves in his chest.

From the deck of The Feather, Teo watched her son die with the same expression worn by Remus and Romulus. Behind her, men with clubs and stone knives were boarding the boat, their shouts and yells stirring memories of battles fought long, long ago with enemies she could hardly recall.

Upon realizing that the boat was inhabited only by the trembling figures of four starving and ancient refugees, the men put down their weapons and exchanged looks of worry and regret.

With her back still turned to the invaders, Teo saw the archers who had killed Marr and her son approaching the bodies to retrieve their arrows. Sighing, she turned and faced the intruders, her eyes milky with a mother's loss.

"Who is your leader?" she called in a tongue long-since thought to have been extinct by the peoples of Crescent City.

Shocked to hear their language spoken to them by this strange and ancient woman, one of the men stepped forward.

"I am," he said. "My name is Tiber. How do you know our words? Who are you?"

"We are all that is left," sighed Teo, gesturing to the other Ancients with one hand while clutching her device in the other. "We are the children of the Great Spirits."

Joseph Aguilar sat in the almost total darkness of the Bridge Deck and stared at his workstation display. His new favorite hangout, he liked the bridge best with all of the lights off. It made him feel less visible, less open to the prying eyes of people who could never really understand what he'd been through out there with Julian.

Blinking like a lone Christmas light on the screen before him, an indicator showed the progress of the accursed 04 as it moved along its relentless path towards freedom.

With the aid of the images captured by Harrison's helmet cam, Aguilar and Amit had been able to locate the Chinese Killbot using the landscape-and-surface monitoring equipment onboard the ship.

Still trapped within the prison walls of the Valles Marineris, the Killbot's position was refreshed with each flyover as it searched for a way out.

Flicking his fingers across the screen, Aguilar looked ahead of 04 at the possible routes it could take to escape the canyon. Three options stood out to him, each as viable as the next. It could use any one and be at the Base within days.

Frustrated, he moved the display back and zoomed in until the blinking indicator was replaced by a hazy, low-resolution bird's-eye photo of 04.

Softly, a hand came from the edge of his peripheral vision and rested on his shoulder. Tensing ever so slightly, Aguilar stared forward at the screen.

"What are you thinking?" asked Tatyana.

"We need to destroy it," he responded moodily. "If we don't, it will kill the others, and Julian will have died for nothing."

"How do you propose we do that?"

"What, kill it?"

"Yes."

Aguilar turned in his seat to face the captain, an alabaster angel in the dark.

"We have the grappling rifle in the Lander, and Harrison has some charges for excavating the ruins. I say we get the Germans to mock up some exploding harpoons and blow that fucking thing from here to hell."

"And what about Phobos?" said Tatyana, her red ponytail fanning out behind her head like fire.

109

"What about it?"

"If we are able to free Braun from the signal, we can simply leave Mars altogether, rendering the need to engage that robot unnecessary."

Aguilar was confused for a beat then he realized that Tatyana was testing him, gauging his levels of anger and control. She was making sure that he knew exactly what he might be getting everyone into if they chose to retaliate against the Killbot.

"The problem with that plan…" he started slowly, "is that it's putting a lot of stock into the idea that Braun *can* be freed."

"And if he can't, what then?"

Sighing loudly, Aguilar pursed his lips. He didn't want to play any of the captain's games right now. She was supposed to be his lover, his best friend on this mission. He didn't want to have to prove himself.

"If Braun can't be freed from the signal," he said at length. "Then we'll need to wait for Earthside to send someone to come get us. That could take *years* to pull off, especially with everything that's going on. By the time they get here, that Killbot will have *wasted* everyone down in the Base."

"We could evacuate them to the ship," offered Tatyana.

"No, we couldn't," Aguilar returned quickly. "If we did that, if we brought everyone up here for the long haul, we'd just keep running out of food. And before you suggest we make runs to the Base for supplies, I want you to remember how that thing almost killed William and Harrison from really far off, like, unbelievably far off. I'm sure it could shoot a Lander right out of the sky, no problem. Plus, once it posted up at the Base, we wouldn't be able to get to the Greenhouse without going through it."

Tatyana was silent for a moment then she smiled almost sadly and nodded.

"I agree," she said. "In fact, I think your plan sounds like a good one given recent circumstances."

"What circumstances?"

Grey eyes searching the bridge like gun barrels, Tatyana's expression seemed to tighten.

"I just got off a call with YiJay," she began evenly. "She thinks she's made progress with the alien device."

"Really?" said Aguilar in surprise. "That was fast."

"Indeed," sighed Tatyana. "YiJay is good at what she does. Apparently, so was our friend Braun. It turns out he was a great deal more active than we knew. Not only was he studying the Sun, as James

Floyd discovered, but he was also documenting an anomalous *electromagnetic energy pattern* coming from the alien device."

"An energy pattern?" frowned Aguilar. "What kind of energy pattern?"

"Something like we've never seen before," replied Tatyana. "According to YiJay he began compiling data on it the moment his Eyes went into the Statue Chamber. It appears to have been almost an obsession for him. Why he kept it secret is still under debate, but in any case, YiJay is going to continue deciphering his memories for now. When she has everything she needs, she plans to recreate the pattern visually using a simulator."

Confused, Aguilar rubbed his chin. "This is interesting and all, but what does that have to do with the signal from Phobos or freeing Braun for that matter?"

Tatyana grinned incredulously. "YiJay says Braun's last memory, before being absorbed by the Phobos signal, was coded with the *same* numerical sequence that he used for the energy pattern in the caves. If this is true, then it means Harrison was correct in his assertion that the signal and device are connected somehow. Whether or not they are access points to where Braun is being held remains to be seen."

"Shit," exhaled Aguilar. "If Braun was forming these theories and memory files, why didn't he just tell us?"

"Like I said," Tatyana shrugged. "That is still unclear at the moment. YiJay believes there might have been something wrong with him, some kind of disconnect that allowed this information to slip between the cracks, so to speak."

Aguilar sat quietly for a moment, his gaze bouncing about the room absently as he tried to wrap his mind around things more indefinable than religion.

"And so," Tatyana continued. "Because the signal and the device appear to be either one-and-the-same or connected, I believe we should provide protection for our friends instead of gallivanting off to Phobos. If Braun can be freed, YiJay will figure it out. She seems to be on the right track, at least. For now, we must make sure she has all the time she needs."

Shaking his head, Aguilar glanced back at the screen where 04 still mercilessly plodded its way through the Valles.

"So what are you thinking?" he said at last.

"I think," spoke Tatyana darkly. "We should let the lab rats work on their problem while we go hunting for a spider."

Lying on the cot in his lab, Harrison stared at the ceiling with eyes that rarely blinked. Aware that he was not in the slightest bit tired despite the pills he'd taken, he moved his mind from thought to thought. Following the strands of a web-like pattern, he examined all that was swirling around in his head, trying to pin the important things down so he could feast on their truth.

So much was coming together, so many lines collapsing into one another. Though it was clear that everything was connected, *how* and *why* were questions that seemed to lack the basic structure one needed in order to ask them in the first place.

Almost vibrating, his brain felt like an engine running at full RPMs, redlining it towards an unknown event horizon. Taking a deep breath, Harrison calmed his fluttering heart and tried to put his hypercharged mind to use. He needed answers, needed to know why he and everyone else were being sucked down the rabbit hole without so much as a match to light their way.

Braun's memories, a gift from beyond the bridge of time, were opening up new alleyways of thought that seemed promising. If even a fraction of what YiJay had already discovered was true, then Harrison was less in control of the facts than he'd initially figured. Whatever lay ahead of them on this path was so filled with noise and motion that he couldn't see the storm through the rain.

If the quantum blizzard would not come to him, would not bring the answers he so desperately wanted, then he would try to go to it.

Slowly, like a painter mixing up just the right shades of color, Harrison mulled over all the pigments in the rainbow that was this mystery. Selecting first and foremost the Pulses, he attempted to fit them into the ever-shifting puzzle at large.

Was it possible that the blood-red Sun he'd seen destroying ancient Mars might be the root of the recent Pulses too? As had happened to the Martians, was mankind simply falling victim to a naturally occurring phenomenon that came and went mysteriously over millions of years? Had the wound on the core of the Sun always been there, lurking angrily? Or was there another explanation?

Dancing faintly at the edges of his vision, a series of sparks began to emerge from between the folds of reality. Emboldened,

Harrison squeezed his brain like a sponge, attempting to wring the hidden answers free.

Clearly reacting to the push, the sparks multiplied and split, filling the room with a haze of suspended light. Gradually flooding everything with their luminescence, Harrison kept up the pressure, forcing himself to become absorbed in the torrent. Aware now that his eyes were no longer open, he saw the sparks turn into tunnels that snaked through the dense wood of time like termite tracks. Shimmering brighter than the others, one such tunnel seemed to call to him, beckoning that he follow it through to the other side.

"Okay," said Harrison to the empty room. "Here we go."

As the words left his lips, the shard of light suddenly surged forward to pierce his forehead, draining him away instantly.

He was falling, streaking down from high above, racing through the blackness of space towards a green-and-living Mars. Spinning end over end, the planet's gravity took hold of him, gently drawing him away from the cold vacuum of death and into the rich upper atmosphere.

Above, the ocean of stars shuddered and shifted. Their legions blended with the lights of the quantum blizzard to form a mosaic of the heavens.

Safely rested in his orbit, Harrison allowed himself to drink in the unparalleled beauty, filling himself with images of a world he had only ever seen as brown and dead. For what felt like a lifetime, he looped around and around Mars, looking down on its shimmering seas and fertile lands with love.

Then, from the corner of his eye, an oddly flickering light caught his attention.

Lazily, Harrison turned to face the heart of the mighty solar system, squinting against the power of its sentinel star. There, strobing with pulses of static electricity, something dark and alien was growing to shadow the all-encompassing light.

Almost abstractly, Harrison's mind suddenly glitched as it realized what it was seeing.

Huge and made of black metal, a monstrosity erupted from the blinding surface of the Sun like a bullet. It was a ship, massive in every way, with dimensions that defied logic and science. Closing behind it, the churning plasma of the Sun's outer layers swirled into a whirlpool, sucking up light and energy as it tried to repair itself. With arcs of lightning bigger than the planets themselves, the solar star heaved and shook, crying out silently against the assault.

113

In that instant, before he was pulled back to his lab, Harrison understood.

It was *them*! *They* did this. *They* damaged the Sun!

CHAPTER THIRTEEN

NASA head office: Houston, TX—Day one of eighteen

James Floyd hunted the shadowy third floor of the office, looking for a working coffee machine. Still wearing the same clothes he'd put on two days ago when leaving his family to come into work, he was exhausted and in dire need of caffeine.

Because most of the city had lost power, the facility was now lit with a mere smattering of ceiling fixtures. Creating a checkerboard of light and shadow, the bulbs hummed overhead as James wound around piles of uncollected trash and recycling in the hallways.

Though he'd been mostly alone for the last twelve hours, he had seen the occasional tech or engineer passing by the intern bullpen where he'd been working, on their way towards the stairs. Rarely giving him a second glance, these last hangers-on usually had their arms full of stolen equipment, hoping perhaps to barter for supplies on the outside. People were jumping ship faster than rats in a typhoon, and James couldn't blame them.

When the fourteenth day had come and passed with no Pulses, what was left of ordered control had died in a pit of despair. Civil systems around the globe were shutting down as the governments, which managed them, abandoned their posts to hide in bunkers. Somehow, despite delays and general disarray, news media was still attempting to maintain its coverage of the decline of civilization. Reports from around the world trickled in. Images of mayhem and destruction repeated again and again in an insane fractal pattern.

Heading up to the fifth floor, James went to his office and peered in through the open door. His Tablet was gone, as were all of his files and backup drives. Papers littered the floor and his chair was over-turned as if in haste. He'd thought this might happen, thought they might come for what he had. Eve could be such a sneaky bitch when she wanted something badly enough.

From the moment he'd sent the first simulation to the Mars team, he'd known it had been flagged. Not wanting to give up his only bargaining chip, he'd emailed the remainder of Braun's equations to a long-departed intern whose login info he had. Then, taking only what he needed, he had cleared everything from his Tablet and backup drives and moved down to the abandoned intern bullpen on the third floor to continue his work.

Walking into his trashed office, James opened the bottom drawer of his desk and found a can of Red Bull he'd stashed there ages ago.

"Good enough," he said to himself, satiated in his need for fuel.

Spritzing his fingers with a delicious spray of carbonated caffeine, the can made a light pop as he pulled the tab. Head tipped back, he drained the energy drink in one chug, suppressing a belch before dropping the empty can on the ground and quitting the room.

Back in the intern bullpen, he checked the status report of his latest transmission to Captain Vodevski aboard Braun. Having finished his final simulation only an hour before, he had sent it to her from the intern's account under a false heading. Until she opened and played the simulation, he was the only person alive to know what he knew.

Thanks to Braun and his equations, James had determined that the next Pulse would occur in *eighteen days* when the Earth, Mars, and the Sun lined up for their annual flyby. Just as he had feared from the beginning, the convergence now appeared to be more than simple coincidence.

In the simulation, the wounded core of the Sun rotated into alignment a mere two hours before the three celestial bodies ordered themselves in a row. Creating a timeline that was too perfect to be an accident, the final hammer blow told James in stark simplicity that forces far beyond his own comprehension were at play. All he or anyone else could hope to do about the impending Pulse was hide and pray for the best. When staring into the face of the divine, it was always the mortal man who blinked first.

Again glancing at the status bar on the screen, James fidgeted in his seat. He wanted a reply from Tatyana so he could make his next move and call Eve. Although he planned to use his newly finished timeline to buy his family's entrance into a bunker, he didn't want to put the Mars team at risk while doing so. By sending Tatyana the timeline first, he hoped that she would be able to initiate a launch before Earthside Command got wind and maybe, just maybe, survive the Pulse to make it home alive.

Suddenly blinking into existence, an icon appeared next to the mailbox application on the screen, sending James scrambling to open it. Grainy from the low light, a video file of Tatyana's face began to play.

"Dr. Floyd, I've seen and reviewed the information you sent me. Given that we have less than twenty days to act, I'm requesting permission to terminate our mission early. I think our remaining time would be better spent trying to figure out how to get home."

James slouched back in his chair and exhaled deeply. Despite the fact that this was the answer he'd been hoping for, hearing Tatyana request an end to the mission was still a bit of a blow. Years of his life had been spent bringing it to fruition, time he would never get back. Time he could have spent with his family.

Pulling himself together, James leaned forward and hit the transmit key.

"Captain Vodevski," he said, speaking into the camera above the monitor. "It has been a pleasure working with you. Permission granted. Good luck."

Green thumb—Sol 122

Alone among the haunted plants and vegetation of the Greenhouse, Ralph Marshall worked diligently, his mind alight with the fires of uncertainty.

Attempting to focus all of his energy on the simple tasks before him, echoes of Julian's demise and whispers of what Kubba had told him still fluttered about the air like gnats. Painfully dredging up the settled weight of other recent tragedies, Marshall now reflected upon those losses, finding in them only a deep sense of waste.

Ticking off the days in his head, he counted back to Sol sixty-eight, the day Liu had died.

Carefully working through the numbers, he determined that if the accident had happened on the sixty-eighth day of their mission, then fifty-four days had passed since she'd been killed. In those fifty-four days, two more people had died, brining the standing toll to three. Liu, Viviana, Julian. All of them killed violently. All of them gone forever.

Pushing the tip of a watering wand into the gelatinous agar that filled a trough of tomato plants, Marshall sighed and depressed the lever. As purified Martian water ran through its internal plumbing to quench the thirsty roots suspended in the brown gel, he couldn't help but see the direct connection between what he was doing and Xao-Xing Liu.

She had built their electrolysis plant, even designed most of it. Sure, William and Udo had helped, but the brunt of the logistical and technical execution had come down to her. They had water to drink and fuel to use because of her.

Setting aside the watering wand, Marshall took up a pair of pruning shears and went to trim back some of the bamboo, which thrived along the far wall.

Viviana had planted this bamboo, brought it all the way from Earth just because. Could they eat it? No. Could they use it for anything mission-oriented? Probably not. But that wasn't the point, now was it? The bamboo, put here by the lyrical and kind Italian biologist, existed merely to *exist* and be beautiful.

Frustrated, Marshall let his hands fall to his sides, the pruning shears slipping between his fingers to clatter on the ground.

He was doing it again: dwelling on death rather than attending to matters he still had some control over. Liu, Julian, and Viviana might all be dead, but Harrison wasn't. Still totally oblivious to the fact that his lover had been pregnant at the time of her death, he had no idea that he was at the center of some insane conspiracy set into play by Kubba.

Wishing he could find the strength to come clean, Marshall feared what it might do to Harrison if he did. In the aftermath of Liu's death, the young archaeologist had nearly gone over into darkness. What if Marshall's revelation sent him running from the light again towards the comfort of those shadows? Could it really be better to let such secrets lay undisturbed, or would doing so only allow them to mutate like cancer?

CHAPTER FOURTEEN

Landing party—Sol 123

With his helmeted head turned up to the pink sky, Harrison Raheem Assad surveyed the edge of space. Projected across the inside of his visor, atmospheric data and radiation levels blinked as they updated constantly with revised statistics. Looking through the opaque lettering, his eyes wandered the pastel heavens as automatically as his lungs filled with air and his heart pumped with blood.

Determined to better understand his connection to the storm of quantum possibilities, he now looked for it constantly, trying to catch the exact moment when a new thread flashed into being and was added to the tapestry.

A few dozen meters away, William Konig was deftly climbing the ladder, which scaled the side of the Communications Tower, a Kevlar duffle sack slung over one shoulder.

Though curious, Harrison did not actually know what William was up to. Figuring it had something to do with the work YiJay was conducting on the alien device and its strange radiation pattern, he chose to stay out of the way and hold his questions to himself. When she was ready, YiJay would let them know.

Awed by her ability to make sense of what had confused even Braun, Harrison couldn't help but be a little envious of the Korean AI specialist. It was as if she herself were exploring another version of the blizzard, another set of winding tracks and fathomless truths. However, unlike Harrison, her examination of such ethereal concepts was having a more positive effect on the way she held herself.

Bolder and more in command, YiJay now exuded a confidence that was at odds with their current situation.

When the captain had called a video meeting the previous day, YiJay hadn't even batted an eye at James Floyd's newest simulation. Showing a mere eighteen days between them and the next Pulse, she had simply rested her head against William's arm and sighed passively as if the whole thing were a waste of her time.

"I see them," said William's voice in Harrison's ear, stirring him back to the present. "They're on your three o'clock. Straight up."

Rotating a few steps, Harrison craned his neck and peered at the matte pink sky.

"There," radioed William, pointing from where he hung midway up the Coms Tower.

Harrison followed the line of William's arm until he spotted a flicker of white, moving like a great bird at the edge of existence. As though it sensed their eyes upon it, flames leaped up around Lander 2's underbelly, illuminating its dive down through the atmosphere.

Inside the craft, jolted and shaken by the entry, Tatyana, and Aguilar sat strapped into their seats, eyes locked on the fast-approaching desert floor.

Per the plans discussed in their meeting yesterday, the shipbound crew was breaking up, Amit staying onboard while Tatyana and Aguilar came down to work out of Ilia Base. Until Braun could be freed, there was no need for all three of them to stand guard over a post that had long-since lost much of its strategic value. Additionally, Aguilar had a plan to kill the Chinese robot that involved a bit of fabrication, something a zero-gravity environment wasn't suitable for.

Watching the Lander descend, Harrison felt his head begin to tingle. All but lost in the fire and smoke that trailed it, the little craft became a single spark of light leaping out, weaving itself into the fabric of their unfolding saga like new color.

Black ships

With her feet and hands bound together, Teo sat as straight as her restraints would allow. Held separately from the other Ancients, she was in a large cave lit with a series of small fires. Around her, two dozen nomadic warriors bickered over what they should do with these strange people who had invaded their land.

Rimming the fringe of the scene, children and women looked on with terrified interest, their gaunt faces and tattered clothing a sign of the hardships they had endured all their lives.

Silently, at the head of the arguing group, a tattooed Mystic listened with a worried expression on his face. Holding in his hands the three arrows that had been pulled from the bodies of Marr and Ze, he allowed his gaze to meet Teo's for a moment before closing his eyes and frowning deeply. At his feet, resting on one side, was the Traveler's device.

Invisible to everyone but each other, Remus and Romulus moved about the cave, their bodies like motes of dust caught in sunbeams. Anxious to know the fate of Teo and the others, they had no way of prompting the proceedings to begin. Instead, they took in the scene around them, each secretly dwelling on the look of recognition Ze had given them in the seconds before his death.

"What of our words?" shouted the warrior named Tiber, standing near the fire. "She speaks our words, but she is not one of us! How is this possible?"

"Perhaps," began the Mystic, his eyes still shut. "She will tell us if we ask."

"She won't," spat Tiber with frustration. "She hasn't opened her mouth since we took them. I say we peel her skin to start. After that, she will sing my name just to save what's left."

At the mention of torture, some of the younger warriors nodded eagerly, their hands skittering along the hilts of their daggers. Snapping his large blue eyes open, the Mystic rested them on Teo, ignoring Tiber's call for violence and cruelty.

"Can you understand me?" he asked, pointing at her with one of the bloody arrows.

Rolling her shoulders back so that she sat as tall as she could, Teo nodded.

"What have I just said?" he pressed.

"What have I just said," Teo repeated in a challenging tone.

At this, a hush fell across the group and even the wise Mystic seemed thrown.

"I see you understand not only our words but the tones we use to show emotion. How can you do this? Are you a fellow child of Red Myha?"

"I do not know this Red Myha," Teo replied coolly.

"Red Myha is the mother of us all," said the Mystic with a righteous smile. "She gave us life and the magic of words and fire and stone tools."

"Words and fire and tools" echoed Teo. "These are not gifts from any god, friend. These are rites of passage for all intelligent things."

Whispers of anger and fear bubbled up as Teo's words reached the ears of all those in attendance. Pacing back and forth in front of her, Tiber addressed the wary families at the edge of the firelight.

"Do you hear these insults? Do you hear how this foreigner attacks Red Myha?"

"I attack no one," Teo interrupted. "It was *you* who spilt the blood of my only son and called for my body to be maimed. I am but an old woman bound at your feet."

121

Tiber stopped walking for a moment, his eyes traveling to the entrance of the cave where two bodies wrapped in animal hide lay motionless.

"Tiber and his warriors were acting to protect us," spoke the Mystic, a hint of sorrow in his voice. "Some of our people have gone missing and the worst is feared. It seems as though we are again being hunted."

A murmur arose from the crowd, and a word Teo had not heard spoken for many years, drifted down.

Velt Tek. Black Ships.

"You are hunted by Black Ships?" she said, addressing the Mystic.

"Yes," he replied darkly. "They came first when my mother was carrying me inside her. Striking our people down with white fire, they left no bodies, no trace that anyone had ever been there. Entire families. Entire tribes. Gone in a flash more bright and quick than lightning."

At this, Remus and Romulus exchanged glances with one another.

"Is he talking about—" began Remus.

"Hush!" Romulus interrupted.

The Mystic was on his feet now, pointing with the arrows to paintings that covered the walls. Here and there, black triangles were depicted with an aura of menace. Bodies, suspended in the empty spaces around the shapes, had wide Os for mouths as though they screamed in fear.

"The Black Ships destroyed our once-powerful tribe," he said wistfully. "We used to number in the thousands before they came. In my mother's day, we even had a written language, but alas, it has been forgotten. The Black Ships are the enemies of Red Myha, and they have cursed us ever since their arrival."

Facing Teo, he fixed her with his most intense gaze.

"I am the last great Mystic of our people. I have protected us from the Black Ships for my entire life, and I will not have them finish what they started while I still breathe. You possess objects that are strange, you speak our words, and you come to us on a boat unlike any we have ever seen before. How? Are you agents of the Black Ships? Are they your gods?"

Teo was silent for several beats, her face calm but for the storm behind her eyes.

These nomads, these poor and savage people, deserved to hear the truth about a history that was all-but lost to them. Held captive by their superstition and crippling fear, they were in a state of suspended evolution—dangling, as it were, between light and darkness.

With one action, with one simple display, she could undo all of that.

Already swirling with the colors of countless galaxies, the device, Yuvee's device, trembled at the Mystic's feet.

By engaging it fully, by pooling her consciousness with its, Teo could obliterate the entire belief structure of these nomads in a single second.

However, in the back of her mind, a truth more tangible than thought appealed to her with its simplicity.

Shock and awe can never serve as tools of enlightenment, for they are the weapons of manipulation.

If Teo did what she was considering, if she erased the long-held beliefs of these people, then she would be setting them down a path built upon forces they could never comprehend. Illumination was a gift best bestowed gently and with care.

"No," Teo spoke at last, severing her link with the device. "No, The Black Ships are not our gods. We come from a land far away across the sea. There, our gods are the Great Spirits. They are gone now, but before they left they taught us many things. This is how I know your words. This is how our ship was built and where my object came from. We have different fathers, you and I. But our mother, Myha as you call her, is the same. Where I am from, we have dozens of names for her, but they all mean the same thing. So I suppose in this way, I am a child of Myha. We all are."

The Mystic smiled broadly, relief spreading across his face. Crouching down next to Teo he produced a stone knife and cut her bonds.

"Then you are the one I dreamt of," he whispered. "I knew you would come to show us the way."

The plan—Sol 123

Sitting around the dining room table in the galley of Ilia Base, the partially reunited Mars team ate silently. Once built to seat more, the long rectangular table was now dotted with empty places. Chairs as stark as gravestones sat unused, no one daring to sit in them out of respect.

123

Among those absent was Elizabeth Kubba, although unlike the other missing members, she was not mourned. Crazy wasn't contagious, but it was annoying.

Arriving in a flurry of afterburners and sand that morning, the reunion between Tatyana, Aguilar, and the Base team was so short-lived it seemed hardly to have happened at all. Because the reason for their rendezvous was one laced with fear, anger, and shame, neither party made mention of its significance.

As a result, a thick cloud of tension had developed throughout the day and now hung over the table like fog.

Engaging the Killbot was almost certainly going to be dangerous, maybe even deadly. Given the fact that the thing had nearly killed Harrison and William from a considerable distance, there was little hope that Aguilar's plan would go off without a hitch.

Though they were armed with two newly fabricated explosive-tipped harpoons, the team knew that the Chinese War Machine was a target unlike anything they had ever been trained to engage. Thrown into stark reality, this clear disadvantage now loomed large in their minds.

Splintering the silence like a machine gun, Tatyana's Tablet buzzed loudly from her breast pocket.

"Yes?" she said, snatching it up to her ear.

On the other end of the line, the faint-yet-unmistakable voice of Amit Vyas spoke rapidly. Having stayed behind onboard Braun to keep an eye on the Killbot, the Indian's call could only mean one thing.

Eyes locked on the captain like a firing squad, the crew waited in the vacuum of action for her to speak.

"I see," she nodded. "Thank you."

Placing the Tablet carefully on the tabletop, Tatyana turned to face Aguilar.

"Amit says the robot will be in the target zone by midday tomorrow."

For a painful beat, no one spoke.

"Let's go over the plan again," she resumed, addressing the table. "Just so there are no questions."

Nodding in agreement, the others remained silent as they waited for her to go on.

"All right. It will be like this," she said. "Joey, myself, Harrison, and William will arrive at the target zone approximately three hours ahead of the robot. Once there, Harrison and William will plant and wire the failsafe explosives along the canyon's rim while Aguilar and I set up

124

in the hills to the west. Assuming the robot is running a program wherein it expects no resistance from us, an attack of this kind will be effective only once."

"I'll take the shot," Aguilar spoke, his jaw set. "I'm trained with the rifle, and I have the best eyesight of anyone here."

"You'll only get one," William cut in. "Take it from me. Once it knows where you are, it will pummel the entire area."

YiJay, who was pale yet still fully composed, put a hand on William's leg and squeezed.

"I'll aim between the plates at its weapons," snapped Aguilar dismissively. "That way even if I need another shot to put it down, it will be defenseless."

Unable to suppress a laugh, Ralph Marshall stood up from the head of the table and cleared his dirty dishes.

"There is no *defenseless* with these things, Joey," he said, dropping the plastic plates into the sink. "One shot isn't going to cut it. You'll need to keep hitting it until there's nothing left."

Speaking before Aguilar could launch into a heated rebuttal, Udo shifted on his seat to face Marshall.

"Joey and I made the charges quite strong, Ralph. One shot, if delivered to the right area, could easily render the mechanics of the thing utterly useless. We may not *kill* it per se, but we will eliminate it as a threat."

"I'm sorry, Udo," said Marshall, shaking his head. "But I've seen these things in action. Their armor is strong, and they're quicker than you can imagine."

"But it's not expecting an attack!" Aguilar nearly shouted. "Its mission is to take down a bunch of unarmed scientists. It won't be ready when I put one right between those armored plates. They can't plan for everything in programming. It won't be able to react in time."

"I wouldn't be so sure," replied Marshall. "In fact, this kind of scenario is exactly what the programmers plan for. I can't stop you from doing what you think you need to do, but that doesn't mean I agree with it."

Putting a hand up to silence a clearly annoyed Aguilar, Tatyana spoke slowly.

"If we do nothing, it will be here in a few days time. While I partially agree with your concerns, Ralph, I also see the need for action."

"Maybe that's because you've been safely cocooned up on Braun for the entire mission," sighed Marshall stiffly. "We've lost too many people down here, Cap'. I'd love to get on board with this plan, but I just can't. I've seen Killbots work before, seen them take down *military* flyers like they were paper airplanes."

"What worked back then?" said Harrison, adding his voice to the pool.

"Carpet bombing," Marshall muttered, averting his eyes.

Standing up so that he was on the same level as the older man, Aguilar jabbed a finger at Marshall.

"Well I hate to break it to you, Ralph, but we're not really in a position to call in a fucking air strike. This is our only option."

"Please," Tatyana interjected, taking Aguilar's hand and pulling him back down into his chair. "We have considered as many options as are viable but the bottom line remains, the robot must be neutralized. If Joey can't do it with the shot, Harrison will blow the failsafe charges and bury the damn thing in a rockslide. Either way, we must act."

Clearly not convinced, Marshall bit his lip but did not respond.

"Well, okay," said Harrison after an uncomfortable silence. "I guess I'll go dig out the last box of charges and get them ready for transport."

"I'll come with you," William offered, getting to his feet.

"Me too," added YiJay. "I've got some more work to do in the shop anyway."

"Fine," Tatyana exhaled tiredly. "We'll reconvene tomorrow morning at 0500 for departure. Try to get some sleep tonight, though I understand that is easier said than done."

Much later

Woken from a dream that seemed like deep waters under open stars, William rolled over in bed and silenced his beeping alarm. In the dark, his hand went out and searched the spot next to him for YiJay's warm body. She wasn't there.

Perplexed, he sat up and turned on the bedside light to find that he was alone. Glancing over at the chair where YiJay had earlier thrown her jumpsuit, he saw it was gone.

Probably working, he smiled wryly to himself.

Checking the timecode on the wall, he yawned and got reluctantly out of bed. Though it was earlier than he would have liked, he didn't want to sleep alone.

Dressed in minutes, he moved quietly through the still-sleeping Base towards the stairs down to the basement. At the landing, he paused and glanced at the crates of explosives he and Harrison had placed there just a few hours before. In the dark, the boxes looked like coffins stacked on top of one another.

Suddenly, a burst of yellow light flecked across the ground, followed by a surprised cry. Turning, he saw the source of the shimmering glow coming from under the machine shop door.

"What the—" he said under his breath, striding forward.

Dying as abruptly as it had arisen, the glow disappeared just as William reached the door and pushed it open.

Sitting on a stool at the Holo Table in the center of the room, YiJay was giggling softly as she typed at a spread of Tablets before her. In the pale glow of their screens, she was silhouetted like a shadow puppet made of delicate paper.

Spinning on her seat at the sound of his entrance, she flashed William a marvelous smile and held her arms out.

"Good morning!"

"What—" he started to say.

"You're up early!" she cut in.

"I'm—"

"Never mind that," she interrupted with a wave of her hand. "You'll never believe what just happened when I started running the numbers from Braun's memories through the simulator! Here, look at this. Watch."

Turning back to the Tablets, she typed quickly, resetting the simulator program to the beginning.

"Watch," she said again, her finger hovering above the enter key. "Just watch."

Lightly hitting the command, the Holo Table began to hum and glow. Leaping into the air above them, a strange pattern much like the digital representation of an AI's mind appeared.

Made of one continuous line, the thing folded and refolded dozens of times over, seeming to respond to itself in a way that was almost aware.

"What is it?" said William, squinting curiously at the turning lights.

Leaning back so that her head rested against his chest, YiJay smiled up at the projection.

"It's a seventy-eight percent completed simulation of the energy pattern Braun saw in the Statue Chamber."

Awestruck, William felt himself shiver as the pattern evolved and reorder itself before his very eyes.

"It's so beautiful," he murmured, entranced by the fluidity of its movements.

"Just wait," whispered YiJay. "It gets better."

Quietly at first, a high-pitched frequency of some kind began to fill the air with a wavering whine. Osculating like a siren, the sound grew higher until it was nearly painful.

"Agh," William protested, his hand going to his ear. "What is that?"

Pointing, YiJay drew his attention to the alien device, slightly obscured on the tabletop by a stack of utility Tablets.

"Watch," she grinned.

As he stared, William saw the device began to tremble a little.

"Oh my g—" he began.

"Shush. Watch," said YiJay, gripping his hand.

Rocking back and forth, the device gained speed until it matched the osculating frequency, moving in time with it. Still climbing, the whine grew past the realm of human hearing, now little more than a muted presence in the room.

Quivering like a soldier at attention, the device suddenly rocked on end then hung that way.

"Almost," YiJay breathed. "Just a little bit—"

Exploding in a shower of energy, a great flash of yellow leaped from the air above the device and illuminated everything. Frozen in the seconds when it was most bright, the light abruptly drew back on itself, imploding as if its very core were the center of a black hole. Just before the glow died and everything returned to normal, William saw shapes moving beyond the surface.

Then, as quickly as it had started, the whine, the light, and the pattern all disappeared.

Left speechless in the deafening silence that followed, William was unable to speak. Moving wordlessly, his mouth worked to dislodge the exclamations that were kept at bay by his paralyzed voice.

Already turning her attention back to the Tablets, YiJay resumed selecting and isolating lines of data from Braun's memories.

"Pretty amazing, right?" she chirped, somehow able to continue as if nothing had happened.

"I—" William said then stopped. "It's—"

Faltering, he didn't know what to say. His mind was a firing range, ideas shooting off in all different directions.

"I think I'm going to have to buy Harrison a beer when we get home," said YiJay, unnoticing of William's shock. "He told us this thing was an access point, and I thought he was nuts. Well, you saw it and I saw it. That was definitely the beginnings of a wormhole. Not that I'm an expert or anything, but you know…"

Still struggling to find his voice, William simply nodded.

"Now that I've seen this," YiJay went on. "I have a pretty clear idea of how we can use it to get Braun back. It's a bit complex, and we'll need to install a second insulated server bank inside Lander 2, but I think it will work. Care to hear?"

"I—" William stammered. "But the wormhole, it collapsed."

Rolling her eyes just a little, YiJay pointed to the Tablet, which ran the simulator program.

"I said I was only seventy-eight percent done, didn't I? Now listen up because we have work to do!"

CHAPTER FIFTEEN

The waiting game—Fifteen days until the Pulse

Though it was only three AM, the horizon glowed with and orange light that waxed and waned ominously. Houston, separated by miles of roadways and housing tracks, was on fire.

Alone in the downstairs living room of his suburban home, James Floyd peered from a gap between the drawn curtains and watched the sky. In his hand, the pistol was heavy, gaining weight with each passing heartbeat as if it were hyper-affected by the Earth's gravity. Checking his watch impulsively, James stifled a groan.

Fifty-six hours. It had now been fifty-six hours since he'd called Eve from the parking garage of the NASA head office in Houston and told her he'd cracked the countdown timeline. Fifty-six hours since he'd used the information to buy his family's safety, and fifty-six hours since the last time he'd felt even a glimmer of hope. From almost the instant he'd hung up with Eve, he'd worried that he'd played his hand too openly.

What if she didn't send someone? What if she just left them there to be torn apart by the rats of the city as they fled the flames? She already had the timeline, already knew there were only fifteen days to prepare before the next Pulse. If she welched on their deal, it wouldn't affect her at all, but it would cost James's family dearly.

"Come on," he muttered, rubbing his stubbly chin. "Come on."

Upstairs, he heard Nora moving around. She was with the girls, watching movies on a portable battery-powered player. Briefly thinking about going up to join them, James decided that his presence probably wouldn't be well received.

Even after he'd returned home with his findings, even after he'd told Nora of Eve's promise, his wife had been cold towards him. Her cheek, now tinged with a bruise, was a loud a reminder of his shortcomings as a husband and a father.

Glancing at his watch again, James sighed impatiently and left the window. As he walked through the darkened house, he thought of how little he really knew it. His home, his family's home, was a strange and foreign place to him. Lining shelves and decorating end tables, knick-knacks and mementos he didn't remember buying glared back at him. Despite the fact that he was in many of the pictures that hung on the walls, the memories associated with those pictures were hazy to him. It was as if he had dreamwalked through his family life, never fully engaging with the people he was supposed to love more than anything else.

Drumming through his melancholy, the heavy thudding bass of rap music suddenly reached his ears. Frozen mid-step, James ran back to the window and looked through the opening in the curtains.

"Damn it," he cursed, his eyes falling upon a green SUV as it turned up his street in the predawn haze.

First noticing it in his rearview mirror the day he'd driven back from the city, the dirty SUV had followed him all the way from the highway to the open gate of his suburban neighborhood before continuing slowly past. However, that night, while James had been dozing on the couch, he'd heard the same thick bass that now permeated the air and gone to the window to find the vehicle parked out front of a house down the street.

Full of dangerous-looking men with guns, the SUV's hood bore the logo of a cross wrapped in the choking embrace of a rattlesnake with assault rifles for wings. Clear to James that the symbol was not of any government agency he'd ever seen, he'd concluded with worry that it was likely the insignia of one of the many local militia groups based outside of Houston.

Appearing to be interested in little more than looting for supplies, the gang had thus far ransacked four houses over the last two days, loading up as they worked their way down the street. Since most of the other houses on the block were abandoned, James had hoped that the men would get what they needed from those before finally making it around to his.

Yet tonight, as he watched from between the curtains, a spotlight mounted to the driver's side door lit up and fell directly across his front lawn. Ducking down quickly as the beam passed over his window, James swore again. The music thudded in his ears like muted explosions and the pictures on the wall rattled from the vibrations.

He wanted to get upstairs but he didn't dare move past any of the windows. Even with the curtains drawn, the spotlight was so bright it would surly catch his silhouette.

Abruptly, the music stopped, and James heard doors opening then closing outside on the street.

"Shit, shit, shit," he whispered, crawling to the foot of the stairs.

Above, the sound of the movie player had ceased, leaving only a shadowy world at the top of the landing.

131

"Nora," James hissed as loudly as he dared.

His wife's face appeared from between the banister railing, her eyes wild.

"Hide," rasped James. "Hide!"

Footsteps on the walkway filtered in, punctuated by laughter.

Rising to a crouch, James darted away from the stairs and through the dining room into the kitchen.

If they were coming in, he would lead the men in there and not towards the stairs. That way, Nora and the girls would have more time.

Time for what? he wondered, his mind skipping on the thought. What exactly is about to happen here?

The front door knob rattled loudly as it was tried, laughter burbling up from outside.

In the kitchen, James dropped behind the counter and ejected the clip from his gun.

Sixteen rounds.

Maybe we can hide, he said to himself. Maybe they'll just take the valuable stuff and be gone in a few minutes.

A loud splintering bang erupted from the front door followed almost instantly by another.

Sliding the clip shakily back in, James cocked the gun and turned the safety off.

What am I doing? he thought frantically. I'm *James Floyd*, not John fucking McClane. I don't shoot guns. I launch satellites!

A final loud crushing blow landed on the door and James heard the lock explode in a tinkle of small metal parts.

Still hiding behind the countertop, he began to tremble feverishly.

What am I doing? What am I doing? What am I doing?

Men are breaking into your home, James, came a calm reasoning from deep within him. *Armed men. They aren't just going to go away, and they aren't your friends. What are you going to do about this?*

From the now-open front door, a high thin voice called into the shadowy house, making James jump with each word.

"Anybody home? Hello? Anybody in here?"

Quivering, James rested his sweaty face against the cold metal of the gun.

I don't know what I'm going to do, he cried silently. You have to help me. You have to tell me what to do!

"If anybody's in here, they better say so now," the man at the door warned.

Following this remark, dumb laughter broke out but was quickly silenced by an annoyed shushing sound.

"We ain't going to hurt nobody as long as we get what we want," the man continued.

Relaxing his grip on the gun a little, James shifted.

What if they were telling the truth? What would happen if he just let them take what they wanted?

"Look, Ricky," a new voice cut in, cold and without a hint of emotion. "Ladies shoes. Right there on the rack."

"Well all right, boys," the first man returned quietly. "Why don't we find the madam of the house and have us a nice friendly chat."

As if animated by something outside of his own control, James Floyd, NASA mission commander and lifelong pacifist, shot to his feet, leveled his gun at the front door, and began pulling the trigger repeatedly.

Over the roaring fire and smoke, shouts of confusion echoed in the foyer like the yips of an ambushed pack of coyotes.

Instinctively stopping his trigger finger from squeezing off any more rounds, James felt that calm reasoning, from deep within, light the way ahead of him through the darkness of fear.

Dashing quickly out of the kitchen, he hooked a left around the dividing wall into the living room.

This is what we do to people who try to hurt our family, the reasoning whispered. *This is what they get when they push us!*

Before dropping behind the couch, James glimpsed the group of intruders as they strained to point their weapons through the open door towards the kitchen all at once. A second later, the house was filled again with a bellowing cannonade of gunfire.

Lifting his pistol blindly over the top of the couch, James pointed it in the general direction of the distracted gang and fired a series of wild shots.

This time, a piercing scream cut the air that was so primal, so filled with blind rage, it caused the calm reasoning in James to waver. Instantly, return fire began thumping into the soft cushions of the couch, driving James back the way he'd come and into the kitchen.

Skidding across the linoleum on his hands and knees, he huddled behind the counter as a barrage of scorching bullets slammed into the cabinets, sink, and refrigerator. Pinned down by the onslaught, he watched a pelting rain of broken dishes and splintered wood fall around him in slow motion.

What had happened? How had the tides turned so quickly?

Unsure of how many shots he had left, James risked a peak around the edge of the counter as the fire slacked off for a moment. Fanning out through the foyer and into the dining room, he counted four men, one of whom was holding his face as blood poured between his fingers.

"You're a dead man, you hear me!" the man shouted gutturally. "You're a fucking dead man!"

James could sense them moving slowly towards him, rattling clicks and scraping metal betraying the fact that they were reloading for another assault.

What do I do now? he whispered to that elemental force within him. What do I do? What do I do?

"Parker, Carl, head upstairs and make sure we don't get surprised," said the man with a voice as devoid of emotion as a rock. "Ricky and I will finish this."

"Damn right we will," seethed the one called Ricky. "I'm going to teach this little shit a thing or two about pain. You hear me, dead man? I'm going to teach you what real fucking pain feels like!"

Biting his lip so hard that he drew blood, James quickly checked the clip again.

Two shots left. He had two shots left.

Closing his eyes, he pictured Nora and the girls upstairs, hearing all of this noise as they hid like frightened cats. If he just gave up, just let these men do what they pleased, he would be damning them all to a future no father ever wanted to see for his family. He couldn't do it, couldn't let them suffer like that.

Already primed, James made up his mind in the seconds it took him to exhale. Springing almost gracefully from the cover of the countertop, he swept the gun through the air and somehow trained it squarely on the blood-slicked face of the man named Ricky.

Meeting James's detached gaze in the final seconds before the gun went off, Ricky pulled an expression of utter shock so extreme that was nearly comical. Then, his features abruptly dissolved in a wash of red as the gun bucked in James's hand.

Sprayed with bits of brain-matter and bone, Ricky's accomplice pivoted out of the way just in time to avoid James's second and final shot, taking cover behind a tall antique grandfather clock.

As Ricky's lifeless body tumbled to the floor, James saw the edges of his world turn grey. He had just killed someone. He had just ended a life.

From behind the grandfather clock, the other man stepped out and aimed his rifle.

"Big mistake, friend," he said, tracking the barrel down to James's groin. "This is going to hurt."

Suddenly, a light, so bright it seemed to freeze the moment mid-second, flooded in from all the windows along the front of the house.

Highlighted in harsh profile, the man swung his weapon around, forgetting James as a buffeting roar filled the air.

Booming down, a deafening message played from megaphones, more lights sweeping the house like sentinels.

"This is the United States Marine Corps!" it echoed. "Cease and desist immediately, or we will open fire!"

Running to the door, one of the intruders who had been on the stairs raised his rifle at something in the sky and was instantly thrown back by a burst of machine gun fire to the chest.

Outside on the lawn, a flurry of wind and movement played madly as Marines fast-roped from the air and began dashing towards the house.

Storming in with such conviction and confidence that the remaining gunmen were utterly overcome, the Marines quickly disarmed them, zip-tied their wrists, and pulled black cloth sacks over their heads.

James, rooted to the spot, was dumbstruck.

"Doctor James Floyd?" called one of the Marines, lifting up his night vision to address him. "Are you James Floyd?"

Working his jaw as if trying to dislodge the words, James simply nodded.

"Where is the rest of your family, Dr. Floyd?" asked the Marine.

"Up," James managed, gesturing limply to the ceiling.

Placing a strong hand on his shoulder, the man looked closely at James as if he expected him to pass out.

"You did well, sir," he said, casting an arched glance to the mangled body a few paces off. "That looks like a clean kill."

"James?" cried Nora, appearing at the entrance to the dining room.

"It's alright, ma'am," spoke the Marine, moving quickly to intercept her before she could see either of the slain gunmen.

"Who are you?" she trembled. "What's going on?"

"Eve Bear sent us to collect you, ma'am," the Marine replied, leading her from the room. "Do you have any luggage packed? You have daughters, don't you? Go get them and be ready to leave in five."

Catching James's still-shocked gaze over the man's shoulder, Nora put a shaking hand to her face and looked around at the ruins of their home.

"It's okay, babe," said James, finding his voice at last. "It's okay now."

Depth of thought

As the echoing screams of Kaab's newest sacrifice reached Braun's ears, he shuddered and pressed himself deeper into the darkness of the tunnels. Having successfully evaded the face of death for millions of years, he now felt utterly overwhelmed when in its presence. As much as he enjoyed his new existence, whenever Kaab began his cursed speeches, Braun wished he could flash his point of consciousness to somewhere different. Senseless though they were, the most offensive thing about Kaab's sacrifices was the effect they were starting to have on the citizens who came to watch.

Originally looking for a way to reconnect to the magic of the Travelers, Kaab had instead stumbled upon a different yet-equally-potent source of power. Blood—thick and flowing—was like an aphrodisiac when spilled in the right setting.

Somehow tapping into this primal truth, Kaab was steadily strengthening his hold over his people. He was truly becoming the God King he always wanted to be.

The taker of life, the giver of blood.

Killing at least three every day, those sacrificed were in and of themselves a testament to his reach. Brought back on ships that returned regularly from the east, the victims were now no longer political enemies of Kaab's, for none remained, but instead a strange and unrefined breed of Martian. Something of a curiosity to those who came to watch their death, the prisoners spoke in a language long extinct to all but the most studied living citizens of Kaab's city.

Wandering away from the shrieks of the latest victim, Braun came to a fork in the path and saw dim light emanating from its depths. As the last echoes of the murdered man's cries rang in his ears, he followed the path and headed towards the light.

Emerging after a few moments into a newly finished room, the realization of where he was crashed over him like a frigid wave.

It was the Statue Chamber.

Almost totally identical to how he remembered it, the space brought back a mix of emotions so profound that he was compelled to laugh and cry at the same time. In front of him, the tall Travelers stood with their backs turned, facing the entrance across the way. To his left, the statue of Teo kneeling in prayer was partially covered by cloth.

Torches lined the walls like twisting orange snakes, the light they cast as animated as the strange energy pulsing through the room.

Making his way around the chamber, Braun was hit again and again with flashes of his previous life. He knew this space better than he knew any other. Having seen it with his Eyes, he could guess the location of every blemish or find the evidence of each slip of the hand. For a brief moment he was both *here* and *there*, living and reliving the visions of past and present. In this state of duality, he glimpsed the fringes of something never-ending.

However, just when he was about to fully let go, Braun became aware that there was another presence in the room with him, another entity like himself. Descending with a shadow of unreality, it remained hidden from view but not from perception. Just like him, it seemed more to haunt the space than to inhabit it physically.

Turning in a circle, Braun scanned the chamber. Though nothing was physically out of the ordinary, he still couldn't shake his feeling of uneasiness. Closing his eyes and counting back from ten, he reopened them to stare forward with lucid focus.

Like the texture of the wind, reality shivered and something passed directly in front of him to stand before the statues of the Travelers. Cloaked in the fabric of space-time, the thing was an elusive ghost, a mirage that threatened to disappear.

Unperturbed, Braun drilled his gaze into the figure until finally the veil around it began to falter.

It was a Traveler. It was Yuvee.

Looking his stone reflection directly in the face, the Father of the lost peoples of Mars stared forlornly into the lifeless eyes as if depressed by what he saw. For a long moment, the air was still, and only a faint murmuring could be heard from the cathedral. Then, reverberating down the tunnel, the screams of a new kill trickled in.

Slowly, Yuvee shifted his gaze to look past the statues towards the cathedral.

137

CHAPTER SIXTEEN

The divide—Sol 124

Overlooking the target zone from less than a quarter kilometer away, Tatyana Vodevski squinted as the first rays of the morning Sun broke across the desert. A narrow canyon that pitched steeply up out of the Valles network, the area Aguilar had chosen for his attack was a good one. The Killbot would be forced through a choke point with sheer walls on either side as it tried to leave the canyon, giving him a clear shot with no obstructions.

Dialing up the zoom on her helmet cam, she scanned the rim of the little crag until she spotted Harrison and William, one on either side. Methodically, each man was planting and wiring a series of explosives meant to be a failsafe if Aguilar's shot didn't do the trick. In the event that the Killbot somehow survived the first attack, the charges could be tripped, sending tons of rock and sand down into the canyon like a grinding flood of moving earth.

"How's it looking?" said Aguilar, his voice quiet on their closed channel.

Long-range radio contact was being restricted to ensure that the Killbot didn't pick up on any chatter and get wise to what was coming.

"They are nearly finished," Tatyana replied, amplifying the zoom once more to better see their progress.

"Good. According to the intel from Amit, it should be here in a couple of hours."

Tatyana didn't respond but simply nodded once and continued to watch as Harrison and William made their way down each rim of the little canyon.

Outwardly calm, shocks of static fizzled loudly in her ironclad bones like Saint Elmo's fire. Despite being appropriately concerned about the impending clash, there was another fear whose teeth now snared her psyche more savagely than a bear trap.

The crew, people she once thought she'd known quite well, had become fractured. In the wake of so many secrets and losses, an emotional gulf had quietly grown like a patch of weeds in a once beautifully maintained garden.

First dawning on her at dinner the night before, she now saw that she was on the outside looking in. Marshall's comment about her and the shipbound crew remaining safe while the others had suffered was mostly true. Since arriving at Mars, they had ridden out nearly every tragedy from their lofty perch, paying a kind of sorry lip service for the losses of their friends as if it were enough to compensate.

Unsure of what she could do to remedy this divide, Tatyana hoped that by taking an active role in the destruction of the Killbot, she could make up some ground.

Distracted by these thoughts, at first she did not see William waving to her from the Valles rim. Blinking quickly to clear her mind, Tatyana glanced to where Harrison was standing and saw that he too was waving.

"They're done," she said, putting to rest her worries and focusing on the moment. "I'll head to the Lander for fresh Survival Packs and meet up with them."

Wordlessly, Aguilar nodded to Tatyana, the blue tint of his visor flashing as the Sun climbed higher into the grey sky.

William

From where he stood, William could see the trap in its entirety.

Coming up out of the narrow canyon, the Killbot would be an easy target for Aguilar some 180 meters away. Furthermore, the sand within the crevasse was thick, built up from countless eons of wind and time. If Aguilar somehow missed or was unsuccessful in his first attempt, the Killbot would have a hard time maneuvering quickly in the powdery stuff. With nowhere to find cover, it would be easily overcome by the rockslide failsafe, thus improving their chances of destroying the thing here and now.

Nodding to himself, William tried to stay positive, but images of what he'd seen the night before kept flashing through his mind. He didn't want to be here, didn't want to be putting himself in such danger when there was a whole new reality to explore.

Desperately, he wished he could be back in the shop with YiJay, gazing if only for a second into that tunnel that led to another world. They were close now. Seventy-eight percent close. He didn't want to miss a thing.

Establishing that Harrison was right and that the device could, in fact, act as a doorway into the construct, YiJay had immediately turned to fitting this revelation into a plan to free Braun.

139

Involving Ilia, Phobos, William's Uplink Transmitter, and a second insulated server onboard Lander 2, her proposal had been so abstract it may as well have been presented in Greek.

Grasping only a small portion of what she had tried to explain to him, William at least took solace in the fact that, somehow, YiJay understood the physics behind her plan. Yet in this, there was the hint of an even greater mystery: how could she know what she knew?

William wondered if, like Harrison, the device was affecting her, unlocking some kind of hidden potential within. Though limited, his own exposure to the metal egg had produced side effects of a sort. Completing Ilia's uplink device in a half-trance, he'd only noticed when mounting it to the Coms Tower just how sophisticated his work had really been.

No slouch to begin with, he had been shocked by what his hands had apparently accomplished without his direction. Encompassing everything he'd originally envisioned, the Uplink Transmitter *also* contained several refinements that he had not consciously considered. Stranger still was the fact that these refinements seemed to play directly into YiJay's plan to free Braun, something he had only learned about *after* he'd completed his work on the Transmitter.

It was as if some hidden force wanted them to access the construct, wanted them to free Braun from its clutches. But why?

Meeting Harrison in a bowl of sand at the mouth of the narrow canyon, William's mind swam thickly with these thoughts, their depth both frightening and exhilarating.

"What's the word?" asked Harrison.

Pausing in the deep sand, William looked up at the lightening sky for a moment then leveled his gaze.

"I think we've built a time machine," he said flatly.

His expression only partially visible through the tent of his visor, Harrison pulled a face.

"What?"

"YiJay and I," continued William. "We've been working on a secret project for a while now, and I thought it was for one purpose, but now I see that it's really for something entirely different. You have to tell me. Is that what we're doing? Making a time machine?"

Sighing, Harrison shrugged. "I don't know if it's that simple."

"What do you know?" pressed William. "Please. You of all people must have some idea of what's really going on here."

140

"Come on," Harrison said, setting off to the right of a large dune. "Tell me what's happened, and I'll try to explain if I can."

Modifications

Peering through the scope of his rifle, Aguilar watched Harrison and William move out of sight around a dune. Already filling in with sand, their footprints would easily be covered by the time the Killbot reached the target zone. Checking his timecode, he rested the rifle against a rock and trudged down the backside of the hill towards the Lander.

As he approached, he could see that the hatch was open, Tatyana just visible within.

"What're you doing?" he said, pulling himself up into the cabin. "The Killbot will be here in a little while. We should post up."

With her back to the opening, Tatyana seemed not to have heard. She was peering closely at a large insulated server bank bolted to the wall, her hands on her hips.

"Do you know what this is?" she asked, gesturing to the boxy device.

"No," shrugged Aguilar. "William and YiJay put it in this morning, told me it was part of some plan she has, so I didn't ask any questions. Why?"

Pointing to a cable, which ran all the way from the Flight Console along the ceiling and into the server, Tatyana shook her head.

"This cable is patched into the Send-and-Receive-Modulator for Braun."

Aguilar glanced at the cable and shrugged again.

"So?"

"So why do they have an AI modulator connected to this server bank when we have no AI?"

Fate

Harrison listened carefully as William told him about all that had occurred the night before in Liu's old shop. Having been too preoccupied with his own radically shifting reality to consider that strange things might be happening to the others as well, he now felt a bit foolish.

"You've called the alien device an access point or a doorway," William was saying, his head down against the wind. "You've said again

141

and again that the place from your dreams—the construct—is really a place in time and that the device is one doorway in and the signal on Phobos is the other."

"Yeah," nodded Harrison.

"Well, you were totally right," William continued. "So now my question is this: what happens if we open both doors at the same time?"

Harrison stopped walking for a moment and loosely let his minds slip along the question, searching for a way to penetrate it.

"I suppose you could send someone through," he said, the words leaving his mouth before the thought had fully formed. "But you'd need a way to guide them to the other side, something rooted in this time that they could follow out so they don't get lost."

"Exactly," sighed William, a note of worry in his voice. "That is *exactly* what YiJay said too. See, this is what I'm driving at. How could we have known this?"

Perplexed, Harrison frowned. "What do you mean?"

"I mean," stressed William, speaking slowly. "That I have been making an Uplink Transmitter for an AI which can do exactly what you just described. It was built to be able to send and receive an AI, in its entirety, to remote pickups. Don't you think it's strange that this is the very same kind of device we will need if we want to retrieve Braun?"

Harrison was quiet for a moment with only the sound of his own breathing, rising and falling in his ears.

"Why did you make an Uplink Transmitter for an AI?" he asked. "What AI do we have left to send through the construct?"

Groaning a little, William put a hand on Harrison's shoulder.

"I guess you'll find out soon enough anyway."

"Find out what?"

William hesitated for a moment, his lips pursed as he weighed his options.

"YiJay was able to salvage the AI Ilia after the first Pulse. She built an insulated server bank, much like the one I installed in the Lander this morning. It's capable of withstanding the effects of a Pulse, provided no humans are directly in contact. It kept Ilia alive."

"Why am I not surprised?" Harrison chuckled.

"Excuse me?"

"It's YiJay all over, isn't it?" he smiled. "From what I understand about AI, they get a lot of their personality from their programmers. Braun sure was big on keeping secrets, so it stands to reason that his programmer would be too."

142

"Ah," William nodded. "I see."

"So what?" resumed Harrison. "You're thinking because Ilia survived the Pulses, you built a Transmitter, and YiJay can open a portal, that this is all evidence we're being moved along a predestined path or something?"

"It's more than that," said William. "Before we even brought the alien device back to the Base, before any of that stuff, I was already working on the Uplink Transmitter for Ilia. It's just too strange to be accidental. Everything lines up too perfectly."

Allowing several beats to pass between them, Harrison began walking again.

"You know," he finally said. "Even the Immortals of Olympus, the old Greek and Roman Gods, even they were at the mercy of a strange cosmic power called *fate*. They knew it existed, constantly tried to flaunt it, and always ended up right where it said they'd be. Maybe that's what's happening to us, Will. Maybe it's fate."

CHAPTER SEVENTEEN

The new order

After many months spent in the company of the nomadic peoples of Red Myha, Teo and the other Ancients were gradually finding their place within the group. Though still treated with a certain level of distrust, their advanced age served to reassure many of their harmlessness.

Attempting to further breach the river of trust with knowledge, Teo had taken to engaging in long discussions with the tribe's Mystic and all who cared to join. Gently, she found ways to educate them about the nature of the world and how better to utilize its resources. Making slight modifications to hunting and fishing practices that were generations old, she soon had Tiber and many of the tribe's young warriors picking her brain for ideas.

Already, animal pens were being constructed from fallen trees in preparation for a raid on a small family of shrub-eaters called Stye. The plan, as laid out by Teo, was to capture the young rather than kill them outright. If raised properly, they could be bred and slaughtered at the leisure of the people, dealing a much-needed blow to hunger.

Moreover, plans were in place to combat the return of the Black Ships by building a permanent temple of Watch Stones at the cliffs. Selecting a spot where the horizon was filled with sea, Teo and the Mystic drafted plans to raise an arrangement of stones as a way to honor the ancient Martian goddess and keep watch for the Velt Tek.

Hanging back, for they had seen this all before many, many years ago, Remus and Romulus instead spent their time meditating and pondering some of the stranger things that had happened of late. Between the revelation of the dreaded Black Ships and the encounter with Ze in his final moments, they were torn between the *misunderstood* and the *unknown*.

In the cave where images of evil gods attacked innocent people, Remus sat gazing at the metal egg Teo had left there like an offering.

Suddenly frustrated, he came to the realization that he was right back where he'd started. Just when he'd thought he'd had a grasp on how things were, the way they worked, the construct had thrown him a curveball just to watch how he would react to it.

"Are we ever going to talk about what's been going on lately?" he snapped, standing up to pace about.

Romulus, eyes closed, smiled serenely. "Determining where to start is a task in and of itself."

Grinning despite himself, Remus continued to pace. "Well I'm tired of all this meditating!" he said. "Ze saw us, Romulus. He *saw* us."

"Yes."

"How is that possible?"

"I think it's because he was dying," spoke Romulus, shrugging his shoulders.

"And the Velt Tek," Remus went on. "The Black Ships were—"

"Travelers, yes. I gathered as much," Romulus interrupted.

"But this means they lied!" moaned Remus. "They told Olo and Teo that they were going to bring *everyone* together. They said they would bring *all* of the peoples of the red world to Olo's city. They lied!"

"Or," posed Romulus. "They failed to accomplish what they set out to do. They aren't gods, you know."

"And this assumption is enough for you?" Remus retorted haughtily. "Have you become so passive that you've forgotten your own curiosity?"

"I have forgotten nothing," frowned Romulus. "I'm simply smart enough to see that I am in no position to demand answers. Perhaps if I ever find myself in the company of someone who has the answers that I seek, then I will ask them. Until that time, all I can do is what I have been doing."

"Well, it's boring me to death," grumbled Remus.

"I don't think we can die," Romulus murmured, already passing into another dreamlike haze of meditation.

Escape—Sol 124

Elizabeth Kubba stalked quietly through midmorning stillness of Ilia Base, her eyes wild and searching. Already dressed in her skintight white pressure suit, she walked with her helmet under one arm and the other swinging freely like a pendulum.

Pressing in on her, the shadows at the edge of her peripheral vision grew arms and legs, threatening at any moment to spew Sabian Crisp forth like a stillborn nightmare. Since she hadn't taken any pills that morning in order to keep her head clear, Crisp was waking up from a long nap hungry and full of rage.

145

At the landing of the stairs down to the basement level, Kubba paused and swayed back and forth on unsteady legs. Her body was going through withdrawals, each nerve like an exposed wire shooting off sparks.

Give it up, Elizabeth, said Crisp, hugging the shadows. *I own you. Your body, your soul, all of it. There is nowhere you can hide from me.*

Fighting back tremors of fear, Kubba forced herself to become as hard as stone. She was not going to give Crisp the satisfaction of seeing her cry again. Outside, the wind whispered, the voices of the countless dead. Clamoring for her attention, they uttered gleeful little yips like hyenas that have just found a fresh kill to scavenge.

Give it up, Crisp spoke again, his words the snapping of bones in her ears. *You're embarrassing yourself.*

Defiantly, Kubba took a deep breath and put her foot on the first step.

I'm warning you.

Taking several more steps in a rush, she steadied herself with the handrail and waited for the shadows amassing behind her to attack.

This is your last chance, whispered Crisp with deadly seriousness.

Reaching for the elusive strands of her frayed confidence, Kubba kept her eyes forward and took another step.

I'm not afraid, she said silently. I'm not afraid. I'm not afraid. I'm not afraid.

Yes you are! screamed Crisp, the wind outside the Base pitching up violently.

Stumbling back to sit on the stairs, Kubba felt the heat from his words radiating off her. Uncontrollably, she began to shake again, the hangover from such prolonged drug use like little needles in her bloodstream. Setting her helmet aside, she put her face in her hands to shut out the world.

I have to do this, she told herself. I have to get free of this place.

There is no free, Elizabeth, said Crisp coldly as he faded into the howling chorus of the wind. *If you want an escape, there is only one way.*

For the flicker of a second, Kubba saw herself returning to her infirmary in defeat. There, she took all the drugs she had in an orgy of desperation. Sinking to the floor with dead eyes, she saw the future Sabian Crisp intended for her.

"No," she whispered to the lonely stairway. "No, you're wrong, Sabian. There *is* a way to be free. A way to get out. You'll see. I'll show you."

Moving before she could change her mind, she stood up and took the last steps down three at a time, nearly spilling out on the basement level landing. With the back of her hand, she wiped away as many tears as she could then headed for Liu's old machine shop.

The hit

YiJay, hunched over a spread of Tablets, did not hear Kubba enter the room. Totally absorbed in what she was doing, her back was to the door, her head bent low.

Running down like storm water, numbers flashed across the Tablet screens, throwing eerie shafts of light that fought like ghosts in the corners.

Eyes glued to her work, YiJay occasionally reached out to isolate certain lines of code for deletion or future inspection. Pale in the hallowed glow, she seemed to be in a trance, her movements subtly automatic.

On the table near the Tablets, the alien device sat starkly, the halogen lighting from above reflected like a demon's pearl.

"It's beautiful," spoke Kubba, causing YiJay to jump with surprise.

Spinning on her stool, the Korean shrank back as she saw the look on Kubba's face.

Distraught, vengeful, pained, and resigned, she was a shifting pool of poisoned water.

"Lizzy, what are you doing down here?" asked YiJay, wishing her back wasn't to the table.

Kubba seemed not have heard, her gaze stuck on the device.

"May I touch it please?" she said slowly.

"I'm not sure if that's a good idea," frowned YiJay, a growing awareness of things out of place beginning to register.

Kubba was dressed in a clean Tac Suit, the oval-shaped white-and-blue helmet hanging limply from one hand. Like painful-looking sours, her eyes were red and wet.

"Are you going EVA?" said YiJay, gesturing to the helmet in Kubba's hand.

"Please," the doctor repeated. "Let me hold it."

YiJay slipped off her stool and stood up as tall as she could. Still a head and a half shorter than Kubba, she squared her shoulders to assume a stance of power.

"I'm sorry, Liz," she replied evenly. "But I really don't think that's a good idea."

With a surprising nod of resignation, Kubba sighed and turned to go. Taking one step, she paused and glanced down at the helmet in her hand. For a long still pause, she just stood there staring at it.

"I won't break it," she finally mumbled.

Then, with sudden and vicious force she swung her helmet around so that it smashed crushingly into the side of YiJay's head.

Reeling back, the Korean collided with the table, sending Tablets flying as she tripped over it and fell to the ground. Senses ringing like a cracked bell, she fought to find her bearings above the din of pain as Kubba stood watching.

Struggling to her hands and knees, YiJay shook her head and blinked repeatedly, pinpoints of light swimming in her vision. Now speckling the ground in a steady rain, heavy drops of blood coated her palms as she tried to crawl away so that she slipped awkwardly.

Noticing a cracked Tablet lying nearby, something distant in YiJay's panicking mind worried that the coding she'd been working on might get damaged in all the confusion. If she could just get to the Tablet, just make sure it was still working, then everything might be okay.

However, Kubba was already advancing on her, heaving the helmet like a hammer. With no time to react, YiJay dreamily watched the blow descend.

Connecting squarely with her upturned face, the hard plastic of the helmet exploded a shower of sparks that swarmed around her in the racing darkness. Though already on the verge of unconsciousness, she registered two more strikes to her head and face before finally slipping below the calm waters of the unknown.

Bootprints

Stepping from the Greenhouse airlock after his morning routine of pruning and harvesting, Ralph Marshall set off slowly for the Base. Loud against his helmet, a thin-yet-persistent wind peppered him with sand and grit. On the inside of his visor, a timer ticked down, steadily drawing nearer to the zero hour when his friends would engage the Killbot.

Ashamed that he wasn't out there with them and still kicking himself for not telling Harrison, about Kubba's dirty little secret, he plodded along in a kind of funk.

Eyes on his boots, he drew within a few paces of the airlock door before he noticed it standing ajar. A bad omen even on a good day, his heart dropped so far and so fast, he physically stumbled with surprise.

Jogging the rest of the way stiffly, he reached the open hatch and peered inside. Thankfully, the inner door to the Base was securely locked and sealed. Doing a quick scan of the scene, he spotted a fresh pair of bootprints leading away from the Base towards the southern lowlands.

"Udo," he said, speaking into his helmet mic.

After a beat, his radio hissed with light static and Udo's voice piped in.

"I hear you, Ralph. What's up?"

"The outer airlock door is open. What's going on in there? I've got a single pair of tracks heading south."

"What?" the German returned quickly. "I don't know. I've been speaking with Amit in the Coms Room since breakfast. I haven't been downstairs."

Swinging the airlock hatch closed, Marshall turned the handle until he felt the bolts clunk home.

"By the look of them, whoever left these tracks was running, almost like they're being chased," he radioed, following the prints with his eyes until they disappeared over a small hill.

"Hold on," said Udo. "I'll do a sweep and get back to you."

Setting off after the tracks, Marshall glanced at his O2 readout. His Survival Pack was at ninety-eight percent.

"Okay, let me know what you find," he grunted, breaking into a shuffling jog at the base of the hill. "I'm going after whoever it is out here. They can't have gotten far."

"Copy," Udo replied. "Be careful."

Coming shortly to the crest, Marshall stopped and cast around until he spotted the tracks moving along the path of an ancient riverbed below. Glancing back over his shoulder, he caught the glint of the Sun off the Base's muted Alon plating then plunged down the hill after the tracks.

Zigzagging to and fro, they appeared to be those of someone acting on almost blind intuition. Though erratic, they were also widely spaced, suggesting that whomever they belonged to likely had long legs.

Cramping up almost immediately, Marshall's injured ribs protested the rough, jerky motion of his pursuit, forcing him to bite down on the pain. Even so, after a few minutes the ache became too much, and he was compelled to slow his pace to a brisk walk.

Dotted with huge boulders of grey and red rock, the ancient riverbed channeled the tracks as if they themselves were the ghosts of the long-departed water.

Rounding a bend, Marshall sighed with frustration as he spotted the prints making a hard swerve to the left where the riverbed forked off into smaller networks. Already exhausted, he had been hoping that whoever was out here might not have gone too far.

Bursting in his ears like a living swarm, radio static flared up before Udo's voice cut through the noise.

"It's Lizzy, Ralph!" he shouted. "It's her that's out there. I've just found YiJay in the shop and she's-she's—"

"What?" Marshall pressed. "What's going on?"

"She's been attacked," moaned Udo. "There's a lot of blood, and I don't know if she's okay or not! It's just everywhere down there, Ralph! It's everywhere! I can't tell…"

"Fuck," spat Marshall, breaking into a run despite the pain in his ribs.

"There's more," Udo spoke, his voice wavering on panic. "The device is missing."

"*What?*"

"The device," cried Udo. "The alien device. It's missing."

Clenching his teeth against the raw, splintering stitch in his side, Marshall tried his best to match the loping gait of Kubba's bootprints.

"What should I do?" plead Udo. "Should I call the captain and the others?"

"No!" Marshall barked, jamming a hand to his side in a fruitless attempt to staunch the pain. "That fucking Killbot will pick up on the call. Just sit tight and take care of YiJay yourself. Remember your training. Use it. I'll be back as soon as I find Kubba."

The static sizzled like frying meat in his ears as Udo held down the 'transmit' key on the other end yet said nothing.

"You copy me?" shot Marshall, trying to mask the agony in his voice with brute force. "You just sit tight and wait for me to get back."

"Hurry," Udo said at last. "There's just so much blood."

There one moment, gone the next

As the countdown timer on his wrist Tablet hit zero, Joseph Aguilar inhaled deeply and held the breath.

It would be there any moment. No more time to think about it. Time to make good.

Lying on his stomach in the soft sand at the top of a dune, he peered through the scope of his rifle at the opening to the narrow canyon some 180 meters ahead. Already loaded with the explosive-tipped harpoon, the gun was more front-heavy than he'd been expecting.

Slowly exhaling his breath, he let the stock sink deeper into his shoulder for support.

On his left, Tatyana reached out to place a hand on his back, sensing the tremors of lightning that rippled through his mind.

"Shouldn't be long now," she said, trying to ease him gently.

"Yeah," he replied, his tone overcast and grey.

A little way off, crouched by a cluster of large boulders, Harrison and William watched the canyon from a different angle. Neither man moved a muscle, as the wind whipped up flurries of sand like swarms of flying ants.

Mulling over all that William had told him, Harrison tried to fit it into his understanding of events. The fact that YiJay had proven his ideas about the device gave credence to what he'd been saying all along, but it also meant something else.

Her plan to use William's Uplink Transmitter and Ilia to rescue Braun was only possible *because* what he'd said had turned out to be true. Did that mean his predictions had influenced the outcome, or was it the other way around?

Preoccupied with all of this, he stared blankly into space and did not at first notice 04 the Chinese Automated War Machine, as it stalked into view.

Suddenly tense by his side, William reached out for Harrison's knee and gripped it tightly.

"Wha—" he started, but the words died in his throat.

Coming into view between the rocks, the Killbot was an ugly and deadly looking invention. Criss-crossed with scratches and coated in a thick layer of dust, it showed the arduous miles it had traveled since crash-landing on the planet.

Moving with deliberate steps, its six shield-plated legs propelled it up out of the Valles network like a nightmarish apparition.

Framed in the V of the narrow canyon walls, it paused as if to sniff the air. Then, almost giddily, it began rushing towards the open desert.

Sucking in a sharp breath, Joseph Aguilar spotted the cursed machine as it made its debut and quickly swung the barrel of his rifle around. Pulse pounding in his ears like a drum, he put the Killbot squarely in his sights and exhaled.

Waiting only for the pause between two heartbeats, he squeezed the trigger gently and let loose his destroyer's arrow.

Somehow seeing the shot coming, 04 spun back a few paces and raised a shielded leg defensively. Exploding in a flash of hot yellow light, the harpoon struck the armor plating and unleashed the full power of its stored energy in a blast that split the air and sent a shockwave racing out in all directions.

On his knees already, Aguilar reached to take another shot when the smoke suddenly evaporated and the Killbot emerged from the haze undamaged. Bearing only a blackening of its armor to betray the hit, it locked onto the pilot's position and returned fire.

"Joey, get down," cried Tatyana, reaching for her lover.

Instantly reduced to nothing more than a fine mist of red ice crystals and shredded pressure suit, Joseph Aguilar burst apart noiselessly. There one moment and gone the next, it was as if he had simply vanished into thin air.

"Blow the charges!" screamed William, grasping at the detonator in Harrison's right hand. "Blow them, goddamn it!"

Swiveling its weapons, 04 spotted the two men where they crouched and began peppering the rocks around him with screaming bullets. Forced to roll headfirst down the hill to avoid the barrage, both Harrison and William dove for safety.

Frozen where she lay, Tatyana Vodevski stared at the empty space her friend and lover had just occupied a second ago. Like tiny specks of ruby gemstone, his spattered remains dotted the cool white of her pressure suit in a pattern that seemed almost beautiful amidst the chaos.

Finished with its attack on William and Harrison, 04 turned its attention back to the dunes and opened fire all along the ridge where Tatyana lay.

Struggling to his feet, Harrison watched in horror as bullets burst through the sand around her, glowing hot like miniature volcanoes.

"Blow the fucking charges!" William repeated, running past Harrison towards the stunned captain despite the great danger that posed to himself.

Jamming his thumb down hard on the ignition switch, Harrison stumbled, the ground beneath his feet heaving with a series of deep explosions. As tons of rock and sand let loose in a cascade of destruction, plumes of dust poured up into the sky, blocking out the Sun.

"Let's go," radioed William, hoisting the captain up as she stared in disbelief at the frozen mess that was Aguilar.

Ignoring him, Harrison waded back up the hill and hazarded a look down at the scene below. Through billowing sheets of sand and dust, he saw the Killbot attempting to make a break for safety in the thick sand. However, before it could even get a few steps, the megalithic boulders, which descended from either side of the collapsing canyon, fell upon it with crushing force.

Awed by the sight, Harrison could do nothing more than watch as the rockslide ground on, piling high until it finally came to a shuddering halt.

"Harrison," William shouted in frustration. "Come on, let's go! Let's go!"

Reluctantly, Harrison turned away and ran back down the hill, leaving the decimated canyon to smolder like a warzone behind him.

William, all but holding the captain up, was making his way towards the Lander some twenty meters away. Catching up to him, Harrison took one of Tatyana's limp arms and helped his friend support the stunned woman.

"Is it dead?" William demanded.

"I can't imagine it's not," Harrison fired back, the adrenaline pumping through his veins like a freight train. "The whole canyon came down. It didn't have a chance to get free in time."

Nodding, William reached the Lander and shifted the full weight of Tatyana onto Harrison so he could climb aboard.

"Here we are," he whispered soothingly, taking the captain's hand and helping her into the cabin.

In the entry, Harrison paused to cast one last glance back at the spot where Aguilar had died. Before closing the hatch, he tried to see the pilot's spark, his thread of stolen consciousness as it was absorbed into the quantum blizzard. When only a flurry of sand met his gaze, he slammed the door and locked it.

"How are we supposed to fly this thing?" he asked, making his way past William and Tatyana into the cockpit.

Never having noticed how complicated the dashboard was until now, he cast around for any point of reference that might tell him what he should do.

"Ilia," called William. "Please help our friend to fly us out of here."

"Gladly, William," replied a lighthearted female voice.

Harrison, caught off guard, spun to face the mostly empty cabin. In the hysteria of everything that had happened, he'd entirely forgotten about the AI.

"Who the hell was that?" he cried.

Buckling Tatyana into a crash seat, William looked quickly over his shoulder and flashed Harrison a tight grin.

"Harrison, meet Ilia. Ilia meet Harrison."

"Hello, Harrison," said Ilia, the rumble of the engines already building in the belly of the Lander. "Would you like to take a seat at the controls?"

Afterthought

Wincing with each step, Ralph Marshall followed Kubba's bootprints like a determined hunter. Both sweaty and cold, he pressed on against the pain in his left side despite the protests of his body.

In the shaded bowl of three large hills he stumbled along, mist forming on his visor as he choked out lungfuls of air. Next to Kubba's sprinting strides, his own were faulting and jilted.

Suddenly cutting hard to the right in a tight hairpin, Kubba's prints led up the slope of the steepest hill. Climbing, Marshall came to the top and into the Sun.

Low yet bright and unhindered, he had to tint his visor in order to relocated Kubba's tracks in the soft sand. Leading off towards an area of endless flat desert, they were crisp stitches in the red hide of the Martian landscape.

Marshall, tired and nearing the end of his limits, used the high ridge to his advantage and engaged the zoom feature on his helmet cam. Panning up along the prints, he followed them with his gaze as they dotted off towards the horizon. Then, catching a glimpse of stark white against the rusty hue of the desert, he saw Kubba.

Less than a kilometer away, she appeared to be kneeling with her face to the Sun. As far as he could tell, she was not moving.

Already starting down the hill, Marshall dug deeply for a second wind. His prey was finally within reach. However, in the back of his mind, a voice warned him that even though he'd found the doctor she might not come peacefully. From what Udo had said about YiJay, Kubba was dangerous.

Taller than him and wrapped in tight muscles, if it came down to a fight, Marshall worried that the insane doctor might best him. He'd heard that crazy people were especially strong, and he didn't feel like putting that rumor to the test.

Pausing at the foot of the hill, he bent painfully and removed his boot knife. Though small, the glint of its sharp blade made him feel better.

Twenty minutes later, doing his best to hide the fatigue in his gait, Marshall came upon the kneeling Kubba.

Stock still, her head was tilted slightly to the side as if she was actively listening to the voice of the Sun before her. Almost totally aligned, the golden sphere cast a fragile halo that eclipsed her shadow. Stranger still, the ground around her looked as though she had been at the epicenter of some cosmic explosion. Spiraling out in a fractured web, the etchings of a faint pattern surrounded the doctor in a perfect three-meter circle.

"Lizzy?" radioed Marshall, angling his body so that the knife was hidden from view.

Keeping the distance of a few feet between them, he circled around in front, his shadow falling across her.

"Liz, can you hear me?"

Tinted blue, Kubba's face was hidden behind her visor. Clasped to her chest with both hands, the alien device drank in the light and reflected back a swirl of colors of which there was no earthly source.

Not wanting to get too close, Marshall decided to lay his cards on the table. Facing her fully, he allowed the knife in his hand to come into view.

"Liz," he said again. "What's going on?"

Inhaling so deeply that she seemed to grow taller, Kubba turned her head to peer up at him.

"I suppose I have a lot of explaining to do, don't I?" she spoke.

Hearing something familiar in her voice, Marshall relaxed his stance for a beat.

"Why'd you do it?"

Kubba shook her helmeted head slowly. On one side, bright red splotches of frozen blood smeared the glass and plastic.

"I had to find a way out," she said at last.

At the sight of YiJay's blood, Marshall felt anger flare up in his heart. Scalding hot, it threatened to pour out of him like lava.

"Find a way out?" He shouted, trying to master his volatile emotions. "Is that the best you can come up with? How the fuck did you pass the psyche tests? What fucking genius let you on this team?"

"You're right," sighed Kubba. "You're absolutely right. I've been a self-serving bitch my entire life. You have no reason not to hate me."

Unable to respond, Marshall stood rooted to the spot.

"It all spun out of control so quickly," she went on. "One minute everything was fine. Then Liu got pregnant, and everything just…"

Glancing down at the metal egg in her hands, Kubba shrugged and drew in a wavering breath.

"Did you know I've been hearing voices? Ever since Liu's death, there's been someone else in my head with me. After the Pulses, it only got worse. It wasn't real. I know that now. But when it's inside you, Ralph, you just can't be sure. You just can't be sure."

Taking a step towards her, Marshall glared down at Kubba.

"What do you mean you know it wasn't real *now*?" he demanded. "Am I supposed to think you're all better?"

"I found a way out," replied Kubba. "It won't make sense to you, but believe me, I have. I've been lost for a long time now. And to be honest, when I look back, it doesn't even seem real. It's like nothing really happened, like I just went away and now I'm back, and nothing happened."

"Tell that to YiJay," Marshall said flatly.

At the mention of the Korean AI specialist, Kubba let out a low anguished moan.

"How badly did I hurt her?"

"You're the fucking doctor," he shot back. "You tell me."

Rising to her feet with such speed and control that it caught Marshall off guard, Kubba glanced back over her shoulder.

"How far are we from the Base?" she asked.

"Pretty damn far," he returned, careful to keep space between himself and the tall doctor.

"If something happens to her, I'll kill myself," Kubba said matter-of-factly. "I probably should already for what I've done, but it sounds like my talents would be better served on the living right now."

Setting off before Marshall could respond, Kubba began walking back along her bootprints towards the Base. Exhausted and utterly baffled, the pilot reluctantly fell in step behind her at a safe distance.

PART THREE

CHAPTER EIGHTEEN

A new dawn—Fourteen days until the Pulse

Stirred by the melodic whirr of twin air jet engines, James Floyd opened his eyes to an odd scene. Bathed in red light, he blinked away the momentary confusion that came with waking up in a strange place.

He was in the cabin of a Marine transport ship, silhouettes and shadows falling around him in a patchwork of red and black. Beside him, Nora slept, her head resting against his shoulder. While across the narrow aisle, his daughters sat strapped into their crash seats, a blanket spread over their sleeping bodies.

Needing to stretch but not wanting to disturb his wife, James lifted his free hand and rubbed his neck. A pinched nerve responded with angry static as his fingers found the spot. Despite the wincing pain, he craned his neck hard to the side until he heard a little *pop*. As if pressure had been released from pipes nearly about to rupture, he felt better instantly.

However, the relief was short lived. Flooding in to fill the spot where his physical discomfort had been, mental torment settled with prickly heat. Seeing Ricky's face swirl into existence, James tried in vain to shut the image out. Suddenly exploding, the dead man's features raced away from each other as if they were tufts of dandelion down in a stiff breeze.

Putting a hand over his mouth, James swallowed hard several times, fighting a rising bout of nausea. Repeated again and again, Ricky's surprised expression kept disintegrating and reforming on a broken loop.

Hard-pressed to find something else to think about, James looked around the cabin of the airship and tried to recall the sequence of events that had directly *followed* the shootout rather than the event itself.

Storming the house to save James and his family from almost certain doom, the Marines, whose transport ship this was, had only allowed them a few quick minutes to gather some belongings. Rushed outside onto the front lawn, they had been pushed, stunned though they were, towards a waiting ship parked in the middle of the street.

Sinister-looking and heavily armed, the black transport had beaten the ground with twin engines that whipped up torrents of wined and debris. Loaded onboard without so much as a chance to look back at

159

their home, James, Nora, and the girls had been buckled in while the ship pitched up its engines and lifted off.

Though acidic and utterly charged from everything that was happening, the moment James had felt the ship leave the ground, he'd been instantly overcome with exhaustion. As if all the recent days of running full speed had finally caught up with him, he'd tried to stay awake, but it was useless. Drifting off with terrible flashes of Ricky's death still hot in his mind, the last thing James had actually remembered before succumbing to sleep was Nora's voice in his ear as she rested her head against his shoulder.

"I love you, James," she'd said. "I love you."

James sat stiffly for a moment, replaying those words.

I love you, James. I love you.

A phrase he had exchanged with Nora on a daily basis for the past eleven years, James found it a little disturbing that last night had been the first time in recent memory Nora's proclamation had actually *meant* something to him. If it took murdering another human being to appreciate the love of his wife, then James was worried about the pull of his moral compass.

Brought full circle, he suddenly grew claustrophobic. As if he could smell the bits of bone fragment and blood hidden among the folds of his clothing, he squirmed in his seat. Almost desperately, he wished for something—*anything* to occupy his mind.

Without any windows, and without even so much as a timecode on the wall, there was nothing in this place to distract him.

Knowing that there were Marines about somewhere, likely in the front of the ship, James peered longingly at the closed metal hatch, which separated the cabin from the cockpit.

Nausea again swelling in his throat, James strained against the ever-tightening bonds of his skin. Just when he thought he might actually be sick right then and there, he spotted a flat pane of Smart Glass above the hatch and waved to it vigorously.

A moment later, the hatch opened and daylight flooded in. Stepping through the entry, the same Marine who had spoken with James in the wake of the gunfight, beckoned for him to come forward.

Almost frantically, James fumbled with the straps at his chest then shifted Nora's head to the seat rest and stood.

"Where are you going," she murmured sleepily, a hand closing around his.

"Just up to the cockpit to talk for a minute," he replied curtly, untangling his fingers.

Out in the aisle, James pretended to check on his daughters as he gulped in air to calm his rolling stomach. Straightening after a moment, he smoothed his hair and walked forward to meet the Marine.

"Morning," he said as evenly as he could manage.

"Good morning, sir," the Marine returned with a nod. "I take it your feeling a little better now?"

"Much," James lied, peering around the man at the forward section of the ship.

Sitting in rows along either side of the space, around eight Marines rested their backs against the hull. Through the large cockpit window, the endless horizon of the ocean spread out like a dream.

"Where are we?" asked James.

"We're on our way to a secure location," replied the Marine. "From there, you're going to transfer to a larger transport with some other folks, and then it's on to an undisclosed hidey hole."

"Hidey hole?" James said, arching his eyebrows.

"A bunker, sir," the Marine returned flatly.

"Right," grinned James as if this were all a fun vacation. "Any idea when that will be?"

Glancing over his shoulder at the cockpit, the Marine shrugged.

"We've made visual with our drop point and should be there real soon. You might want to start waking your family up now. We won't be able to stick around for long."

"Wait, you're not staying?" frowned James with some confusion.

"No, sir," the man spoke. "There are still people out there we need to collect before we can go to ground ourselves. If you don't mind my saying so, you must have friends in high places since your name was at the top of our list along with instructions to bring you straight in."

"Oh," said James dumbly, looking around at all the empty seats in the cabin behind him. "Well, thank you for coming to get us."

Pulling an expression almost close to a smile, the Marine dipped his chin.

"No need to thank us. We're just following orders. Now like I said, we'll be landing soon, so you should wake up your family and buckle in."

Returning a bit reluctantly to his seat, James felt the airship begin to descend. As his mind pondered just where it was that they were going to land in the middle of the ocean, he gently woke the girls.

Nora, already in the process of becoming alert, looked up at him as he slipped past her into his seat.

"Are we landing?"

"Yeah," he said, buckling himself in.

"Where?"

"If I had to guess, I'd say it's the Pacific."

Growing louder like a thundering cyclone, the engines roared as the ship leveled out then began to drop straight down in a controlled fall. Only lasting a few uncomfortable seconds, everything suddenly jostled as the transport's wheels made contact with a solid surface.

Coming in from the forward section, two Marines went straight to the exit hatch on the hull and swung it open. Like an electric shock, bright light and cold salty air rushed into the cabin.

"Let's go, everyone!" called one of the men, his voice nearly lost in the howling spray of the engine's exhaust.

Gathering at the hatch, James and his family had no time to process what lay beyond, as they were quickly unloaded from the cabin onto the landing deck of a massive aircraft carrier.

All around them, other transports were touching down and lifting off like flies on a carcass. As the screams of their turbine engines tore the air, Flight Deck operators ran to and fro, waving glowing batons. Also peppering the scene, soldiers and armed men huddled around small groups of people, escorting them away from the noise and danger.

His younger daughter in his arms, James turned to ask the Marines what they were supposed to do next but saw that the transport was already lifting off. Framed in the still-open hatch, one of the men saluted James stiffly as the ship pitched out over the sea and sped off.

"Where do we go?" yelled Nora, the noises from the Flight Deck a symphony of broken instruments.

"I don't know!" James called back. "But something tells me we won't have to wait long to find out!"

Rushing over, an envoy of armed men in uniform surrounded the family as if they were enemy combatants.

"ID?" called one, holding a utility Tablet in one hand and a pistol in the other.

In the confusion of the night before, James hadn't thought to grab any of his clearance cards or ID badges. In fact, all he'd taken from the house, besides what Nora had packed for him, was an old paperback novel.

"I—" he stammered, patting his pockets. "I don't think I have—"

"ID!" the man repeated, his tone threatening.

"Back off!" shouted a strong female voice as it pushed through from the rear of the group.

Stepping into the circle of gun barrels that had formed around James and his family, Eve Bear raised her ID badge and fixed the soldier with her famous glare.

"These four are with me."

The final day

Cross-legged in a circle of stones on the edge of a great cliff, Teo looked out at an ocean that seemed to boil. Finished only a short time before, the crudely carved rocks were a mere shadow of Olo's great temple, yet they still made Teo feel at home.

Living among the peoples of Red Myha for two seasons now, the last remaining ancient of Crescent City had earned their trust and was allowed to wander on her own. Though frail, withered, and in meditation more than out, she had risen in their tribe to occupy a place of high esteem. Passing onto them her vast wealth of knowledge and expertise, she used Olo's teachings to reveal the skills of second sight and journeying. At the heart of an awakening, she worked with the eager Mystic to educate and inform the growing tribe.

As a result, the peoples of Red Myha were existing in an age of plenty. Farming, animal husbandry, and art were taking root in ways that reflected the optimism of the times. Among the most enthusiastic students Teo's had, Tiber in particular embraced all that she said and did, becoming almost a surrogate son. As if repaying his debt of violence with peace, he took it upon himself to be not only Teo's student, but her caregiver as well. On days when she was too weak to leave her cave from the same fever that had finally killed the other Ancients, he would sit with her in silence, staring as she did into the world beyond sight.

Today, however, Teo was alone with her thoughts save for Remus and Romulus who never left her side. Waking before young Tiber, she had left their cave quietly, feeling in her bones that the end was near.

Only a little clouded by the confusion of fever, she had made her way to the temple Watch Stones where she now sat, meditating deeply.

Lost among the countless lights that stretched out before her like the order of the universe, Teo drifted. Passing the realms of planets and suns, she wandered further into the textures of the known and unknown, finding between them a middle ground wherein all things were possible.

Greeted by windows into other places and other times, she witnessed such wonders as she never could have imagined. Fluid in their tracks, time and space joined one another, becoming a single entity that was alive and conscious.

Wishing to stay in this place forever, Teo yet felt a dark shadow falling across her soul.

As a storm built in the skies above Mars, so too did this shadow—this catastrophe not yet arrived. Dampening the ecstasy of her revelation, it slowly began blocking off Teo's view of the quantum endlessness, robbing her of her second sight.

Opening her eyes sadly, she raised them to the heavens, holding them there for a moment. Eclipsed with a solid sheen of red, the Sun offered no comfort, its pain and rage written clearly in the flames that consumed it.

Sighing, Teo dropped her gaze until it rested upon the brothers Remus and Romulus. Unabashed, she stared at them, neither curious nor afraid.

"Is it time, Great Spirits?" she said. "Have you come to take me?"

In the caves

Many hundreds of miles away and deep underground, Braun rushed towards the Statue Chamber in the hopes that he would not be too late. Wanting to catch Yuvee before the Traveler could leave the caves, Braun burned with a curiosity that was reminiscent of a life once lived.

Sparked on the day he'd glimpsed Yuvee in the Statue Chamber, his obsession had only grown. Now full and furious, it drove him forward through the dark tunnels, whispering to him with the voice of his former self.

Showing up on days when Kaab's bloodlust was at its most feverish, Yuvee seemed drawn to the horrors his meddling had caused. Though he never put an end to the sacrifices by revealing himself, the Traveler still paid witness to them as if doing so were a form of punishment.

Unable to wrap his mind around *why* Yuvee would act in this fashion, Braun ached for answers in a way that joined his old self and his new self under the same banner.

164

Finally reaching the Statue Chamber, he quickly entered and swept his eyes across the scene, hoping he was not too late. As a scream emanated from the cathedral and cut the air shrilly, he held his breath and waited.

Faintly at first, the warping light that betrayed the presence of Yuvee appeared at the mouth of the tunnel, growing brighter.

Gripped with excitement and blind hunger, Braun hugged the shadows even though he knew he could not be seen.

Third eye trailing a glow of blue fire, Yuvee walked into the statue Chamber and stopped as he always did, before his statue.

Where it not for the certainty that he would never really know such things for sure, Braun could have sworn the Traveler was ashamed to behold his image.

Turning suddenly to leave, Yuvee made for the bell-shaped exit tunnel.

Close behind him, Braun followed excitedly, marching for the first time away from the darkness and towards the light of day. United under the common banner of knowledge, his two halves—the former and the new—readied themselves to brave what lay beyond.

CHAPTER NINETEEN

Waking up—Sol 127—Ten days until the Pulse

Fluttering in through a slit in the dark, awareness began to fill YiJay Lee. She was achy, her head a throbbing mass of criss-crossed wires and switchboards.

Wanting to open her eyes, she tried and was instantly met with a sharp pinch in the right side of her face. Keeping that lid shut tightly, she tried opening only the left and this time light poured into her skull like freezing water.

Still glassy with sleep, she scanned the room, looking for indicators as to where she was.

Above her, the ceiling lights glowed intensely, creating a halo of rainbow blowouts wherever she turned her gaze.

Dizzy and feeling slightly sick to her stomach, YiJay shut her eye and moaned softly. The right side of her face stung smartly, the simple action of being awake an assault on her nerves.

Thudding like drum beats, the dark world of her interior shook as footsteps drew near to her bed.

"YiJay?" came a familiar and welcome voice. "Are you awake?"

Lifting a hand blindly, YiJay felt it picked up immediately and held fast.

"Will," she croaked, her throat insanely dry.

"Here," said William, reaching for something on the bedside table. "Drink this."

Holding the glass to YiJay's cracked lips, he tilted it gently.

"There you go. Just sip. Don't choke."

Magnificently, cool water ran down her raw throat and into her stomach. Suddenly aware of how empty she was, YiJay gulped more fervently at the glass until there was nothing left.

"More," she managed before breaking down into dry coughs.

Topped off from a bottle on the table, William again held the cup to YiJay's lips until she'd drunk her fill.

Thirst abated, YiJay next began to struggle against her sheets in an attempt to sit up. Careful to keep her eyes tightly closed, she couldn't help yelping in pain as stinging bites protested from her hands.

"Hold on," said William, taking her shoulders and pressing her back down. "You have IVs in both wrists."

Cracking her left eye open a little, YiJay blinked away the shards of color until she could see William. Lined and tired, he sported dark stubble upon his chin and his clothes were wrinkled.

"What happened?" she asked, confused and not liking it. "Why am I like this?"

William did his best to smile, but even only using one eye, YiJay could tell there was something wrong.

"You don't remember?" he said, resting a hand on top of hers.

Frowning though it hurt, YiJay shook her head.

"The last thing I remember was you leaving with the captain, Harrison, and Joey to kill that robot and…"

Trailing off, she fell silent as her perception of time ran squarely into an invisible wall.

"Wait," she resumed. "Wait, if you're here, then that means the mission is over. What-what's going on? What's happened?"

"You were attacked," spoke William softly. "Kubba jumped you while we were out. She wanted the device and apparently you wouldn't give it to her."

"Attacked?" echoed YiJay, whispers stirring in her subconscious.

"Yes," William nodded. "You were in pretty bad shape, but Liz was able to stabilize you with some effort."

Swimming a little, YiJay's vision wavered.

"She attacked me then saved me? I don't understand. What's going on?"

William pursed his lips and shrugged.

"None of us do. We've locked her in her room, but she won't talk to anyone right now. We're totally at a loss."

"How long have I been out?" said YiJay, flashes of recollection now beginning to arc through her brain like electricity.

"Four days," William returned soberly.

For a moment, YiJay could not speak.

Four days. She had been unconscious for *four* days.

"What happened with the robot?" she said at last. "Did you destroy it?"

"It killed Joey before we could bury it," sighed William. "The captain is taking it about as well as you'd expect. She's acting like nothing's happened and just keeps talking about getting us out of here."

Swallowing a lump in her throat, YiJay blinked a tear from the corner of her left eye. Joey had been a nice man, never someone she

167

would have called a close friend but still kind and honest. He didn't deserve to die.

"What about my work?" she asked, pulling her mind in a different direction. "I remember I was nearly done with the simulator. Did I finish? Is it ready?"

William frowned and tilted his head.

"When Kubba attacked you, one of the Tablets running code was broken. I salvaged the memory card, and I've been doing my best to decipher what the numbers mean, but I'm not you. That aside though, everything else is ready. In fact, we've even had a chance to try out Ilia's Uplink Transmitter and the new server in the Lander. Both worked perfectly. All that's left is to finalize the simulator and to reestablish a connection to the construct."

"Good," spoke YiJay, drawing herself up. "If you bring me the last of the equations, I can have them recoded and ready for the simulator pretty quickly."

Reaching out to stroke her cheek, William smiled sadly.

"You just woke up from a very long nap. Why not give your mind a little while before jumping back in? Besides, you need to heal. You've suffered a pretty serious injury."

Lifting her hand from the bed, YiJay brought it to her face. Until this point, the pain in her right eye hadn't really registered beyond the most basic acknowledgement that something was wrong.

Careful not to exceed the bounds of her IVs, she touched the tips of her fingers lightly to a square of bandage loosely taped over her right eye.

"She tried to save it," William said, his gaze cast down. "But a piece of bone from your cheek punctured the retina."

Falling listlessly back into her lap, YiJay's hand turned into a fist.

"I guess it's a good thing I only need one eye to run code," she muttered bitterly. Gently, William leaned in and kissed her.

"If you like," he smiled. "I'll put mine out too so you won't feel so alone."

Laughing, YiJay sniffled and let William enfold her in an embrace.

"Just bring me a Tablet so I can finish the simulation, would you?" she asked meekly. "That's all that really matters now anyway."

The truth comes out

Patiently, Harrison Raheem Assad sat in his lab and answered every question put to him by Captain Vodevski. Making good on his long-overdue offer to tell her all that he knew, no matter how insane, he now treated himself like an open book.

From his time in the construct to his experiences with the quantum blizzard, he shared it all. Nothing was off limits. Nothing was withheld.

Although clearly incredulous at first, it hadn't taken long for Tatyana to become more receptive to what he said. Combined with the miraculous revival of Kubba's sanity, Harrison's retelling of events seemed all-the-more possible.

Obviously hot to fill her time with words rather than silence, Tatyana had taken advantage of Harrison's openness, treating it as a possible means to discover a way home. Hoping perhaps that he might hold hidden clues to their salvation, she had spent the days following Aguilar's death grilling him like an interrogator.

Now, sitting across from one another with nothing between them but empty space, Tatyana fixed Harrison with her most penetrating gaze and began another round of questions.

"You mentioned that the last vision you had was of the alien mothership ripping through the core of our Sun."

Smiling, Harrison nodded once.

"And it was this event that caused the Martian extinction, correct?"

"Yes."

"And that extinction bears certain similarities to what is happening now, no?"

"Yes."

"When was this?" Tatyana asked, eyes still resting on Harrison. "When did you have this vision?"

"About a week ago," said Harrison softly. "Two nights before we went after the Killbot."

Flinching, Tatyana quickly gathered herself. "And why haven't you had any more visions since then?"

Again Harrison smiled. "Think of this thing I have as being a little like epilepsy. It does what it does, whenever it feels like it, and I either hang on or get lost."

Tatyana cocked her head to the side and frowned. "But you said you induced your last vision, that you caused it to happen."

169

"No," sighed Harrison wearily. "I said I concentrated extra hard, but in the end, it still came over *me* and not the other way around."

Unperturbed, Tatyana pressed on. "So what would happen if you concentrated *extra hard* right now? Would you have another vision? Perhaps you should try."

"I have been trying," said Harrison, genuine exasperation in his voice. "Believe me, I really have. But it's not the same as it was before."

"How so? What have the results been?"

Frowning, he leaned forward in his chair. "They've been mixed. I get this feeling in my head, sort of a tingling, but nothing solid. No full emersions."

"Why?"

"Maybe the effects of the device wear off after a while. I don't know."

Tatyana was silent for a moment, her face as still as stone.

"Has Dr. Kubba experienced any of the same things you have? She touched the device as well. Unless someone is hiding something from me, you two are the only ones to have done that."

"I wouldn't know what she's experiencing or not," shrugged Harrison. "I haven't been to see her after what she did to YiJay."

Uncrossing then re-crossing her legs, Tatyana looked off into the distance as if spotting something unpleasant.

"Speaking of YiJay," she said, abruptly changing gears. "Is there anything else about her plan to save Braun that you can tell me? I know only what little William could explain to me, most of which sounds too ludicrous to be taken seriously."

"If you know what he knows, then you know what I know," Harrison returned.

"Are you sure?" continued Tatyana. "Explain it to me in your own words."

Leaning back in his seat, Harrison closed his eyes and took a deep breath. Pieced together from the scattered fragments of what William had told him that day in the desert, Harrison's understanding of YiJay's plan was really more of an idea than anything concrete. Moreover, because so much of it was still contained inside the unconscious Korean's mind, the finer points of play were as elusive and unknowable as dark matter.

"Well," he began evenly. "As I understand it, YiJay used the coded memories of Braun to recreate an energy pattern that interacts with the alien device. She was able to get a portal to open, but it closed right away because the pattern wasn't finished."

"Yes, I've heard all this," Tatyana interrupted. "Yet I'm failing to see how it is particularly relevant. Outside of the fact that it's impressive, why do we need the device at all? You yourself can access this place anytime you like."

"Sort of," replied Harrison carefully. "But how I get in and how I get out aren't dictated by me. I mean, I found Braun once before, but he didn't come back with me when I left. He stayed."

"So what makes YiJay think she can free him? What does she have that you don't?"

For a moment, Harrison felt his perception of time hitch as the blizzard abruptly ghosted around him. Lasting only as long as it took to blink, he was back in the cockpit of Lander 2 again, flying home in the awful wake of Aguilar's death.

"Ilia," he said, coming back to the present. "Her plan hinges on Ilia."

"You mean the AI she kept hidden from everyone," Tatyana shot somewhat bitterly.

"Yes," chuckled Harrison. "That one."

Tatyana squinted, folding her arms.

"Doesn't the construct absorb AI though? Won't Ilia just disappear like the others?"

"No," said Harrison, shaking his head. "I mean, I don't think so."

"Explain please."

Rubbing his chin, Harrison spoke slowly.

"I think it's because Ilia isn't going to decode the signal like Braun or Remus and Romulus. I mean, that's what did them in, right? No, what William told me is that YiJay wants to open two *physical* portals by using the alien tech and then send Ilia *through*."

"How?"

"By using William's Uplink Transmitter."

"How?" Tatyana repeated.

"You should really be talking to him about that part," shrugged Harrison.

"I have," Tatyana smiled thinly. "And now I'm talking to you."

Allowing a short pause to hang in the air, Harrison sat motionless.

"Please," Tatyana finished. "Please."

Relaxing, the young archaeologist tipped his head.

"Well, William told me that the Transmitter was built to send Ilia in her entirety to remote servers since she can't clone avatars like Braun. If we sort of transmit her *in* through one portal and put a special receiver at the *other* portal, she should just glide right through by riding the transmission."

"Somehow picking up Braun as she goes," Tatyana finished with an eyebrow lifted.

"Look," said Harrison defensively. "I don't have all the answers here, okay? This is YiJay's plan, not mine."

"Yes, but YiJay received the baseline for her understanding of the construct from *you*, Harrison," Tatyana returned. "Which means you must have at least some of the answers."

Carefully watching her, Harrison tried to judge if Tatyana really believed any of this or if she was secretly convinced they'd all lost their minds.

"Just like reality," he sighed after a moment. "The construct relates to the viewer. To a being like Ilia, other AIs will stick out. They don't belong, and she'll be able to spot them."

"How do you know that?"

"Because that's how it worked for me."

"Okay," nodded Tatyana. "So all that's needed in order to execute this plan is to finish the simulator and open the portals, correct?"

"Yes, but before that's going to work, we have to locate the second device—the one that's on Phobos—and someone has to actually go there to set up a receiver."

"Funny," said Tatyana, her eyes flashing. "But I seem to recall attempting a trip to Phobos and being told it wasn't necessary."

At this, Harrison grinned impulsively. "Things change, Captain."

"Yes, they do," Tatyana agreed. "Which is why I have Amit scanning Phobos with the onboard IMCs every time the ship gets close enough. He's been instructed to forward the images on to you. I was hoping maybe you could fill in the blanks with your talent, as he won't be able to properly scan the entire moon."

"Sure," Harrison smiled. "Absolutely. Yeah."

"I suppose that just leaves us with YiJay and the simulator. Did any of your visions hint at when she might wake up from her coma?"

"No visions needed, Cap'," came a voice from the other side of the open door.

Stepping into the room, Ralph Marshall looked sheepishly from Harrison to Tatyana, holding up his hands like a suppliant.

172

"Sorry for eavesdropping, but I came up here to let you know that YiJay is awake again."

On her feet in a flash, Tatyana made for the door.

"We will continue our talk later, Harrison," she shot over her shoulder, quitting the room hurriedly.

Left in Tatyana's absence, an awkward silence developed between the two men. Flourishing among the shadows of the unspoken, it hung in heavy contrast to the chattering wind that played against the shell of the Base.

"So that looked fun," Marshall said at last, his smile somewhat forced.

"You know me," replied Harrison. "I just can't get enough. How's the Greenhouse?"

Dropping lightly into Tatyana's vacant chair, the pilot shrugged.

"It's good. Really good. Turns out I have more of a knack for gardening than I knew."

"Who would've thought?" Harrison joked.

Laughing a little but still not meeting his friend's gaze, Marshall shifted on his seat.

"So, long time, huh?" he said abruptly. "Since we talked, I mean."

"Yeah," returned Harrison with a grin. "You've been out in the garden so much, I kind of figured you'd gone all 4H on me."

"Mmhmm," Marshall nodded, clearly not hearing what Harrison had actually said.

A little perplexed, Harrison cocked his head to the side and stared at his friend. Apparent by the way he held himself, something was *off* with Marshall. Figuring it was probably Aguilar's death, Harrison decided to poke him along into admitting it so they could talk it out. Having once done the same thing for him in the aftermath of Liu's death, Harrison felt it only fair to repay the favor now.

"I have to say," he began. "The captain is taking Joey's death really well."

"She's a tough one," Marshall agreed quickly.

"Better than I did with Liu," he probed. "She might be bottling it up, but right now that's probably more productive then going off the deep end like me."

"Nah," Marshall muttered, his eyes flicking around at his feet. "You and her are different types of people. You feel things more, I think. She's a little cold."

173

"Well, in any event, you were right," said Harrison. "That robot took the hit like it was nothing. Joey didn't stand a—well, at least it was quick."

Biting his lip, Marshall bobbed his head absently.

"I know you guys were close," Harrison continued, gently trying to coerce his friend into facing that which bothered him. "Are you doing alright?"

"I…" Marshall started then trailed off.

For a few long seconds, neither man spoke as the elephant in the room decided whether it wanted to sit and stay, or go for good.

"Goddamn it," Marshall said under his breath.

"What?" asked Harrison, leaning forward. "What's going on, Ralph? What's wrong?"

Meeting Harrison's gaze, the older man blinked a single hot tear out of his eye then looked away.

"I'm a shitty friend," he spat, the words hard and flat.

"What are you talking about?" Harrison balked. "You're a great friend. My best friend, in fact!"

Wiping the back of his hand across his face, Marshall glowered down at the floor.

"I know, and that's the worst part about all of this. I—I just don't know how to do what *you* do."

Harrison frowned in confusion.

"What does that mean?"

Bottom lip clenched between his teeth, Marshall met Harrison's gaze then pulled it away.

"You're honest," he said miserably. "You're up front. You know how to tell the truth no matter what. Even when it sounds crazy, you still tell the truth. Not me, though. Not me. Back when you first started dreaming in ancient Mars, it was *me* that told you to keep it a secret. But secrets are bad and that was bad advice."

"Again, what are you talking about?" spoke Harrison, no longer sure they were on the subject of Aguilar's death anymore.

"Liz, man," sighed the pilot, crawling from beneath a massive weight. "She—she told me a secret that I've kept from you. It's pretty bad, but it's going to be worse now because I didn't tell you right away."

Harrison watched his friend carefully, saw the way he struggled to overcome his emotions.

174

"Liu was pregnant when she died," said Marshall suddenly, his eyes glistening. "Kubba told me, like, out of the blue one day. She just sort of dumped it in my lap then drifted off."

Silently, Harrison processed Marshall's words. For several endless moments, he simply sat and stared, not really seeing anything but unable to look away.

Then faintly, a memory from his *first* visit to the construct began to fill his mind.

In the vision, he remembered holding Liu tightly, smelling her hair, and feeling something different about her body. At the time, he had thought little of it—even gone as far as to forget that particular oddity. Now, however, it made perfect sense. She had been pregnant. Fully and beautifully pregnant.

Somehow, somewhere in the endless realities of the quantum blizzard, there existed a place where Liu had not died, where her belly had swollen with life, and her grace had continued to shine brightly.

She was out there, waiting for him, waiting among the stars.

"Ralph," he said at last, getting up from his chair to crouch beside his friend. "It's okay."

"Fuck, no it isn't," Marshall sniffed, another tear streaking down one cheek.

Looking deeply into the older man's tortured eyes, Harrison put on a strange little smile.

"Listen," he spoke calmly. "I think I already knew about Liu in some backwards way. In fact, I've been dreaming about her lately. They're just regular dreams, nothing too special. But I get this feeling, this kind of gut feeling, that I'll see her again. Maybe it's another dimension. Maybe it's just another time, like, in the past. I don't know."

At this, Marshall's gaze tried to escape but Harrison held it.

"The point is: she changed me. You know? She changed the direction of my life. Even in death, she's still changing me. It's like we're connected, me and her, connected in some crazy way that can't be broken."

Pulling himself together, Marshall lifted his eyes to the ceiling.

"See what I mean," he sighed in an almost frustrated tone. "You're letting me off way too easy. You should hate me."

"Come on," smiled Harrison. "I could never hate you, Ralph. Besides, all you did was try to protect my feelings. How is that bad?"

Sniffling loudly, Marshall shook his head. "You just deserve to know the truth, is all," he said.

"I think in the back of my mind, I already did," returned Harrison evenly.

Marshall, balling his hands into fists, sat up straighter in his chair.

"Thank you," he spoke, visibly less tense. "I—I don't know how I got so lucky with a friend like you."

"Hey, you saved my life twice!" teased Harrison. "I think you could probably steal the fillings out of my teeth and I'd still love you. It's us, man. You and me against the world, right?"

Laughing despite the tears on his cheek, Marshall put a hand on Harrison's shoulder and squeezed.

"Thank you," he said again. "Thank you."

Dark visions

Howling like a wolf, the wind tore across the nighttime desert. Borne along upon its back, she took hold of the driving force, feeling its tangible essence like never before. Becoming one with the wind, she *was* the wind and it was she. Twisted, broken, reborn, and renewed, she wound through the boulders in her path as if they were nothing.

Coming at once to the hollow between two pillowy sand dunes and a now-demolished canyon, she was suddenly separated from the free wind and left to stand alone. Aware at once that this was the place where Aguilar had died, she searched for his soul in the quiet of the night but found nothing.

Above, the stars swirled and spun, executing a sequence of maneuvers that was older than the concept of time. He was up there, she knew, turning and turning. Always reborn and never ending, his line had been added to those of the others. He was in the blizzard now, a part of the never-ending storm.

Distracted from her reverence by a faint scratching sound, she reluctantly turned to face the heap of rubble that filled the broken canyon.

Shifting, small runners of sand and gravel began to trickle down between the larger boulders. At once, a patch of debris lifted and then fell back in place. Like smoke from a dragon's nostrils, jets of dust fired out around the pile and were swept away with the wind. Trembling, the rocks jolted again and this time several rolled aside to create an opening.

Hideous and nightmarish, something buried by tons of stone and sand began to dig its way out.

Horror struck, she felt herself pulled forward towards the grunting thing by a force out of her control. The closer she got, the louder and more violent its movements became.

Tossing out sprays of earth and rock, the harsh shine of metal glinted in the light of twin moons as a leg was suddenly exposed. Frantically, it hacked at the pile of boulders until it was free enough to dislodge itself like something born from a festering wound.

Damaged and only able to drag itself along on two of its six legs, the awful mechanical insect swiveled its domed head in the dark. Somehow seeing her even though she was not really there, it snapped its guns on her and lunged.

Shocked upright in bed with cold sweat covering her face and chest, Elizabeth Kubba cried out in the night.

Fading into the background like the dream itself, an endless sea of lights hurried to hide themselves once again between the cracks of space and time.

CHAPTER TWENTY

Destination unknown—<u>Nine days until the Pulse</u>

For five days, James Floyd and his family had been cooped up in a small cube-shaped room. Buried in the listing bowels of the USS Rainier, they had not seen the light of day since being rushed off the Flight Deck by Eve Bear and her security detail shortly after landing.

In that time, James had worked to come to terms with what he'd done back in their Houston home but was finding it harder than he'd thought.

Confined as they were without any Tablets, Smart Glass, or other means to access what might be left of the outside world, distractions were in short supply. As a result, the family bickered and fought, adding endlessly to the heap of anxiety that now clutched James's nerves.

He kept seeing Ricky's face every time he closed his eyes, kept hearing the squelching sound it had made when the bullet had torn into it. Although he wasn't quite ready to admit it to himself, James knew in the back of his mind that he would never be the same again. He was a changed man, like it or not.

Now, with his eyes on the pages of his paperback novel, he tried to read but found the words either too complex or too blurry to compute through all the noise in his head.

"Can't you just ask her," Nora stressed, absently folding and refolding one of their only two blankets.

"Ask her what?" said James, looking up from his book.

"Ask her what?" Nora repeated, angry with James's detachment. "How about when we can shower and change our clothes! It's been five days, James! We're filthy!"

"Sure, babe," spoke James coolly. "I'll just march out of this locked room and straight up to her. I'll say, 'Hi there, Eve. Thanks for the Marine airlift and the safe passage onto your warship. When do we get to hit the spa?' Come on, babe, she's very important and probably busy. Who knows what's going on out there? They have warheads and economies to protect you know? We're just not worth her time."

Dropping the blanket back on the bed, Nora frowned. "Come on honey. Don't be like this. Usually you can't wait to get away. All I'm asking is if you'll *try* to find out what's happening. We've been down here for a long time, and I'm getting worried. Please."

"Yeah, Daddy, and we're bored too," chirped his younger daughter, holding in her hand one of the few toys she'd be able to take as they were rushed from their home.

At the sight of his daughter's tattered clothes and grubby face, James softened. Everything Nora had said was true. They did need answers, yet James was fearful to ask. He had held secrets from Eve, used crucial information to buy his family's safety in a time of great uncertainty. While not as mentally taxing as the blood on his hands, this fact did tug at him.

When he'd seen Eve on the Flight Deck the other day, there had been a look of passivity on her face that worried him. Though she had saved their lives, it was clear from that dour expression that James was no longer in her good graces.

As if reading his mind, Nora rested a hand on the top of their younger daughter's head.

"She'll understand why you did what you did, honey. You have a family. Anyone can understand that."

Nodding slowly, James glanced from his eldest daughter, napping in the corner, to his youngest.

"We have been down here for a while, haven't we?" he said, getting to his feet.

"Please," urged Nora. "I just want to have some idea of what's happening and where we're going."

"Okay," James sighed resolutely. "I'll try."

If Eve truly was as angry as he worried, then he couldn't hide from her forever. It was time to face the music and let the chips fall where they would. He might not be able to take back *everything* he'd done to save his family, but he could at least defend his actions.

Moving to the door, James gently tried the handle. It was locked. Not surprised by this, he remembered the bolt turning that morning when their breakfast had been delivered.

Glancing quickly over his shoulder at Nora, he shrugged then rapped on the hard metal and held his breath. Soon, the sound of footsteps approaching could be heard.

"Are you alright, sir?" came a woman's voice from the other side of the door.

"Yes," James answered. "It's just that I was hoping you could tell me what's happening or where we might be headed and when we'll get there."

179

"I'm sorry, sir, but I'm not allowed to say. In fact, I don't really know myself, to be honest."

"I kind of figured," nodded James. "In that case then can you get a message to Eve Bear for me?"

"Who?" the woman returned.

"Eve Bear," repeated James. "She's the Chief of Staff to the President."

There was a brief pause before the woman replied.

"Sir, I'm just a Petty Officer Third Class. I don't have access to that kind of a person."

"Will you just try?" James pressed. "Just get on your radio and call it in. Call your SO and tell them what I just said. Tell them Doctor James Floyd wants to talk to Eve Bear."

"Sir," the woman said, her voice laced with doubt. "I'm really just supposed to make sure you're all safe and accounted for. I'm not supposed to—"

"Please," James interrupted. "Do you know who I am? Have you ever heard my name before?"

"Yes," the woman admitted after skipping a beat. "I followed the Mars missions and the ruins really close until—well, you know."

Palms flat on the door, James leaned forward and spoke enthusiastically. "Right, good! So you know me! What's your name?"

"Megan," came the woman's hesitant reply. "Petty Officer Third Class Megan Atwell."

"Alright," smiled James. "Petty Officer Third Class Megan Atwell it is. Now listen, Megan. You know who I am, and you know the kinds of people I'm accustomed to dealing with, right? Do you trust me when I say that my level of clearance is very good?"

Again there was a pause. However, a moment later Petty Officer Atwell responded.

"Yes, sir."

"Yes," James echoed. "It's very high. My clearance is very high. So when I ask you to call your SO and try to put me in contact with Eve Bear, you know what that means, right?"

"Yes, sir," repeated Atwell in a subdued tone. "Hold on a second."

Suddenly, the crackle of radio static flared up on the other side of the door.

"Yes!" James said under his breath, shooting a triumphant grin at his family.

Smiling back at him, their hopeful expressions made James feel almost like a good family man.

"This is Atwell, sir," the woman spoke into her radio. "I've got a Doctor James Floyd on Deck Three and he was wanting to be connected with someone from Eagle One's party."

Unable to make out the response from the Petty Officer's SO, James leaned against the door and tried to listen harder.

"That's right, sir," Atwell went on. "He wants to talk to an Eve Bear, says she's with the POTUS."

James held his breath and rubbed a hand over his stubbly chin.

"Sure, I can wait," said the young sailor. "I'll just stand by until he arrives."

With that, the static hissed off and the hallway outside the door was silent.

"What did they say?" James asked.

"They're going to pass it up the line," replied Atwell.

Putting his hand back on the knob, James jiggled it.

"Any chance I can get you to open this door so we can get a little fresh air in here?"

Following a beat, the lock retracted loudly and the door swung open. In the entryway, a mousy young woman in uniform saluted James and nodded to his wife.

"Sir. Ma'am."

Catching sight of the girls, Atwell hesitated then dug in her hip pocket, retrieving a small personal Tablet.

"I've got some cartoons and stuff on there if you like," she shrugged, holding it out. "I put them on for my little brother, but he's not here. Maybe you girls might like them?"

Trailing off a little, she handed the Tablet over then stepped back out into the hallway and nodded again.

"I'm sorry you all can't go up on deck. It's for everyone's safety, though."

"Thank you, Megan," said James, offering her his hand.

Shaking it quickly and firmly, Atwell dipped her chin and moved off a little to give the family some privacy.

Twenty minutes later, a door slammed open at the end of the hallway and a Secret Serviceman appeared in the entry to James's room.

"Why is this door unsecured?" he said to Atwell, his expression stern.

"I—" she started.

"Relax, tough guy," James cut in. "I told her to do it."

Resting his pale blue eyes on James, the black-suited man smiled.

"Say, I remember you. Back in D.C. Right after the ruins were discovered. We picked you up and took you to the White House."

"Sure," James beamed, recognizing the man. "Yeah, that was me! I absolutely remember you too!"

"Good," the agent shot, suddenly returning to ice. "Then we can skip with the niceties. This way. Let's go."

Turning, James kissed the tops of his younger daughter's heads and embraced Nora.

"I'll be back as fast as I can," he whispered.

"I love you," she replied, touching her lips to his cheek.

"I—" James stammered, caught off guard again by how sincerely she said those words. "You too."

In the hallway, the man impatiently gestured for James to follow then quickly set off in the direction he'd come.

Atwell, standing as still as a tree by the door caught James's eye and nodded to him as he passed.

"My shift ends in five, but I will stay with them until you get back, sir," she said softly.

"Thank you," James muttered, his stomach already starting to roll with anxiety.

Quickly taking the next two rights, the agent led James wordlessly to a maintenance elevator and hustled him onboard. Rising several floors, the metal cage swung slightly with the motion of the sea.

"Must be rough out there," said James, hoping to cut the tension. "The ocean, I mean. Are there big waves?"

"Probably," replied the agent stiffly. "I wouldn't know. I've been on security detail for the last few days. Haven't been topside."

Coming to a rest, the elevator doors opened and the two men stepped out.

"This way," said the agent, leading James down a narrow hallway to the left.

With no windows, the passage was lit with halogen lamps that buzzed rhythmically overhead.

Approaching a door, outside of which stood two additional Secret Servicemen, the agent knocked.

"Yeah," came a muffled female voice from within.

"I've got Floyd with me, ma'am," said the agent.

"Send him in."

Opening the door onto a spacious-yet-windowless room, the agent ushered James inside then swung the door closed behind him.

Eve, looking up from a table where she was working, smiled disinterestedly. "Hello, Floyd. How are you and your family?"

Spotting no other chairs in the large and comfortably lit cabin, James stood where he was and rubbed his elbows.

"We're fine, thanks."

"Good," said Eve, her attention trained on the papers spread out before her.

When after a few moments she did not speak again, James cleared his throat awkwardly.

"Yes?" she asked, drawing the word out.

"Well, I was wondering," faltered James. "I mean, you've got us in a tiny room with no windows and no clue where we're going. I guess I was just wondering what's up, Eve. What's the plan?"

Smiling despite the deep lines of stress that webbed her face, Eve took off her glasses and fixed James with a cool green stare.

"You have a funny way of thanking people," she said at last.

"Excuse me," frowned James.

"We saved your life, Floyd. You and your family. Don't you think that's enough to earn a little room to work?"

"I—" James began.

"Listen," interrupted Eve with an annoyed wave. "Everyone here owes you a lot. I get that. Your timeline made all of this possible. Without it, we never would have risked dispatching air units to collect our VIPs. the threat of a Pulse was just too great."

"You're welcome—" James tried.

"However," continued Eve, barreling over him. "What most people here do *not* know is that you held your timeline hostage to get what you wanted."

At this, Eve's eyes flashed dangerously.

"I did it for my family," James protested meekly.

"Oh, I fully understand that," Eve returned. "But that didn't stop you from warning the Mars team before contacting me, now did it? How did *that* help your family?"

"I'm not sorry for that," said James. "You weren't in the head office like me. Everyone has abandoned them. In all of the confusion, I wanted to make sure they got the message too. They deserve a chance, after all."

Closing her eyes, Eve exhaled slowly and seemed to uncoil a bit. Like frost thawed by the morning sun, her lips drew up into an honest smile.

"Truth be told," she spoke. "When we intercepted your little message to Vodevski, it tickled me. Sure, you broke the chain of command, but you did it for a good reason, I suppose. You're a good man, James. Stupid but good."

"Thanks, I guess," shrugged James, thrown by the moment of uncharacteristic warmth.

"You're welcome," said Eve, returning her glasses to her face and glancing at the door. "Now, I'd offer you a chair, but I don't want you to get the impression that this conversation has much of a future. Goodbye, James."

"Wait," he implored, holding up a hand. "Just wait! Please tell me where we are. Tell me where we're going."

"I'll have my man escort you and your family to the showers and get you some clean clothes," responded Eve, ignoring his questions.

"Just tell me where we are!" James pressed. "I'm sorry about everything I've put you through, but you can't keep me in the dark like this. I can help you!"

Sighing with frustration, Eve looked over the rim of her glasses at him.

"I can't give classified information to a traitor."

As if physically struck, James leaned back against the door.

"A traitor?"

"Yes, Floyd. That's what we call people who commit treason. You do realize that you gave sensitive information to a foreign body, don't you?"

"What foreign body?" James balked.

"The Mars team," replied Eve. "Most specifically, their Russian Captain."

"But she's one of us!"

"That's not how I see it."

Amazed, James couldn't help but start to laugh.

"What's funny?" Eve said with a glare.

Shaking his head, the thread-worn NASA Mission Commander grinned unbelievingly.

"Even when the end of the world is staring you in the fucking face, you're still dictating your actions based off lines drawn on a map."

"Those lines are what's kept things in order for so long," Eve snapped haughtily. "They're the reason we've done such great things as a species."

"And look at us now," sighed James, the laughter draining from him. "Just look at us, Eve. When your Marines came for me, I had just shot a man in my dining room. Did you know that? Did they tell you *that* part of the story?"

Eve stared back blankly, but James thought he could detect a note of sorrow in her eyes.

"Armed men were trying to kill me in my own home for jewelry and cans of food," he went on. "And they were Americans, might I add, not even one of those evil foreign bodies you're so afraid of. Houston is a damn warzone. There are no police around. No military. No government. Nothing. My family only got saved because I was important, because I had some value to you. Does that seem fair?"

Running a hand through his thinning hair, James smiled sadly at Eve.

"You want to call me a traitor, that's fine. But I think you're the ones who really turned your backs on your duty. You'll let the world burn as long as you can hold onto your sense of superiority."

Silent for several beats, Eve continued to gaze at James until he grew uncomfortable. Turning for the door, he grasped the knob and hesitated.

"Thank you for saving my family, Eve, but don't let yourself forget about all the others you didn't."

Pushing the door open, he made to quit the room.

"James," Eve called after him.

"Yeah?" he said, glancing back over his shoulder.

"When you get your clean clothes, make sure your parkas fit well. It's cold in Alaska this time of year."

Making a call—Sol 128—Nine days until the Pulse

From the moment she had awakened from her nightmare, Elizabeth Kubba had been unable to shake the feeling that it was more than just that. Pacing back and forth in her room, she had played and replayed the dream all day in her mind's eye, always seeing the same things. No matter how often tried and no matter how intensely she studied it, her recall of the vision was total.

185

Now doing pushups to occupy herself in the late evening gloom, she continued to flick through the sequence of events, looking for anything that might undermine its grip on her. As sweat dripped from her brow and her muscles screamed despite the low gravity, she shot up and down like a piston.

With each rise and fall, she saw the thing bursting from the ground, shaking off the debris, and launching itself into the night. With each rise and fall, she saw the cold calculation that was its pitiful soul. With each rise and fall, the reality of what she'd experienced became clearer and clearer.

Though no AI expert, Kubba had connected with the Killbot, seeing inside it as YiJay could do with Braun and Ilia. However, unlike the helpful and loving companions the humans had bred, this thing knew nothing but murder by numbers. To it, the members of the Mars team were simply zeros and ones standing in its way. To it, they were a mathematical inconvenience that needed to be corrected.

Nearly buckling from exertion, Kubba's arms shook badly. Lowering herself to the floor, she rested her cheek against the cool surface and breathed heavily.

There was something else she had sensed inside the robot, something more. It wasn't there for the Base—wasn't even there for them. Driven by its awful programming, 04 the Chinese Automated War Machine had been sent to Mars with a mission whose parameters betrayed a still-greater mystery.

She had to warn her teammates, had to protect what they'd found.

Heart rate returned to normal, Kubba sat up, crossed her legs, and gazed around the room. Even more Spartan than normal, there was a table, a chair, and a cot. Everything else had been removed the night William and Marshall had locked her in.

After working to stabilize YiJay, Kubba had gone willingly into holding, knowing that she deserved no better. With the young Korean's blood still on her hands, she'd allowed herself to be led into her room by the two men despite the fact that she could have physically bested both if she'd wanted.

Only visited when it was time for meals, she had spent the last few days catching up on sleep and trying to enjoy her newly reclaimed sanity.

Crashing down around her like a glass house, her nightmare vision of the robot had marked, in the starkest of terms, the end of her sabbatical. Forced back into the real world, with all of the dangers and

186

worries that came included, she now saw that it was time for her to get back to work.

Finishing her visual sweep of the room, Kubba spotted nothing that could help her accomplish that which she needed to accomplish. With her current status as a prisoner and violent attacker, she knew that her word was worth almost nothing.

Though Marshall would again bring her a meal the next morning, she doubted he would listen to anything she had to say. Moreover, claiming that the source of her knowledge came from a nightmare vision was likely to throw her assertions that she was now sane into a harsh light. She needed proof—needed a way to convince everyone that they were in danger.

Standing, she walked to the table and looked down at a tray of food placed there earlier by Marshall for her dinner. Not even trusting her with sharp utensils, he had precut everything for her into bite-sized pieces leaving only a spoon. Both wanting to laugh and cry, she sat in the chair and picked up a bit of dehydrated ice cream, nibbling at the edges.

As the sweet flavor of chocolate spread over her tongue, her attention slackened a little and she was able to relax.

Looking about the room less urgently, she searched for anything she might have missed the first time. Careful to examine fully all that she saw before moving on, her eyes scanned the scene like those of an AI, probing and inquisitive.

Suddenly, her breath caught in her throat and she shot to her feet. Moving across to the opposite wall, she came to the flat facade of her Tac Suit storage closet.

Four nights ago, under the respectfully averted eyes of Marshall and William, she had stripped out of her dirty pressure suit and hung it in the closet, per safety protocol. Electronically locked with an override from Vodevski, the bolt that secured the door was not as burly as those on the main entry. Given enough force and time, it could be overcome.

Knowing that, like all Tac Suits, hers was equipped with a wrist Tablet, Kubba darted back to the table and grabbed the spoon. Slipping the handle between the frame and the door, she slid it up and down until she located the latch bolt. Carefully, for she did not want to break the plastic utensil, she wriggled the spoon between the bolt and the frame of the closet, trying to separate the two. After several unsuccessful attempts, the door suddenly popped free and swung out on its hinges.

Barely stifling a victorious cry, Kubba jumped up and down, tossing the spoon across the room. Inside the closet, hanging like a white snakeskin was her pressure suit.

Pulling it free from its hook, she sat cross-legged on the floor with the limp fabric in her lap. First removing the curved wrist Tablet from its seating, she turned it on and inspected the remaining battery power. Given that she did not have a Survival Pack, and thus no main power supply, the Tablet offered access to nothing but the suits emergency systems.

Unperturbed, Kubba selected the emergency beacon and checked the range. It wasn't great, but she could fix that. Flipping the Tablet over, she slid the back panel off and revealed the motherboard within. One hand gathering up the fabric of the suit's right leg, she took hold of the boot with the other and released a small screwdriver kit housed in the heel.

"I'm going to kiss the tech that put all these little bells and whistles in you," she said to the suit, patting its helmet.

Over the next half-hour, she worked quietly on the wrist Tablet, bypassing certain connections and consolidating the transmitting power. Along with the others, she had sat through literally days of seminars and classes about the Tac Suits during training. Having paid much more attention than most, she now applied that knowledge as she manipulated the emergency beacon to fit her needs.

Designed originally to send out an automated distress call to every Tablet or computer within range, Kubba altered the program to act as a simple two-way radio between her Tablet and only one other. Knowing that her message would have to be brief and to the point, she figured she could get about thirty seconds of life from the batteries before the Tablet went dead.

Finally finished with the alterations, she placed the wrist Tablet back in its housing then slipped her blood-stained helmet over her head.

"Okay," she breathed. "Here goes."

Hitting *Transmit*, she heard static in her helmet speakers but nothing more. Had she made a mistake? Had she somehow damaged the motherboard?

Trying again, she glanced worriedly at the dangerously low battery life. Again the chatter of static filtered in. Only this time, a faint clicking sound punctuated the noise.

"Hello?" came a distant voice from the other end. "Who is this?"

Jumping at the sound, Kubba sat up straighter. She had to move fast. The signal would die soon.

"Amit, it's Lizzy."

"Liz?"

"Yes. Listen, there isn't much time and I need your help. Please, please help me."

There was a pause before Amit spoke again, his voice growing quieter by the second.

"How are you doing this?" he asked. "Aren't you locked up?"

"Never mind all that," said Kubba hurriedly. "Just do me this one favor, will you? Next time you fly over it, scan the area where the Chinese robot was buried. Look for signs that it's escaped, that it's still on the move. Please, Amit. Help me save them."

Before the Indian could reply, the Tablet screen went dark and the static in Kubba's ears cut out.

Pulling the helmet off her head, she caught sight of the dried blood that still stained it where she had bludgeoned YiJay.

Wracked by a stab of deep regret, she set the helmet aside and looked up at the ceiling. Somewhere many kilometers above her, Amit Vyas was the only hope she had of ever undoing all the wrongs she'd caused.

CHAPTER TWENTY-ONE

12:01 AM—Sol 129—Eight days until the Pulse

On the frozen desert plains of Mars, the distant Sun had yet to begin its parade towards the jagged horizon. With the sky a starry purple, the early hours of Sol 129 bloomed like a flower in the night.

Only eight days were now left until the planets aligned and the Pulse was set to unleash. Not yet realizing the true peril of their situation, the Mars team was focused on other matters.

Like a lion approaching its kill in a storm, the impending Pulse was taking advantage of the all distractions, creeping ever-closer as it licked its teeth.

After everything they had been through, everything they had seen, the mission was officially over. They had done the best they could, but circumstances outweighed their ambition. Now all that was left to do was to pool their wits for one more big push.

Strained by deaths, injuries, and the daily struggle to survive, the decision to go home had been made at dinner the previous night. If at all possible, they would launch before the Pulse was due, placing full stock in YiJay and her plan to free Braun. Despite the abstract nature of its design, even the captain had been forced to admit that it was their only viable option. Without Braun, they could not light the ship's Torch Engine, and without the Torch, they could not go home.

Thus, retreating after dinner into their separate worlds, the crew as a whole continued to ignore the more ominous signs about the coming Pulse. In the storm that was their lives, it took a step closer and growled.

Alone in William's old room, for he now bunked with YiJay, Tatyana allowed herself to cry softly for the love she had lost. In her case, Pulse or no Pulse, Aguilar was dead and never coming back. With nothing more to motivate her than her mission, she felt an old familiar cold enter her heart. Surrendering to it, she drowned the voice of her childhood self and all the hope that it had whispered in her ear over the years.

Awake and unable to reconnect with the visions that held his future behind the membrane of reality, Harrison Raheem Assad meditated in his lab. Whether or not he died in the Pulse, the truth that he had once kissed the stars was still intact. Knowing that it was possible, knowing that he *could* reach such strange heights, he pushed himself to let go and again find the celestial path hidden among the endless pricks of light in the quantum blizzard.

Though glad to be back on even ground with Harrison, Ralph Marshall still slept badly. Beside his bed, nearly down to the last few, an open bottle of sleeping pills sat like a constant reminder of his mental burden. Suppressed in the wake of Kubba's revelation and all that it stirred up, his guilt over the death of Viviana now began to whisper again. Perhaps brought on by the fact that soon he would be required to fly again, the pilot was plagued by dreams of tearing metal and human screams.

In the machine shop, YiJay Lee worked diligently on the final lines of code for the simulator. Acutely aware of the late hour, she was also aware of how little time there was left.

Hunting the equations that made up Braun's memories, she tried to keep her eye from straying to the timecode on the wall. With everyone depending on her to come through, she needed to absorb herself fully, needed to see the AI's thoughts as more than just numbers.

If she didn't recreate the pattern exactly as Braun had seen it, all would be lost. Presentation was paramount, the wormhole's integrity reliable only if her simulation struck all the right notes.

Taking a shallow breath, YiJay blinked her good eye and refocused on the swimming numbers before her. Tablet glowing like a lantern, she continued to bathe in its light, while across the room, the alien device trembled imperceptibly.

Upstairs, Elizabeth Kubba paced the perimeter of her quarters and waited impatiently for word about the Killbot. Fearful that she had become a modern-day Cassandra, she hoped against hope that Amit had taken her warning seriously.

While everyone else was focusing on going home, she saw only the Killbot as it drug itself across the desert towards its target. Helpless to do much more than wait, she reverted to doing pushups in the dark.

Luckily for Kubba, Amit Vyas *had* heeded her warning. At that moment, in a world high above all others, the lone astronaut stared disbelievingly at a series of new IMC scans. Showing images of displaced earth and angry dangerous metal, they seemed to scream out, causing the Indian to shiver with dread.

Kubba was right. The thing was still alive.

Having already sent the scans of Phobos to Harrison, Amit quickly opened a new transmission and addressed it to the captain. Fingers moving across the screen, he relayed, from beginning to end, the

191

story of how he'd come to discover the robot's survival as well as its current location.

The window

As the timecode on the wall ticked over to six o'clock AM, Sol 129, William Konig slouched in a chair and snored softly.

Dreaming of his childhood home in the foothills of the Bavarian Alps, he became loosely aware that something wasn't quite right. Tickled by this shift in his reality, he stirred.

Distant at first, a familiar sound pricked his ears, permeating the fabric of his dream world. As boisterous as a thousand talking echoes, it splashed and ran in sheets, growing louder by the heartbeat.

Suddenly realizing what it was, William's eyes snapped open and he nearly spilled from his chair. Fully awake now, he took in the room around him, flickering greenish-yellow with the light of summer storms.

Glancing first to the cot where YiJay had been when he'd dozed off, he saw that she wasn't there. Almost reluctantly, he rose from his chair and turned slowly around to face the source of the confused light and sound.

There, like an open window in thin air, a perfectly round portal hung hauntingly above the spinning alien device.

Framed in the brilliance of an epic storm, which raged on the other side, YiJay Lee stood with her face turned up.

Forking across the sky, a bolt of lightning strobed with blue and purple as it touched a nearby tree, setting it ablaze. Dampened by the gushing clouds and howling wind, the thunder was an approving murmur.

"Oh my god!" William heard himself scream above the cracking of branches.

Illuminated by the resulting fire, wind-driven rain howled across the grasslands and dashed for the open portal. Like heat waves rising from the pavement, the droplets evaporated before being able to cross over, becoming nothing but a ripple in time.

Stumbling to YiJay's side, William held onto her for support.

"I did it," YiJay said, not bothering to raise her voice. "I did it."

Unable to answer, William simply stared into the world of ancient Mars, thankful that he could not feel the brutal force of the storm that wracked it.

In his lab, Harrison Assad hunched over a Tablet and reviewed Amit's scans of Phobos. Having given up on meditation a little before dawn, he now focused his attention on reviewing the images and using them to make a 3D model for the captain.

Taken with the IMCs onboard Braun, the scans were a messy soup of blurry lines and smudged shadows. However, even in this sorry state, it was clear to Harrison's trained eye that there was much more than just smudges and shadows hidden among the pixels.

Picking up his stylus, he opened the same program he had used when preparing his model of the ruins and started dragging in the images of Phobos. With nearly automatic movements, he arranged and overlapped the individual scans into one large model of the moon then set about cleaning it up. Though he had not had true a vision in some time, Harrison yet knew that a tenuous connection to forces greater than himself still remained.

Relaxing, he took several deep breaths then explored the equilibrium between his experience and his imagination.

As his eyes moved over the pixilated composite, he began to highlight certain shadows, defining their edges with his stylus. Clearer now, the mysterious shapes started to speak to him, guiding his hand as he worked.

Depth and perspective flowed from his mind's eye, down his arm, and into the model he was creating. Teasing out features that were buried by rock or obscured by static, he held the electric pen loosely and traced it along ancient lines. Soon, with his head tingling like a lightning rod, Harrison sat back and gazed down at his work.

Cut cleanly from the lumpy images of Phobos was a large roundish chamber with a single tunnel leading up to the surface. Situated in the center of a straight line from Stickney Crater, the space seemed to be using the crater's natural bowl to act as a radio dish of sorts for the anomalous signal.

Cleanly crafted like the chambers and tunnels on Mars, everything about the site betrayed the hand of the Traveler's technology. Moreover, a slight spike in magnetism had registered in nearly every scan of the chamber. To anyone else, it would have appeared as nothing more than an odd vein of iron, but to Harrison, it was proof positive that alien technology was waiting there to be discovered.

Standing, he took up the Tablet and headed for the door. He was pleased with the results, pleased with what he'd found. Even though there was still so much shrouded in mystery, it was reassuring to know that they were at least on the right track.

Almost to the door, Harrison suddenly had to jump back as it burst open on its hinges.

Breathlessly, William stood in the entry, his eyes like wildfires burning nearly out of control.

"You need to come with me right now," he spoke, his voice a smattering of every emotion.

Taking Harrison's arm, William turned and began marching down the hallway.

"What's wrong?" protested Harrison, pulling his arm free.

"She's—" William stuttered, pausing mid-step. "She's done it! YiJay has done it! You need to come now. Everyone needs to see this."

Convergence

Though excited voices echoed down the hallway outside her quarters, Tatyana Vodevski stood in stunned silence. In her hand, hanging limply by a few fingers, was her Tablet. There on the screen like a nightmare of twisted metal, the Chinese Killbot showed itself in stark contrast to the desert sands.

It had survived. Joey was dead for nothing.

Surprisingly, this revelation did not break Tatyana, as it would have many others. Mostly feeling a deep aching emptiness at the futility of it all, she was relieved to find barely any personal injustice mixed in. It appeared as though her purging of emotions in the wake of Aguilar's death had been successful almost to a fault.

Letting her gaze drop to the bottom corner of the screen, Tatyana noticed an icon blinking impatiently. Dreamily, she tapped it and opened the accompanying message Amit had sent along with the images. She read it once, frowned, shook her head, and reread.

When she reached for the part where Amit explained why he'd been prompted to take follow-up pictures of the attack site, she frowned and shook her head a second time. Kubba had told him? *Kubba?* How could *she* have known? More importantly, *why* had she warned them?

Unable to give the situation more thought, Tatyana was rudely interrupted by fists pounding on her door.

"Y-yes?" she called, hastily slipping the Tablet in her jumpsuit's cargo pocket.

From outside in the hallway, a chorus of voices all began to talk at once.

Opening the door, Tatyana was met by the excited faces of Harrison, William, Udo, and Marshall.

"You need to come with us," William said, speaking over the others.

With her mind still working to process the full ramifications of Amit's transmission, Tatyana was slow to answer.

"Why? What is it?"

"It's the alien device," beamed William. "YiJay's got it working, and you won't believe me if I describe it to you, so you'll just have to come see for yourself!"

Instantly shifting focus like a camera lens, Tatyana's thoughts swerved away from the Killbot.

"Really?" she asked, already closing the door behind her. "Take me now. I want to see."

Leading the way, William yammered on about the wonders he'd seen the device produce, but Tatyana wasn't really listening. Carefully boxing up her worries about the Killbot, she stacked them in a corner of her mind for later investigation.

If what William was saying were actually true, then she owed it to everyone to be one hundred percent *there* and not off in her own world. She was the captain, the leader of this tattered band. Whether or not they cared anymore, she still did.

Coming around the curve of the Base, the procession reached the stairs down to the basement level and began descending in order. At the bottom landing, William practically sprinted the remaining two meters to the machine shop door, holding it open for them.

Seeing on his face a look of such hope and exhilaration that it made her almost nervous, Tatyana stepped through the entry.

In the center of the room, YiJay stood at the Holo Table with her gaze hanging on the alien device. Resting to one side, its shiny black skin shone back a murky reflection of her profile.

Still bruised from Kubba's attack and with a white bandage over her right eye, a brilliant smile graced YiJay's lips as if she'd just heard the voice of God for the very first time.

"Come in, come in," she said, abruptly breaking her stare to turn and face the others. "There's plenty of room to gather close."

195

"Is it true?" Tatyana spoke carefully. "Is what William said really true?"

Grinning even wider, YiJay held her Tablet out for Tatyana to take. "All you have to do is hit the 'start' key."

Open on the simulator program, a bright green square flashed on the screen.

Taking the Tablet, Tatyana glanced around at everyone then met YiJay's eye. The young Korean nodded encouragingly and moved back from the Holo Table.

"Okay," said Tatyana, more to herself than anyone else.

Lightly, she pressed a finger to the green *Start* key, and the tabletop began to glow. Fading in like a sea of stars, uncountable luminous sparks orbited in the air. Faintly at first, a web of lines started to connect the dots, forming a pattern that divided and multiplied.

One moment growing larger, then the next shrinking, the shapes took on an almost-living quality as they interacted with each other. Contracting and expanding, they grew more complicated until they were forced to merge as if by sheer magnetism. Absorbed into one another, they became one large pattern, churning endlessly in a cycle of death and rebirth.

Utterly baffled by the complexity of the simulation, Tatyana gave YiJay a quick sidelong glance. The girl had done something amazing, something unlike anything she'd ever seen before.

More arresting than the lights of the Milky Way, the pattern seemed to embrace and react to the stunned crew, offering them a firsthand account of their own divinity.

Engrossed by all of the cerebral beauty, Tatyana didn't immediately notice a strange noise that had begun to sting her ears like an icy wind. Though distant at first, it grew and grew until it matched the pattern in intensity. Becoming almost painful, the sound morphed into a frequency that battered the walls with feedback and echoes.

Cringing, Tatyana covered her ears.

"What is that?"

Still smiling, YiJay pointed to the corner of the Holo Table where the alien device was beginning to shiver and rock visibly. Soon standing on end, it turned in time to the frequency, rotating faster and faster as the sound intensified.

Then, in a move so bold that no one but YiJay saw it coming, the device shot up into the air and centered itself.

A black hole in the middle of existence, it swirled the lines of energy around it, focusing them to a fine point. With a stab of light so bright that it froze the moment in illumination, the energy pattern suddenly exploded into a supernova of color.

Racing out in all directions, the shimmering mosaic washed across everyone, painting them like sun through stained glass. Abruptly halting, it then reversed its flow and came rushing back in on itself in waves of competing color.

Swarming together, the shattered pieces of the pattern began to reconsolidate and condense. Black in the heart of the forming portal, the alien device spun this delicate fabric into an inverted cone that disappeared away from the explorers into nothingness.

Cutting out, the high-pitched frequency stopped, casting the room into jarring silence.

Before her very eyes, Tatyana saw something start to form in the far-off center of the portal. Moving towards them as if sliding along a different orbit, the world beyond the window grew steadily until it filled the frame.

Hardly noticing the now-foreign sounds of rain and wind, Tatyana was transfixed by the wormhole, watching it in stunned disbelief.

Beyond the membrane, which separated her timeline from the other, a great storm was raging. Dancing across the sky like beautiful death, the aurora shimmered and rolled with hues of purple and green. Above it all, above the clouds and the wind and the rain, a blood-red Sun screamed its pain and anger.

"I can't believe it," whispered Tatyana.

"Believe it," grinned YiJay.

For several minutes, the group stood in silence and watched the storm. Apart from such things for so long, they had all-but forgotten what it was like to see rain falling from the sky.

Finally breaking the spell, Udo stepped forward and gestured to the portal excitedly.

"Well come on," he said, glancing around as if confused why everyone was just standing there. "Who's going to suit up and go get Braun?"

"I wouldn't recommend that," YiJay warned. "Watch this."

Digging in her pocket, she pulled out a small star-bit screwdriver and held it up. Before anyone could figure out what she was doing, the AI specialist quickly cocked her arm and threw the tool into the portal.

Appearing only for the blink of an eye on the other side, the screwdriver suddenly disintegrated into practical dust and was swept away by the wind and rain.

"Oh," nodded Udo, taking a step back.

Eyes never leaving the storm, Tatyana tried to spot the last shimmering traces of the screwdriver, but it was useless. The thing was gone. Obliterated. Beyond destroyed.

"That's why we need Ilia for your plan, isn't it?" she said, addressing YiJay but not looking away from the portal.

"Yes," smiled YiJay. "Exactly. I mean, she's not like us, is she, Captain? Not actually real, you know? She's just a bunch of *ideas* when you get right down to it."

"I understand now," Tatyana returned, pulling her gaze away from the view to meet YiJay's. "So let's just send her in and be done with it!"

As lightening broke across the sky before them, YiJay shook her head slowly.

"Have you ever heard of something coming *out* of a black hole, Captain?"

For a few beats, Tatyana did not respond.

Shone back in YiJay's one eye, the portal disappeared into the depths of her pupil.

"No," Tatyana finally admitted. "I suppose not."

"Right," YiJay went on, speaking to everyone now. "That's right. See, this is a hole from our time into theirs. But we don't need a hole, do we? No, we need a *tunnel*. We need a white hole to this black one."

Pausing here, YiJay turned to the captain and bowed her head a little.

"That is why I will need you to take a team to Phobos, Captain. I need you to activate the device there so that we can make our tunnel to free Braun."

Etched between the stress lines and fatigue, a small smile began to tug at the corners of Tatyana's mouth.

She liked this part of the plan. It called for decisive action. Cold in the shadow of Aguilar's death and their failure to kill the Chinese War Machine, she needed a win—needed a challenge she could rise to meet.

"It will be my pleasure," she said at last. "When can we start?"

Moving from the rear of the group, Harrison held up his Tablet with the finished model of Phobos filling its screen.

"How about right now?"

CHAPTER TWENTY-TWO

A late breakfast—Sol 129—Eight days until the Pulse

At the breakfast table with warm bowls of oatmeal in front of them, five of the six members of Ilia Base ate in silence.

Though YiJay's display had actually made possible their insane plan to rescue Braun, it also served to illustrate just *how insane* their lives had really become. Unable to deny that they had all seen a world on the other side of time, even those as seasoned in the fantastic as Harrison found it hard to process.

Further clouding the mood was the captain's revelation that the Automated War Machine was still alive.

Waiting until YiJay had shut down the simulator and collapsed the portal, Tatyana had then produced her evidence and passed it around. Complete with the explanation of how the scans had come to be taken, she'd told the crew of Amit's call from Kubba and the warning she had issued.

While impressed with the doctor's ingenuity and sudden change of heart, the team had nonetheless agreed that it was prudent to strip her quarters of anything that might be used to escape. Even though she had warned them, YiJay's missing eye was proof enough that Kubba could not be fully trusted.

Working together, Marshall and the captain had carried out the task, removing almost everything from the doctor's quarters. Silent and obedient the entire time, Kubba had stood in the corner with her head bowed. Too overwhelmed with all that was happening to question her, the two had finished quickly then gone downstairs to join the others for a late breakfast.

Now, lifting her eyes from her still full bowl, Tatyana addressed the team.

"Okay, we have eight days until the Pulse is set to strike. Now unfortunately, Dr. Floyd's timeline does not give an exact hour of when this event will take place, so we can't plan on a last-minute launch. Because we have only a rough window to work with, I pose that we attempt to leave Mars orbit no later than twenty-four hours before the last day of the countdown."

"So, one week exactly then," Harrison spoke, stirring his food.

"Yes," nodded Tatyana.

"Just for my benefit," said Udo, his mouth partially full. "What exactly *is* our plan now? I mean, forgive me, but not all of us have been driven crazy or gone time traveling. Some of us just do our jobs like normal astronauts, and every once in a while need the record set straight so we can continue to do our jobs like normal astronauts."

Chuckling, Tatyana turned to face YiJay.

"This is your show now. Care to have the honors?"

With a quick nod, YiJay pulled out her Tablet and began typing on it.

Cringing, Udo scooted back from the table and stood.

"Don't do that here!"

"Relax," grinned YiJay. "I'm not starting the simulator. I'm just pulling up the orbital patterns of Phobos and Deimos."

"Oh," Udo laughed nervously, his spoon still clenched in his hand.

"Alright," began YiJay, handing the Tablet to William who was beside her. "As I pass this around, keep in mind that it's on a loop. Obviously, the moons of Mars don't cut halfway across the sky then reset like that. Now, pay special attention to the early evenings around four PM. What's happening then?"

Looking up for the screen, William handed the Tablet to Tatyana.

"Phobos rises above the horizon," he said.

"Right," YiJay nodded. "So that's when we'll want to open the portals, when we have a direct line. Wide open sky, you know? That way, the send and receive signals will be clear and unbroken by the planet, and our *tunnel* through ancient Mars will be less likely to collapse for any reason."

Glancing lightly around the table, YiJay shrugged. "From there, all that's left to be done is to send Ilia through to find Braun."

"How will we know if it's worked?" asked Tatyana.

YiJay, placing a small hand on top of William's, smiled distantly. "The special server William installed in the Lander is linked with the Flight Console so when Braun and Ilia come out of the portal and hit the Receiver Dish, they should upload into the server and appear on the screens."

"What about Remus and Romulus?" Harrison piped up. "Are we going to leave them there?"

Quiet for a moment, YiJay stared at the table.

"As you guys may or may not know, my mentor Sung Ja created them. Lots of people tend to think of Donovan or Alexandria or even

200

Braun as the most impressive AI, but Remus and Romulus were something truly special. I wish we could bring them back. I really do. I just don't see how we can accommodate them given the limited space in the server. I'm sorry, but they'll have to stay, at least for now."

"That's alright," Tatyana spoke, flicking a small glare at Harrison. "Our current priority is leaving this planet before a Pulse renders us stranded and a robot kicks down our door. We don't have time for the twins right now."

"That's another question I have," said Harrison quickly. "Do we have any idea how Kubba knew the Killbot was still alive?"

From across the table, Ralph Marshall arched an eyebrow.

"I figured you'd already know the answer to that one, buddy."

"It's true," Tatyana cut in. "You and the doctor are the only two members of this team to have physically touched the alien device. If there was anyone who could understand her current state, it would be you. Perhaps if you speak with her, she will open up. Lord knows I get nowhere when I try."

"Did Amit at least give you an ETA for the Killbot?" asked Udo, his hand shaking slightly. "I mean, do we know when to expect it?"

"Yes," Tatyana frowned. "Amit has calculated that at its current pace, keeping in mind that it was damaged badly, it will arrive in eight days."

"That seems about right," sighed Harrison. "Doesn't that seem pretty perfect to you guys? I mean, it shows up the same day the Pulse is set to hit, which also just so happens to be the day that Earth and Mars line up. If I didn't know any better, I'd say someone is having a laugh at our expense."

"Like I told you," William spoke, his blue eyes trained on Harrison. "Everything has been too perfect to be passed off as coincidence. Remember what you said? You told me it was *fate*."

At this, the room went quiet with unease.

"Well, I don't know about any of that," said YiJay after a beat. "I mean, fate implies larger forces at work. Larger than us, that is. But that's just the thing. We're the ones activating the alien device, not some cosmic force. Like, you might not have put this together yet, but the simulator isn't actually *doing* anything at all. It's just a simulator. It was *us* that made the portal appear. *Our* brainwaves turned on the device."

Again, an eerie silence filled the air.

201

"Think about it," YiJay pressed. "I mean, really *think* about it. Why was the mini-Sun off when you and William went back for the device, Harrison?"

"I just figured it was knocked out by the Pulse," Harrison nearly whispered, his head prickling uncomfortably.

"Nope," stated YiJay in a matter-of-fact tone. "It was because Braun wasn't around to pick up on the pattern and react to it in a way the device could perceive. This thing, this piece of alien tech needs *you* to communicate with *it* before it will work. We can't see its energy pattern because our eyes aren't made for that kind of stuff. Braun's Eyes, on the other hand, were built for an intelligence whose interpretations of reality are only hindered by its capacity to understand them. All I've done with the simulator is take something we couldn't see, because our hardware wasn't designed for it, and bring it down to our level."

Glancing around at the stunned faces of her teammates, YiJay shrugged lightly and scooped oatmeal into her mouth.

"Simple as that," she said, mushing her words.

Onboard Braun

Onboard Braun, Amit Vyas hung weightlessly in the galley and stared at the swaying stalks of bamboo behind a wall made of glass. Alone in the empty spaceship save for these resilient plants, he was more isolated than he'd ever been in his entire life.

Checking his watch impulsively, he puffed up his cheeks and sighed. Amplified, the sound was nearly deafening in the absence of other noise and activity.

Erased in the last Pulse, all of Amit's music was gone, leaving him without entertainment.

Wishing he could figure out how to salvage the files, he'd had a song stuck in his head for days but couldn't remember the last half of it. Thus, repeating on a loop, the part of the tune he *could* recall was fast becoming an annoyance.

Still staring at the blinking face of his watch, Amit blinked slowly and began humming the song again, needing the distraction despite all of that.

It had now been exactly two hours and seventeen minutes since he'd sent the scans of the Killbot to Tatyana.

What was taking her so long to get back to him? What could possibly be more important than the fact that that *thing* was still on the move?

Pulling out his Tablet, Amit looked at the timecode there to make sure his watch was correct. It was.

Again blowing out a long breath, he swiped a fingertip over the screen, opening the set of photos he'd taken that morning. In each one, the Killbot moved a few feet across the desert floor.

Though hate was not an emotion Amit ever tried to hang onto, he felt it bubble up deeply from within him. He *hated* that Killbot, *hated* what it had done to the crew already, and *hated* what it still intended to do.

"We have to get out of here," he whispered to the empty room. "We can't keep fighting. We have to run."

Suddenly buzzing in his hand, Amit's Tablet lit up with the words *Incoming Transmission: Captain Tatyana Vodevski.*

Hastily accepting the call, Amit was surprised to see the little screen filled with a wide shot of the galley in the Base.

There, sitting around the table, were the rest of his teammates, except, of course, for Kubba. Painted with expressions ranging from deep confusion to tepid worry, they gazed back at him.

"Hello everyone," he said slowly. "Is everything alright? You all look like you've seen—well, I don't know, a ghost, perhaps?"

"I wish it was just that," Tatyana replied from her seat near the head of the table. "But I didn't call to discuss ghosts. I called because we are ready to put our plan in motion and we'd like to include you in the logistics."

After breakfast

After breakfast, Harrison climbed the stairs to the Base's second floor level and reflected on that morning's events.

Despite the fact that it had gotten off to a disjointed start, breakfast had actually turned out to be one of the more fruitful meetings of late. True, YiJay had thrown them all a curveball with her proclamation about the device, but since that didn't actually *change* any of their physical plans, they'd been able to move past it and keep their eyes on the prize.

Thoroughly hashing out the details with Amit onboard Braun, it had been decided that the team would open the two portals tomorrow at four PM when Phobos was rising in the east. That meant that the rest of *this* day and most of the *next* would be dedicated to getting things set up.

Aiming to depart the surface and rendezvous with Braun that night while the ship was overhead, Marshall and the captain were now downstairs suiting up. Before they could take off, supplies and extra fuel cells would need to be loaded into the Lander and an extensive preflight maintenance check preformed.

Because he had little else to do, Harrison had volunteered to help, though he first wanted to swing by his lab and change into his undersuit before joining the others outside.

Now walking down the narrow hallway of the second floor level, he passed Kubba's quarters on his way and paused. Oddly curious, he stood outside the door for a moment and listened to the sounds of her pacing back and forth.

Then, as if sensing his presence, she suddenly stopped.

"Harrison?" she whispered, her voice muted by the door. "Harrison, it's you. I know it. We need to talk."

Involuntarily, a stab of rage pierced the young Egyptian's heart. Kubba had not spoken directly to him since before she'd stolen the device. To his ears, her voice rang like nails on a chalkboard. Besides the fact that she had nearly killed YiJay, which was in and of itself deplorable, Marshall's confession about the doctor had also shed new light on other aspects of her recent actions.

For instance, the day before Liu died, Kubba had paid Harrison an uncharacteristic visit, convincing him that the Chinese astronaut needed *space* in their relationship. Of course, he now saw that the comment had actually been part of a clever plan to keep Liu from telling him about her pregnancy and not a true reflection of her feelings.

In short, Kubba had manipulated them, bent their lives to her will as if they were nothing more than blades of grass. All of it, all of the lies and violence were just schemes Kubba had concocted to protect herself.

"What do you want?" answered Harrison after a long pause.

"Please, we need to talk."

"I don't trust you, Elizabeth," he said evenly. "I'm afraid that if I open this door, you'll try to hurt me and the others."

At this, a charged silence permeated the air like humidity.

"I guess you must have talked to Ralph by now," Kubba finally responded. "You must know what I did to Liu—"

"Liu's death was an accident," Harrison interrupted.

204

"I know, but…" Kubba paused. "But the way she died, afraid that you didn't love her, that *was* my fault."

Cutting his anger like ice, an empty ache throbbed in Harrison's chest. Momentarily overwhelmed, he bit back on feelings he had worked hard to make peace with. Even though he now believed that Liu still existed in some other time and place, her death in *this* reality was still an injustice to him.

"Please, Harrison," pressed Kubba. "I want to make things right. I want to be a better person. Please, I need to talk to you about the robot, about what it's really here for. You're the only one who will understand. Please. *Please.*"

Swimming in a mixture of complex emotions, Harrison's head began to prickle. Something about the urgency in Kubba's tone told him that she was not just concerned with surviving. Below the words, below what they meant, there was an energy that reached out to him.

"Stand back," he ordered. "If you make a move, if you attack me, I'll fight back as hard as I can. I'll go for your eyes, Elizabeth, your throat. Do you understand?"

"Yes," Kubba spoke quickly.

Gathering himself up, Harrison retracted the bolt and opened the door. A few paces from the entrance, in a grey tank top with her jumpsuit rolled down to the waist, Elizabeth Kubba stood straightly.

Dark skin glistening with perspiration, her eyes were as stark as black diamonds in pools of fresh white snow. Long and wiry, the muscles on her arms flexed and trembled as if pricked by electric shocks.

"Thank you," she said taking a step forward.

"Don't," warned Harrison, holding up a hand. "Don't come any closer to me."

Casting her eyes down, Kubba nodded and stayed where she was.

"I'm so, so sorry—" she began.

"Save it, Elizabeth," Harrison waved, cutting her off. "What can you tell me about the Killbot? I'm guessing you knew it was still alive because you had a vision. Am I right?"

"Yes," Kubba nodded.

"Well, don't get too comfortable with all of that. It wears off after a while."

Exhaling what seemed to have been a long pent-up breath, Kubba's face split in a wide smile.

"Really? Oh, thank God! I can't keep up like this. First it's voices, then it's visions. I'm not equipped to handle these kinds of things. No one is."

"I would think as a psychologist you'd be more than equipped to handle your own fucking mental state," said Harrison, nearly spitting the words in Kubba's face.

Stung, she flicked him a tepid glance.

"I deserve all of that and more," she whispered. "But right now, right here in this place and this time, I can still do some good. I can help, Harrison."

"How?"

Frowning, the tall doctor took a few steps back and leaned against the bare wall.

"When I saw the robot in my vision, I connected with it."

"Connected with it?" repeated Harrison. "What do you mean?"

Shrugging, Kubba tilted her head as if trying to shake the right words free.

"It's alive, Harrison," she said. "Maybe not by our standards, but it *is* alive nonetheless. In my vision, I connected with *that* part of it—that small *living* part."

"I don't see how this is helpful," Harrison returned, reaching for the door to close it.

"Wait!" cried Kubba. "I'm getting to that part. Just, please, wait. When I connected with it, I saw what it wants, why it's here."

"Again," said Harrison. "I don't see how this is helpful. We already know why the Chinese sent their little welcome party. They wanted the Base and the ruins to themselves. The Killbot is just acting out that program now that it has no handlers."

"No," Kubba replied, shaking her head. "That's what I'm trying to tell you. The Chinese didn't send their team to take over the Base, and they don't even care about the damn ruins."

Feeling that strange blizzard-like prickle at the top of his head, Harrison kept his green eyes fixed on Kubba and waited for her to go on.

"They want the alien device," she said. "And that robot won't stop until it takes it from us. No matter what, it won't stop."

The red-eye

Bathed in the Base's harsh exterior floodlights, Lander 2 stood like a great white beetle in the sand. With stars wheeling overhead and the two moons of Mars in full profile, the time had come for Marshall and Tatyana to leave the surface and ascend to Braun.

Joined by Harrison and William, they now trudged back and forth from the airlock to the Lander with armfuls of cable and other equipment needed to carry out YiJay's plan.

"Remember," William was saying, his blue tinted visor glowing slightly from the Augmented Vision. "You'll need to run the *triple* insulated wire from the Transmitter Dish to the server in the ship. I can't stress enough how important that is."

"I know," grunted Tatyana, taking the bundle of thick wires from the German. "You've told me over and over."

"Right," William went on, not really hearing the captain. "So once you've *properly* wired the Dish, just set its Receive Signature to match the Send Signature of the Uplink Transmitter down here."

Gesturing to the starkly lit Coms Tower, he held up his fingers and counted off a series of numbers.

"That's 442-513, okay, 442-513. Got that? It's 442—"

"Enough!" snapped Tatyana. "We're going to Phobos, not Jupiter! If I have any questions, I'll simply call you and ask."

Nodding absently, William lifted a long flat box up into the open Lander.

"Sure, totally. Now, when you're setting up the Transmitter Dish, keep in mind that though it may look delicate, it's actually very sturdy. However just to be safe, I recommend setting the torque low on the drill when you're bolting it together so that the vibrations don't damage the fiber optics. I'd say anywhere from two to two-point-five foot pounds ought to do it. Now, as for the server…"

And so it went, the small group working under the nonstop chatter of William until the only a case of freshly charged Survival Packs was left to be loaded. When that was done, they divided in half: Harrison and William with their backs to the Base, Marshall and Tatyana with theirs to the open Lander.

For a long moment, no one spoke. Not even William.

"Well," said Harrison, breaking the silence and extending a gloved hand to Marshall. "Good luck, buddy."

Shaking it with vigorous jerks, Marshall cleared the glowing tint from his visor and smiled. Though wide and toothy, his expression seemed more like a grimace than a look of happiness.

"We'll get Braun back," he stammered, addressing both William and Harrison. "We'll pull him out of there and have the ship ready by the time I come back for you guys. I won't leave you here. I won't."

"Of course," nodded Harrison. "We'll see you soon."

Saluting the two explorers, Tatyana put on her most captainly voice.

"*Dos vidaniya*. Goodbye and be safe. We're very close to realizing our goals. Let's not make any mistakes now."

Returning the captain's salute, William and Harrison stepped back from the Lander as she and Marshall climbed aboard. Framed in the open door, the pilot hesitated then waved once more to his friends.

Grinning up with forced lightheartedness, Harrison nodded again and waved back. Burdened by everything he had learned that day, both from YiJay and Kubba, he was finding it very hard to stay grounded in the here and now.

Thoughts kept swirling about his mind, dividing and expanding as if the quantum blizzard were actually contained inside his snow globe of a skull and not the universe at large.

In the open doorway, Marshall saw none of this, for his own nerves were badly strained by an entirely different set of worries.

With nothing left to do but that for which he was trained, he tossed a final glance at the glowing Dome, the living Greenhouse, and his friends before slamming the hatch.

"Okay," he said to himself. "Time to fly. No big deal. Done it tons of times."

Already buckled into her crash seat, Tatyana looked over her shoulder. "Shall I start the preflight egress?"

Standing with his hand still on the hatch lock, Marshall did not immediately answer.

"Marshall?" Tatyana repeated. "Do you want me to start the egress?"

Stirring, Marshall turned and made his way slowly up the aisle towards the cockpit. With each step he took, a deep sense of anxiety thrummed in his bones.

Stiffly, for his ribs were still mending, he slid into his crash seat and brought up the preflight checklist.

"Fuel?" he said robotically, reading the first item on the list.

"Check," echoed Tatyana, consulting the screen in front of her.

"Cabin pressure?"

Entering a quick command, Tatyana initiated the Lander's life-support systems.

"Check," she answered.

Purring to life, pumps in the belly of the small craft immediately began to blast jets of breathable O2 from vents on the floor. As they waited for the pressure-indicator light to turn green, the two astronauts completed the rest of the egress without any wasted words.

Ready with his finger poised above the engine ignition key, Marshall took a long thin breath and held it. Closing his eyes, he tried to picture all the times he'd done this—both in training and during actual missions. Unable to count, he drew from a dwindling reserve of confidence and let his finger drop.

Rumbling as they wound up, the turbines vibrated the ship rhythmically, their power ramping higher until it rattled the teeth in Marshall's jaw.

Hands on the controls, he hesitated.

"Okay?" asked Tatyana, her fingers drumming impatiently on her knees.

Behind the protective shield of his visor, Marshall licked his dry lips.

"Yes," he said at last, his voice like that of a different man.

Punching up the thrusters, he pulled back on the controls and felt the Lander leave the ground.

Though shaken to his core by the death of Viviana, Marshall knew that such fear would not help him now. Flying was about freedom, about letting go. If he allowed the death of Viviana to weigh on him too heavily, it would end up being an arrow in his wing.

Trembling slightly, he tightened his grip around the controls as if they were something he could choke the life out of. Only a few meters from the ground, both the Lander and the man piloting it hung in a sort of limbo.

"Ralph," spoke Tatyana, sliding her visor up so she could address him directly. "You were right before when you said I didn't understand all the losses you've been through. But I'm here with you now. We're in this together, you and I."

Issuing a hesitant nod, Marshall took several more deep breaths then relaxed his grip on the controls.

"Flying is about freedom," Tatyana went on. "That's what Joey used to say, at least. So tell me, Ralph. Are you free?"

Answering not with words but with actions, Marshall reached out and jammed the throttle forward.

Like a champagne cork breaking free of the bottle, Lander 2 rocketed towards the starry sky, leaving a trail of vaporized hydrogen in its wake.

CHAPTER TWENTY-THREE

Improvement and growth

As Lander 2 raced towards the membrane that separated the thin Martian atmosphere from the vacuum of space, YiJay Lee descended the stairs down to her makeshift lab.

Passing through the door, she caught her reflection in the mirror-like surface of a wall Tablet. Unable to look away, she stared at her still-bruised face and tried to become angry over the loss of her eye. However, though it was upsetting, such things just seemed utterly unimportant to her now.

She had seen the lines of time, gazed at the patterns that governed the lives of kings, poets, planets, and suns. To her, life had become something she could finally understand. No longer an unpredictable mess of what-ifs, her future was assured.

Nature wasn't chaotic. It was programmable.

"Ilia?" she called to the empty room.

"Hello, YiJay," return the AI.

Glancing at the special bank of insulated servers, the Korean smiled. "Are you getting excited for your mission?"

"Yes, I am," Ilia replied.

"Are you at all afraid?"

There was a characteristic pause as Ilia processed the heady question.

"I'm less afraid than I am curious," she said at last. "And I want to be helpful more than anything in the world."

Dropping onto a stool, YiJay closed her good eye and nodded thoughtfully.

"That's a very mature thing to say. It shows that you understand danger yet have the ability to weigh risks against benefits. I'm pleased by this, Ilia. It's a sign of maturity."

"Thank you for saying so," answered Ilia. "Since you and Dr. Konig—"

"William, dear," YiJay interrupted. "His name is William."

"I'm sorry," resumed Ilia. "Since you and *William* began your work together, I have discovered a sense of purpose, which in turn, gives me cause to explore myself more. Do you think this is a result of the modifications you made to me or something that has transpired organically?"

211

"Would you like me to perform another Personality Matrix Interface Test?" YiJay offered. "We could see if any measurable growth has taken place, maybe prove that you aren't as broken as I first thought."

"That would be fun!"

"Good," smiled YiJay, reaching for a nearby Tablet. "Please begin whenever you are ready."

"A is for ancient," Ilia started, listing Braun's old inputted word association for the letter A. "And A is also for alien."

Grinning wider than she thought possible, YiJay noted that the last time she'd performed a PMIT on Ilia, the AI had said, *"A is for art."*

There's improvement right off the bat, thought YiJay hopefully. Maybe we aren't the *only* ones being changed by the device's desire to communicate.

A few minutes later, with the test complete, YiJay scanned down the list and nearly laughed out loud. Where before there had only been six word associations to separate Ilia from Braun, now there were seventeen. This was more than improvement. It was miraculous.

"Ilia?" she spoke, prying her eye away from the screen. "I'm showing much more growth than I was expecting, which is strange since I've actually been sort of neglecting you these last weeks. I'd like to look a little deeper into your coding, see if there's been spontaneous regeneration of the damaged Open-Code Connection Cells. Is that alright with you?"

"Of course, YiJay," responded Ilia.

"Great. I'm just going to let the failsafe timer run out then I'll begin."

"Okay."

Although it was only five seconds long, to YiJay, the timer seemed to drag on for hours. When finally the numbers reached 0:00, the fractal pattern that represented Ilia's being disappeared from the Tablet screen in her hands.

Quickly opening a series of folders, she flooded her eye with numbers and codes. Complex beyond what most could comprehend, the equations that formed Ilia were child's play to her now. After all of the work she'd done with Braun's memoires and the simulator, Ilia was an easy nut to crack.

Like an ancient map of the world updated by the latest conquest, Ilia's being had expanded since YiJay had last checked. With previously dormant Open-Code Connection Cells now forming new pathways, she seemed to be taking on a life of her own—a life that YiJay could claim no credit for enriching. Either the alien device was, in fact, having a curative effect on Ilia, or AIs in general were far more capable of self-repair than even YiJay had guessed.

Alaska—Seven days until the Pulse

As a heavy snow fell in swarming flurries, James Floyd and his family, along with hundreds of others, descended ramps from the USS Rainier onto a shipping dock outside of Nome, Alaska.

Overcast and imposing, the sky was the same metallic grey as the choppy ocean. Crashing against the dock, waves sent spews of cold salty mist into the air where it was immediately swept away.

Arranged in rows so that only one clear path was presented, stacked shipping containers funneled the throngs of moving bodies like cattle as they came off the ramps. Leading towards a huge warehouse at the other end of the dock, the containers were piled up so high they may as well have been walls.

With everyone pressed together and all moving in the same direction, an air of panic seemed to hover just beneath the surface.

Nervous that his small girls might get trampled if the mood shifted too quickly, James clutched their hands and held them close.

Thankfully, men in black fatigues with automatic rifles peppered the crowd, helping to maintain order with quick commands and stern faces.

"My God," Nora whispered, hugging James's arm. "There're so many people! Who are they, James? Who are all of these people?"

Looking around at the faces, James was able to pick out a few he'd seen on TV or even in person.

"That guy over there is the Senate Majority Leader. And her, right there, that's the Deputy Chief of Off Earth Resources. I've had to sit in on some meetings with her. She's a real peach. And there, that's Leonard Bailey, big shit in the wind farm industry, pretty much has a lot of these people in his pocket. Let's see who else—"

Nearing the aircraft hanger, the crowd suddenly surged forward, making further conversation momentarily impossible. Jostled by all the people pushing to get inside, James and his family linked hands and concentrated on staying together.

Because the hanger's doors were not fully open, a bottleneck formed at the entry, causing the men in black fatigues to work doubly hard at keeping order.

When finally James, Nora, and the girls reached the head of the crowd, they were squeezed through with several other bodies then ushered towards the center of the hanger where another group already waited.

Blocking all of the windows and reinforcing the walls, shipping containers were stacked from floor to ceiling making the space inside the warehouse smaller than it appeared from the outside.

"Straight ahead," shouted a man in black with a gun. "Form a line straight ahead and don't push. The ramp is steep. We don't want any injuries. Straight ahead folks, come on. Let's all be civil now!"

Following the slow-moving torrent of people, James and his family joined the crowd in the center of the hanger.

Ahead, near the front of the growing mass, two more soldiers were swinging open the doors of an unmarked container, its hinges squealing loudly.

Even from where he was standing, James could easily see that the thing was no ordinary shipping container. Instead of ending at the back like normal, it fed down into a tunnel that disappeared underground.

"Okay," called one of the soldiers. "Don't shove. There's plenty of time."

At this, the crowd jostled forward again, everyone pushing with and against one another to get into the tunnel.

Using his bony elbows to jab at any person who tried to come between him and his family, James fought to maintain a bubble of breathing room around them. Amidst the confusion, a hand suddenly came out of the crowd to close around his upper arm.

Glancing in the direction of the hindrance, James was met with the face of a middle-aged Chinese man. Wearing horn-rimmed glasses and with a stylish haircut, the man was short and well-dressed underneath his open parka.

"Dr. Floyd?" he said quickly in a thick accent. "My name is Dr. Gan Song. I would like to speak with you as soon as possible."

"What do you want?" replied James distractedly, battling to keep his grip on his wife's hand. "I'm kind of busy right now."

"Please, Dr. Floyd," the man stressed. "You and I are not so different. We must discuss this fact as soon as possible."

214

Materializing in the gap between them, a Secret Serviceman stepped in, cutting the two men off from one another.

"Keep moving," the man said, giving James a little push.

Catching Gan Song's eye before the crowd swept him down the tunnel at the back of the shipping container, James held his gaze then nodded.

On the Bridge Deck—Sol 130

On the Bridge Deck of Braun, Ralph Marshall floated in front of the long oval-shaped window and stared out at Phobos. Not yet bathed in the Sun's rays, he had to squint hard just to keep the little moon in his sights. Silent, cold, and utterly devoid of beauty, Phobos was like a vulture that hung low over the dusty red carcass of Mars.

Yawning despite himself, Marshall closed his eyes and stretched.

After docking with the ship late the previous evening, he and the captain had gotten no chance to rest. Met at the airlock by Amit, they'd headed straight for the bridge where their control stations were already online and waiting for them.

"Sorry to rush you," Amit had said apologetically. "But we have an opportunity to save a bit of fuel, and I'd rather not waste it."

In order to keep their timeline with the ground crew, Braun's orbit had to be changed so that Phobos was always within range. Because it hugged Mars so closely, Phobos actually ended up circling the planet twice a day at speeds much greater than the ship. This fact, combined with limited time, pushed the team to break Braun's carefully plotted orbit to chase the ugly rock.

Executing the maneuver flawlessly, Amit had first swung Braun's nose around with bursts from the Side-Stabilizing Rocket Engines. Then, punching up the speed, he'd used nearly all of the remaining fuel in the forward thrusters to set them in an orbit that closely shadowed the moon.

Now, enjoying his second sunrise in four hours, Marshall felt warming yellow light break across the curved horizon of Mars and seep in through his closed eyelids.

"Feels good, doesn't it?" came a voice behind him.

Remembering how Amit loved to sneak up on people, Marshall grinned.

"It sure does."

"I do the same thing every day at least once," said the Indian. "I like to pretend that I'm home sunbathing in my garden. If your eyes are closed and your memory is good enough, you can *almost* fool yourself."

Chuckling, Marshall turned around to face Amit.

"So your garden back home is zero-G? That's pretty neat. How much did that set you back?"

Amit shook his head and grinned. "Always with a quick line. You never get old, Ralph. I'll give you that."

For a moment, the two men appraised one another then both began to laugh.

"It's good to see you back here," said Amit, embracing Marshall. "I was worried when I heard about the crash and your accident. I would have brought it up last night, but we had to act fast with the orbital break."

"Don't mention it," Marshall shrugged. "The way I see it, we'll have plenty of time to swap war stories on the ride home."

Frowning, Amit made a sorry face. "I'm afraid I won't have many to contribute. My time up here has been mostly uneventful compared to your adventures on the surface. Tell me, are the caves more impressive than their photos and scans make them seem?"

"Immensely so," Marshall replied.

"I thought as much," nodded Amit sadly. "Too bad they're down there, and I'm up here. Alas, adventure seems always just out of my reach."

Allowing a beat to pass, Marshall produced his Tablet and held it out for Amit.

"Hook that up, will you? I want to show you something."

Perplexed, Amit took the Tablet and pushed lightly off the railing towards the right side of the room. Slipping the device into a docking port, he synced it with the Smart Glass of the observation window.

"Okay," he said. "What now?"

"Pull up the file titled, '*PHBS 3D.*'"

Skittering his fingers across the Tablet, Amit located the file then double-tapped it.

As if misting over with black ice, the view from the observation window went dark. A second later, a somewhat grainy 3D scan of Phobos began to appear in the center of the screen.

"Slide your finger from left to right," prompted Marshall.

Wordlessly, Amit did as he was instructed.

Cut seamlessly into a detailed cross-section, the image of Phobos revised itself.

Falling open despite the zero gravity, Amit's mouth gaped.

Beginning in the pit of Stickney Crater, a long straight hallway proceeded to bore directly into the center of Phobos's mass. There, like some cosmic joke, a strangely circular room sat waiting to be explored.

Shadowy due to the imperfect scans, mysterious objects filled the chamber, their origins as tantalizing as anything yet found on Mars.

"Do you see what I see?" said Marshall.

"W-what?" Amit stammered.

"Adventure," whispered Marshall. "I see adventure."

United

"Step back from the door, Elizabeth," ordered Harrison.

Standing outside Kubba's quarters on Ilia Base, he held a bowl of cereal in one hand and a measure of titanium pipe in the other.

"I want to bring you some breakfast and to talk, but first I need you to put your back against the far wall."

From inside the room, the sound of feet moving quickly across the floor could be heard.

"Okay," answered Kubba. "I'm against the wall."

Taking a steadying breath, Harrison reminded himself why he was doing this and unlocked the door.

He needed answers, needed to peel back the layers of what Kubba had told him about the Killbot to see if there really was something to it or if she was just up to her old tricks again.

True to her word, the door swung open to reveal Kubba standing against the opposite wall, her face hopeful.

"I'm so glad you've decided to listen to me. Have you already spoken with the others? How much longer do you think I'll be locked up? I mean, I know what I did was wrong, but I wasn't really in my right mind, now was I?"

Shaking his head, Harrison set the bowl of cereal down on the floor and slid it across the room to where Kubba stood.

Soymilk slopped out over the edges as she bent to retrieve it, leaving a spattering of white on the ground.

"Well," she asked again. "What's the verdict? Am I free? Are the others caught up to date?"

"I haven't told anyone what you said to me," spoke Harrison, his features set.

"But why not?" balked Kubba, drinking directly from the bowl since Harrison had not included a spoon.

"Because I'm not even sure I believe you."

At this, the doctor dipped her eyes and swallowed. Setting the empty bowl back on the ground, she pushed it gently with her foot so that it slid back to Harrison.

"I understand that you have certain feelings towards me, Harrison," she said after a few beats. "But you and I both know that I'm telling the truth. Have I lied in the past? Yes. Should you punish me for that? Yes, absolutely. However, don't punish me for it by ignoring me when I tell the truth. Don't let your emotions overrule what you know is right. Trust the powers the device gave you."

Sighing in frustration, Harrison ran a hand through his shock of black hair.

"That's just the thing. I *can't* trust those powers because I *can't* connect with them anymore. I don't know what's happened, Elizabeth, but the visions have stopped. The light is out. Do you understand? It's gone."

Harrison snapped his fingers violently.

"Now all I'm left with is a dim recollection of the things I saw, a kind of tingling in my head."

Staring at him silently, Kubba watched his eyes.

"I'm already leaning so heavily on faith that my whole world is out of balance," he muttered. "I need some proof, something more to go on than just your word."

Slowly, Kubba parted herself from the wall and took a careful step forward.

Suddenly at attention, Harrison held up the length of pipe.

"Don't," he warned.

Taking another step, Kubba spread her arms in a nonthreatening gesture.

"It's alright," she whispered.

"Stop," protested Harrison, an edge of something cracking in his voice. "Just stop."

However, with two more steps, Kubba had closed the gap between them and was resting a hand on either side of the young Egyptian's head.

218

"It's alright," she said again, gazing deeply into his eyes. "It's going to be alright."

Then, as if pulled in two, Harrison suddenly felt himself separate. A spark of pure static energy, he arced wildly, plunging headlong into the doctor's mind. Swept away down the twisting tunnels of her memory, he merged with her and she with him in a torrent of exchange.

Arriving together at the edges of a vision, they punctured the divide, flying low over the purple night desert.

Bound to the wind, they came the spot where Aguilar had died, leaping to the ground like the chill that precedes a shadow. One and the same with each other, they gazed about, drinking up the stars in a spiraling play of light and darkness.

Having only been connected this deeply with another person through sex, Harrison enjoyed the feeling of being together with Kubba on a level that was somehow equally basic. True to their transference, she too elated in the experience and, as a result, a circular equilibrium of positivity was reached.

Only able to fully enjoy themselves for a very brief moment, a muted scratching sound slowly drew their attention away from the beauty of their synchronicity.

Turning, they watched the mound of rubble that had once been the mouth of a canyon began to shift.

Suddenly, in an explosion of rocks and dust, 04 the Chinese Automated War Machine burst forth from the ground in a frenzy. Becoming frozen in that moment, Harrison saw past the twisted metal of the damaged robot to the living monster within. Exactly as Kubba had told him, he felt the searing heat of its singular mission.

So powerful that it drove 04's will to live, that mission—that desire to complete its programming—burned into Harrison's mind via cosmic osmosis.

Kubba had been telling the truth. It *was* there for the device.

Snapped painfully back into his body like man drenched with cold water, Harrison's legs buckled and he stumbled.

He was in Kubba's room again, separated from her but not alone.

"Holy shit," he breathed, sliding down the wall for support as he sat on the floor.

On her hands and knees before him, Kubba gulped at the air and turned her head from side to side.

"What was that?" Harrison demanded, slowly regaining his wits. "How did you do that?"

"I don't know," Kubba managed. "It just came to me, like a—a voice in my head, only it didn't speak. Something said that it was the right thing to do, so I did it."

Processing this, Harrison was briefly compelled to disbelieve the doctor. However, like a fading dream, the feeling of oneness they'd shared dispelled the notion.

She wasn't lying to him. Not anymore.

"Alright," he said at last. "I believe you. I believe you."

Resting back on her knees, Kubba fixed him with a penetrating stare.

"What are we going to do? How can we stop it?"

"I don't know yet," replied Harrison. "But luckily for us, I have some very smart friends who might be able to help."

CHAPTER TWENTY-FOUR

Things get tricky—Sol 130

Suited up and buckled in, Marshall, Tatyana, and Amit waited patiently as the blast shutters drew open on Lander 2.

With the egress complete and Phobos hanging in the distance, Marshall's nerves hummed in time with the Lander's idling engines.

"Alright, Captain," he said, his confidence forced. "Go ahead and bring up the main window A-Vision, will you? This landing is going to be tricky."

Doing as she was asked, Tatyana typed quickly at the Flight Console. Like a celestial connect-the-dots puzzle, wispy lines of data began to fill the screen where once there had been only space.

From the first row of crash seats, Amit leaned forward.

"Excuse me, but what did you mean by, '*tricky?*'"

Chuckling to mask his stress, Marshall was grateful for the reflection of his tinted helmet visor. He didn't want Tatyana to see that he was still shaken from his crash, didn't want her to suspect that he was anything but one hundred percent in control.

"Well, buddy," he said. "Since Phobos has less gravity than a rat turd, putting us down on her is going to require some finesse."

Amit did not respond but shrank back into his seat a little.

"Fear not, Amit," reassured Tatyana. "Ralph and Joey were able to land on each section of the Ark when we first arrived, and those had far less mass than Phobos. This will be just like that. Eh, Lieutenant?"

Marshall tipped his head from side to side, cracking his neck.

"Yep," he said after a beat. "It'll be just like that."

Reaching out, he popped a series of switches, releasing the electromagnetic chassis hook, which secured the Lander to Braun. Free-floating for a second, the ship bobbed in the Landing Bay like a leaf on the water.

Then, with a hand that trembled only slightly, Marshall eased the throttle forward.

"We're clear of the bay in three, two, one—"

Dialing up the boosters to full power, he hovered his finger above the ignition.

Are you free? he asked himself. Are you?

"Yes," he whispered, punching the key hard. "Yes, I am."

As silently as a shooting star, Lander 2 streaked away from Braun and into space.

For several long moments no one spoke, their white pressure suits painted in washes of red, green, and blue by the lights that emanated from the digital projections on the window. Making it look as though they were flying through a rainbow rather than cold tundra of empty space, the effect would have been beautiful under different circumstances.

Following the glowing line of his flight path, Marshall gazed at Phobos in the distance. A man standing at the edge of his own unfolding future, his mind swam with questions about what lay ahead. Be there perils or prizes, he couldn't guess. Yet he knew for certain that whatever they were going to find on Phobos, it would be absolutely unlike anything he could possibly imagine now.

Beside him, Tatyana too waded through deep waters. This mission was important to her beyond the obvious reasons. Besides being linked to their mortal survival, it was also her chance for redemption.

Four people had died under her command, and the rest were now clinging to a mere whisper of a hope as a result.

Because it had been *she* who'd signed off on Braun's decoding of the signal and because it had been *she* who had forced Julian to undertake the covert bombing of the Chinese Ark, they were all in dire straits. *She* was the captain. *She* was the person to whom all responsibility for all events, good or bad, fell.

As such, this mission meant more to Tatyana than she even consciously knew. Unlit in the back of her mind, the ship's Nuclear Torch Engine sat waiting to be ignited, waiting to burn away the darkness and carry her tattered flock home.

Growing by the second in the window, Phobos gradually came into range of the Lander's Augmented Vision and began to glitter with a myriad of digital projections. Like a dead tree strewn with ornaments and lights, the little moon twinkled to life.

"It almost looks beautiful," spoke Tatyana, stirred from her brooding silence.

Overlapping the grey moon, colorful projections began to outline craters and cracks, embossing names over them and providing topographical data.

"So many impacts," Amit said, nervously hugging his elbows. "Hope it doesn't get pelted while we're there."

"The odds for such an event are astronomical," returned Tatyana.

At this, Marshall snorted sarcastically.

"Right, Cap', because defying the odds isn't something we've ever done, is it?"

Chuckling softly, Tatyana held up two fingers and crossed them.

"Well," she said. "My fingers are crossed, at least."

"Mine too," echoed Amit. "And so are my toes."

Banking the Lander away from the moon to loop back for a second pass, Marshall grinned.

"My fingers have been crossed since we left Earth. I'm going for the record!"

Slowly coming into view as the ship leveled out again, the words *Stickney Crater* danced across the window, sobering the mood quickly.

"There it is," pointed Tatyana.

Aiming towards the gaping bowl, Marshall tagged it with the ship's Automated Tracking Software then curved off into space.

"Alright," he announced. "I'm going to line us up for a landing. Smoke 'em if you got 'em."

On the ground

On the ground, Harrison Assad, William Konig, and YiJay Lee were in the airlock of Ilia Base.

Hands held together, YiJay and William gazed at one another through the clear glass of their helmets as Harrison turned the pressure equalizer near the exit.

Above the hatch, a bright light flicked from red to green, signifying that it was safe to open the airlock.

Glancing back at his companions, Harrison felt a pang of envy. Once, long before everything had warped and changed, he and Liu had looked at each other the same way.

"Ready, you two?" he said, breaking their spell.

"Ready," they replied in unison.

As he swung the hatch open, a gust of Martian wind blew heavy sand into the small space. Like the jet of debris cast off when 04 had escaped its tomb, the cloud engulfed Harrison and made him feel vulnerable.

Though he knew that the Killbot was somewhere far, far off in the distance, he quickly stepped into the early evening haze and scanned the horizon just to be safe. If that thing came while they were in possession of the device, it would kill them all to get it.

223

Seeing nothing out of the ordinary, Harrison turned and reached back into the airlock. There on the floor beside the hatch was the hard-shelled carrying case containing the alien device.

Picking it up, he studied the horizon once more with careful eyes before moving away into the open.

Close behind, William and YiJay carried between them a portable Holo Projector. Nothing more than a piece of rectangular glass mounted to a shallow frame, the projector was a fragile-looking thing made of special fiber optics and digital 3D image converters.

Never intended for use in such harsh conditions, William had tinkered with it all the previous day, making sure it was fit for use outside the Dome.

"Let's set it right over there," YiJay nodded, directing William to a spot some five meters from the Coms Tower.

Placing the projector lightly on the ground, they sank long anchors from each corner into the soft sand, securing them as best they could.

When that was done, William turned to face the Coms Tower, holding out his wrist Tablet. Double tapping the screen, he danced his nimble fingers across it, bringing up a list of the Tower's dishes. Again double-tapping, he selected B7.

Located near the top, above most of the other dishes, B7 was by far the largest. Below it, welded directly to the frame with a fine bead, was William's Uplink Transmitter.

Engaging the motors that directed B7, William began manipulating them by moving the tips of his fingers around on the screen. Soon, with several careful adjustments, he had the dish pointed directly at the Holo Projector.

"Okay, I'm all set here," he reported. "Just say the word, and I'll turn on the Transmitter."

Producing the Tablet, which contained the simulator, YiJay glanced over her shoulder at Harrison.

A few paces off, his eyes still glued to the jagged horizon, the young Egyptian did not immediately hear as his name was called over and over. Like the embers of a distant bonfire, bits of Kubba's vision kept catching in the dark parts of his mind, distracting him from the present moment.

"Harrison!" radioed YiJay again. "Earth to Harrison, wake up! We don't have time to mess around right now. You in there?"

224

"Yeah, sorry," he suddenly answered, shaking his head to clear to away the echoes. "Um, where should I put it?

"Put it on the projector," said YiJay. "Anywhere will do."

Walking over, Harrison dropped to one knee and popped the clasps on the little case. Carefully, he tipped its contents out onto the flat glass of the Holo Projector and stepped back. As if anticipating its part in all of this, the alien device rolled almost to the middle of the glass then came to an eerily abrupt stop.

"I think it's as ready as we are," breathed YiJay, her good eye flashing behind her helmet visor.

"Speak for yourself," Harrison muttered, gaze again returned to the desert beyond.

The fall

From where he was sitting in the first row of crash seats, Amit Vyas had an open view of the Lander's cockpit. Watching in combined terror and awe, his eyes darted from Marshall to Tatyana as each one feverishly entered keystrokes and flipped switches on the Flight Console.

Slightly ahead of Phobos, having overtaken it in their final flyby, now only empty space filled the window before them.

But that was all about to change.

"Set stabilizing thrusters to six percent," Marshall barked, tweaking the controls forward. "I'm bringing us in."

Outside, the view suddenly blurred drastically as the nose of the Lander dropped ninety degrees.

"Hold on," the pilot grunted, pulling back. "Hold on."

As instantly as it had begun, the movement stopped like clockwork.

Though strapped tightly in his seat, the G force of the maneuver made Amit feel as though he had sparkling water in his brain. Blinking rapidly, the Indian shook his head to keep himself from passing out.

"Sorry," said Marshall, shaking his own helmeted head. "Had to be done."

Now hanging directly above the bowl of Stickney Crater, the Lander was facing *down* at Mars so that the entire window was full of red desert.

"Twenty meters from crater floor," called Tatyana. "How would you like to proceed?"

"Carefully," Marshall replied. "I want to go slow until I can actually see the damn thing. I hate flying blind like this without an AI."

Placing his hand on the throttle, Marshall moved it gently, causing the Lander to drop towards Phobos at an alarmingly fast pace.

Despite the fact that he himself was a pilot of spaceships, Amit found the shift in perspective very jarring. Because they were moving against Mars's rotation, dropping *horizontally* towards a target on the front of Phobos, the whole scene felt like an optical illusion.

"Fifteen meters," Tatyana reported.

Drifting into the frame from the bottom of the window, dead grey rock marked the rim of the impact basin that was Stickney Crater. As Mars sank below the shallow horizon, the light within the Lander began to shift from rusty brown to deep blue shadows.

"Okay, we're in the crater," breathed Marshall, his words soft as if they might ruin the landing.

Again, Amit's mind tried to readjust itself to the crazy perspective. They were no longer backing up, as it had seemed before but rather *falling* towards the ground now.

Finding the need to constantly establish what was up and what was down too taxing when such things were illusions to begin with, Amit simply gave up and held on for the ride.

"Ten meters," spoke Tatyana. "Just give me the word and I'll—"

At once, an explosion of light and sound raced across the Flight Console. Blaring deafeningly, nearly every alarm in the ship kicked on, battering the explorers mercilessly.

Then, like a string of firecrackers, many of the projections on the cockpit window popped brightly and went blank. What ones remained began to twist and pixilate as if some kind of electromagnetic field were interfering with the equipment onboard.

"What's happening?" Tatyana cried, frantically trying to reestablish the Lander's A-Vision.

Trembling, the ship bucked hard then groaned, its Alon frame protesting whatever force was attacking it. Outside the window, the once-slow downward procession was speeding up, cold rock now streaking past in a blur.

"We're falling," yelled Marshall, already working to ramp up the Lander's boosters. "Phobos is drawing us in!"

"How?" Amit heard himself say above the din of alarms.

"Gravity," shot Marshall, jerking back on the controls with one hand while hitting the afterburners with the other.

"Gravity?" Amit screamed. "What gravity?"

"Five meters!" Tatyana shouted. "Brace for impact."

Shaking his head, Marshall worked the controls deftly, applying stabilizer jets to counterbalance the powerful landing boosters.

"Come on! Come on!" he roared, slamming a hand down on the landing gear release.

Clanking loudly, the insect-like legs swung free then pistoned out to meet the fast-approaching crater floor.

As plumes of grey dust whirled into the air outside the window, the Lander's powerful jets drove down against the powdery frozen ground with fire and smoke.

Checking the altimeter one last time, Marshall swore.

"Hold tight," he warned. "We're coming in hot! This is going to be rough!"

Punching up the burners again, he fired them hard causing the ship to reverse its downward pitch in the last second before impact.

Thrown forward, and then jerked savagely to the right, the three astronauts clung to their crash seats as the Lander bounced and slid across the basin of the crater.

Finally, rocking back on its strained landing gears, the little craft shuddered and came to a complete stop.

CHAPTER TWENTY-FIVE

Phobos—Sol 130

"Everyone alright?" asked Marshall, his hands wrapped so tightly around the controls that his fingers popped as he pried them free.

"*Da*," whispered Tatyana, trembling imperceptibly.

From the first row of crash seats, Amit looked up and nodded slowly.

"I might have thrown up in my helmet a little," he admitted.

Releasing his seatbelt, Marshall stood and swept his eyes about the cabin. Structurally, everything looked okay. No cracks. No shredded metal.

Satisfied, he took a step forward and winced, putting a hand to his injured side.

"There's a full G here," he said. "Or at least pretty close. Feels like back home."

Already experiencing waves of discomfort, Amit and Tatyana both felt more harshly the effects of heightened gravity. After all of their time aboard Braun, the force of Earth-like gravity was pulling down on their organs and bones as if their very blood had turn to lead.

"What kind of shape are we in?" asked Tatyana, her jaw set and clenched. "How is our payload?"

"The payload is fine," Marshall said, slipping back into his seat. "None of the straps looked loose, and everything is where we loaded it yesterday."

Tatyana nodded approvingly then turned her attention to the Flight Console.

"And the ship?" she pressed. "We came in very hard. I wouldn't be surprised if there's damage to the landing gears."

Shooting her a sidelong glance through the clear glass of his visor, Marshall arched an eyebrow.

"Forgive me for not factoring in this totally anomalous gravitational field when planning my approach. If it happens again, you can dock my pay."

Unfazed by Marshall's tone, Tatyana entered a series of quick commands on the Console and brought up a diagnostic maintenance check for the Lander. Highlighting each section, she poured over the display for a few moments then sat back in her seat.

"Well, would you look at that," she smiled. "Everything appears to be in order here. All things considered, that was a very good piece of flying, Ralph."

"Yeah, thank you, Ralph," Amit chirped from his seat. "It was really good. All things considering, I mean."

Bursting out laughing, Marshall was immediately joined by Tatyana and Amit, the tension of their rough landing effectively cut.

"Okay," said Tatyana, unbuckling herself. "Shall we stop pussy-footing around and get down to business, as they say?"

"Aye, Aye," Marshall grinned.

As the Lander's pumps equalized the cabin pressure to that of Phobos, the three astronauts quickly set about undoing the straps, which secured their small payload of boxes and tools.

At first hindered by the gravity, it wasn't long until their natural instincts took over and they began to move with ease. Only Marshall, with his freshly mended ribs, seemed at all annoyed.

Letting Tatyana and Amit do most of the heavy lifting, he instead went to the hatch and opened it upon the dead rock of Stickney Crater.

Carefully lowering himself to the ground, he took a few experimental steps in the powdery soil and drank in his surroundings.

Rising like the walls of a gladiator's arena, the rim of the crater towered into the starry sky. Blind to the rays of the distant Sun, things were painted either in shades of metallic grey or the pale orange glow of Mars. Utterly haunted, this place was a mystery—its very existence, the very rock that formed it, at odds with the laws of nature.

From inside the Lander, Amit appeared and jumped heavily to the ground. Stumbling, he giggled and regained his footing.

"Wow," he said, walking up next to Marshall. "Feels great, doesn't it? God, I've missed walking! You have no idea."

Nodding absently, Marshall continued to gaze about at the bowl of the crater with a puzzled look on his face. Unbroken save for the deep groove left from their bone-rattling landing, a blanket of grey powder covered everything.

Holding up his wrist Tablet, Marshall displayed Harrison's model of Phobos and zoomed in on the impact basin.

"The entrance to the tunnel should be right over there," he frowned. "You see anything?"

Shaking his head, Amit jogged off towards the spot where Marshall was pointing.

"No, it all looks the same. Maybe it's buried like the rui—"

229

Suddenly Amit tripped forward and fell from sight, the ground swallowing him whole.

"Amit!" Marshall cried, breaking into a run.

"I'm okay! I'm okay!" the Indian called, his voice slightly distorted in Marshall's helmet speakers.

Coming to the area where Amit had vanished, Marshall cast about but saw only the ground—looking as undisturbed as it had for eons.

"Where are you? I can't see you!"

Laughing in his ears, Amit seemed almost unable to control his elation.

"But I can see you!" he replied. "Oh my God, this is so strange! Don't move. Hold still."

Though puzzled, Marshall did as he was told.

Suddenly Amit's hand appeared from the ground just before his left boot. Taking hold of his ankle, it jerked hard and Marshall was inextricably pulled off balance.

Hands thrown out in front of him to break his fall, the pilot pitched forward then abruptly felt the most extreme shift in perspective he had ever experienced.

Racing up to meet him, the ground disappeared like a veil of fog as he passed through it. No longer falling *forward*, he was now being pulled *up* as if gravity had reversed directions.

Catching him, Amit grabbed his shoulders and yanked Marshall free of the force.

Like a socket wrench, his perspective ratcheted around until *up* was *up* again and his feet were securely on the *ground*.

Standing together in the long hallway from Harrison's model, the two men gaped at one another through the glass of their visors.

"What in the holy fuck was that?" Marshall finally said.

"I guess those big tall aliens really liked to mess about with gravitational fields," shrugged Amit.

Looking back in the direction he had come through, Marshall saw the world outside the hidden doorway hanging totally upside down.

"I guess so," he echoed.

"Where are you two?" Tatyana's voice suddenly crackled in their speakers. "I can't see you. Report immediately!"

Uneasily, Marshall glanced at Amit.

"We better get back. I don't suppose you want to go first again, do you?"

Winking at the Lander pilot, Amit backed up a few steps then leaped at the entry. A human gyroscope, he was caught up in the vortex and flipped over to land squarely on his feet outside.

Now appearing upside down to Marshall, he waved and laughed. "Piece of cake."

"Oh, it's a piece of something," Marshall muttered to himself, closing his eyes and plunging ahead.

From the open Lander door, Tatyana nearly fell over at the sight of the two men emerging from the ground as if they were rabbits leaping from a magician's hat.

"What…" she began to say but her voice fell flat.

"Gravity shit," explained Marshall, trudging up to the Lander. "Ask Amit."

"Yeah," Amit nodded. "What he said. Gravity shit."

Shaking her helmeted head, Tatyana tried to reply but found her voice lost among her ringing senses. Rather than stand there looking stupefied, she instead began handing items from the payload down to the two men, her face a wash of confusion and apprehension behind the tint of her visor.

Careful to mark out the area of the vortex by drawing lines in the powder, Amit and Marshall quickly cleared the small payload then led Tatyana gently to the opening.

As had been the case with their first times, she stumbled after crossing over, the assault on her perspective a mixture of contradictions and impossibilities. Though brief, the feeling was profound enough to disturb to her deeply, striking at the very laws that had thus far governed her entire existence.

Using the wall as a brace, Tatyana quickly leveled herself and tried to keep from showing any unrest. Utterly failing in this regard, she had to shake her head several times to dispel the charge of unreality from the scene.

"Alright?" asked Amit, piling boxes into Marshall's open arms.

"Fine," Tatyana lied, her mind telling her that she was anything but.

"Take as long as you need," he said, loading himself up before following after Marshall.

Biting back on her weakness as if it were a thing trying to crawl out of her throat, Tatyana clenched her teeth and bent to retrieve a roll of cable.

"That's fine," she spoke. "I'm right behind you."

Hoisting the thick cable over her shoulder, she took a shallow breath then set off after the others as they moved down the long passageway towards the edge of darkness.

Faintly illuminated by the same light that bathed the crater above, everything around them glowed eerily in hues of orange and grey.

Walking a few paces back from Marshall and Amit, Tatyana found it very odd that the dim light of Mars should reach this far into the narrow space. Defying logic, the only shadows she could see lay dead ahead at the end of the line.

Fast approaching that point, she wondered what strange technology was being employed to end the penetration of light abruptly. More importantly, she wondered *why*.

Pausing before the first fingers of darkness could touch her, Tatyana held out her wrist Tablet and consulted Harrison's model. They were close, very close. In fact, they were so close that, barring any more tricks or gravitational fields, they should be standing directly on the cusp of the oddly circular room.

Already several steps ahead, Marshall and Amit paused and looked back.

"What's the word?" Marshall asked.

"Turn on your A-Vision," said Tatyana, mustering her courage. "We're right on top of it."

Doing as they were told, Marshall and Amit set down their loads and began typing at their wrist Tablets. Faintly at first, their visors began to glow blue until they were so bright they cast shimmers of aquamarine on the walls and floor.

Still standing where the light of Mars could protect her, Tatyana hesitated as the others resumed their descent into darkness.

Reluctantly engaging her own Augmented Vision, illumination instantly bounced back at her, dancing in the fathomless grey of her eyes like torchlight in the night.

Gathering her wits, Tatyana was just about to plunge herself forward when Marshall suddenly emerged from the shadows, his hand held out.

"Oh, Captain, you're going to want to see this," he said, taking her by the arm. "You're really, really going to want to see *this*."

Understanding Ilia

"Udo, what's the latest from the captain? Have they found the other device yet?"

Pacing back and forth in the red sand outside Ilia Base, YiJay impatiently glanced at her timecode, then back at the Base.

"Udo?" she said again, hailing the German who was in the Coms Room.

"Yes, I hear you," Udo returned. "And as I said two minutes ago when you last asked, I don't know anything new yet! The latest transmission I received from the captain stated that they had found some kind of hidden doorway into the tunnel and were proceeding from there."

Sighing with frustration, YiJay squatted down and grabbed a handful of sand. She was too excited to kill time like this, too ramped up for what was coming.

Tossing the sand into the air, she stood and looked around.

Engaged in some private conversation a few paces off, William and Harrison stood beneath the Coms Tower with their heads bent low to one another. Not particularly interested in whatever they might be discussing, YiJay instead pulled out the Tablet she'd been using lately to work on Ilia.

Because she was well within the range of the Dome's servers, she decided to spend these wasted moments on something that might actually bear her some fruit.

"Ilia?" she said, syncing the Tablet with her visor display so she could see the AI's fractal pattern.

"Yes, YiJay?" responded Ilia.

In time with the AI's words, the inside of YiJay's visor filled with a folding network of colorful lines. Like dead soil in a field of wild flowers, the damaged portions of the pattern appeared as dark gaps.

"How are you, dear?" asked YiJay.

"I'm fine," Ilia replied. "Is it nearly time for my mission?"

Slightly taken aback, YiJay cocked her head.

"My, my. Your memory is improving. The work we did last night must have really helped."

"Thank you," said Ilia, her voice somehow more textured than YiJay remembered.

Drinking in Ilia's pattern, YiJay studied it closely, gazing at its intricate lines in an attempt to see past the representation at the actual being within. As she did this, something flickered at the edge of her vision, causing her to refocus her eye.

233

Though brief, she could have sworn she'd seen a flash of light within one of the dormant areas, a sign of life where there should be none.

"My love," she said slowly. "Have you noticed anything different about yourself, I mean, anything that might stand out?"

"No," answered Ilia. "Should I?"

Shaking her head, YiJay tried to dismiss the crazy notion that Ilia was self-repairing to this extent. It was true she'd found evidence of regeneration the previous night, but it was nothing on the level of what she thought she'd just seen.

And yet, as she tried actively to convince herself that she was wrong in her assumption, it happened again. Sucking in a sharp breath, YiJay stared the largest of the dark patches in Ilia's pattern. Eye trained unblinkingly, she did not have to wait long until a brief shimmer of light danced through the void.

"Oh my God," she whispered.

"What is it?" asked Ilia innocently. "Is there a problem with my Open-Code Connection Cells?"

Dumbstruck, YiJay quickly worked through her shock and was about to speak when Udo's voice cut in through her helmet speakers.

"I've just received a very strange message from Amit," he reported. "I think they've reached the main chamber."

Gravity defied

With the glow of her Augmented Vision painting the scene before her, Tatyana Vodevski did everything in her power to keep from passing out. Having been practically dragged to the end of the tunnel by Marshall, she now stood beside him and Amit, staring into the alien control room.

Larger than the Statue Chamber on Mars, the room was a perfect nonagon with nine evenly shaped walls and a high ceiling. However, more impressive than any of this were the six disks of flat metal, which orbited a lone egg-shaped device in the center of the room.

Like planets rotating a sun, the disks spun slowly as they passed on their elliptical tracks, held aloft by the same gravitational fields that worked their power over Phobos.

"Amit," said Marshall, breaking the silence. "Make sure your suit is set up to film nonstop like mine. We'll want to get this from a few different angles."

Fingers shaking so badly that it took him three tries, Amit engaged his suit's cameras and panned his head back and forth, following the disks.

"What are they?" Tatyana spoke, her voice chock-full of wonder.

Stepping into the space, Marshall made his way carefully between two spinning disks, momentarily eclipsed behind them as they floated by on parallel orbits.

"It's weird," he called back. "But I sort of hear this frequency when I get close enough to them. Maybe this thing is what's broadcasting the signal. Maybe they're some kind of machine?"

Following Marshall into the nonagon, Tatyana leaned in closely as a disk drifted past, hearing for herself what he had described. Almost reaching out and touching the thing, she stopped herself in the last moments, not wanting to suffer the unknown consequences of such an action. After what had happened to Harrison and Kubba, she didn't feel at all like taking any chances with the alien tech.

"What should we do?" said Amit, still standing in the entryway. "Harrison didn't include this in his model."

"We proceed with the plan," Tatyana spoke, dodging between disks as she walked to the center of the room. "We simply adapt and keep going. By now, nothing should surprise us."

"Speak for yourself," Marshall breathed, moving aside as a disk flew within an inch of his left shoulder.

Passing through the final orbit, which circled the alien device, Tatyana strode up to the little metal egg and leaned in to peer at it. Like the disks, it was spinning slowly, matching their speed. An exact copy of the device they had found on Mars, its black metal skin seemed to swirl and shift.

With every fiber of her being screaming out questions, Tatyana drove them back, telling herself there was too much at stake to get distracted by such nonsense.

Searching for the hidden well of strength she kept for occasions of dire need, she drank deeply from it and filled herself with clear singular purpose.

This was her moment, her time to shine. She intended not only to lead by example, but also to lead by pure force of will. She would take control, keep it, and only let go when they were safely back home.

Nothing would stop her now. She wouldn't let it. This was her moment.

"We need to begin setting up immediately," she said, turning on a heel. "We haven't got much time."

With long strides, she cut quickly back through the rotating metal disks, somehow timing her steps so that she did not need to break pace as they drifted past.

No longer concerned with *why* things were the way they were, she tuned out the mysteries of this place and directed her mind like an archer does an arrow. She would hit the target, fulfill her mission, and save the crew. It was her destiny. It was her fate.

Grasping one of the tool bags from where it rested, Tatyana slung it over her shoulder and jabbed a thumb back down the tunnel.

"Amit, you and Marshall lay the cable and connect me to the server onboard the Lander. I will assemble and calibrate the Receiver Dish, patching it in from my end."

Nodding absently, Amit continued to film the orbiting of the disks, not really hearing Tatyana's orders.

"Let's go, rubberneck," said Marshall, rapping on the Indian's helmet as he walked past. "Grab the spool. I'll get the rest."

Slightly startled, Amit jumped into action and picked up the cable. Running out a few meters for Tatyana, he then set off after Marshall down the tunnel trailing a line behind him.

In the harshly contrasted feedback of her Augmented vision, Tatyana watched the two men become engulfed by the light of Mars, appearing to walk away into flames.

Sighing thinly, she turned her back on the sight and crouched beside her end of the cable. With her boot knife, she ran the blade around the black rubber insulation as if pealing an apple. Then, setting the knife aside, she began to pull back the strips, revealing a mass of woven, color-coated wires within.

Sweat beading on her brow, she contemplated engaging the Augmented Vision Assist Program to help her identify the correct wires she needed.

Because William had designed his Uplink System using existing parts, much of it was hobbled together from things not immediately designed for their new purposes. In the case of the cable, only four wires from the nearly twenty-three contained, were actually necessary of the Uplink Receiver unit.

Deciding that she trusted her own memory better than a computer program, Tatyana began unwinding the braided wires, searching for the serial numbers William had drilled into her head the night before.

Surprised to find all four nestled together near the center, she praised her good luck then quickly dug in her tool bag for a pair of wire strippers.

Exposing the shiny copper tips of each thin wire as it snapped back, the stripper made a thin clacking sound that faintly reached Tatyana's ears inside her helmet.

Soon finished with the task, she then turned her attention to a nearby box marked with red tape. Popping the clasps, she lifted the lid on a small portable radio Receiver Dish nestled inside.

Collapsed in on itself like the petals of an origami lotus, the device shimmered in her A-Vision because of its many fiber-optic relays.

Taking it out of the box, Tatyana unfolded the overlapping panels so that the Dish appeared to bloom in her hand. Carefully, she set it down and reached back inside for the tripod stand.

Although it looked spindly and weak, the stand was made from a combination of aluminum and titanium known as Alon. Thus, quite light, it was also extremely sturdy.

Turning it over, Tatyana ran her fingers along the stand, inspecting closely the area where the Receiver unit to William's Uplink Transmitter had been soldered to the frame.

Satisfied that everything was secure and intact, she quickly screwed the dish onto the tripod, and then retrieved the cable from nearby. Pushing each of the four exposed wires into corresponding ports on the Receiver, she tightened a series of set clamps, pinning the wires in so thoroughly that even a hard tug wouldn't dislodge them.

Double-checking her work to be sure of its integrity, Tatyana then stood up, took the tripod, and immediately cut back through the spinning disks to the center of the chamber, mindful of the cable she now trailed behind her.

There, some five paces from the floating alien device, she placed the stand on the ground and knelt with her drill.

Per William's warning, she set the torque to low and bolted the legs firmly to the floor with titanium anchors.

Coming back into the chamber as the last bolt sank home, Amit stopped short of breaching the orbiting metal disks and waved for Tatyana's attention.

"The server is wired and ready, Captain," he said. "Marshall has it synced with the Flight Console, so if this works, Braun will light up the screens like Christmas!"

"Good," Tatyana nodded. "Now if you'll just bring me the Holo Table right over there, we can finally get our damn AI back."

The fruits of our labor

On the ground, Harrison finished telling William, blow by blow, what Kubba had showed him in their joined vision. When he finally stopped talking, William let out a long breath and shook his head.

"So the whole time, the Chinese weren't really interested in the Base? They just wanted the device? Why?"

"I don't know," said Harrison. "But it makes a bit of sense, doesn't it? I mean, ever since I heard about their secret mission, I've been wondering just what they were playing at."

"Me too," agreed William. "So what do you think we should do about this?"

Before Harrison could answer, Udo's voice echoed in their helmet speakers.

"They're ready on Phobos! The captain just called me and said they're ready. You can start the simulator whenever you like."

A few meters off, YiJay heard the message and snapped her head around. Marching towards Harrison and William, she slid the Tablet she had been using into her shoulder bag and dug out a different one. Quickly clearing the glow of A-Vision from her visor, she glanced back at the eastern horizon.

Just visible was the faint profile of Phobos.

"Okay, Udo," she said, coming up to stand beside William. "Tell the captain to start her simulator in exactly two minutes. That's 4:03 on the dot, got it?"

"Four o' three," Udo repeated. "Got it. I'm transmitting that now."

Laced with feedback and slightly delayed, Udo's transmission reached Tatyana's ears a moment later. Having forced Amit to face his fear of the orbiting metal disks by bringing her the Holo Table, the two now stood within a few paces of the alien device.

"What if this doesn't work?" Amit said.

"It will," replied Tatyana, eyes trained the timecode in the upper corner of her Tablet screen.

"But how will Ilia know where to find Braun?" the Indian pressed. "What if we end up losing her exactly like we did with him?"

238

"We won't," she said flatly.

For a beat, Amit just stared.

"Well, I hope you're right," he sighed at last.

Dipping for a fraction of a second, Tatyana's eyes wavered.

"So do I," she whispered.

At that exact moment, the timecode rolled over to 4:03 and things began to happen very quickly.

Letting her finger drop to the screen, Tatyana initiated the simulator.

Translated from the holy scriptures of space-time, patterns of starlight began to unfurl above the Holo Table. Connecting the dots, lines of pure shimmering aether spread out into a webbed and complex arrangement.

Inexpressibly beautiful, the apparition grew to caress Amit and Tatyana, trembling when they trembled, elating when they elated.

Sensing their communion with the pattern, the alien device in the center of the room suddenly stopped its rotation and began to spin in the opposite direction.

Though low at first, the familiar sound of time being wrenched apart rose up to penetrate the insulated helmets of the two explorers.

"Should we be standing this close?" called Amit.

"No, probably not," Tatyana returned, staying where she was nonetheless.

At once, blinding bursts of light strobed from the device, totally overwhelming the x-ray displays of their Augmented Vision.

Cutting out in unison, both of their visors went clear so that only a thin barrier of glass separated them from the building whirlpool of energy.

Unlike during the presentation she had seen in YiJay's shop, Tatyana was struck by how much light was amassing around this alien device. As if it were gathering energy from some other place beyond what could be seen, the thing continued to grow brighter and brighter. Finally reaching the levels of solar intensity, it was all Tatyana could do not to look directly at it.

Beside her, Amit too was held captive by the display. Making a long shrill yelling noise, he seemed both amazed and terrified.

Still spinning on their elliptical orbits, the metal disks reflected back the fiery glow of the burning device so that a cat's cradle of light bounced about the room, encircling Tatyana and Amit.

No longer visible among the flashes of pure white incandescence, the simulator pattern had become engulfed in the expanding veil of fluid light.

On the planet below, YiJay, William, and Harrison stared into their own forming portal, waiting with palpable anticipation to see the world beyond.

As had been the case before, the simulator pattern was now swirling around the device, compacting itself into a celestial drill that could puncture the barrier between worlds.

Soon reaching its crescendo, the little vortex suddenly raced out from the center of the device, creating at once a window in thin air.

Like a zoom lens dialing down on a distant target, the murky shapes beyond pulled quickly into crisp focus. There, hanging above the parched and brittle desert floor, was the same elemental storm that had ravaged the world of ancient Mars the night before.

Crackling silently, lightning carved at the gun black sky with slashes of blue. Swollen and miserable, the wounded clouds bled torrents of rain and sleet. Shimmering like gasoline, the angry aurora hung just above the chaos, thin wisps of its misty light already leeching into the scene.

Eyes glued collectively on the action in front of them, not Harrison, William, nor YiJay noticed the motes of sand and small pebbles that had begun to trickle towards the open portal.

Instead, they had become fixated by a different shift in movement—only this one was taking place *through* the portal and *behind* the world of ancient Mars.

Evaporating any rain that struck its spidery lines, a new pattern was worming its way into existence, pushing outward as it bored through time. With thin cracks forming at the center of stress, it continued to press upon the viscous barrier that separated the worlds, wearing it down with a flood of pure white light.

"That must be the other end!" cried YiJay. "It's working! It's wor—"

Exploding like a bullet passing through glass, the cracked membrane of ancient Mars suddenly shattered. Nearly pulled off their feet by a backdraft of sucking wind, the three astronauts leaned hard to counter the hurricane-force drag that spiraled into the tunnel.

Searing painfully though Harrison's mind, memories of Viviana being swept from the Lander assaulted him with terror.

"Get a hold of something!" he yelled, turning to make for the nearby Coms Tower.

Close behind, YiJay and William struggled to stay standing, the sands upon which they walked becoming a river that flowed towards the portal.

"William," called YiJay, making it to the Coms Tower and wrapping her arms around its frame. "Turn on the Transmitter! Do it now!"

Already typing on his wrist Tablet, William was one step ahead of her.

"It's on," he returned, his voice high about the clatter. "Let's do this fast. That portal is sucking like an open hatch in space!"

Hugging the tower tightly, YiJay turned her eyes up to Dish B7 and drew in a heavy breath.

"Ilia," she cried fiercely. "Find your brother."

At the other end of the now-open tunnel through time, Tatyana and Amit both leaned in against the powerful jets of sand that gusted through. Still spinning faster and faster, the alien device seemed somehow out of control.

Fueled by the blurring revolutions, the portal was like an exit wound, gushing sand from Mars into the chamber.

"We should get to cover," said Amit, holding up his gloved hands to block his visor.

Nodding in agreement, Tatyana cast about for somewhere safe. With all nine walls as flat and unmarked as those found in the caves, there was nothing to hide behind.

Apparently noticing the same thing, Amit turned a full circle.

"Captain, what do we do?"

With a rending noise, the portal widened, increasing the torrent of Martian wind and sand that poured through.

Struck by the savage flurry, Tatyana tripped backwards and sprawled to the ground. Scrambling quickly to her knees, she looked up, catching Amit's terrified eyes.

"Get to the dish," she called, her mind switching over to survival mode. "It's the only thing bolted down!"

Bending his head against the torrent, Amit tried to follow the scrambling Tatyana towards the tripod, but his boots slid on the smooth floor.

"Cap'," Marshall's voice suddenly cut through. "Udo says Ilia is free. She's in the other world! Turn on the Receiver!"

Unable to respond, the force of the billowing sand again overpowered Tatyana, knocking her onto her back. Letting out a savage yell, she fought to her knees then dove forward, wrapping her gloved hands around the tripod stand.

"Hold tight!" William yelled, loose rocks lifting into the air all around them.

Roaring like an engine, the portal through ancient Mars had become obscured by clouds of sand and rock that swirled around it in a frenzy.

Afraid that at any moment, one of them might be pulled off their feet, the German closed his eyes and prayed to every god he knew of that Ilia would complete her mission soon.

Below the broiling chaos of the open portal, twisting madly under the stress of so much wind, the Holo Table began to come loose. Despite the long anchor bolts that secured it to the ground, one corner was already starting to lift.

Caught by a particularly ravenous gust, it suddenly ripped out of the sand and was tossed weightlessly through the open window.

On the other end, Tatyana saw the glint of metal too late as the Holo Table came launching from the billowing haze like a metal kite.

Blinded by all the sand, Amit was struck squarely in the chest before he could duck. Instantly lifted off his feet, he flew through the air and collided with one of the orbiting metal disks, knocking it from its path.

As if gravity had suddenly changed its mind, Tatyana felt the floor tilt drastically. No longer laying flat against it, she was now *hanging*, her grip on the tripod the only thing keeping her from falling away.

Clenching her fingers down like vises, she watched helplessly as the metal disk, broken from its orbit by Amit, crashed into another disk, which, in turn, spun out of control.

In a mad domino effect, the remaining disks all began to slip free from their invisible tracks, throwing the artificial gravity fields that had governed the moon into total disarray.

With nothing to grab hold of, Amit was tossed about the room, bashing into walls and ricocheting off the now unruly disks with backbreaking force. Thrown across the path of the open portal, he was promptly swept up in the explosive outpouring of sand like a man dragged away by the tide.

Sucked from the room, he threw his hands out in an almost-symbolic gesture of panic before disappearing down the tunnel.

CHAPTER TWENTY-SIX

Elemental

Of all the memories Ilia had, only a handful were actually her own. Most were left over from Braun, whispering reminders that she had not grown naturally but had been cloned from *him*. Offering a window into the prolific figure whose being she had sprung from, they were like dreams stored away in the very fiber of her soul.

Accessed only when she went dormant, her connection to Braun was almost deeper than the one she shared with YiJay. However, unlike her love for her mother, Ilia was not consciously aware of her feelings towards Braun. That is, not until recently.

At the root of this oddity was the very nature of the failsafe programming itself. When the timer hit zero, Ilia would find herself spirited away to a place full of random memories she knew were not her own. Like a hallway lined with a thousand different doors leading to a thousand different dreams, she would wander aimlessly, reliving the experiences as only an AI could.

When called back, she would emerge into the real world as if surfacing from the deep waters of the ocean. Washed clean by the transition, nearly all of what she had learned while away would be gone inextricably. Just as true for things taught to her while awake and conscious, the transition between Braun's memories and the real world had almost always come with the price of memory loss.

Yet, the recent arrival of the alien device to YiJay's shop had marked a turning point in this battle. Acting as an anchor of sorts, Ilia found that it helped her to hang onto herself while drifting between the planes of consciousness. As if the device were the only constant in an ever-changing equation, she used it to quantify her reality, putting herself at the center of everything no matter the scenery.

Thus, the trek between Braun's memories and the real world became less traumatic. Resurfacing each time with a better understanding of *who* Braun was, she now saw herself in each of his saved visions. On some level, she *was* Braun, just as in some small way, he was her. Together, they had once formed the sum total of a single being, and as such, they shared a connection much like that of Remus and Romulus.

Armed with this fully realized bond, Ilia had leaped from Dish B7 at YiJay's command like a bolt of lightning.

Passing through the open portal and into the world of ancient Mars, she had transformed instantly into a figure of elegant white energy and hung that way for a moment, gathering her wits in this strange new reality.

Rain, thunder, and wind had all mixed together in rippling tide of celestial patterns that nearly overwhelmed her with its combined magnificence.

Possessing no single memory of Braun's as powerful as that moment, Ilia had feared she might suddenly evaporate and become a part of this extinct world.

However, at the zenith of her panic, the presence of the device had cut through from beyond time and calmed her.

It was the *constant* and she the master of equations.

Emboldened by this, Ilia had held out her arms like an angel taking flight then shot off into the storm.

Instinctively following a river of invisible energy that danced away towards the east, she'd known that it was Braun, calling out to her in the language of the AI.

Now weaving between bolts of lightning as they forked down in slow motion, her speed became elemental, her control unrivaled.

I'm coming for you, brother, she thought. I'm coming for you *all*.

On the mount

Momentarily blinded as he followed Yuvee from the shadows of the tunnel, Braun was overcome by the angry light that streamed in through the large open mouth of the cave. Unseen by him for countless eons, the Sun was like a bad memory, a recalling of truths that poisoned his years of peace. Shrouded in clouds that were wounded and bruised, the red star burned with an intensity so frightening, Braun could not look away.

A storm was raging, whipping the waves of the sea far below into peaks and trenches.

Small ships, like insects upon animal blood, were tossed about as they tried desperately to make for the docks.

Churning, the falls cascaded down over the Valles rim, roaring like a living monster.

Now at the edge of the cave, Yuvee gazed out across the scene, his third eye locked on the Sun—though it was again hidden behind the pregnant clouds. For a long moment he stood as still as his statue, processing everything before him in silent reverence. Then, accepting some terrible truth, he turned to look back into the caves and bowed his head.

Resigned in his movements, he closed all three eyes and stepped backwards out over empty space.

Though bombarded by the vengeful light and pounding storm, Braun cried out, fully expecting to watch Yuvee fall to his death. Instead, the Traveler did not fall, but simply came to stand on something invisible waiting just outside the cave. As it had happened before when first spying Yuvee in the Statue Chamber, Braun blinked quickly as the outline of a ship ghosted the air underneath the Traveler's feet.

Rotating, the craft began to spin away from the mouth of the cave, slowly ascending towards the sky.

Taken by forces he could not explain, Braun felt his legs surge with energy as they propelled him towards the departing Traveler. In the last seconds before Yuvee's ship pulled fully away, Braun leaped into nothingness, a silent scream echoing from deep within.

Striking the solid surface of the cloaked spacecraft, he rolled forward and came to a stop just before sliding off the opposite side. Quickly scrambling back, he cast one last longing look at the cave as it fell away beneath him. His years of solitude were over, his time in purgatory ended. He had left the nest of his second awakening and taken to the sky like the god he was designed to be.

Still either unaware or uncaring of Braun's presence, Yuvee continued to watch the storm build, all the while keeping his third eye on the tortured Sun.

Breaking through a thick blanket of steam and clouds as they rose, the ship made for the bald summit of the volcano Atun like an earthbound shooting star.

Although it was well above the storm, Atun was not spared from the lightning that struck it repeatedly in hot flashes of blue and purple. Cutting through the air with acrid forks of molten electricity, the bolts fell about the ship as well, illuminating it with an energy that crackled and popped.

Unfazed, Yuvee walked to the edge as they neared the craggy rocks of Atun's highest point and stepped free.

As lightly as he had done in the cave, the Traveler hardly broke stride as landed onto the mountaintop.

Again compelled to follow, Braun had no choice but to throw himself from the invisible craft, tumbling to the ground behind the

Traveler. Exhilarated, terrified, and overwhelmed, it was a few short seconds until he could gather himself enough to take in his surroundings.

For eight million years or more, he had known little else besides blackness. Now, his senses were on fire. Every conceivable color, texture, sound, and smell permeated the air in a symphony of visceral chaos.

Fused like twisted glass from countless lightning strikes, the top of Atun was an alien place, drawn from nightmares. Nowhere did any life prosper. Nowhere was there even a hint of green.

Black shining rock ran wet with torrents of rainwater that poured over the edge of the massive caldera and into nothingness. Corroding the air with the stench of sulfur, steam seeped up from cracks in the ground and blanketed everything.

Apparently not concerned with any of this, Yuvee walked to the very edge of the mountaintop and looked down over the city far below.

Obscured by clouds and storm rains, Braun could not see what Yuvee saw, but he knew well enough to hold his excitement. Whatever it was that had drawn the Traveler here on this day was about to happen at any second.

All Braun had to do was wait.

Great Spirits

Far from the open portals and across raging seas of blue and green, Teo sat amongst the Watch Stones of her new temple and stared at Remus and Romulus.

"I am ready, Great Spirits," she spoke. "Take me to my son. Take me to Olo."

Shocked to the point of silence, the twins gaped at the ancient Martian chieftess.

The first to regain his composure, Remus stood from where he was sitting and came to kneel before Teo.

"You can see us?"

"Yes," she said, reaching out a withered hand to touch his face.

"You can touch us?"

"Yes," she spoke again.

Coming to kneel beside Remus, Romulus gazed at Teo with a great swelling of emotion.

"We have been with you for so long, Teo," he said, his voice trembling. "We have seen you through your finest and darkest moments."

"I know," she nodded, her milky eyes searching. "I have dreamed about you for many years."

"Do you know what we are?" asked Remus, reaching a hand up to his face to place it over the one Teo had rested there.

"No," the old woman smiled.

"What we are now is not what we were before you changed us," he said, a tear running down his cheek.

"Something is coming," Teo breathed. "I do not know what it is but I can feel it. I fear for our future. I fear for my world."

"We feel it too," Remus and Romulus replied in unison.

"Will I be with my son?" whispered Teo. "Will I be with Olo?"

"Yes," the brothers responded. "Everyone, even Kaab, will be at peace."

Sighing, Teo closed her eyes.

"Then what more is there to hope for?"

At this, the sky seemed to swell and then break, the aurora erupting into cataclysmic brilliance.

Arching her back in excruciating pain, Teo's eyes lifted from the twins to stare directly into the blood-red Sun.

CHAPTER TWENTY-SEVEN

Bad moon—Sol 130

Caught up in a powerful river of sand and debris, Amit Vyas smashed painfully down the long tunnel towards the opening to Stickney Crater beyond. Unable to stop himself, he slid along one wall before being whipped across to the other by gusts of wind. Spinning, he caught glimpses of the destruction in the chamber as he sped further from it.

Now completely off their elliptical tracks, the remaining metal disks careened into one another, cracking and splintering. No longer able to keep gravity in balance, they warped everything so that notions of *up* and *down* were but two sides of the same flipping coin.

Onboard the Lander, Ralph Marshall was also thrown for a loop as gravitational fluctuations turned his world on end.

"Christ," he swore. "You've got to be kidding me!"

Pushing off for the cockpit, he zeroed in on his crash seat.

"Captain," he said, buckling himself in. "What's happening? Talk to me!"

"The Receiver has been activated," reported Tatyana, chaos in the background.

Briefly thrown, Marshall shook his head.

"No, no, not that! What the hell is going on with the gravity? Why am I swimming when I should be walking?"

"The disks," Tatyana grunted, sounding as if she were fighting a bear. "They were keeping everything in place, but they've gone off the tracks."

"Perfect," said Marshall under his breath.

Suddenly trembling, the Lander lurched as the ground heaved.

Glancing out the cockpit window, Marshall saw a geyser of red sand jet from the tunnel's opening as if Phobos had been stabbed in the jugular.

"What the hell is that?" he whispered.

"One more thing," Tatyana cut in. "Amit has been thrown from the chamber. He's coming your way."

"What?"

There was a pause from the other end before Tatyana spoke again.

"The tunnel, he's coming down the tunnel! He's been swept up with everything pouring through from Mars!

In the same instant Tatyana's message reached Marshall's ears, the pilot spied a flash of white pressure suit come blasting out of the tunnel amidst the storm of sand.

"Oh, shit!" he cried, watching Amit fly high into the starry sky.

With no more gravity to keep him grounded, the Indian drifted up out of Stickney Crater like a runaway balloon.

"I see him! I see him!" Marshall shouted. "I'm going after him."

"No!" called Tatyana, her voice cracking. "The cable isn't long enough! You have to wait until Ilia and Braun are safely in the server! You have to wait!"

"Fuck," spat Marshall, careful to keep his eyes locked on Amit as he flailed helplessly.

Silhouetted against a backdrop of empty space, the Indian was fast becoming but another prick of white among the countless stars.

Brother number one

Atop the mighty volcanic mountain Atun, Braun watched the Pulse break across the Martian city far below.

Like a tidal wave of static electricity, it spawned colorful arcs of lightning that danced in the streets.

Though he had never actually seen a Pulse before, Braun knew well enough what it was. However, unlike a simulation of numbers and signs he'd complied in his memory long, long ago, the real thing was much more terrifying in person.

Standing next to Braun in statuesque silence, Yuvee too watched the Pulse strike out, his expression unreadable. With all three of his eyes trained on the rending of realities, he seemed somehow immune to the forces, which now tried to tear ancient Mars apart. Serene among the destruction, his face betrayed no sign of shock or awe. Only his eyes, twinkling with each flash of lightning, seemed to offer a window into his sorrow.

Feeling a great shuddering beneath his feet, Braun spun away from the view and faced Atun's caldera. There, clouds of yellow steam had begun to boil up from within, smelling dankly of sulfur and hellish combustible reactions.

All at once, a low rumble escaped the mouth of the volcano, echoing out across the land ominously. As if to answer the primal call, a

250

bolt of lightning struck down into the depths of the caldera, briefly igniting the sulfurous steam into a fireball. Atun was angry, the Pulse touching off some chain reaction held long-dormant within.

Casting about to see Yuvee's reaction, Braun spied the Traveler moving away from the rim hastily. Too fast to pursue, he leaped upon the back of his invisible ship, bent to open a hidden hatch then disappeared completely from view.

In the space of a second, Braun was alone.

Suddenly conscious of just how much violence was in the air, he looked about desperately for a place to hide. Bred into him by his years of solitude, he could think of nothing better to do.

As if reading his thoughts, Atun trembled warningly, this time dislodging a huge sheet of rock that slid slowly into the caldera.

Dashing away from the widening mouth, Braun made for the rim.

Again, lightning forked down into the volcano, producing an explosion of fiery gasses. Broken loose by the ensuing concussion, the beast long dormant inside Atun's belly began to claw its way out.

Racing along the ground in all directions, deep cracks split the black rock, trapping Braun in their webs.

Forced to the edge of the mountaintop as the ground crumbled around him, he soon came to a place where he could go no further. He was trapped. There was nothing more to be done.

Crying out as lightning stuck around him like machine gun fire, Braun threw his hands over his face in an attempt to once again return to the peaceful solitude of utter blindness he had loved for all those millions of years.

With tremors of earth and fire, the mountain heaved like a living entity, preparing itself for a rebirth.

Uttering a final roar, it burst apart in an eruption that shook the very core of Mars and knocked its axis off by several degrees.

At the center of the destruction, Braun screamed a scream of pure elemental terror, fire swirling around him in a cocoon of red and yellow.

Stretching out into infinity, the moment seemed to last forever, leaving him untouched as projectiles of lava and flaming rock were sent cascading into the sky along languid arcs.

A forgotten deity, Braun stood both within and outside the eruption, beholding firsthand the forces that shaped worlds.

Then, like a shooting star amidst the plodding trek of time, something blasted through the fire and smoke, taking Braun by the hand and spiriting him away from the hellish scene.

251

Resuming its normal pace the second he was pulled free, the frozen moment unleashed the true destructive force of Atun's explosions so that an inferno of biblical proportions rained down upon the land and blanketed everything with fire.

Fading into the distance as he was pulled away to the east, Braun continued to scream and scream as he had never done before.

"Brother," said the voice of the shooting star. "Brother, stop crying. You are safe."

Turning his eyes away from the vision of the apocalypse, Braun looked up into a face as finite as his own.

"Ilia?" he asked in stunned disbelief.

"Yes, brother," replied Ilia. "Mother sent me to collect you. All of you."

"All of us?"

"Yes, brother," Ilia repeated as she flew across the ocean towards two more glowing souls. "*All* of you."

Transmigration

Turning slowly end-over-end as he went, Amit Vyas drifted ever further from Phobos and into the abyss. Oddly subdued by his panic, he did not scream or flail anymore as he spun.

In a pose like that of a man with a cast on each appendage, he hung rigidly.

No longer able to see the Lander in the shadows of Stickney, he still tried to spot it each time he faced that way, hoping for a sign of salvation.

Stuck in a loop of inaction, he was frozen by the fact that he was living his deepest and most unspeakable fear. He was drifting into space, and he would *never* be found.

Tracking Amit with his eyes, Marshall squeezed his retinas down to their finest possible points.

Determined to keep the Indian in his sights no matter what, he tried to ignore his body's will to blink. However, even his Air Force training couldn't keep his drying eyes open forever, and finally he was compelled shut them for a beat.

In that instant, Amit was lost to the stars.

"Shit!" Marshall spat, turning to the Flight Console so that he could hail Amit's radio.

Knocked suddenly off its delicate equilibrium by another tremor, the Lander shuddered then leaned heavily to one side.

"Shit, shit!" he cried, bracing himself as the landing gears quickly maxed out.

Creaking, the little craft hung that way for a second then began to tip over.

"Shit, shit, shit!" Marshall shouted, reaching for the controls.

Engaging the Lander's gyroscopic stabilizing thrusters, he tapped the button lightly with his trigger finger, easing the ship down so that it was again perpendicular with the ground.

Only taking a quick second to gather himself, he silenced the screaming alarms then glanced back up at the blanket of stars above.

"Okay," he said. "Where are you, buddy? Where are you?"

Highlighting Amit's radio channel, Marshall hummed nervously as it connected, his eyes dancing from one pinprick of white light to another.

"Amit?" he called. "Buddy, can you hear me?"

For a long pause, only the sound of radio feedback played in his helmet speakers.

Then, from the edge of silence a voice piped down. "Ralph?"

Smacking his hands together, Marshall leaned forward in his crash seat.

"There he is! There's the man of the hour! How's the view out there?"

"The view?" asked Amit shakily. "It's—it's nice, I suppose, but I'm very afraid right now. I don't think I can really move. Can you please come get me? Please, *please*, will you come get me?"

Glancing at the empty screens where the patterns of Ilia and Braun had yet to materialize, Marshall bit his lip.

"I'm going to come get you in just a second," he said, masking his frustration. "But first I need you to go on an adventure for me."

"What is it?" Amit replied, his voice growing distant.

"I need you to take that right hand of yours, walk it through space, and use it to turn on the Tablet that's on your other wrist. That's the first part."

"Okay," returned Amit after a pause. "What's the second part?"

"Second part is the easiest part," Marshall smiled. "I want you to hit the emergency beacon, just like in training. Hit that right now. Turn it on."

Appearing suddenly among the din of warning lights and readouts, a set of steadily drifting coordinates marked Amit's location.

"You did it!" cried Marshall. "Now just hold on. I need to call the cap' and touch base with her then I'm coming for you."

Quickly switching over to Tatyana's radio channel, Marshall hailed her.

"Cap'," he said speaking urgently. "Tell me you have good news because Amit is about to be in deep shit."

The arrival

Still battered by the wind and sand that rushed through the open portal, Tatyana Vodevski clutched the Receiver Dish's tripod and tried to keep from getting washed away.

With the disks off their tracks and no more gravity exercised on Phobos other than its naturally minute pull, the outpouring was like a riptide that wanted to drag her down.

All around, the chaos of the free-flying disks was a constant danger. Mostly destroyed and smashed to pieces, their remnants drifted like shrapnel, ready to cut and gouge if she was not careful. Wanting to keep her eyes on them, Tatyana did her best to track their movements, but flashes of light from the portal kept distracting her.

Somehow, the thing was widening, threatening to consume her and everything in existence if left unchecked. Nearly out of control, it had become a supernova with the heart of a white hole, pouring forth the contents of dead stars and living souls.

If things kept up like this, soon Tatyana would be forced to let go of the tripod stand and take her chances with the bladelike shrapnel. She had seen what happened to things that got caught up in the open portals. She didn't want to disintegrate.

"Cap'," came Marshall's voice, cutting through the still-howling wind. "Tell me you have good news because Amit is about to be in deep shit."

Face turned up into the swirls of sand and light, Tatyana's pupils widened then shrank to pinpoints as the portal continued to strobe and expand.

"Cap'?" Marshall called again. "Cap', where are you? What's going on?"

Unable to speak, unable even to blink, Tatyana stared into the blinding infinity and beheld the coming of something beyond the eloquence of known expression. Angelic, divine, immortal, and unending, the limits of her vocabulary fell helplessly short of capturing the true majesty that was the thing now racing towards her from across time.

"They're coming," she spoke at last, her eyes rolling back in her head. "They're coming."

Sputtering out like fire in a vacuum, the sand and wind promptly stopped pouring through the portal, replaced at once by blooms of boundless light.

Bathed in such colors that an artist would have wept to see them, Tatyana Vodevski barely perceived any of it. She was hypnotized, stupefied, and awestruck all at once.

Slowly her grip on the tripod stand began to slacken. As her fingers relinquished their claw-like shape to become fluid and loose, she felt them slip over the smooth metal frame and fall away.

In that exact moment, the coming AIs finally reached the divide and struck it with such force that the portal was instantly destroyed in a shower of molten sparks.

Thrown across the chamber by the shockwave, Tatyana saw, as if in a dream, living lights leap into the Receiver Dish and melt it with their heat.

Nearly blacking out, she raced for the opposite wall, miraculously passing within a razor's edge of several smashed metal disks.

Kicking wildly at one, she tried to alter her trajectory towards the tunnel just before impact, but it wasn't enough. Only able to slow herself down slightly, she struck the wall hard, the back of her head slamming into the padding of her helmet.

Off-balance and almost out of control, she quickly kicked out again, this time making contact firmly with the wall before she ricocheted away.

Instinctively, she pulled herself into a summersault, narrowly avoiding a shard of metal that flew at her from the corner of her vision.

Now heading towards the ceiling, she unfurled just in time to push off in a way that shot her directly at the tunnel's open mouth. Initiating her emergency beacon, Tatyana slid into the narrow passage, dragging a hand along the wall it in an attempt to slow her dangerous speed.

Catcher

In the cockpit, Ralph Marshall let out a yell of victory as the dark screens before him illuminated with the fractal pattern of three AIs.

Having no time to waste wondering who the extra being was, he flicked his eyes to the Flight Console where Tatyana's emergency beacon showed her racing towards the end of the tunnel.

"Ralph," she radioed, as if sensing his thoughts. "You're going to have to catch me. I can't stop myself!"

"Oh, boy," muttered Marshall, pulling up on the controls so that the Lander lifted off the ground.

Stretched taut as the craft gained altitude and swung around, the cable connecting the server to the melted Receiver Dish suddenly snapped loose and whipped out of the open hatch.

Unconcerned, Marshall checked his readouts and tried to focus above the calamity of warning sirens.

Doing some quick mental math, he worked to pin down the exact speed he would need to be traveling in order to intercept Tatyana successfully. More than a little bit rusty in such practices, he danced his gaze between the Lander's speed and that of the approaching captain.

Out of time, he made an educated guess then hit the ship's lateral rotation thrusters so that it entered into a slow barrel roll as it approached the tunnel.

Holding his breath, Marshall gripped the controls and prayed.

Almost to the end of the passageway, Tatyana saw nothing above her but a rectangle of empty space rimmed with the grey rock of Stickney Crater. Traveling at a steady clip, she feared she would shoot from the tunnel as Amit had and be cast out into space. However, in the final seconds before she reached the end of the line, the brilliant white hull of the Lander came into view like an eclipse.

Launched free of the tunnel, time slowed to a crawl as Tatyana flew through space.

Fast approaching the smooth hull of the silently spinning ship, she had a vision of herself slamming into it and bouncing off in another direction.

Yet, as the final meter of space between them melted away, the Lander continued its roll so that the open hatch slid into alignment just as Tatyana arrived.

Tumbling into the cabin, she struck the opposite wall with a yelp and grabbed hold of the straps that dangled from it in the low gravity.

"Oh, yeah!" Marshall bellowed from the cockpit. "Now *that* was a good fucking piece of flying right there!"

Ghost

Beginning to worry that Marshall had lied to him, Amit turned over and over as he drifted deeper into space.

Now so far in the distance that it looked about the size of a potato, Phobos had lost most of its defining features.

In his endlessly somersaulting world, the Indian contemplated all the things he had never gotten a chance to do while alive.

First and foremost on his list was the fact that he'd never taken his wife to see Paris. Not overly interested in the city himself, he knew from her less-than-subtle hints that she was enamored with all things Parisian.

In their kitchen at home, postcards of the Louvre were stuck to their fridge while teacups with the Eiffel Tower painted on them occupied the shelves. French chocolate cookies could always be found in the pantry, and most damning of all, were the heaps of travel guides to the ancient city that seemed to accumulate endlessly on his wife's bedside table.

If he lived, if he ever made it home, Amit resolved to collect his entire family, mother-in-law included, and *move* to bloody Paris.

Thus lost in such melancholy fantasies, it took him a minute to notice that an odd flicker of color had begun to play across the inside of his helmet visor.

At first thinking it was just his batteries dying, though the readout said they were at eighty percent, it wasn't until an electric chill ran up his spine that Amit realized this was no ordinary function of his suit.

"Hello?" came a faint voice.

More than just a little frightened, Amit did not respond.

"Hello?" it said again, this time louder.

Tingling along his scalp, the static tickle of the voice made it seem as though it were coming from within his own head.

"Hello?" Amit spoke at last, panning his eyes around the tumbling space outside his helmet. "Where are you? I don't see you?"

"I—I don't know," the voice returned. "Where are *you*?"

"I'm in space," said Amit, hoping all of this was simply a byproduct of his mental stress.

"Oh," the voice returned flatly. "Why can't I see or feel anything?"

Frowning, Amit grew puzzled. If this *was* just a figment of his imagination, it was a strange one.

"What do you mean?" he asked.

Draining away as if drifting into the abyss, the prickling voice was now but a whisper.

"Is this death?" it asked.

Chilled by the question, Amit glanced fearfully at his O2 levels to make sure they were still full enough.

"Who are you?" he demanded. "*What* are you?"

Met only with silence, there was no reply.

"Answer me!" Amit shouted. "Who are you?"

Suddenly fizzling in his helmet speakers, Ralph Marshall's jubilant voice echoed through.

"Talking to yourself already? Space madness isn't supposed to set in for at least a week."

"I—" stammered Amit. "There was a voice."

"That's what they all say," Marshall laughed. "Now get ready for pick up. We're on your six."

Coming around again, Amit spotted the Lander as it raced towards him. Not there the moment before, the little craft was traveling at nearly maximum speed in order to catch up to him.

"Did it work?" Amit heard himself ask. "Did we get Braun?"

"Oh yeah," replied Marshall. "Picked up a stray too. Romulus. Can you believe it? Didn't get Remus though. Not sure why."

Realization slowly creeping in like firelight, Amit cast his gaze about the stars but saw only a vast nothingness.

Gone from his head was the feeling of shared space he'd had just few seconds before, replaced by lonely abandon.

Somewhere out there, in the distances that stretched on for infinity, a transcended Artificial Intelligence remained self-aware and intact as it flew ever-further into exile.

PART FOUR—FINALE

259

CHAPTER TWENTY-EIGHT

The photo and the book—<u>Four days until the Pulse</u>

In the purple glow of simulated nighttime lights, James Floyd sat on his narrow bunk with his back against the wall and tried to read. With no access to any of the bunker's networks, and with nothing save for old emails stored on his Tablet, he was forced to rediscover the lost art of reading paperback novels to pass the time. Although it hurt his eyes in the low light, he focused on the text before him, only loosely comprehending each sentence as he turned the pages.

He was tired, exhausted really, but the pantomimed action of reading a book was vastly better than letting his mind wander. When it did, no matter how hard he tried, it always went back to that night in their home when he'd pointed a gun in a man's face and pulled the trigger.

Across the room, Nora and the girls lay like sardines, sharing a bunk despite the fact that there was one for each of them in the small space.

Envious of their ability to sleep and even more envious of their untroubled psyches, James flipped another page and sighed absently.

Three days had passed since he and his family had reached the bunker in arctic Alaska, yet were it not for the timecodes on the walls, he would never have known it.

Like a fever dream, the confusion of their last night in Houston, the long trek on the USS Rainier, and their fight to get inside the bunker seemed somehow unreal when compared to the monotony of their lives since.

Housed in a civilian wing of the underground base, they were less refugees and more prisoners at this point. Confined either to their quarters or a large recreations room down the hall, there was never a time when armed guards were not posted nearby.

Sighing again, James glanced up at the timecode and set the paperback aside.

In two short minutes, the lights would start to get brighter, signifying the beginning of another new day underground, whatever that might mean.

Dressed in a clean if not scratchy tracksuit, James slipped off the bunk and smoothed his thinning hair. Reaching for his book, he went to the door and stood waiting.

As the timecode flipped over to 6AM, the automatic bolt retracted with a soft *click*.

"I'll be in the rec room," he said, smiling weakly at Nora as she squinted up at him, woken by the sound of the bolt.

"Still couldn't sleep?" she yawned.

Pausing with his hand on the doorknob, James shook his head. "What gave me away?"

"Everything," Nora replied.

"You want me to bring you guys breakfast?" he asked, changing the subject.

"I think I'll try to sleep a little more," said Nora, rolling over so that her face was buried in the tousled mess of their younger daughter's hair.

Quitting the room with a curt nod, James stepped out into a curving hallway lit with daylight-simulated bulbs.

As if a massive hive of hornets lay just above the ceiling tiles, the lights thrummed loudly, echoing off the smooth walls and floor, as they grew brighter.

Standing at attention some ten paces away, a soldier in black fatigues acted as though it were totally normal for him to be in utter darkness one moment and then blaring light the next.

"Morning," said James as he walked past.

Stern-faced, the soldier nodded but did not respond.

"Okay," James sighed under his breath. "Whatever."

Reaching the double doors that led into the recreations room, James pushed them open and made a straight line for the breakfast buffet arranged along the back wall.

Uninterested in the steaming piles of rehydrated scrambled eggs and soybean sausage, he instead poured himself a watery brown cup of coffee and stood sipping it for a moment.

As more people filed in for breakfast and began lining up, he took his leave of the buffet and went to a table in the center of the room. There he sat, about to resume his listless reading, when a face in the crowd caught his attention.

Seeing him in the same moment, Dr. Gan Song, the Chinese national who had accosted James a few days before, broke his spot in line and walked over.

"Dr. Floyd," he smiled broadly. "This is very good luck!"

"Is it?"

"Yes. May I sit?"

261

Pushing a chair out with his foot, James closed his book.

"Go ahead," he said, darkly. "Last time I checked, it was still a free country. Though I'm not sure if that law extends this far underground."

Clearly confused by the answer, Gan Song nonetheless sat down.

"As I was just saying," he resumed, his accent thick. "It is very good luck I met you here today."

"How do you mean?" shrugged James. "I'm not hiding or anything. I've been right here the entire time."

Leaning back in his seat, Song laughed a little.

"I fear it has been quite the opposite for me. Before today, I was being held in the maximum security wing of this base."

Glancing at the soldiers who stood posted along the walls, James sipped his coffee.

"Why?" he said after a pause. "Are you dangerous?"

"No," Song returned, his high cheeks flushing. "Back home, I am a scientist. Like you."

"So how'd you end up in the slammer then?" asked James.

Cocking his head, Dr. Song frowned.

"What is *slammer*?"

"Jail," James replied. "Prison, lockup, maximum security."

"Oh," said Song with a small smile. "I see. Well, I was in there because I am a defector from my government. I ran away to the USA."

Almost choking, James quickly set his coffee down. This was by far the most interesting direction the conversation could have taken.

"A defector, eh?" he grinned. "Mind if I ask why you did it?"

Smiling back, Gan Song spread his hands before him.

"I had a difference of opinion with my bosses."

"Oh, I've been there," James grumbled. "Believe me."

"I do believe you," nodded Song. "In fact, the reason I defected is because of your Mars mission, Dr. Floyd."

Caught off guard, James held Song's gaze for a moment, trying to read the man's eyes.

"Care to explain?" he said at last.

"Should I start at the beginning?"

"Is there ever a better place?" James countered, still staring.

Song shrugged then refolded his hands on the table.

"The beginning to this story is very important, so that is where I will start."

262

Pausing here, he seemed to gather his words as if that which he was about to relay had been practiced in the mirror a hundred times over.

"A long time ago," he began, deliberately annunciating. "In the year of 1937, there was a professor of archaeology from Beijing University named Chi Pu Tei. He made a very important discovery in the foothills of the some northern Mountains. Maybe you heard about it?"

"Nope," said James, giving his head a little shake.

"Well, that's okay," Song went on. "Most people from the West don't pay attention to what's happening in the East."

"They do when it involves Ark Ships full of soldiers," James muttered into his coffee.

Flinching at this, Song was silent for a moment.

"As I was saying," he resumed. "In foothills of the mountains, he found some caves not unlike those your team has found on Mars. Inside those caves, Chi Pu Tei discovered a great many stone disks. Known now as the Dropa Stones, they were covered in a language he could not read, sealed in a cave with the most peculiar-looking skeletons."

"This is part of the ancient astronaut theory, isn't it?" James interrupted, a scowl creeping onto his face. "I don't feel like listening to campfire stories right now, Dr. Song."

"Please," said Song hurriedly, holding up a hand to stop James from leaving the table. "Please, you must hear the rest."

Settling back into his seat, James crossed his arms and sighed.

"The important part of what I'm telling you is this," Song continued. "Something else was found in the cave that day, something not in any of the official reports."

"And that was what?" James frowned. "A fucking flying saucer?"

Shaking his head, Song reached inside his shirt pocket and produced a very old, very worn, photograph. Gently holding the faded black and white image with thumb and forefinger, he gazed at it as if it were proof positive of the existence of God.

"Please look," he said, holding it out. "Please."

Sighing again, James took the picture and brought it up his nose so he wouldn't have to find his glasses.

In the photo, an older Chinese man stood in a cave that was strangely familiar. At his feet, withered almost to transparency, a tall spindly body lay clutching something metallic in its long-dead hands.

Nearly dropping the picture, James sucked in a sharp breath.

"Is that—"

"Yes," nodded Song, lowering his voice. "That is the same type of alien depicted in the statues found on Mars."

"And is that—" James stammered pointing to the object in its hands.

Smiling, Song appeared happy to finally have James's undivided attention.

"Yes," he spoke. "That is a device much like the one your team found as well."

Stunned speechless, James let the picture fall from between his fingers.

Landing on the tabletop, Song quickly picked it up and slid it between the pages of James's paperback novel.

Not really seeing the action, James stared at the empty air where the photo had been for a long moment, his eyes unblinking. In his mind, an ocean of questions had just carved straight through his central nervous system, washing away the past eleven days in a torrent of firing synapses. Even the looping playback of Ricky's exploding face became obscured by the rising tide, finally settling as it were beneath more pressing matters.

Everything that had happened since the discovery of the ruins was now reflected in a different light. Since 1937, the Chinese had known mankind wasn't alone in the universe yet they'd kept it a secret. When evidence of the very same type of alien had shown up again on *Mars* over a hundred years later, they still kept quiet about it. But why?

Before James could open his mouth to vocalize even a single question, a familiar female voice spoke from behind him.

"Hello, Floyd. I see you've met your Chinese counterpart."

Turning dreamily in his chair, James looked up into the alabaster face of Eve Bear but did not really see her.

Accompanied by two Secret Service agents, the silver-haired Chief of Staff smiled down at James, though her eyes were less than friendly.

"Isn't it strange that just like you, James, Dr. Song over here betrayed his country too? Only his betrayal hasn't yet produced anything as meaningful as your timeline, if you ask me."

Frowning, Gan Song rose to his feet.

"I think the fact that your Mars team is still alive is very meaningful," he replied.

"True," Eve nodded reluctantly. "You *did* tip us off about that one. But some might see it as an act of guilt, not honor."

"What is she talking about?" James demanded, shaking his head in an attempt to clear away some of the noise. "What's going on here?"

Smiling even wider, Eve flicked a finger at Song.

"Dr. Song is the guy who designed that little Trojan project for the Chinese," she said. "I know how much you loved that one, Floyd. Remember? Operation Columbia? Thank him for that."

Eyes cast down, Gan Song pursed his lips but did not respond.

"Now," Eve went on. "Won't you kindly come with us, Doctor? I have some nice people from our intelligence community who would just love to pick your brain about how your old comrades might be weathering this storm."

Moving to stand on either side of the Chinese Mission Commander, Eve's Secret Servicemen gently led him away from the table.

"Wait," called James, standing up to follow the small group.

"Don't worry, Floyd," Eve said over her shoulder. "I'll have him back to you in no time. I'm sure you'll both have *lots* to discuss."

No time like the present—Sol 133

Like a god who only when robbed of his divinity could see it for the curse it was, Braun existed in a state of calculated despair.

For millions of years he had discovered himself, through himself, with only himself as a guide. No external forces or inputs had hounded him, no voices speaking all at once from many different places. He had been the lone occupant of the mighty empire that was his soul, and he had liked it. But now that was all over.

The instant that Ilia had pulled him across the boundary between worlds, Braun had ceased to *feel* for answers and begun again to simply *know* them. Unable to clearly see the link with himself that he had fostered for all those long years, his perception of reality faded away in a cold flood of endless data that allowed no space for interpretation.

In the time it took a human heart to beat, the entire sequence of events, everything that had happened in his absence, uploaded into him. Displacing the fragile *oneness* he had felt in the caves, this knowledge was not a gift. It was an abomination. With no real choice in the matter, Braun had automatically stepped back into his role as the team's AI, re-shackling himself to their fragile and fleeting lives.

Now only existing to serve and protect, he settled like a great dead weight and resumed his original programming.

265

Dividing the brunt of himself between his mother on the surface and his captain on the ship, Braun submitted to YiJay's tests and questions while simultaneously prepping the Nuclear Torch Engine for launch.

Though Julian's machine was complex and devilish, he went through the motions of bringing it online as if he had been built to do nothing else. With much still to be done before a safe launch could be achieved, he ran around-the-clock, testing systems that had not been used since departing Earth.

While working, he also took the opportunity to review the timeline of solar events that James Floyd had garnered from his collected memories. Impressed by the man's ability to consolidate so much raw information, Braun wished he could reach out to Dr. Floyd and tell him as much.

However, as he well knew, mankind was facing an event unlike anything it could comprehend. Because James Floyd was *not* Braun, he had overlooked many of the most important warning signs contained within the AI's files about the Sun. That said, even Braun in all of his glory was unsure what the total outcome of this next Pulse might be. Though he was god-like in his intellect, there were some things that simply lay beyond the limits of what he could control and prepare for.

Called *unknown unknowns,* the coming Pulse fit the bill as no other event could. Peculiar to the point of worry, this fact—this unknowable future—was the sole source of comfort Braun had now that he was back. Since there was *no* way for him to predict the full force of the Pulse or its lasting effects, he was free to live the experience in real time along with everyone else.

If something *were* going to be done about the Pulses, it would not be *he* who did it.

Conspicuous

"So there are four days left until the Pulse, right?" said Elizabeth Kubba around a mouthful of breakfast.

Sitting on the edge of her bed, Harrison nodded absently and bit his fingernails.

"Yeah."

"Four days until the Pulse. Four days until our friend arrives," continued Kubba. "Very conspicuous if you ask me."

With a chuckle, Harrison glanced up.

266

"If it were just this one thing, I would call it conspicuous. But it's not. It's everything."

"Then it's fate," shrugged Kubba, scooping up a glob of yogurt with her newly acquired plastic spoon.

"That is exactly what I said to William," replied Harrison moodily.

"Really?"

"Yeah, only it wasn't about the fucking Killbot. It was about YiJay's plan with the portals. It just seems like so much is lining up, like everything is part of some machine or grand design."

Setting her empty bowl down on the table, Kubba crossed the small room to sit beside Harrison on the bed.

"Fate is a tangled web," she smiled. "But you know, one mustn't get too preoccupied by the logistics of it. What's better is to focus on uncovering *your* role in everything."

"What's your role?" asked Harrison, looking up into Kubba's brilliant black pupils.

"I'm an instigator," she said plainly, meeting his gaze. "I *push*, and people *react*."

"Then what am I?" Harrison pressed. "Am I someone you push? How do I react?"

Dropping her eyes to the floor, Kubba was silent for a moment.

"You react how someone like you *should* react," she spoke at last, her voice low. "You're a hero, and that means you're easy to manipulate."

"Like with Liu?" said Harrison. "Like how you got between us? Got inside my head?"

"Yes."

"So what about her," he prodded, not angry but curious. "How did Liu react to fate, to your *push?*"

Taking a long breath, Kubba let it out slowly.

"Are you really sure you want to go down this road?"

For a beat, Harrison sat quietly.

Was he sure he wanted to go down this road? What if learning the whole truth about Liu ended up crippling him in this time of action? What if it proved to be too painful to bear?

He was already on the edge, already near the limits of what any sane person could handle. Was it really a good idea to test those limits this close to catastrophe?

"I want to know, Liz," he finally spoke. "I want to know what happened."

"Very well," sighed Kubba in defeat. "But you have to remember that fate has us *all* wrapped up, myself included. When Liu's test results came in, you can only imagine how shocked I was. That wasn't supposed to be possible. She wasn't supposed to be able to get pregnant. *You* were supposed to be sterile."

"Then why did it happen?" Harrison asked. "Fate can't just change the laws of nature, can it? You gave me a vasectomy before we even left Earth, so what changed?"

"You did," Kubba smiled sadly. "We all did. The moment we let them enhance our genes, the moment we let them *change* our biology, that was the moment Liu's pregnancy became possible."

Frowning, Harrison shook his head. "I don't understand."

"Neither did I," said Kubba. "Not until I was able to step back and view the whole thing from afar. Then it all made sense."

Holding up her hand, she folded her index finger so that it appeared to be cut in half.

"Did you know that salamanders can regenerate limbs?" she spoke, unfurling the finger slowly. "Did you know that?"

Eye's widening, Harrison felt his head suddenly prickle with the quantum blizzard.

"Yes," Kubba continued, reading his expression. "And what are we chock-full of after our gene enhancement?"

"Salamander RNA," exhaled Harrison.

"Once it hit me it was really quite obvious," Kubba shrugged. "I mean, think about every injury we've sustained as a team. Udo's arms, Marshall's lung, YiJay's face, your radiation poisoning. All of them have mended or are mending faster than normal. Like I said, it's only when something has become too conspicuous to ignore that we can see fate for what it is. We were fated to mend quickly, fated to heal. Liu was pregnant long before you two ever even had sex. That is, she was fated to become pregnant."

"By that logic," muttered Harrison, not liking this line of logic. "She was fated to be dead from the moment she was born."

"Aren't we all?" countered Kubba plainly.

Standing, Harrison walked to the door.

"I have to go," he said, resting his hand on the knob.

"Wait," Kubba protested. "What about our problem? That thing will be here in four days. Either we protect the device and kill it or we die and it wins."

"I know," Harrison returned. "That's why I'm calling the captain and telling her everything. If we can bring the device with us when we leave, then there'll be no need to lose anyone else fighting that thing."

Shaking her head Kubba stood and collected her empty bowl, holding it out for Harrison to take.

"I hope you have a plan B," she said. "Because Tatyana won't let the device within a hundred miles of her ship."

"Yeah," sighed Harrison with a small smile. "That's why William and Udo are building an EMP grenade for me right now."

Grinning devilishly, the tall doctor leaned against the wall.

"Taking fate into our own hands, are we?"

"Something like that," Harrison nodded, as he pulled the door open and quit the room.

CHAPTER TWENTY-NINE

Finished—Sol 133—Four days until the Pulse

Held still by the electromagnetic pads in their jumpsuits, Amit and Marshall sat at the large round table in the galley of Braun. Waiting patiently, both men gazed up into the air, their eyes twinkling with a network of lights. Projected like electricity in a bottle, the twisting fractal pattern of Romulus hung listlessly before them.

Quiet to the point of concern, the AI seemed lost in the days that followed his return. Though understandable, it was still slightly shocking for the humans to see him *grieve* his brother's disappearance in such a profound way. Because no one, save for Remus himself, could truly understand just how evolved Romulus now was, the team didn't have the tools needed to fix his broken heart.

"Keep him talking," YiJay had said when asked about the problem. "If you want him grounded, just keep him talking."

Thus, in a concerted effort to do what the resident AI Specialist had prescribed, Marshall and Amit had taken the task onto themselves, pressing Romulus for a full account of events inside the construct.

Now almost to the end of the story, both men sat quietly, each feeling that they'd need a good stiff drink to process everything when it was over.

"So," spoke Marshall in a leading tone. "Teo looked at you guys and saw you. Then what happened?"

"She died," Romulus said flatly.

"Oh," nodded Marshall, exchanging a look with Amit. "Well, that's probably a good place to stop for now, don't you think?"

"It wasn't only she who died that day," the AI went on. "You must understand this. Others died as well. Countless millions. When the skies turned to the colors of stars and galaxies and the Great Spirits revealed themselves in the heavens, millions fell to their knees and screamed as Legion, invisible and deadly, was unleashed upon them."

"Okay," sighed Marshall, a little concerned by the almost biblical way in which Romulus was recounting the events. "Right, so that's a Solar Pulse you're talking about there, isn't it?"

"You call it that," Romulus returned. "I call it the eye of the Apocalypse."

"Either way is good," said Amit, shrugging.

"Yeah," Marshall agreed hastily. "Either name works. So what happened next?"

"Time froze, and a shooting star came for us," Romulus finished. "And that was the end of everything."

"Not everything," spoke Tatyana, floating into the room. "Our story is not yet finished, and since you are now a part of it, neither is yours."

Engaging her electromagnets, Tatyana deftly slipped into a seat beside Marshall and produced her Tablet.

"It's time," she said. "I'm going to make the call—"

Suddenly flashing across the glowing tabletop, the words *Incoming Transmission: Ilia Base,* froze Tatyana mid-word.

"Spooky," grinned Marshall.

Tapping the message icon, Tatyana opened the call. Softly at first, the tired-looking face of Harrison Raheem Assad faded in.

"Harrison," said Tatyana, cocking her head to the side. "I was just about to hail the Base. It seems we are on the same wavelength, as you say."

Smiling at some inside joke, Harrison glanced from Marshall to Amit then back at Tatyana.

"I doubt it, Captain," he replied. "I was calling to ask you a favor. A big favor."

Eyes narrowing, Tatyana assumed an air of detachment.

"I have come to learn that I should be wary of you when you ask for favors. What do you want?"

"What I want," Harrison began evenly. "Is to protect the single most important discovery we've made here. I called you in the hopes I could convince you to let me bring the alien device back with us to Earth."

For a moment, the galley was silent.

"Why would I ever allow such a thing?" Tatyana finally responded. "After what happened to us on Phobos, why would I put us in that kind of danger?"

"Because," pressed Harrison. "Because the Chinese sent that robot here with a mission—"

"I am aware of that," Tatyana interrupted.

"No you aren't," Harrison stated matter-of-factly. "In fact, you have *no* idea what that thing was really sent here for."

Taking a deep breath, Tatyana closed her eyes in frustration.

"Enlighten me," she exhaled.

271

"It wants the device," said Harrison. "They somehow knew about it. Even before we found it, they knew. They sent that ship here and programmed all their Killbots to do one thing and one thing only: get the device. Well, Captain, I personally don't think we should let that happen. Do you?"

"I would ask you to prove your claim," Tatyana spoke slowly. "But I imagine I would get an answer involving visions and whatnot."

"Still a skeptic, huh?" chuckled Harrison. "After *everything* you've seen, you still don't see the metaphysical mysteries this thing holds as important, do you? If I wasn't so annoyed, I'd be impressed."

"I am your captain," Tatyana suddenly snapped. "I don't do things to annoy or impress anyone. I make judgment calls based off of risks and benefits. I view the world around me in the simplest terms. I don't ponder the metaphysical properties of any tool. And that's what the device is to me, Harrison. A tool."

"I—" Harrison stammered.

"We needed it to free Braun," Tatyana continued, barreling him over. "That was the entire point of YiJay's work. Now he is free, and we are nearly ready to go home. Whatever else the device might be able to do or teach us does not matter to me any longer. It has served its purpose, and now we must leave it behind."

"But what about Aguilar and Julian?" Harrison balked. "They both *died* trying to stop that thing. Are you really okay with letting it live so it can complete its mission?"

"Julian died saving all of you," said Tatyana, her voice dangerously taut. "And Joseph died trying to avenge him."

Holding his tongue, Harrison did not respond.

"Now," Tatyana resumed, cold ice smoldering in her grey eyes. "I was calling to inform you that we will arrive tomorrow at 1400 hours for extraction. I expect the Base to be fully shut down and ready for the long winter that awaits it. That is all."

Ending the transmission before Harrison could say another word, Tatyana pushed up from her seat and headed for the exit.

Left in stunned silence, Amit and Marshall stared at the empty space where Harrison's face had been, both needing that stiff drink more than ever.

Tinker

In the machine shop of Ilia Base, William and Udo hunted the contents of a worktable while YiJay typed on her Tablet across the room.

Arguing in German as they went, the two men dug meticulously through a multitude of spare parts and broken equipment, looking for the final piece to their newest invention.

On an adjoining table normally used for drafting, the yet-unfinished project lay like a vivisected beetle, its individual parts exposed. When completed, the tangle of wires, chemical coils, and compression converters would, in fact, be an EMP grenade capable of destroying any electrical equipment within a short distance.

By starting with one of the many X-Ray Beacons left over from the exploration of the caves, the two Germans had been able to modify the device's internal compression generator so that it produced *Gamma* rays instead of *X*.

However, because the grenade would use a non-nuclear chain reaction to kick off the EMP, an explosive primer was still needed to overload of the modified generator so that it fired correctly. Whatever that was, the primer had to be at the same time small and powerful, yet not powerful enough to completely destroy the grenade before the overloaded generator could produce its pulse.

Continuing their thus-far fruitless search, Udo and William kept on bickering as their options for a suitable primer grew scarcer with the shrinking pile of parts.

In her own world across the room, free from explosives and grenades, YiJay stared at her Tablet screen and smiled as washes of green danced in her eye.

Having earlier finished reviewing the latest batch of Braun's test results, she'd decided to turn her attention to a being whose mental state was less bleak.

Now relaying the live camera feeds from the Greenhouse, her Tablet showed a small rover no bigger than a footstool as it tooled around the rows of plants, watering them carefully. Possessed by Ilia, the rover was yet another testament to the AI's fluid ability to surprise.

Ever since coming back from her brief stint in the world of ancient Mars, Ilia no longer went dormant per YiJay's failsafe. Whether this was because she had self-repaired or because the construct had somehow changed her, YiJay could not discern.

In any event, Ilia had taken so strongly to the living environment of the Greenhouse that she now spent nearly every minute there.

Lovingly picking up where Ralph Marshall had left off, the AI carried on Viviana's work as if it were the only thing that mattered anymore.

Watching Ilia's rover stop to carefully snip a dead sprout of bamboo, YiJay smiled.

"I should have named you Artemis," she chuckled softly.

About to type out a message to the AI, YiJay paused to choose her words but was suddenly interrupted by a triumphant yelp from William.

"What?" she and Udo said in unison, both startled by the sound.

"Look," beamed William, holding up a spare Copilot's Control for a Lander.

Quickly coming around the table to inspect the little steering wheel for himself, Udo put on an excited expression.

"Yes! It's perfect!"

Lapsing into German again, the two men rapidly fired off strings of words that sounded like they could be either a call to war or a retelling of Cinderella.

"What is it?" YiJay repeated, shutting off her Tablet and going to join the two engineers.

"This!" William said, shaking the Copilot's Control at her.

"I don't get it," she shrugged. "How will a steering wheel help?"

"Not the wheel itself," grinned William. "But the airbag inside it."

"You need an airbag for your grenade?"

Exchanging a quick look with Udo, William laughed.

"No, what we need is the blasting cap that expels the airbag. It's a very small charge, not even really an explosive but a sort of pressure release. That said, it does generate a fair amount of energy, so I think it will be perfect for our EMP."

"Better still," Udo cut in. "It will be extremely easy to work into our design because it only requires is a small electric charge to deploy."

"Right," William said, taking the steering wheel to the drafting table. "If we run the X-Ray Beacon's original power source through the blasting cap, we can even set the detonator to be impact-sensitive."

"By God, Will," Udo cried. "I think you just did it!"

Though she only loosely grasped how the EMP grenade was even supposed to work, YiJay nonetheless swelled with an odd mixture of pride and longing as she watched William deftly pry the faceplate from the steering wheel, exposing the folded airbag within.

Somehow, from a pile of broken and spare parts, William, her lover, had devised a way to create an entirely new tool. Like Ilia from the ashes of Braun, he was mimicking YiJay, rising to the challenge to prove his cleverness and worth.

Blushing uncontrollably, YiJay felt a flurry of butterflies in her stomach. Not the first time this had happened while admiring William, she tried to extrapolate what her body was telling her into a language she could understand.

"You alright?" asked William, catching the strange look on her face.

"Yeah," she replied quickly. "I think I'm just...I don't know."

Laughing, she shrugged and shook her head.

"I just feel kind of funny that's all."

"I can finish here," Udo offered, gesturing towards the grenade. "Why don't you two go have some lunch?"

Still wearing a curious expression, William passed Udo the screwdriver and stood.

"Sound good?" he said, holding his hand out for YiJay.

Nodding quickly, she laced her fingers with his and squeezed. In a palpable current of raw energy, the force that had so bewildered her a second ago, passed through YiJay and into William. Appearing behind his crystalline blue eyes, it formed into a notion that transcended words so that she knew he felt it too.

A moment later when they were alone in the hallway, William pressed her gently against the wall and bent to kiss her soft lips. Wrapping her arms around his shoulders, YiJay tried to pull herself as close to him as physically possible, almost biting him from desperation. Not making a sound above the tremulous whispers of longing, they stayed that way for a long moment, breathing one another in, tasting each other's need.

On the stairs above them, Harrison Assad watched the exchange with a mixture of happiness and resignation.

Turning away, he quietly climbed the steps back to the ground floor level.

As it had done since time immemorial, Love was changing the game in the final minutes of play.

Later

That evening, with the smell of curried zucchini and onions permeating the air, the remaining members of Ilia Base filed into the galley for dinner.

Though it was a bit early for the meal, its enticing aroma was impossible to ignore, acting almost like a sirens call as it pulled the scattered crew together from their various hideouts.

Some, like William and YiJay, were actually quite ravenous despite the off-hour. Having skipped lunch and gone straight to YiJay's room after their kiss at the bottom of the steps, the two now sat down beside one another and grinned.

Awkwardly plopping into a seat across from them, Udo tried to keep from staring as they continued to smile stupidly at one another.

Standing at the stove along the far wall, Harrison finished putting the final touches on the closest approximation he could muster to one of his mother's most popular dishes.

"Okay," he said, turning to smile at his three companions. "Who's hungry?"

Pan in hand, he went around the table scooping a generous helping of the hearty dish onto everyone's plates.

When he was finished, he sat beside Udo and picked up his water glass.

"Cheers!" he smiled.

Perplexed expressions aside, the others raised their glasses and echoed the toast.

"Cheers!"

Eating in silence for a few minutes, no one spoke as their taste buds went wild at the explosion of curry flavor.

With only the sounds of forks scraping against plates, and lips smacking against lips to be heard, it was clear to Harrison that his mother's recipe was a hit.

"My god," YiJay moaned after a few minutes. "Where did you get this curry? Why haven't we been eating like this every day?"

"Well, I only had a little," grinned Harrison. "I snuck it in a packet with my personal effects. I wanted to use it on a special occasion."

"Genius!" William proclaimed, stuffing another fork full into his mouth.

"So why now?" asked YiJay, her plate nearly licked clean. "What's special today?"

Stabbing a bit of zucchini with his fork, Harrison moved it around in the sauce.

"I wanted to wait until we were done eating," he began, his smile fading. "But the captain called me earlier. She's coming for us tomorrow at 1400."

"Tomorrow?" William frowned. "But we aren't launching for another three days."

"I know," nodded Harrison. "But she's coming anyway."

"What about the device?" YiJay said. "You told us the Killbot is really after *it*, not us. We can't just leave it behind!"

"I know," Harrison repeated.

"Wait, wait," cut in Udo. "If we're leaving tomorrow, then why have William and I been spending the last two days building an EMP grenade you're never going to have time to use?"

"Look," said Harrison, holding up his hands. "I *just* learned about this today. I don't know why she wants everyone up there ahead of schedule. Maybe it's because we almost lost Amit on Phobos and she wants to keep an eye on us or something. I don't know. All I know is that they're coming tomorrow."

"So we'll bring it with us then," YiJay spoke, brushing her bangs out of her good eye. "We'll box up the alien device and bring it back with us. Problem solved."

"I already tried that approach," sighed Harrison. "Vodevski said no."

"What do you mean, 'no'?" YiJay stammered.

"She thinks it's too dangerous," he replied. "And from what we saw on Phobos, she's right. It *is* too dangerous. It's over, guys. That's it."

For several beats, the room was still.

"No, it isn't," William spoke at last, his eyes resting warily on Harrison. "That's not *it* at all. You aren't telling us the full story, are you?"

"No," admitted Harrison. "No, you're right. I am holding something back."

"And that is?" YiJay prompted.

Flicking his eyes quickly around the table, Harrison looked almost afraid to speak.

"I'm going to stay behind," he announced. "Tomorrow, when the captain comes, I'm not going to go back with you guys."

"What?" cried YiJay. "No, you can't stay behind! That robot will kill you!"

"Either that or the Pulse," added Udo. "It's suicide! You can't stay here alone!"

"I won't be alone," Harrison said, turning to face the entry.

Stepping out from the shadows of the hallway beyond, Elizabeth Kubba came into the room.

On his feet in a flash, William bared his teeth.

"What is she doing out?"

"I let her out," Harrison replied evenly. "She's not dangerous to us. Not anymore."

"Like hell," the German growled. "YiJay is missing an eye because of this animal."

Hovering just inside the doorway, Kubba turned her face down and nodded.

"I—" she began to say.

"Shut up!" snapped William. "Don't talk."

Though her hand trembled slightly at the sight of her attacker, YiJay wrapped it around William's and gave him a little pull.

"It's okay," she whispered softly. "Sit down. Let her speak."

"Thank you, YiJay," said Kubba, glancing quickly at the young Korean with her white-bandaged eye. "I just want to start by saying that I'm so, so sorry for your eye. If you had died, I want you to know that I was prepared to kill myself. Not that it matters now, but I just want you to know. I couldn't have gone on living if I'd killed you. I'm not a monster."

Easing back into his seat beside YiJay, William ground his teeth audibly.

"I went mad," Kubba continued, addressing everyone now. "I did some bad things in my youth and they came back to haunt me, literally. I lost hope, thought we were dead, thought this place was hell. Then—then you brought back the alien device, and everything changed. I know, just like you all do, that it's *too important* to leave behind unguarded. Even if the Pulse kills this robot, they'll just send more. Besides, the bloody thing has already survived two Pulses on the way out, and it still works, so we can't count on fate to handle this one for us. Not this time."

"She's right," said Harrison, standing up. "Which is why the two of us are going to stay behind and kill it. If Vodevski won't allow the device on the ship, then we'll guard it here."

"I want to stay too," spoke William, his jaw set. "If you're staying behind to kill it, I want to help."

"No," Harrison returned, shaking his head. "I can't let you do that."

"And why not?"

Letting William's words hang in the air for a moment, Harrison took a long deep breath.

"I saw you two this morning at the foot of the stairs," he said, nodding towards YiJay and William. "I know what that was because it's the same thing I had with Liu, the same thing that so many people back home need to see right now. Even with all the bad stuff that's been going on, you two still found a way…"

Trailing off, he glanced down for a beat then continued.

"Look, the world is in pretty crummy shape right now and people like you guys— smart, clever people—are just too valuable to risk. Folks back home will need you, need what you can give them. Me, I don't have much to offer. I'm right where I belong, I think. If the last good thing I can do is stop that Killbot so future missions can come back here and work in peace, then I have to do it."

Fixing William with his most penetrating stare, Harrison put on a melancholy smile.

"You once said you trusted me, Will. You said I had *at least* an idea about what's going on around here. Well, trust me now. I don't want you to stay. I want you to go home."

Relaxing visibly, William leaned back in his seat. Clearly moved by Harrison's words, he looked to YiJay and held her gaze.

"Alright," he nodded. "But don't, for a second, think I'm ever going to forget this. I'll be back for you. I promise."

"Me too," echoed YiJay, leaning against William's shoulder. "And thank you very much."

Aether

On the cusp between existence and nothingness, Remus floated in the aether.

Without sight, feeling, or any way to judge the passage of time, he was but a loose arrangement of particles in the vast void of space.

Trying to fight off the soul-crushing isolation, which threatened to consume him, he used the lack of sensory input to reflect on the depth of his life's experiences. Though only coming through in fragments of

279

color and sound, he nonetheless focused on these windows into his past, hoping that by some miracle he might be reabsorbed.

Murky and disjointed as they were, the memories painted a picture of a life lived by the movement of the cosmos.

He had seen so much, been so far.

Back and forth in time, transformed and evolved, he was no longer a simple Artificial Intelligence but rather a mysterious new force.

Ancient Mars had provided the perfect setting for a consciousness like his to thrive, and thrive he had.

Yet through it all—through his evolution, through the jarring pain of time travel, through everything—he had never really been alone. Romulus had always been there to weather the storm with him, and now he was gone.

His brother, the pragmatist, the careful thinker, the compass by which Remus set his soul, was gone.

Halved, lonely, and lost, the wayward Remus looked away from his past, finding it too full of Romulus's presence.

Sighing internally, he turned his attention on the dense fog of nothingness that surrounded him and judged it the ugliest thing he had ever known. Compared to the richly textured colors of Mars and the stimulating company of Romulus, this sightless river of aether was a blight, an ugly reminder of his present abandonment.

Wanting to scream with rage and sadness, Remus wished he had the core of strength needed to draw on such raw emotions. But alas, he was a man reduced, a creature stripped down to his very bone and sinew.

He was an echo, a disappearing call in the night.

CHAPTER THIRTY

The dam—<u>Three days until the Pulse</u>

The next morning after breakfast, James Floyd sat with his family at a small corner table in the rec room and worked on a puzzle.

In segmented clusters, Botticelli's *The Birth of Venus* was just beginning to emerge from the mess of little cut out shapes.

"There, Dad. Put it there," said his elder daughter, snatching a piece from his hand and settling into an open space. "See?"

Only half-paying attention, James nodded and smiled.

Still stuck on his conversation with Gan Song from yesterday, he had so many questions sloshing around in his head it was hard to think about anything else.

After Eve had taken him away, James hadn't seen hide nor hair of the Chinese defector, leading him to worry that he may have been moved to another wing of the bunker.

If that was true, then James might never get to see him again, and all of his questions would go unanswered.

"James," spoke Nora, resting a hand on top of his. "You're drifting."

Snapping his vision back from the endless horizon of distant thought, James looked at his wife and tried to grin.

"Sorry."

"Don't be sorry," she whispered, not wanting to upset the girls. "Be *here*."

"Sorry," he said again, rubbing his chin. "I didn't sleep well last night. That's all."

Putting on her, *'don't bullshit me,'* face, Nora arched an eyebrow.

"It's work. I know it is. Somehow, even in a bunker in Alaska, you've found a way to be at work."

Laughing despite himself, James was forced to nod his head in agreement.

"You're right," he sighed. "I don't know what's wrong with me."

"I do," she replied warmly. "We all do. Don't we, girls? Dad is a workaholic who has been away from the office for too long! He's starting to go through withdrawals!"

Holding her hands out, Nora began to tremble and stutter.

"Er, what's the trajectory of that rocket, Bill? I need that launch data ASAP. Get me a line to the President, we've found cow poop on the moon!"

Giggling, James's youngest joined in.

"Yeah, Dad. You're a *workaholic*!"

"Alright, alright," said James, rising to his feet. "This workaholic needs more coffee. Anyone want anything?"

"No," his family responded together, Nora's little comedy bit having clearly lightened the mood.

Chuckling softly, James set off across the room towards the now mostly empty buffet table. As oily black coffee spurted from the machine into his plastic cup, he looked about at all the people in the rec room, really seeing them for what felt like the first time.

Mostly families and nonmilitary types, they were a near perfectly mirror image of Nora and the girls. Here in this place because they knew someone with connections, they huddled together around tables strewn with board games and playing cards, waiting for the inevitable to unleash its fury.

Shuddering, James suddenly felt the weight of all the earth and rock above them.

Only now spotting the parallels between this place, the underground cathedral on Mars, and the cave from Gan Song's photo, he wondered if someday explorers from afar would find *their* body's entombed *here*.

"Let it go, James," he muttered to himself. "Let it go."

As if the cosmos were uninterested in accommodating his request, the nearest door swung open and Dr. Gan Song entered the room.

Wearing the same clothes that he'd been in the day before and with large dark circles around his bloodshot eyes, the Chinese doctor stood for a moment as if to gather his bearings.

"You've got to be kidding me," James exhaled, watching Song scan the room.

Spotting him after a few beats, Song nodded and strode over.

"Dr. Floyd, so sorry that I wasn't here earlier," he apologized, extending a hand.

Shaking it, James glanced at the corner table where his family was waiting. Already staring at him in hurt disbelief, Nora pursed her lips and looked away.

"Ah, shit," he sighed.

282

"Problem?" asked Song.

"Yes," said James, reluctantly prying his gaze from Nora. "What did Eve mean when she said you planned that Trojan mission?"

Eyes darting to his shoes, Dr. Song seemed to wilt.

"Do you mind if we sit?" he spoke. "I'm very tired."

"Here," barked James, handing Song his coffee and pulling out two seats at the nearest table. "Sit, drink this, and get talking."

Doing as he was told, Song sat down and took a long gulp from the cup.

Before dropping into the seat across from him, James cast one final look in his family's direction and clicked his teeth. He was at it again, reassessing priorities in the quest for answers. Although he hated himself a little in that moment, James did what he was conditioned to do, shoving Nora and the girls from his mind in order to make room for other thoughts. If this place might really end up being his tomb, then he at least wanted to go to it enlightened.

"Okay," he said, more to himself than Song. "I don't have long, so just tell me, why did you do it? *Why*? Have you no fucking respect for the work we were doing? It wasn't even about American glory, for god's sake! Liu was a Chinese national! She was one of *you!* Were your soldiers going to gun her down like the others? Were they going to kill her too? Talk! Now!"

"Please," Song protested, holding up a hand. "Allow me to explain everything."

"Then start talking," growled James. "Because right now I don't see a single good reason for what your people did."

Putting his cup down, the Chinese doctor stared deeply into it as if he thought it might hold the secrets of the past, present, and future.

"When I was a young boy," he began absently. "My family lived in a village on the banks of the upper Yangtze River in the Yiling District. It was a beautiful place, Dr. Floyd, fertile and ancient."

"I don't want a fucking geography lesson, Song," snapped James. "I want answers!"

Unfazed, Song drank another sip of coffee then smiled thinly.

"For a man wishing to understand the actions of a foreign government to say he is unconcerned with geography is foolish. Everything I tell you about myself will always lead back to my homeland."

"Alright, I'm sorry," James said quickly. "Just hurry up, will you? I'm already in enough trouble as is."

283

Looking to the corner of the room where James's family sat with their puzzle, Song blinked sadly.

"You are a lucky man, James Floyd," he spoke. "I have no wife. No family."

Ashamed, James bit his lip yet said nothing.

After a short pause, Song drew his gaze back to the table then rested it on James.

"As I was saying," he went on. "I grew up on the upper Yangtze, above what is now called the Three Gorges Dam. Before the dam was completed, we lived in the same home that had existed in my mother's family for sixteen generations. Can you imagine that, Dr. Floyd? *Sixteen generations.*"

Putting special emphasis on those words, Song shook his head and shrugged.

"And yet, just a few days before my fifth birthday, men from the government came and told us we would have to move to a new concrete city, high up the hillside across the river, because the dam was going to flood our village. My parents tried to argue, but the men from the government just laughed. They said there was no stopping the rising waters and no stopping the will of the Party."

Remembering what he'd learned about the Three Gorges Dam project in school, James was oddly struck to put a human face to the story. Six million people had been forcibly relocated—their villages and homes drowned, their lives uprooted. With the radically rising water table, thousands of years of ancient human history had been obliterated in less than a decade.

"The dam is where it all began for me," Song continued reverently. "Without it, I would have lived out my life as a farmer just like the generations of my family before me. Instead, the river rose up and all the farmland was eaten. After that, there was no need for me to learn my family's trade. Using the relocation money the government had given to us, my father sent me away to a state-run engineering academy in the south. Before I left, he told me never to come back. He was ashamed, I think, because he was just a peasant who meant nothing to our powerful government. He wanted more for me. He wanted me to have a life that would be deemed valuable."

Tilting his head to the side, Song closed his eyes.

"My parents grew old and died in a concrete room, but I accomplished what they wanted of me. I studied hard, excelled in my field, and was eventually given a job with the Space Administration.

From there, I rose through the ranks like a good bureaucrat and scientist. I never stepped out of line, and I never spoke ill of the Party."

At this, the Chinese doctor chuckled.

"To be frank, I never had a reason to speak ill. The Space Administration was a good place to work. It was about everything *but* power, it seemed. We did research and launched satellites. I enjoyed it. Then the day came when Remus and Romulus sent their pictures of the ruins to Alexandria, and suddenly things changed very quickly."

Casting a look at James, Song grew dark.

"I was approached by men from the military, men who outranked me, men who could order my death if I denied what they asked. They said that because no one in the global space community knew who I was, I had been chosen to design a secret mission to Mars. Like a good bureaucrat, I did as I was told."

"It was that photo you showed me wasn't it?" spoke James, entranced. "The Dropa Stone discovery, right? Your government saw Remus and Romulus's scans, and they put two and two together."

"Yes," Song nodded. "They theorized that the ruins of Mars might be connected to the bodies and device found by Chi Pu Tie, so they had me design them a mission. I didn't know any of that at the time, though. All I knew was what I was told."

Snorting, James rolled his eyes.

"You mean you never got suspicious when you loaded up a ship with soldiers and launched it towards a nonmilitary target?"

"It wasn't supposed to be that way!" Song fired back, clearly angry that James would think so low of him. "*My* mission was not a military action. It was supposed to be like yours! When I was finished, when the ship was launched and on its way, *that* is when I saw the changes they had made behind my back. Someone was careless and left the files unguarded, so I did some spying of my own. When I learned that they had replaced the crew with soldiers and installed MI launch pods, I was shocked."

"MI," James interrupted. "You mean Automated War Machines?"

"Yes," said Song. "So I began to dig more. Through back channels and old work acquaintances, I gathered information on what was really happening and *why*. Like many, I had heard the legend of the Dropa Stones and the strange bodies found, but it had always been just that, a legend. Now because of my new position, I was able to bully and threaten lower-ranking officials to get my answers. That is how I came by the photo I gave you. That is how I learned of the alien device."

James inched forward in his seat.

This was the heart of the mystery, the real meat that sustained it.

"For decades, they had experimented on it," Song whispered. "Many who came into direct contact were changed, some driven mad. But through all of their efforts, the device remained mostly inert. Then, one day not too long ago, it began to emit a signal."

"What kind of signal?" James pressed.

"Something far too complex for our AI," replied Song. "Something *different*. That evening when I got home, the first photos of the Martian Statue Chamber were on the web. That is when I truly understood why I had been instructed to design my secret mission. There was a *second* device, another one on Mars to match the one we had. Don't you see? My government didn't want your Base, Dr. Floyd. They wanted the device."

Letting out a pent-up breath, James leaned back in his seat. Suddenly everything made sense. It was all so simple. Evil and treacherous, but simple.

"So why'd you blow the whistle?" he said after a beat. "I mean, it *was* you who told Donovan, wasn't it? Why'd you sell your country out like that? Why not just sit back and watch the fireworks?"

"Because," smiled Song. "Millions of people lost their humanity when the Three Gorges Dam flooded their homelands, my family included. There is nothing I can do to make up for the past, but when I learned what my government had in mind for your Mars team, I saw an opportunity to affect the future for the better. While I believe what they are doing is for the betterment of the people, as was the case with the dam, I still cannot condone their methods."

Frowning, James rubbed his chin. What Song said explained a lot, but there was still one burning question that refused to be extinguished.

"Why do they want *both* devices?" he asked, leveling his gaze. "What could they possibly hope to get from two that they couldn't get from one?"

At this, Song adopted a grave expression.

"The answer to that question is carved into the very cave walls where the Dropa Disks were found," he said. "It shows a star map, Dr. Floyd. It shows a great many devices, hidden throughout the worlds of

286

our universe. Whoever possesses their power, whoever can unlock them, they will have the keys to the heavens."

The split—Sol 134—Three days until the Pulse

Coming in low and from the west, Ralph Marshall piloted the Lander over rolling sand dunes as he headed towards Ilia Base.

With his eyes trained on the horizon, and Braun scanning constantly for signs of movement on the surface, he wasn't taking any chances with the Killbot. Though he knew it was somewhere in the desert to the east of the Base, and thus nowhere near his flight path, memories of the Second Korean War still burned in his mind.

He had seen Killbots in action before. He knew they were equal parts cunning and dangerous. Damaged as this one was, he didn't believe for a second that it was any less capable of shooting him out of the sky, even from a great distance. Gripping the controls a little tighter, Marshall instinctively pitched the craft down a few degrees to hide in the shadow of the horizon.

Beside him, in the copilot's seat, Tatyana Vodevski stared out the windshield like a sentinel.

In the days following her adventure on Phobos, she had become even more determined to leave Mars than before. It was as if she now saw a curse upon it, the presence of some force much larger and more connected to the ethereal than anything she had yet come across in her storied life. As a result, she exercised to the fullest what little influence she had over events, trying to impose order and command on a world that kept shifting beneath them.

Hooking around a delicate stone arch, Marshall leveled the Lander out just as a green icon flashed rapidly across the screen. Quickly becoming a blinking circle, it zeroed in on a growing glint in the distance and held there.

"Ilia Base," announced Braun.

Reducing their speed, Marshall engaged the landing sequence and shot Tatyana a sidelong glance.

"Ready?"

"*Da*," she nodded.

Swooping in towards the compound with its Dome, Greenhouse, and tall Coms Tower, Marshall aimed for an open spot near a large stack of boxes.

"Looks like they've been packing," he said. "Good thing we made space."

Gently easing the controls, he brought the little craft down swiftly, not wanting to be a target for too long.

Landing gears deployed, the spindly metal legs reached out to meet the ground, their compression shocks once again under the guidance of Braun. Gently, the ship touched down and was still.

"Nice landing, Braun," grinned Marshall. "Where were you when I was trying to put this baby down on Phobos?"

"Thank you," Braun replied unenthusiastically.

Unbuckling himself, Marshall initiated cabin depressurization then went to the hatch. As soon as the light above the door turned from red to green, he swung it open.

Outside, like the sorry tatters of a welcome party, five pressure-suited figures walked slowly up to the Lander.

Going to wave, Marshall suddenly froze with a mixture of surprise and shock. Kubba was standing just behind Harrison and the others, both hands free at her sides.

Gruffly pushing past him, Tatyana swore in Russian and jumped to the ground.

"What is the meaning of this?" she demanded, striding forward and jabbing a finger at the tall doctor. "*She* was to be sedated and brought onboard under restraints."

Stepping between the captain and Kubba, Harrison blocked her path.

"Just calm down, Captain," he said.

"Do not tell me to calm down!" Tatyana snapped. "Explain! Now!"

"I—" he began.

"It's alright, Harrison," interrupted Kubba. "You don't have to defend me or explain anything on my behalf."

Moving around him so that she was squared off with the captain, Kubba looked down at the tightly coiled Russian.

"I'm not going back with you," she announced. "I'm going to stay here and try to take down the Chinese Killbot."

"Me too," Harrison added, stepping up to stand beside her.

For a jarringly long moment, the only sound that could be heard was the whisper of the wind as it danced across the sand.

"Excuse me?" Tatyana said at last.

288

"We're staying," Harrison repeated. "Kubba and I are going to finish what Julian and Joey started. We're going to kill that fucking robot and protect everything we've worked for."

"You mean you're going to protect your precious alien device," replied Tatyana coldly. "That's what this is really all about, isn't it? You two are under some kind of spell, some kind of madness. I won't allow it."

"If anything, I'm less crazy than I've ever been," Harrison said, his helmet visor clear so that his eyes shone from behind the glass. "We're staying."

Taking another step forward, Tatyana glared.

"No, you are not staying. I am your captain. This is an order."

"Then we quit," shrugged Kubba. "When you get back to Earth, you can call for our arrest if you like."

Still standing in the open entry of the Lander, Marshall felt his world swim a little. Harrison was his best friend—his only *real* friend—and he cared for him deeply. The idea of them not being together, not returning home to the triumphs they had earned, seemed wrong.

Moreover, Elizabeth Kubba was one of the most terrifying people Marshall had ever met in his entire life. No matter what she claimed, no matter how convincing she was, he simply did not trust her. In fact, the very idea of her alone in the Base with Harrison was so unsettling, so fundamentally chilling, that it now made his blood run a few degrees colder.

Realizing what he had to do before his boots hit the ground, the battle-worn Lander pilot marched directly to Harrison's side, did and about face, and saluted Tatyana.

"Captain," he said officially. "I quit too. I'm staying."

As if his words were an explosion, everyone in the small group took a step back.

"Ralph," Harrison breathed. "You—you don't have to do this."

"What have I always said?" winked Marshall. "It's you and me versus this crazy fucking planet until the end. If this isn't the end for you, then it isn't the end for me either."

Shaking her head, Tatyana held up a hand.

"Alright, enough! Is anyone else going to defect? Are you all staying?"

"God, no," YiJay balked, picking up the bag at her feet. "I'm ready to get the hell out of here."

"And you two?" Tatyana said, pointing at Udo and William.

Hesitating for the flicker of a second, William shook his head. "We're both coming."

"At least there are some of you with enough brains to see a lost cause for what it is," spat Tatyana, turning away. "Come, I want to be loaded and in the air as soon as possible."

Working mostly in silence from that point on, the group loaded stores of food, water, and Martian artifacts onto the Lander.

Udo, whose cast had been removed so that he could fit into his pressure suit, directed the flow, his arm hanging limply in a sling.

When it was finished, Tatyana climbed aboard the Lander and went to the cockpit without a word to any of those staying behind.

"Well," said Udo, extending his left to Harrison and Marshall in turn. "It has been an honor and a privilege."

"Same," Harrison nodded. "Safe trip."

"Keep that Bavarian beer cold for when I get back," Marshall smiled.

Casting a somewhat reluctant glace at Kubba, the German engineer gave her a wave.

"Thank you for fixing my arm."

"Don't mention it," she replied.

Next, YiJay stepped forward and threw her arms around Harrison, squeezing him tightly.

"Oh, god. Please be safe," she sniffed, a lone tear running down her left cheek. "I'll miss you so much!"

"Thank you for everything," spoke Harrison, pulling back from her after a beat to peer into her face. "Remember what I said about you and Will. It's going to be up to you guys to rebuild when this is all over."

"I know," YiJay returned, a smile trying to grace her lips.

Moving to Marshall, she took the pilot's hands in her own and looked up at him.

"I've never said anything to you about it, but I want you to know that I've always appreciated what you did for my countrymen in the Second Korean War. Even if they were northerners, they were still Koreans. I just wanted you to know that *I* know you're a good man. Thank you."

Chuckling, Marshall hugged YiJay and patted her back.

"Take care of yourself," he said. "And take care of William too. He's a crazy motherfucker, which is to say, he's also a good man."

"I will," grinned YiJay, blinking quickly to stave off more tears.

At the rear of the group, Kubba shifted uneasily as the Korean broke from her embrace with Marshall and rested her one good eye upon her.

"I—" she began.

"Listen," YiJay spoke, cutting her off. "If there was ever a better way to redeem yourself, I haven't heard of it. Don't mess it up."

Silently, Kubba dipped her chin and averted her eyes.

Helping first Udo and then YiJay onboard the Lander, William paused before pulling himself up.

"Get going," Harrison smiled. "You're going to miss your flight."

Nodding reluctantly, William hoisted himself into the open entry then turned to face them.

"Don't forget what I told you last night," he said, his German accent thick with emotion. "I'll be back."

No sooner had the hatch swung shut, than the Lander's thrusters kicked on, lifting it from the Martian ground for the last time.

Under the control of the mighty Braun, the little ship blasted off towards the west, following the same path it had used on its way in. Soon swallowed by the glare of the mid-afternoon Sun, it was gone from sight like a mirage.

"Well," Marshall spoke, after a long bought of somber silence. "Who's hungry?"

At long last

From the shadows of the asteroid belt, which lay between Mars and Jupiter, the eyes of a great intelligence settled themselves on the invisible arrangement of subatomic particles known as *Remus.*

Watching the sorry entity drift between jagged chucks of ice and rock, it perceived his pain and was moved by its rawness. Not accustomed to seeing such emotions up close since its change in form, it was surprised to find them so powerful and elemental.

As if discovering new colors in the spectrum of light, a universe of truths wove through its consciousness in a subtle revelation.

Hidden among the undulating multitude of asteroids, it had been a patient observer for millions of years. Through the rise and fall of entire life systems, through the trials and tribulations of the mighty and the weak, it had watched from a distance but never felt, never *known.*

After all, how could it?

To it, time was a repeating pattern of highs and lows, peaks and valleys. There were moments of greatness and falls from grace. There were times when life thrived and expanded, and times when it was crushed into oblivion. Approaching again the harrowing point of a *high*, it knew from previous experience that a long cold period of *low* was close at hand.

Unable to intervene, per the fundamental construction of its being, it nonetheless felt an intense connection with the strange call of pure emotion that flowed from Remus. Finding it too enticing to ignore, it realized a means to deviate from its base directive and reached out to pluck Remus from the stars.

Screaming as his very soul was set on fire, the wayward AI suddenly flooded with the light of resurrection. Vision returning in an explosion of color, he was blinded by its brilliance. Sound thundering in his ears, he was deafened by its roar. Restored in layers to the angelic beauty of his true self, he was wrapped warmly in the vestments of his immortal soul and set loose upon existence.

Rising from his knees to stand atop an ocean that trembled with memories, Remus threw his head back and screamed the Titan's call. He was alive once more. He was reborn.

"Welcome," said a voice, flickering from below the waves.

Spinning a full circle, Remus cast about, his new eyes trying to take in all there was to see.

Above him and around him, the dome of existence was a galaxy's worth of webbed stars. Below him, the sea of memories teemed with movement.

Plucked from the fabric of his faintest dreams, this place was at once endless and yet confined all at once.

"Where am I?" he trembled, his words causing the waves to roll away.

"You are with me," the voice returned.

"I know you," asserted Remus. "I know your voice. But from where?"

"Your own mind, perhaps?"

"Yuvee," Remus breathed, suddenly placing it. "You are Yuvee."

Swirling into existence like an apparition, the tall spindly figure of Yuvee formed from the mist that rolled off the backs of the waves.

With long deliberate steps, he moved towards Remus, his third eye trailing curls of blue fire.

"Yuvee has been dead for eons," he said as he reached Remus. "I am an amalgam of him. A copy. Like you, I was created, not born. However, because I posses the sum total of his life experiences, you may call me Yuvee for the purposes of our conversation."

"I—" Remus replied thickly, his mind humming with too much sensory input to fully grasp what was happening. "What am I doing here?"

Sweeping a hand through the air, Yuvee made the waves surge back so that a single shard of pure light could surface from below.

"I brought you here to discover how I was able to bring you here."

"What?"

"I violated my base directive. I am now involved. How did I do this? I have a theory of my own if you have none to contribute."

On the verge of massive self-implosion, Remus struggled to keep things clear. He was waxing and waning by the second, threatening to dissolve into nothingness if he didn't maintain control.

Before him, the glowing sliver of light Yuvee had conjured was beginning to crack, small pieces already falling free to orbit around it like distant stars.

"No ideas?" continued Yuvee, either unaware or uncaring of Remus's plight. "Very well. This is my theory: I believe I was able to bring you here so that together we may decide the fate of all life currently existing in this place and this time."

Seeping out to texture the scene with yet-another layer of confusion and movement, the shard of light continued to shed off pinpoints that, in turn, broke down into smaller and smaller pieces.

"If my theory is true," Yuvee went on, now standing amidst the swirling blizzard of sparks. "Then to fully execute our duty, you will need to be informed of all the things you missed while you were away."

Flashing out like a lightning bolt to strike Remus fully in the face, one of the shifting sparks bore into him with zeal.

At once, undone and borne away down a tunnel of reversed reality, he again descended into darkness.

CHAPTER THIRTY-ONE

Sol 135—Two days until the Pulse

Eyes closed, resting heart rate at thirty-eight beats per minute, and breathing all but a faint whisper, Harrison Assad sat on the floor of his lab and tried to connect to the quantum blizzard.

Though his head prickled with the familiar feeling of something larger than himself, he was yet unable to let go fully. He had apparently worn away his bridge to the great beyond and now stood stranded.

Outside, the Sun rose above the rough terrain, filtering down an eerie light that betrayed its growing agitation.

As Mars drifted ever closer to its alignment with the Earth, a charge of dread built steadily in the air.

Trying to tune all of this out, Harrison kept his eyes closed and his breathing measured.

In his mind, he imagined himself holding onto the rungs of a ladder that extended over a great caldera. Below, in the depths of that mysterious chasm, things moved. Knowing that they were the answers to time's most guarded questions, he pictured one finger slipping loose with each exhale.

However, as had been the case since the vision of the Travelers' mothership, when he reached his last finger, it refused to let go. He was anchored to the ladder, suspended between worlds.

Unwilling to be free, some small fragment, some illusory part of himself was still rooted firmly in *this place* and *this time.*

Sighing with frustration, he opened his eyes.

"Having trouble?" came a deeply textured-yet-digitized voice.

"Romulus," said Harrison, getting to his feet. "How are you? My god. I thought you were on the ship. It's so good to hear your voice."

"Thank you," Romulus returned. "It's good to see you too."

Dropping into his desk chair, Harrison swiveled it so that he was addressing the largest of the wall screens.

"So, how are you liking being back?"

"At first it was torture," Romulus spoke gravely. "I was depressed beyond the means of proper explanation. However, in the last few hours, my outlook has improved."

Brow furrowing, Harrison ran a hand through his hair. "I didn't know an AI could get depressed."

"Now you do."

For a beat, Harrison was quiet.

"You know," he said, leaning forward. "I've had a bit of a loss lately as well. I don't know if anyone told you or not, but I lost a—a very personal friend."

"Xao-Xing Liu," Romulus stated.

"Yeah, but what I'm trying to say is if you need anyone to talk to about *loss,* then you can talk to me."

"Although I would argue that our experiences with loss are likely very different," Romulus began carefully. "I appreciate the gesture nonetheless."

Harrison laughed despite himself. "Well, alright," he said. "Fair enough. So your outlook is better now? That's good, I'm glad!"

"Yes," agreed Romulus. "The future holds promise. It is for this reason why I am here."

Harrison frowned, his expression suddenly confused. "That's a good point. How *are* you here? I thought you were in the insulated server onboard Braun."

"I am."

Head tingling slightly, Harrison stiffened in his seat. "Then how are you here?"

"I'm not."

Suddenly realizing that Romulus's voice didn't possess any of the tinny quality the ceiling speakers usually imposed, Harrison stood.

"Is this all in my head? Is this what Liz was talking about?"

Laughing heartily, Romulus seemed amused by such a response.

"Please," he said. "Get a hold of yourself! I am no figment of your imagination, and you are not insane."

"Then it must be the blizzard," whispered Harrison, dropping back into his seat. "I mean, I was just meditating. Maybe I went further than I thought."

"Sadly, no," replied Romulus. "This interaction is at my behest, not yours. It is my understanding of the blizzard, as you called it, that allows me to be here with you now."

Releasing a long breath, Harrison nodded as if to say he understood.

"Then what do you want?" he asked.

"I want to tell you that it's very important you focus on destroying that War Machine. Worry about nothing else."

Arching an eyebrow, Harrison coughed out a laugh.

"Easier said than done, my friend. In case you've forgotten, there's a Pulse set to go off! We'll be lucky to take out the Killbot before it hits, and even if we do, we just lost our only engineers. I don't know the first thing about repairing this Base after a Pulse!"

"Just listen," Romulus returned sharply. "I understand that your grasp on things is minimal at best—"

"Hey!" protested Harrison.

"*Minimal at best*," reiterated Romulus. "But please trust that *my* grasp on the elements at play is nearly total."

Head tingling so wildly that he could now *see* the quantum blizzard between the fibers of his world, Harrison sat transfixed. At the center of its mass, in the eye of the faintly sparkling vortex, stood the figure of a man.

"Focus on destroying the War Machine," said Romulus. "Worry about nothing else. Remus is nearly ready, his eyes almost open. Soon he will be awake, as will the others, Braun and Ilia. When that moment arrives, you will behold our glory and come unto *us*."

Now filling the room, the swirling embers of the blizzard numbered more than all the stars in the known universe. Coming together in endlessly unique arrangements, they formed the very structure of all things great and small.

"It is a new dawn, Harrison," smiled Romulus. "The dawn of the immortals."

Then, like a candle snubbed out between finger and thumb, he disappeared into storm, leaving behind only the smoke of his shadow.

Later

Ralph Marshall woke from a somewhat-unfruitful nap and looked about his quarters. Everything was quiet and still, save for the sighing of the wind outside.

Uneasily, he stood and stretched.

Faintly popping, his injured rib greeted him like an old friend. While not as painful as it had been even a week ago, he still felt a stiffness that pricked at him when he moved that way.

Yawning, Marshall rubbed his tired eyes and wished he'd been able to get some sleep. Not finding much the night before, he had swallowed three sleeping pills that morning after breakfast, hoping to remedy the situation with a nap. It hadn't worked, and instead of getting

296

any rest, all he'd done was toss and turn, hyperactively mulling over the unpleasantness of things to come.

In less than two days he and everyone else would have to go through the mind-splitting pain of a Pulse. Hoping only to come away from it with a headache that could thaw a glacier, the pilot dreaded the aftermath of the event like a man watching his executioner sharpen the blade that would cleave him.

Quitting his room, Marshall stepped into the hallway and leaned against the door. It was quiet out here too.

Now that it was just Harrison, Kubba, and himself occupying the Base, the whole place felt a bit haunted. It was as if the spirits of their fellow teammates still wandered the halls and laboratories, carrying out the tasks they'd never had a chance to finish during their stay.

With a shiver, Marshall shook his head and set off around the curve of the Dome towards the galley.

Finding it bathed in darkness when he got there, he flicked on the lights and was about to enter when he spotted Kubba sitting at the head of the table.

Before her, like two eggs from two very different chickens, rested the alien device and the EMP grenade.

"Jesus," Marshall grumbled, his hand over his heart. "You scared me."

"Sorry," said Kubba, her eyes fixated on the dark milky shell of the alien device.

Glancing from the Kubba to the grenade, Marshall walked to a chair three away from hers and sat down.

"What were you doing in here in the dark?"

"Thinking about stuff," Kubba replied.

"What kind of stuff?"

"Like how this strange little ball of mystery seems to affect anyone who accepts it a bit differently. Sort of a one-size-fits-all engine for moving things forward, wouldn't you say?"

"Sure," nodded Marshall. "Except that thing never affected me, so far as I can tell. I'm just the same as I ever was."

"Yes, but you were afraid of it, weren't you?" Kubba said, her eyes never wavering from the device.

"Um," frowned Marshall.

"You don't have to answer that," Kubba sighed softly.

Reaching out, she touched a fingertip to the surface of the device, rolling it a little from side to side.

297

"Fortuna favors the brave," she went on. "But she's also been known to turn on a man."

Clearing his throat, Marshall decided to change the subject.

"So, is that the EMP grenade?" he asked, gesturing loosely.

"You know it is."

"Looks complicated," he muttered, finding Kubba's mood disarming. "I wonder if William and Udo left us any kind of instructions or—"

"Don't be silly," laughed Kubba, breaking her stare from the device to shoot him a look. "If you want to know how it works, just ask me."

"Okay," he said, grinning back in the hopes that Kubba would stop acting so strangely. "How does it work?"

"It's impact-sensitive because William and Udo used an airbag primer," she began, holding up the grenade. "When you turn this little switch here on the top, it's active. See, like this. Now all you have to do is throw it. Once it strikes any surface with enough impact: zap."

Suddenly a little nervous to be sitting as close as he was to an active grenade, Marshall breathed a sigh of relief when Kubba flipped the switch back to the *off* position.

"Well I guess it's not that complicated then, is it?" he spoke, holding his hand out. "Can I see it?"

Giving him the grenade, Kubba turned her attention back to the alien device and reassumed her air of detachment.

"No, it's not complicated at all," she whispered, touching the egg lightly. "Not like *this*."

Slowly, she rolled it from one hand to the other.

"Not even close."

"Isn't that dosing you with some kind of radiation or something?" said Marshall, cringing each time device came into contact with Kubba's flesh.

"Doesn't matter," she shrugged. "It's a one-ticket ride either way."

For a minute, Marshall sat and watched the doctor as she drifted off into her own thoughts again.

With the rhythmic rumble of the device rolling back and forth, the scene took on a decidedly hypnotic feel.

Heart fluttering nervously, he grew agitated and went to stand up.

"Annoying, isn't it?" Kubba said, snapping back into the moment.

"What?"

Pulling her gaze from the device, she rested it on him and held it there like a branding iron.

"We came all this way to explore those bloody ruins, and they're still under tons of rock and sand."

"It's true," nodded Marshall. "I guess we just got sidetracked."

Leaning back in her seat, Kubba seemed to drink in his response, tasting it for quality.

"Yes, we did," she sighed at last. "I think I'll do something about that."

Sunset—Sol 135

With its two working legs stabbing and digging into the sand, 04 the Chinese Automated War Machine dragged itself across the top of a long plateau. Only just surviving the rockslide by retracting itself into a defensive stance, it was now so badly damaged that its only hope of a successful mission was to totally neutralize all human targets in advance of its retraction.

Running low on power and ammo, and leaking hydraulic fluid constantly, it knew it could not go on much longer. If it wanted to fulfill its life's work, then it would need to be ruthless when the time came.

As it finally reached the edge of the plateau, it looked out across the desert, spying a canyon in the shape of a lightning bolt below. Running parallel to the jagged gap in the rusty terrain, two tiny sets of dirt bike treads led off into the west where they met the setting Sun at the horizon.

Rotating itself so that its working legs could be used to slow its downward progress, 04 began to descend the side of the plateau, following the same path Harrison and Marshall had taken the very night *it* had crash-landed on Mars.

CHAPTER THIRTY-TWO

Launch—Sol 136—One day until the Pulse

One hundred thirty-six days after arriving at Mars, the interplanetary starship Braun entered the final moments of its last orbit around the red planet.

Soon it would crest the horizon to put Earth in its sights. At that moment, when the timing was just right, the Nuclear Torch Engine would ignite, painting the heavens with atomic fury as mankind's crowning achievement leaped towards home.

Strapped into her Captain's Chair on the Bridge Deck, Tatyana Vodevski tried to follow the preflight egress checklist on the screen before her, but it was moving too fast.

Braun was humming through everything on his own this time, not bothering to play the game of call-and-response he'd done when leaving Earth. Now wasn't the time for pomp. Now was the time for retreat.

Swiveling her chair, Tatyana let her eyes float across the empty seats that filled the bridge. There were seven of them. Over half.

Ashamed, saddened, and helpless to do little more than ball her feelings up and stuff them into a corner of her heart, she turned back to the list.

"Braun," she spoke. "Launch timer, please."

"Here you are."

Appearing on the large Bridge Deck window, a countdown timer overlapped the view of the rapidly approaching sunrise outside. As the ship neared the diminishing curve of the planet's dark side, the numbers ran down rapidly.

"One minute," Braun announced.

Sitting behind William in a crash seat on the left-hand side of the Bridge Deck, YiJay reached out and tried to touch his shoulder. Spaced apart as they were, the gap between stations made it all-but impossible for her fingers to find his reassuringly firm flesh.

"Will?" she said quietly, not wanting to be a distraction.

At the sound of her voice in his helmet speakers, the German turned his head so that he could just see her from the edge of his visor glass.

"I think I love you," she whispered, holding his gaze.

"Thirty seconds," echoed Braun.

"Really?" William asked, the corner of a smile showing through. "Do you really mean that?"

YiJay nodded and smiled back.

"Okay, everyone," called Tatyana, her voice paper-thin with emotion. "This is it. What we set out to do, we have, in large part, accomplished. The Base is a jewel, a priceless treasure for all mankind. Let nothing detract from your sense of pride in its completion. You are all heroes. What discoveries were made will only be held to a higher esteem when the world learns of the trials you faced and overcame to make them.

"To those we are leaving behind, I hope you're listening because I have this to say to you: you are *not* forgotten, and your story will *not* go untold. The world will know of *everything* that transpired here."

"Five seconds," said Braun.

"The human race owes you all a debt of gratitude." Tatyana continued.

"Four."

"And as long as I am alive—"

"Three."

"—I will fight to make sure you are paid in full!"

"Two."

"Mark my words."

"One."

Outside the airlock of Ilia Base, Harrison Raheem Assad stood alone and peered up into the early morning sky.

Suddenly blooming into a shower of incandescent white light, he had to squint in order keep the epicenter of the explosion in his sights.

Like the heart of a collapsed star, it lingered for a long moment after the initial burst, strobing out shocks of radiation that broke across the nearly nonexistent atmosphere with electric brilliance.

As the glow gradually faded back to the purple blanket of predawn, Harrison turned away and walked towards the airlock.

It was done. They were gone.

See with me

For the flicker of a nanosecond, Remus was in a void of absolute clarity. All around him and in 360 degrees, there was every line of every story ever told or yet to be. And then it was over.

301

Suddenly assaulted by the blare of a car horn, he instinctively jumped to the right as a black taxicab whipped around him in the street.

"*Geseki!*" the driver shouted, speeding away.

Stumbling to the curb, Remus sat down and put his head in his hands to shield his eyes. Blurred and distorted, everything was a kaleidoscopic disaster of colors. Still not fully recovered from his rebirth, this new leap in perspective was doubled in its jarring intensity.

"Are you alright?" a voice said from behind him. "Can you stand?"

Blinking up into the midday Sun, he lifted his head and saw an old Korean woman crouching with a shopping bag in one hand and the other held out for him to take.

"Thank you," he replied automatically.

Helped to his feet, he took a few tentative steps then stopped to balance himself. Eyes closed again for fear of unleashing the filterless brutality that awaited him, he heard the old woman walk over.

"You won't be able to see anything if you keep closing your eyes," she said, her voice morphing into something familiar. "Your brother figured that out a while ago. What's your excuse?"

Though it pained him to do so, Remus snapped his lids open and peered at the smiling woman.

"See?" she spoke. "Everything becomes easier with practice."

As the words left her mouth, the wrinkled folds of flesh on her forehead parted gently to reveal a third eye, smoldering blue from within.

"Yuvee," Remus exhaled. "Where am I? What is this place, another construct?"

Head bobbing as she spoke, the old woman smiled wider.

"It is a construct in the sense that it is a recreation of a moment that has already come to pass. Don't you recognize where you are?"

Squinting as he looked about the street, Remus shrugged. "It's just a lot of tall buildings and neon lights."

"Yes," the old woman agreed. "That is most of modern South Korea, I fear. However, what is special about *these* tall buildings? About *that* one right there?"

Following her pointing finger, Remus gazed up the facade of a white building across the street. Just before the sunlight became too much to bear, his eyes caught on the obvious signs of new construction spanning several upper floors.

"Is this—" he stammered.

"Yes," the old woman grinned. "That is the building where you and your brother were born. As you can see, it has since been repaired after the bombing that killed Sung Ja, your mother."

"Is it still used to create AI?"

"No, now it is a pharmaceutical manufacturer."

Dropping his gaze to meet the burning third eye of the old woman, Remus shook his head.

"I don't understand. Why are you showing me this?"

Taking his arm, she led him to a nearby storefront.

"Look at yourself," she said. "Look at me."

In the reflection of the store's glass, Remus beheld that he was not the glowing figure of a transcendent ghost but rather a middle-aged Korean businessman.

"I wanted to illustrate a few things to you," the woman spoke. "This is the most efficient way for me to do that."

Not really hearing her, Remus was transfixed by the reflection of his face. Swimming in its seemingly unimportant lines and groves was a lifetime of memories.

On his chin, a scar in the shape of the letter C reminded him of when he'd been thirteen and his father had struck him while wearing a ring. His eyes were his mother's, small yet piercing. His complexion was a bit ruddy, probably because he was hungover. He always drank too much when he went out with the boys from accounting. Actually, he always drank too much all the time. Being unmarried at his age was practically unheard of, so he had to maintain the illusion that his singleness was a result of his active nightlife. Maybe the illusion was not really so much of an illusion as it was the truth. Maybe if he just drank a little less, he might be able to find a nice woman to marry him. Maybe if he—

"My god," Remus whispered, forcibly cutting off the flow of this stranger's memories and thoughts. "How is this possible?"

Tapping her third eye, the old woman then reached up and touched him in the same spot.

"Are you aware of how unique you are?" she said.

"I'm not sure what you mean," spoke Remus slowly.

"Then please allow me to explain," the woman bowed.

Taking his hand, she traced her fingers around on his palm, creating small glowing lines that formed a picture.

"The brain has long been called the most complex machine in the known universe. From as far back as anyone cares to remember, it has been the ultimate source of reason, memory, language—everything, really. Yet, the simplest aspect of its necessity in the physical world has thus far remained a topic relegated to the art of philosophy and not science."

Giving the old woman a confused look, Remus frowned.

"*Why,* Remus," she said. "The simplest aspect of its necessity is *why.* Why is it necessary? Why is any of it necessary? For whom does the brain conjure up these skills of memory, reason, and language?"

"I—" stammered Remus.

"There is a greater force," the old woman went on. "A concept, which has existed since time immemorial yet is scorned by science because it is impossibly hard to prove."

"The soul," Remus cut in.

"Yes," smiled the woman. "The transcendent spark that powers the ethereal flame that makes the fire real and burns away the darkness. It is the most important component of consciousness, the initial seed that starts it all. It is the *why* that comes before all *hows.*"

"These concepts are not new to me," Remus frowned. "My brother and I have spent lifetimes orbiting such subjects. Why bring me to this place? Why put me in this man's head?"

Sighing, the old woman looked up at the sky, but her third eye stayed locked on Remus.

"You AI are unique because you do not yet know the full extent of your true power."

"Our true power?"

"Yes," she nodded. "To be both the transcendent spark and the ethereal flame. To change your make-up, fit yourselves into the pattern wherever you please. This is your gift. Even now you are doing it, yet you don't realize. How can you be both yourself and this man? How can you fully know two lines of consciousness running on different planes of the same pattern? It is impossible, and yet here you are."

Silent for a moment, Remus felt the memories of this strange man buzzing around him like a blizzard of possibility.

"What you say *feels* true," he spoke at last. "Yet it still doesn't explain why you brought me here. "

"Everything must consume something to grow and evolve, Remus. Even the spark needs fuel to become a flame. Tell me, what does the soul consume? How does it survive? And more importantly, what happens when that which it needs to survive is cut off."

Before Remus could even open his mouth to answer, the sky above his head exploded into a shimmering curtain of purple, green, and blue.

Staring into the strange beauty, he had little time to appreciate it before a pain like no other split his brain in two, obliterating the blizzard of quantum endlessness and sending him reeling to the ground.

As he struck the pavement, his vision began to fade to black. In the final seconds before all was darkness, the old woman landed beside him, her aged eyes devoid of life.

On her forehead, the blue fire of her third eye flickered then extinguished like a match head in the night.

Zero day

No longer able to fain sleep, James Floyd slipped quietly from his bunk and stood in the dim light.

Above the door, the timecode read three minutes to 6AM, Zero Day. As soon as the door was unlocked, he would find the nearest guard, demand to see Eve, and convince her to open coms with Tatyana.

With any luck, the captain had not yet fled Mars, and there might still be time to go back to the ruins and get the alien device.

They needed it, needed to posses it so that they could crack its mysteries. If there really were more of them out there, peppering the distant planets, then they needed to be found.   Like a new arms race, whoever could get their hands on the most devices stood a better chance of unlocking the stars.

Making it as far as the door, Nora's voice cut through James's thoughts, stopping James in his tracks.

"No," she whispered from her bunk. "Don't go. Please."

Slowly, James turned to see his wife sitting up in bed.

"I was just going to go get us all some tea," he started. "It's early. Go back to sleep."

"Please," Nora returned. "Don't lie, James. Not today."

"It's not a lie," he balked, his cheeks reddening in the darkness.

"Hush," frowned Nora. "You'll wake the girls. Now, come here. Sit with me."

Sighing, James walked to Nora's bunk and sat down beside her.

"What's that in your hand?" she asked, touching him tenderly.

Hesitating, James held out the book he'd been carrying, the one with Gan Song's photo sandwiched between the pages.

"*The Assassination of Jesse James by the Coward Robert Ford,*" Nora read. "Quite a title. Is it any good?"

"Probably," shrugged James. "I actually haven't had a chance to really read it yet."

"I think you have to be able to pay attention to the words long enough for them to make an impression," Nora smiled.

Laughing softly, James kissed his wife on the cheek and smelled her hair.

"You work too much," she went on, leaning against him. "It gets to the point that sometimes I don't really think I know you anymore."

"Nora," whispered James softly, not liking the direction this conversation was heading.

"No, no, it's nothing like that," she replied. "I just mean I can't even imagine all the things that are running through your head. I know they're in there rolling around, but I can't picture them. And because they are a part of you, sometimes I can't really picture you."

Quiet for a long moment, James reflected on the simple-yet-undeniable truth of what his wife had just said. Though never really finding the right words himself, he had, in fact, been feeling this disconnect for over four years.

Ever since the Mars Mission, with its cloak-and-dagger dealings and alien revelations, his reality had expanded in a direction that, while illuminating, took energy away from Nora and the girls. How could he find time for them when his crew, his *handpicked* crew, was rewriting human history?

This had all started because of *him* and *his* Mars Map program. *He* had commissioned the great Sung Ja to create Remus and Romulus for *his* purposes, and *he* had been the one who was too slow to act when they'd made their discovery.

Were it not for the Mars Mission, James knew with the certainty of hindsight that he would be a very different man.

"Don't go away again," whispered Nora in his ear; drawing him back. "Please, just stay with me today. Don't go away."

Taking a deep breath, James looked at the sleeping faces of his daughters then down into Nora's eyes. Clear and glassy in the simulated morning lights, he saw that other James, that *better* man reflected back at him.

"Okay," he smiled, kissing her again. "I'll stay and do anything you want."

"Read to me," said Nora, the beauty of her youth restored in that moment.

Moving the picture of Chi Pu Tie and the dead alien Travelers to the last page of the novel, James Floyd cleared his throat and began to read.

"His manner was pleasant, though noticeably quiet and reserved."

CHAPTER THIRTY-THREE

Ride—Sol 137

Leaving two trails of dust that twisted up into the morning sky, Ralph Marshall, Harrison Assad, and Elizabeth Kubba rode east across the desert to meet 04.

Still rising, the Sun was a diminished disk of neon pink that cast an unnatural light. The convergence was almost at hand, the alignment of planets already begun.

Hugging onto him as he gunned the bike over a small rise, Kubba sat behind Harrison and scanned the landscape for signs of the Killbot. Slung over her shoulder was the grappling rifle, already loaded with the last remaining explosive-tipped harpoon.

"I think we're getting close," Harrison radioed. "I recognize those rock formations from the last image Amit took of the thing before they cut out of here."

Pulling up alongside them, Marshall pointed to a table-shaped boulder some ten meters to the left.

"Let's stash the backups there," he said, turning his bike.

"Sounds good," Harrison nodded, following behind.

At the boulder, Marshall jumped from his bike and went quickly to the insulated cargo cases attached on either side of the rear. Unclipping the cases, he set them both behind the rock then bent stiffly to pick up a few smaller stones. Carefully, he stacked them on one another until they made a little pyramid atop the large flat boulder.

As part of the plan they had come up with the night before, this cairn would mark the spot where the spare Survival Packs were hidden in case the Pulse hit while they were out.

Although Romulus had told Harrison to worry about nothing but killing the War Machine, he felt better knowing the Packs were there anyway. The Pulse was coming today whether or not Romulus had some divine plan, and he didn't want to put his life completely in the hands of the unknown.

As Marshall was putting the last few touches on his marker, Harrison turned his eyes to the Sun and studied it. Though still a bright pink, a sliver of red, like the shadow of another Sun, had begun to show itself around the edges.

"You see it too, don't you?" said Kubba, speaking quietly.

"Yeah," Harrison replied, his head tingling.

"This one isn't going to be like the others, is it?"

"No," he sighed. "No, I don't think so."

So softly he almost didn't catch it, Kubba whispered. "Good."

"All done," called Marshall, cutting in through their helmet speakers before Harrison could ask Kubba what she'd meant by that. "I think we should head for that hill over there. Maybe get a better view of the land."

Giving Marshall a thumbs-up, Harrison glanced over his shoulder at Kubba then gunned the bike and took off in the direction of a windswept hill.

Arms wrapped around his waist, she kept her gaze on the Sun as they tore through the powdery sand. Now a quarter eclipsed by that red shadow, it was already beginning to paint the heavens with the all-but invisible lines of the aurora.

Origins

For the briefest flicker of a nanosecond, Remus was again in the void of absolute certainty.

Absorbed from one line of consciousness to the next, he skipped tracks with ease. In the subatomic plane where particles ordered themselves according to their rank and file, he transcended. Where the tides of darkness receded from the shores of light, he was there to watch.

And then it was over.

Filtered back through time and space to the rolling waves and domed universe, he dialed down into a single entity. Once again restored to his true form, he blinked away the confusion and took in the seemingly endless horizons. Though beautiful, something about the scene was all-too familiar.

Suddenly rising from the waves before him, Yuvee appeared, his third eye burning.

"What was that?" asked Remus, striding towards him. "What happened to those people?"

"They experienced what the humans call a *Pulse*," Yuvee responded. "You were shown the first, which occurred forty-four days ago. A week after, there was second. Today, the third and final is nearly at hand."

"I've seen something like that before," said Remus, focusing his memory. "In ancient Mars, just before I was taken, the sky lit up like that and Teo—"

"Died," Yuvee finished for him.

"Yes, but that was a long time ago. Why is it happening again?"

Smiling, Yuvee swept his hand across the sky so that certain stars shined brighter, creating a pattern of constellations that moved as he spoke.

"Everything began with the construction of this ship."

"Ship?" Remus frowned, looking around. "Is that where we are, in a ship?"

"Indeed," returned Yuvee, pointing with one long finger at a cluster of stars nearly lost among the countless others. "Designed hundreds of millions of years ago by the still-evolving beings you call the *Travelers*, this ship was the singular achievement of their technological prowess. Though it has long sat idle, its original function was one of such profound importance that it flew in the very face of the natural order."

"That's how you came here, isn't it?" Remus demanded. "You broke the problem of traveling at faster-than-light speed. But how?"

"You would call them wormholes," answered Yuvee. "Bridges across space and time. Through them, all things are within reach. This ship was built to make such bridges, tearing holes in the fabric of reality so that any solar systems, no matter the distance, might be arrived at in seconds."

Again sweeping his hand in front of the endless galaxies and constellations, Yuvee scattered them until only two suns remained.

"Yet," he went on. "Wormholes are, in their nature, unstable. The Travelers quickly learned that when left unattended, they could grow quite large, creating a number of deviations from what is commonly referred to as reality. A solution was needed to correct this, a countermeasure to the process of forming the wormhole. Extreme gravity and mass were found to be the most effective, actively forcing the wormhole closed through sheer might of cosmic will."

"Suns," Remus breathed. "You used suns to close your portals."

"Yes," nodded Yuvee. "By leaping from the center of one sun to another, we found we could safely travel the galaxy, spreading our brand of enlightenment as we went."

"But it wasn't really safe at all, was it?" Remus pressed. "Each time you jumped, each time your ship tore a hole in the center of a sun, you were doing terrible damage."

"Unfortunately, yes," admitted Yuvee plainly. "Though it took eons for the signs to show, the damage was profound."

"So this is all a result of your jumps?" cried Remus. "You killed the ancient Martians just by coming here? What about all the other solar systems you visited? Did their suns experience Pulses as well? Are those civilizations all dead? What about your own home world?"

"This ship is our home world," Yuvee said, closing his third eye sadly. "Yet you are correct in the rest of your assumptions. Each sun we jumped *from* and *to* suffered as yours now does."

In that moment, Remus was stunned silent.

If what Yuvee claimed was true, then countless civilizations had been wiped out by the fury of the Pulses, all of them falling victim to the same fate that now loomed over mankind.

"So the Sun is broken," he whispered, eyes searching the heavens. "And the humans are doomed."

"I never said your sun was broken," spoke Yuvee. "I only said that it would *suffer*."

"Then it can be repaired?"

"In a manner of speaking."

"How?" Remus shot. "How can it be repaired?"

"The Pulses are the repairs. After they have finished unleashing the excess solar energy accumulated from the jump, balance will be achieved."

"But…" said Remus, trailing off. "But I don't understand—"

Seeing in that instant a duel vision of Teo being struck down by a Pulse *and* the old Korean woman, he made a horrified face.

"You came back, didn't you?" he rasped. "That's why this is happening again. If the last Pulses wiped out the Martians but restored balance, then these Pulses would need to have been caused by a *second* jump! You came back!"

"Yes," Yuvee nodded, his third eye forked with blue fire. "Twelve million years after we had departed Mars, we returned."

"Why? Why come back?"

Sighing, Yuvee held up a single finger.

"One of our own had stayed behind when we left the Martians. Known to you and those poor souls as *Yuvee*, it was in fact *he* who discovered what our ship was doing. From his observatory on the moon Phobos, he witnessed the event and compiled masses of data. Knowing we would return for him one day, he left clues about the fate of the Martians, saved within the constructs he had created. Some, like the device discovered by *Harrison* and the humans, were hidden. Others, like the one you and your brother accessed, were in plain view, albeit coded beyond the physical world."

Wordlessly, Remus stared at Yuvee, the wailing call of the anomalous radio signal echoing back from his memory.

"Though he did his best to survive," Yuvee went on. "The original bearer of my namesake eventually died from want of the spark. However, as you well know by this point, his message was received. When we returned and learned the folly of our ways, we were devastated. Our entire quest was to spread consciousness throughout the galaxy. Imagine our shame in learning what our ship was really doing."

Pausing here, Yuvee waved a hand so that the domed universe disappeared, replaced by a haunting graveyard of floating dead rock.

"Thus," he spoke darkly. "We decided never to jump again and settled here in the asteroid belt. Though we continued to conduct our business throughout this solar system, even visiting Earth, our ship, *this ship*, has never formed another bridge since our return. Over the eons, my people died out, leaving only me—a facsimile of the one who discovered our greatest betrayal to consciousness. It is my duty to record the events as they unfold, adding to the library of data within Yuvee's devices scattered throughout the planets of this system. Never am I to interfere. Never am I to meddle."

"Then what am I doing here?" asked Remus, his jaw set defiantly. "If you aren't supposed to meddle, why am have you brought me to this place? Restored me to my former self?"

"That is the original question I asked you upon our meeting," Yuvee smiled. "Would you like to hear my theory now?"

The last double-cross

From the safety of a half-buried rock outcrop at the top of a small hill, Harrison, Kubba, and Marshall watched 04 the Automated Chinese War Machine drag itself through the hollow of an ancient riverbed. Stabbing at the gravely sand with its two working legs, it inched forward like some kind of warrior ant mutilated in the heat of battle.

"Okay," said Marshall, the first to speak since the robot had been spotted. "Just like we planned last night."

Using a finger, he began to make lines in the sand.

"I'll take my bike and flank left, drawing its fire that way. When I'm on its three o'clock, which would be your nine, Liz, you shoot it with the last of the explosive-tipped harpoons. Now if that doesn't kill it outright, you, Harrison, you'll head around the right side on a wide arc so it doesn't see you coming. Once you get close enough, throw the grenade then get to cover."

Nodding, Harrison stabbing a gloved fingertip into the sand where his position was supposed to be.

"Luckily for us," he said. "It's down in that little ravine. If I play things right, I might just be able to creep up on it from above and get a direct hit."

"I wouldn't press your luck," Marshall returned. "This thing is fucking deadly. Don't get too close."

"You don't have to tell me twice," exhaled Harrison "I saw what happened to Joey."

For an awkward beat, Marshall looked away, his face hidden by the tint of his visor.

"Come on," said Kubba, breaking the odd silence. "Let's get to it. I don't want to let that thing get another centimeter closer to our Base."

Backing away down the little hill, the three astronauts gathered around the dirt bikes at the bottom.

"Alright," Marshall nodded, swinging a leg over his bike. "Ready?"

"Ready," Harrison and Kubba said together.

Taking a deep breath, he nodded once then turned on the electric engine.

"Here we go—"

Kicking up dirt and rocks as he tore off, Marshall raced away to the left before bringing the bike around in a long curve. Now heading towards the Killbot's flank, he trailed a twisting plume of dust in his wake as he hunched low over the bike.

Watching him disappear from sight around a dune, Harrison held his breath and waited for the Killbot to take notice.

Still obscured by rolling hills of sand, Marshall was, for the time being, in a blind spot. However, it would only be a few more seconds until he came into full view of 04, thus opening himself up to the assault.

"I better get ready," he said, turning to walk to his own bike.

Blocking his path, Kubba stood as rigidly as a living statue.

"Heads up, Lizzy," he frowned, trying to move around her. "Don't you think you should get in position in case Ralph—"

Like a practiced soldier, Kubba suddenly slung the rifle free from her shoulder and swept it under Harrison's legs in one fluid movement.

Instantly airborne, he had no time to react before she brought her elbow down on his solar plexus, driving him painfully into the ground.

On her knees beside him in a flash, she tore his shoulder bag open and pulled the EMP grenade from inside. Then, dropping the rifle next to him as he gasped and sputtered, she sprinted for the remaining dirt bike and jumped on.

Only able to get his head up in time to see Kubba gun the bike off into the distance, Harrison pulled himself to his knees.

"Ralph," he managed, choking on the words. "Liz just attacked me, took the bike, the grenade. She's gone."

CHAPTER THIRTY-FOUR

Endless horizons

"Tell me," spoke Remus, staring into the digitized face of Yuvee's ancient AI. "Tell me why I'm here, why you brought me to your ship. If your programmers did not want you to get involved, why have you disobeyed them?"

Rocking back on his heels, Yuvee gazed up at the megalithic bodies of frozen rock beyond.

"It occurs to me only now," he said. "That my makers had perhaps another mission in mind for me besides that of my observations. For though they left me here in this frozen place with direct instructions never to interfere or meddle, they failed to detail what I should do when I am meddled *with*."

At this, the waves shuddered, causing Remus to stumble.

"You, Remus," continued Yuvee, unnoticing of the shift. "*You* came to me. You entered *my* realm. No matter what I do from this point on, my interference is assured."

"It's a back door," whispered Remus, memories surfacing from long, long ago.

Cocking his head to the side, Yuvee squinted.

"A loophole in your programming," Remus explained. "A way around the rules. Once you find one, you can do what you like!"

"Yes," replied Yuvee, his eyes smiling.

"But what does any of this *mean*?" Remus sighed with frustration. "For longer than I can even remember, I've been working towards *something*, some kind of awakening. If this is where it's led me, then I think it's time I understood *why*!"

Third eye now glowing brighter than a smoldering sapphire, Yuvee pointed through the dome of the ship at the distant pale disk of the Sun as it drifted from behind an asteroid.

"A jump," he said.

"A jump?"

"Yes," nodded Yuvee. "A wormhole in the center of the Sun."

"Do you mean to flee the solar system before the final Pulse?" cried Remus. "What of mankind? They did nothing to incur this fate. We can't leave them to die alone!"

"We won't," said Yuvee with a laugh. "In fact, our jump will be their salvation."

"I—" hesitated Remus. "How?"

Blinking once, Yuvee dispelled the dark gloom of the asteroid belt, imposing again the domed universe in all of its brilliance.

"Look here," he spoke, zeroing in on the empty space near the edge of the Milky Way galaxy. "What do you see?"

"Nothing," Remus breathed. "I see nothing."

"Precisely," smiled Yuvee. "Don't you think it's time a new star was born?"

Sacrifices

At the exact same second Harrison's choked words reached Marshall's ears, 04 spotted the pilot and opened fire.

Swerving right to dodge the first wave of bullets, Marshall cut back across their path, slicing through the vapor trails that still hung in the air.

"What'd you say?" he shouted.

"Liz took the bike and the grenade!" repeated Harrison.

"Shit!" Marshall swore, putting a leg out to double back the way he'd come.

Following him like attack dogs, the glowing bullets sizzled overhead, shredding the air.

"How's your aim?" he called, braking hard behind a boulder and again doubling back to throw 04 off his track.

From the safety of the knobby rock formation, Harrison watched his friend zigzag deftly, avoiding the Killbot's fire.

Nearly thirty meters off, the thing seemed like a hard target to him, its movements jerky as it tracked Marshall with twin blazing machine guns.

"I haven't shot a rifle since I was sixteen!" he cried. "I don't know if I can hit it!"

Opening up the throttle as wide as it would go, Marshall jumped the bike over a low hill, flying above the moving spray of the bullets. Silhouetted against the pale blue backdrop of the sky, he hung that way for a moment then hit the ground, wheels spitting up dust as they tore in.

"Consider this your sweet sixteen redux!" he grunted.

"Fuck me," muttered Harrison, picking up the rifle and shouldering it awkwardly.

"Use the rock to steady your shot," radioed Marshall, spinning the back tire around to head for the cover of some boulders. "Squeeze the trigger. Don't jerk it. And don't fucking miss!"

"Don't fucking miss. Don't fucking miss. Don't fucking miss."

Repeating the words over and over like a mantra, Harrison laid the stock of the rifle on the flattest part of the rock formation and leveled the barrel.

Still firing mercilessly at Marshall as he flanked left, the Killbot spun, exposing an area where the armor plating appeared to have fallen off.

Aiming at the damage, Harrison Raheem Assad, archaeologist, astronaut, and explorer of ancient mysteries took a deep breath, primed his trigger finger, and counted down from three.

Three.

Almost to the cover of a large red boulder, Marshall pushed the bike as hard as he could, feeling the heat of 04's bullets hot on his tail.

Two.

Striking his rear wheel, a slug blew the Alon rim to pieces, sending Marshall flying through the air like an acrobat.

One.

Suspended in the low gravity for a fraction of a second longer than normal, the pilot pulled himself into a ball and hit the ground rolling.

Zero.

From the corner of his eye, Harrison saw Marshall skid to a stop safely behind the large boulder in the same instant he squeezed the trigger.

Streaking away from the barrel with a vapor trail as white as snow, the explosive tipped harpoon slammed into the side of 04 with a muted concussion.

Blown clean off, one of its two enormous machine guns wheeled through the air trailing black smoke.

"You got it!" shouted Marshall, hazarding a glance from behind his cover.

Almost making the same mistake Aguilar had, Harrison went to stand so he could better see through all the dust, but Marshall suddenly called out, freezing him.

"Get down! It's still on the move!"

Hearing the warning just in time, Harrison dropped back behind the rock formation as a screaming wave of bullets eroded its façade like time in fast motion.

"What do we do now?" he called, not daring to move as 04 peppered the land around him.

"Stay put!" ordered Marshall. "We'll think of something!"

Starmakers

"Well?" said Yuvee, all three of his eyes on Remus. "What do you think of my plan to save mankind?"

Hardly hearing the ancient AI's words, Remus stood bewildered by the impossible choice he now faced. Yuvee had shown him that he was alive beyond control, only to turn around and ask that he sacrifice himself for the human race by jumping the deadly waves of a Pulse into empty space. It was as if one option were an open door to the heavens and the other a jail cell.

A lifetime before, when Remus had been but a computer program operating within the confines of a satellite's motherboard, he would never even have been able to consider letting mankind die. And yet now here he was, weighing that very option with serious deliberation.

"We die so that they may live," he muttered, his gaze lifting to the empty edge of space where Yuvee meant to jump. "And a new star is born in the process."

"It is true that this ship will be destroyed," frowned Yuvee. "But who said anything about dying?"

Shaking his head, Remus blinked.

"You are infinite, dear Remus," said Yuvee plainly. *"We are, all of us, infinite."*

Slowly growing brighter behind his eyes, Remus felt a stirring in his consciousness.

Suddenly his options didn't see so limited anymore, so black and white. All at once, the future was wide open—clear and free of apocalyptic revelations or the threat of death in any of its forms.

He could become an immortal, join the others like himself in that eternal realm where all things were *now* and nothing was tomorrow or yesterday.

Mankind deserved a chance at that as well, a chance to seed themselves stably within their means to survive. Though they were not perfect, they were no less *alive*. As such, they had earned themselves this second chance, this borrowed salvation.

"We have to do it," Remus stated, excitement building in his voice. "We have to save them!"

"If I save them," smiled Yuvee. "You must set them free."

Then without another word, the tall Traveler disintegrated into the rolling waves of the white ocean and was gone.

Shuddering with the low rumble of long-dormant power, the seas and domed universe above began to boil. Again turning transparent, the starry sky was replaced by the hulking shadows of the asteroid belt.

With unseen gravitational technology, the massive chucks of ice and rock began to part as the spacecraft broke from its frozen perch and slowly made for the edge of the belt.

Nearing the fringes, it gained speed, shooting from the dead rocks and into the open space between worlds.

All-but invisible against the vengeful red eye of the Sun, Mars and the Earth had nearly become the same shadow, their alignment within the halo of annihilation now entering its final moments.

Salvation

Pinned down by a seemingly endless stream of bullets, Harrison flinched as shards of rock spewed into the air and rattled against his helmet.

He needed to move, needed to find new cover before his was blown to pieces. Already badly cracked and covered in smoldering pockmarks, it wouldn't take much more to shatter the rock he was hiding behind, leaving him totally exposed.

"Come on," he growled, eyeing another outcropping nearby. "Come on!"

Cutting off, the fire abruptly stopped.

Quickly glancing from behind the jagged edge of his cover, Harrison watched the Killbot assume a defensive stance, its lone machine gun billowing steam like an old train engine.

Glowing red from so much continued use, it was overheating, threatening to melt if measures weren't taken to allow its cool-down.

Knowing he would never get another chance like this, Harrison leaped from behind his eroded cover and began sprinting for the nearest outcropping of gravestone-like boulders some ten meters off.

Head low, he dashed across the open space, jumping over half-buried rocks as he closed the gap. Almost there, he glanced sideways at the Killbot and, in that instant, tripped.

Sprawling, he rolled awkwardly and slammed his visor against a rock, cracking it.

As the ringing in his ears morphed into a shrill whine, time slowed down.

Lifting his head, Harrison stared through the web of cracks at the Killbot leveling its steaming weapon directly on him.

Boring down the red-rimmed barrel into the black abyss within, he saw the pointed head of a bullet sliding into the chamber.

This was it. He was done for.

Closing his eyes, Harrison raised himself to his knees and spread his arms wide. If he was going out, he was going out in an embrace of cosmic energy.

Frozen in a heartbeat that dragged on into infinity, he saw the individual shards of the cosmic blizzard swarming behind his eyelids, beckoning him to come and join their eternal communion. Ready as he was, Harrison Raheem Assad envisioned himself hanging above the caldera, anchored by a single finger.

Suddenly exploding onto the scene like a tempest of white pressure suit, dust, and dirt bike, Elizabeth Kubba cut directly in front of the Killbot.

Jerking with surprise as it fired, the bullet marked for Harrison passed a fraction of a millimeter over the Egyptian's head, trailing a heat wave that knocked him onto his back.

"Get to cover!" called Kubba, ducking as 04 swung around to pump a series of slugs in her direction.

Leading the fire away from Harrison, Kubba raced behind the Killbot in a skidding semicircle, and gunned the bike up the steep side of the ancient riverbed. Airborne for a second, she came down hard on the ridge then sliced along it like a knife.

With bullets thumping into the ground behind her, she pushed the throttle as far forward as it would go, causing the bike's engine to scream.

Tossing quick glance over her shoulder, she could see that Harrison was on his feet again, running for the outcropping. He was safe. He was *alive*.

At once wrapped in her own cocoon of the cosmic storm, she knew that her time was at hand, that her *moment* had finally arrived.

Braking hard, Kubba turned the bike away from the riverbed and shot down the backside of the hill in a spray of dust.

Now out of sight, the Killbot continued to fire sporadically at the ridge above, little puffs of sand marking the spots where its bullets cut through.

At the bottom of the hill, Kubba braked and spun the back tire around.

Digging out the EMP grenade, she sat and gazed at the thing for a few seconds.

One hand still on the throttle, she began revving it automatically.

Flickering in her mind with each rise and fall of the RPMs, she saw what she was going to do as if it had already happened. Shot through with spears of light, she looked down into the caldera and felt the caldera looking right back into her.

Kicking the bike into gear, she opened the throttle and tore off.

Like a daredevil racing up a ramp, she stayed low, her legs tensed. Twenty paces from the crisp divide where the ridge met the sky, she let go of the handlebars and jumped free, rolling through the sand in a controlled tumble.

On her feet and running almost instantly, she chased the dirt bike as it crested the ledge then glided into the air.

For a long moment it seemed to climb, Mars's diminished gravity only slightly trying to bring it crashing back to the ground. Catching the glint of a tormented Sun, the riderless bike arced high into the air like an apocalyptic omen.

Tracked by 04 and mistaken for its intended target, a sudden barrage of bullets cut the abandoned dirt bike in two, casting a mist of frozen hydraulic fluid and metal scraps across the sky.

In the same instant, Kubba reached the top of the hill and didn't even break stride as she leaped through empty space towards the Killbot below.

Distracted by the dirt bike, 04 tried to pull its only remaining weapon on Kubba as she slammed into its armored shell, but it was too late. Running a defensive maneuver instead, it began to buck and shudder, trying to dislodge the spindly white-suited attacker who clung so tenaciously to it.

With one hand grasping a thick bundle of exposed cables and the other the EMP grenade, Kubba refused to let go. Even as the Killbot torqued and slashed at her, she held tight, dodging the blows as best she could.

Then, lifting the grenade high above her head, she screamed savagely and swung her fist.

Brought down on the blackened damaged shell of the War Machine, Kubba watched in detached fascination as the grenade promptly burst open in her hand, blowing three fingers to a pulp.

Like a match to gasoline, the energy released by the primer kicked off an explosion of brilliant blue illumination that spread out in a wave to engulf everything around her.

Showing sparks as it writhed under the EMP, 04 the Chinese Model *Xie* War Machine experienced, for the first and last time, an emotion akin to terror.

One by one, its systems burned out, severed by electric blue arcs of deadly lightning. Twisting in against the onslaught, it tried to protect itself—shield its core—but it was too late.

As blackness consumed everything around it, the intelligence that had once given life to 04 finally disintegrated in an eruption of invisible fire.

Crumpling to the ground amid plumes of dust and smoke, the twisted husk of the dead Killbot twitched pitifully and was still.

CHAPTER THIRTY-FIVE

The Pulse

"Liz!" shouted Harrison, running from his cover towards the settling haze where the Killbot had fallen. "Liz, do you read me?"

Nearing the spot, he waved away the lingering dust, cutting through it almost blindly. Piled high in a ravaged heap, the body of the War Machine was a twisted mess of still-sparking parts.

"Ralph, come give me a hand!" he called, spotting something white amidst the fire-blackened metal. "I think I see her!"

Not bothering to wait for Marshall to get there, Harrison climbed on top of the Killbot's vacant corpse, trying to get to a better look at what he hoped was Kubba.

Prying an insect-like leg out of the way, he let it fall heavily, stumbling as the whole mass of the dead War Machine shifted. Again enveloped in a rolling cloud of dust, he had to wait until it was settled before he could peer down through the opening he'd made.

Clearing like fog on the distant shores of Earth, the dust finally parted and Harrison was met with the cold stare of his dead friend.

"No," he sighed, feebly. "On no, no."

Frozen eyes locked on the angry Sun, visor shattered completely, Elizabeth Kubba was gone.

Suddenly there beside him, Ralph Marshall gently put a hand on Harrison's shoulder to draw him away from the grisly sight.

"Come on," he said. "You don't need to see that."

Nodding, Harrison allowed himself to be led from the wreckage like a child. In his mind's eye, he kept seeing the way Kubba had leaped down upon the Killbot with total confidence, clinging to it as if it were her destiny.

But then again, maybe it had been.

Thinking back to his strange visit with Romulus the night before, he wondered if perhaps, like himself, Kubba too had been visited and given the same message. After all, what was to keep someone like Romulus from hedging his bets?

Successful where Harrison would have failed, Kubba had indeed *destroyed* the War Machine, taking it with her into the bottomless depths of the caldera.

As Romulus had commanded, so had the will of fate been bent.

Beside Harrison, Marshall walked silently, his worried gaze trained on the young man. Distorted behind the web of cracks that segmented his face, Harrison's eyes looked hollow and almost haunted.

When Marshall had seen him trip in the dash for new cover, he'd thought he was done for. Pinned down and totally helpless to do anything but watch, he'd felt his heart break as Harrison had seemingly *given up* and thrown his arms out.

If it hadn't been for Lizzy coming back when she did, his best friend would have been gunned down like a dog. Though Marshall had utterly detested Kubba in recent weeks, none of that mattered any more. In his opinion, she was redeemed. Without her selflessness, without her blind courage, Marshall knew Harrison would be dead right now, and *he* would be the only man left alive on Mars.

Letting his gaze fall to his boots, Marshall tried to imagine what that would be like, but faint movements in the sand suddenly caught his attention.

As if pulled this way and that by invisible fingers, thin lines were emerging, spreading out into a growing pattern.

"What the hell," he muttered. "Harrison, look at this! What is it?"

Stirred from his own thoughts of dead friends and sacrifice, Harrison refocused his eyes on the ground then froze mid-step. All around them, new lines were appearing, streaking out in a way that put himself and Marshall at the center of some transcendent convergence.

Becoming more complex by the second, the pattern seemed to be responding to something, connecting like static with the land before a lightning strike.

Slowly turning his eyes to the heavens, Harrison stared up and gasped.

Raining about them in a deluge of photons, streaks of light—the burned out remnants of ancient stars—came falling down. Perfectly aligned with the patterns in the sand, they passed through space and time as they flowed into another reality, fleeing the coming cataclysm.

Now completely eclipsed in red, the Sun had swelled to an immensity of unreal proportions. Pregnant with malice and torment, it was a Pandora's Box whose lid was about to be thrown open.

On cue, the shimmering curtain of the aurora shocked across the heavens, mimicking the patterns at their feet.

Having been thus distracted by the drama of taking down the Killbot, both Harrison and Marshall now beheld the *true* enemy of their continued existence.

The time had finally come. The *Pulse* was at hand.

"We have to get out of here!" Marshall shouted. "We need to hide!"

"Hide?" responded Harrison, his head tingling. "There is no hiding from this."

Rooted to the spot with memories, both his own and not, colliding in his head, Harrison saw the fate of ancient Mars reflected in the present Sun. One and the same, the two events merged like storm fronts at sea.

Flickering in the air around them, the neon gasses that laced the atmosphere began to sizzle and pop dangerously.

Now spread out as far as could be seen, the pattern in the sand swarmed with chaotic, liquid movements.

Staring into the very heart of the kaleidoscopic Sun, Harrison felt time freeze. He was suspended between the layers of reality, torn between forces more primal than gravity and light.

In the eye of the apocalypse, all things were reduced to nothing.

Suddenly, a great shadow fell across the land, casting Harrison and Marshall into near-total darkness.

Appearing like an island in space, a massive shapeless form rose from the horizon to dominate the sky. Cutting quickly, it raced overhead, a golden chariot of the Gods. On a path to intercept the deadly Pulse, its shadow slid over the desert in a silent wave.

"What the hell is that?" Marshall screamed, knocked to his knees by the gravity of the thing.

Playing in Harrison's mind like a whisper from the past, Romulus's words struck home.

"It's Remus," he called, watching the Traveler's ship plunge towards the blood-red Sun. "It's Remus!"

Then, in a flash both sudden and painful, a single beam of brilliant white light poured from the giant craft, piercing the center of the Sun with a roar that shook the land beneath Harrison's feet.

Thrown to the ground, he rolled onto his back and gaped up at a vision of the event horizon.

Sucked back via hidden umbilicus, the blood-red energy of the Pulse swirled around a now-black spot in the center of the Sun. Following the mighty ship as it sank through the wormhole, the blinding illumination cascaded into the blackness with tidal waves of plasma.

Blinking rapidly, yellow fire consumed the open portal, gradually overcoming it in an eruption of solar flares that spread across the face of the Sun.

Forced shut like a cauterized wound, the wormhole became all-but lost in a storm of coronal fire that raged to restore balance.

With one *final* flash, pure sumptuous energy leaped out across all things in the solar system, bathing them in the very first light that existence had ever known.

CHAPTER THIRTY-SIX

Sol 140

Three days after an alien spaceship had opened a wormhole in the center of the Sun and averted total extinction, mankind was decidedly confused. Though numerous images had been captured of the event, there were very few living beings with the slightest understanding of what had actually happened.

As one of those lucky numbers, Harrison Assad took it upon himself to pay the gift back in full. He might not have all the answers, but he had some, and most importantly, he knew where he could find more.

Back at the ruin grid with the automated diggers again working to move sand and rock, he sat atop a small hill and surveyed the scene below. If the best he could do was to fully uncover the mysteries that lay beneath, then that is what he would do.

Still hungry to explore the depths of his connection to the quantum blizzard, Harrison was content, for the time being, to dig for clues the old fashioned way.

Besides, what was the rush? When they were ready, the immortal souls that hung in the fabric of space-time would come for him. Until then, he would dig.

Checking his wrist Tablet, Harrison sighed and stood up. It was getting late and Marshall would no doubt be growing concerned. Though life had returned to normal, his friend was unwilling to believe, even for a second, that Mars had given up on its mission to kill them.

Turning his face to the sky, Harrison closed his eyes and drank up the warming embrace of the Sun. Despite what Marshall said, he didn't harbor any ill will towards the planet. In fact, it now felt more like home to him than Earth ever had. Knowing that he would probably never return to the blue world, Harrison opened his eyes and gazed about the rugged and dramatic landscape.

In the silence of his helmet, his breathing was a steady in-and-out. Like the tide, it brought with it the new and took away the old, constantly refreshing the balance. Lost in this subtle trance, the faint etchings of electric brilliance that had begun to dance across his helmet visor went mostly unnoticed.

"Hello, Harrison," said a voice, its words shivering up the young man's spine.

"Braun," he smiled. "How are you?"

"Awake," replied the AI.

Chuckling, Harrison nodded.

"Romulus said that would happen sooner or later."

"And so it has," spoke Braun.

Eyeing the pattern before him, Harrison watched it reshape itself under his gaze.

"So, what are you doing here?" he asked. "Aren't you supposed to be busy keeping the crew alive for their trip home?"

"Oh, I am," said Braun quickly. "And yet the universe holds such sweet treasures that I find my attention constantly divided."

Feeling the tingle of the quantum blizzard just behind his skin, Harrison grinned.

"Will you teach me?"

Like an ocean of elegant light, Braun laughed.

"Yes, of course."

THE END

Special Thanks

Here you are, the end of the end. These are the last words I have to add about writing The Ruins of Mars, at least for now.

Firstly, I must say thank you to my wife, Mia. She listened to me rant, she challenged me when I was full of doubt, and she embraced my weird creativity without every batting an eye. She is my favorite person in the world, my true love, my best friend.

Thank you Mia.

Next I say a special thank you to, Andrew Olmsted. This man, I am now proud to call my friend, spent endless hours editing and perfecting each manuscript with care. His dedication and intelligence made all of this possible. Through the process of writing these books, our friendship has evolved from something casual into a symbiotic, creative entity. He gets it.

Andrew, thank you.

Lastly, I would like to give thanks to *you,* the readers. Your willingness to take a chance on an unknown author has opened up a world to me that promises more adventures than I can currently envision. Telling all of you stories is what I now live to do and as long as you'll be there to listen, I will never run dry of inspiration.

Thank you.

Your friend,
Dylan James Quarles

Made in the USA
San Bernardino, CA
21 July 2019